THE WITCH AND THE WOLF

Also by Lindsey Kelk

I Heart series
I Heart New York
I Heart Hollywood
I Heart Paris
I Heart Vegas
I Heart London
I Heart Christmas
I Heart Forever
I Heart Hawaii

About a Girl series
About a Girl
What a Girl Wants
A Girl's Best Friend

Standalones
The Single Girl's To-Do List
Always the Bridesmaid
We Were on a Break
One in a Million
In Case You Missed It
The Christmas Wish
On a Night Like This
Love Me Do
Love Story
Christmas Fling

Savannah Red Trilogy
The Bell Witches

THE WITCH AND THE WOLF

LINDSEY KELK

Magpie Books
An imprint of
HarperCollins*Publishers* Ltd
1 London Bridge Street
London SE1 9GF

www.harpercollins.co.uk

HarperCollins*Publishers*
Macken House,
39/40 Mayor Street Upper,
Dublin 1, D01 C9W8
Ireland

First published by HarperCollins*Publishers* Ltd 2026

1

Copyright © Lindsey Kelk 2026

Map and interior illustrations © Nicolette Caven 2026

Lindsey Kelk asserts the moral right to
be identified as the author of this work.

A catalogue record for this book is available from the British Library.

ISBN: 978-0-00-860987-0 (HB)
ISBN: 978-0-00-860988-7 (TPB)

This novel is entirely a work of fiction.
The names, characters and incidents portrayed in it are
the work of the author's imagination. Any resemblance to
actual persons, living or dead, events or localities is
entirely coincidental.

Typeset in Sabon by Palimpsest Book Production Ltd, Falkirk, Stirlingshire

Printed and bound in the UK using 100% renewable electricity by CPI Group (UK) Ltd

All rights reserved. No part of this publication may be
reproduced, stored in a retrieval system, or transmitted,
in any form or by any means, electronic, mechanical,
photocopying, recording or otherwise, without the prior
written permission of the publishers.

Without limiting the exclusive rights of any author, contributor or the publisher of this
publication, any unauthorized use of this publication to train generative artificial
intelligence (AI) technologies is expressly prohibited. HarperCollins also exercise their rights
under Article 4(3) of the Digital Single Market Directive 2019/790 and expressly reserve
this publication from the text and data mining exception.

For Kevin Dickson, wolf to my witch, witch to my wolf,
whatever works for you.
Off to the cave we go . . .

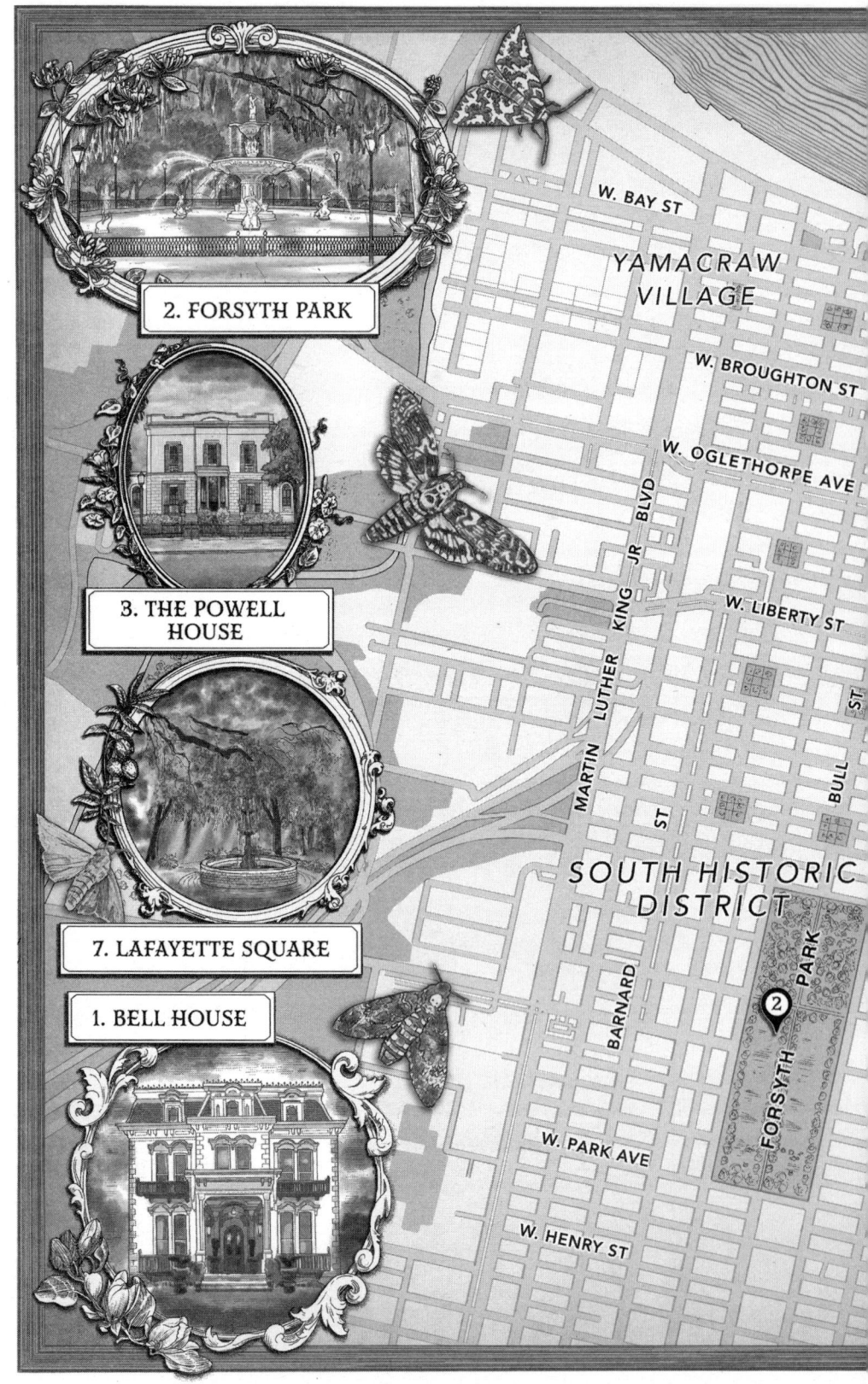

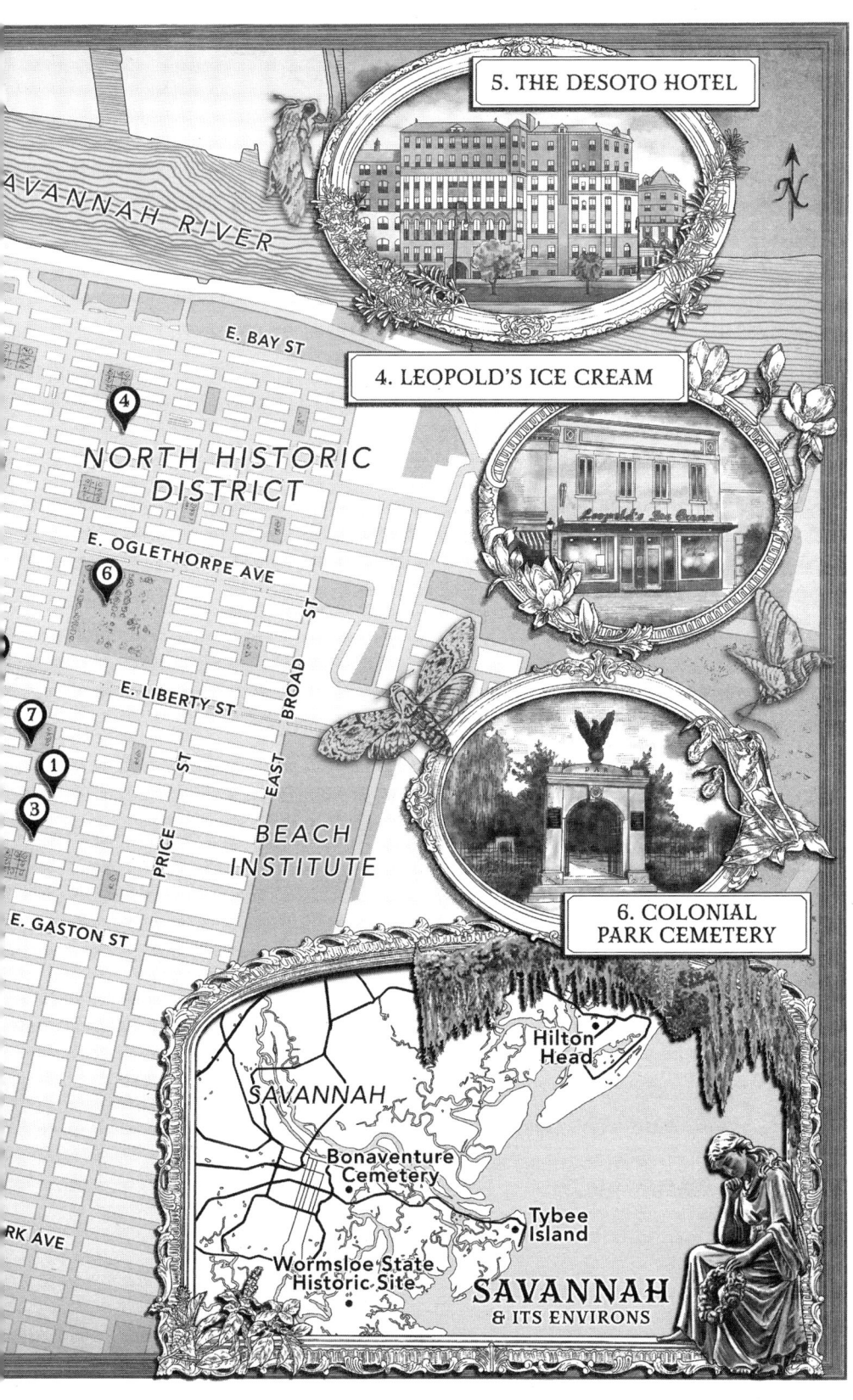

Do you remember the first lie you ever told?

Not so long ago, if you'd asked me the difference between the truth and a lie, it wouldn't have felt like too difficult a question. Lying is wrong. Telling the truth is always the right thing to do.

These days, I'm not so sure.

I can't remember the first lie I ever told but I'll never forget the worst.

I only hope it was worth it.

The Truth

Chapter One

Bell House was too quiet.

I never really understood what people meant when they said a place was too quiet, not until I arrived in Savannah. Bell House, my home, was over two hundred years old and overlooked a busy city square. There was always something, inside or out. Cars rumbling by, voices on the street or the reassuring creaks and groans of my old home's bones. But today, there was only silence.

The house knew I needed to concentrate.

Closing the double doors of the parlour behind me, I took a moment. It still didn't seem real. I couldn't believe this beautiful place was my home, that I actually got to live here. The walls glowed with a soft sheen from the silk wallpaper and the heartwood pine floorboards, as old as the house itself, held onto the memory of every person ever to have set foot in this room. Generation after generation of my ancestors had collected and curated everything I laid my eyes on, lovingly selecting the paintings and ornaments, every single stick of furniture, from the antique Austrian crystal chandelier above my head to the hand-knotted Persian rug beneath my bare feet. It all came together with breathtaking beauty. To anyone who cared to look, the parlour, like the rest of Bell House, was picture-perfect from every angle.

But as I knew all too well, looks could be deceiving.

I took a deep breath in and crossed the room to place a terracotta pot on the low marble coffee table. Inside the pot was an orchid, fully in bloom, its tall, slender stem supporting six blooms with petals that faded from a deep cerise at their heart to a whisper-soft pink around the edges. So pretty. Lowering myself to the ground, I sat back on my heels, knees pressed into the rug before closing my eyes and calming my thoughts. Present, mindful, centred. No noise to distract me. Holding my hands out over the orchid, I envisioned the change. Nothing super fancy, nothing drastic, all I wanted was to change the colour of the petals from pink to blue. It was simple magic. Persuading a plant to change colour should've been intuitive for an apothecary witch like me. With my eyes still closed, I saw the flower before me, pictured the shift in hue. The tips of my fingers tingled, the merest hint of a sensation, as though someone had brushed a feather over my skin. My magic manifesting.

But when I opened one eye in a squint, the pink petals were still pink.

'That's OK,' I said to the orchid as I rubbed my hands together to reset myself. 'Take your time.'

Some plants needed a little more persuading than others but knowing what could be done was half the battle when it came to magic, and I knew I could do this. I was Emily James Bell, I was a Bell witch.

As the thought crossed my mind, something inside me shuddered.

Not a Bell witch. The Bell witch.

The only one.

Without warning, my whole body was aflame and a series

of images raced through my mind, dragging me away from the task at hand; Catherine in a white gown, standing beside a towering stone archway. A huge silver wolf, Wyn enduring his first phase wrapped in silver barbed wire and howling in agony. The full moon, a black sky, and a dozen red-haired women with emerald eyes the same as mine staring down at me as I bled out on a stone floor.

'No!' I said aloud, shaking off the dark thoughts, eyes still squeezed shut.

That was the past. I had survived, and there was nothing to be gained by replaying it over and over in my head. With renewed focus, I squeezed the golden locket that hung around my neck to bring myself back to the present moment, then dipped back into my magic. Present, mindful, centred.

Then something else flashed in front of my eyes, a warmer, softer memory. Green-grey eyes, with flashes of bronze. Golden sunshine skin and dark ash hair, waves curling against his cheekbones. His features were a blur, too close for me to focus, but I heard the catch of a breath in the back of his throat then felt his lips brush over mine, soft and searching, a question and a promise.

I love you, Emily James.

Smiling, my fingers rose to my mouth to press the phantom kiss to my lips. This time I shivered, my skin tingling beautifully from head to toe. This was the past too, but it was also the future. My future with Wyn.

When I opened my eyes again, the orchid on the coffee table looked exactly the same as it had when we started.

But I couldn't say the same for the parlour floor.

There were flowers everywhere. I gazed around the room in shock. Not a single square inch of heartwood pine or Persian rug was visible under the carpet of blossoms I'd conjured. They sprouted up from between the floorboards, fighting for space as they bloomed brilliantly, turning towards me like I was the sun itself. Roses, tulips, violets, azaleas, lilies, peonies, dahlias and daisies, every single flower I could think of . . . everything except a blue orchid.

Almost a month had passed since my birthday. Four whole weeks since I turned seventeen, discovered the truth about my grandmother and came into my full magic, just in time to save my own life and the lives of the people I loved the most. It was, to be fair, not the seventeenth birthday I'd been expecting. Mostly I'd been hoping to get a car, not the manifest abilities of every Bell witch who had lived before me. And certainly not to find out I was most likely the subject of a world-ending prophecy as vague as it was terrifying. I'd gained a past I could never have imagined and a future I wasn't ready for.

So here I was, practising. Trying to hone my skills and control my magic, only to find out that magic didn't want to be controlled. Giving up on my orchid, I lay back in my private indoor meadow, watching as full-grown oaks, elms and a silver birch joined the flowers, stretching towards the ceiling, their branches curving this way and that in order to miss the light fixtures. They were thoughtful at least. Magic didn't come with a guide book. Every day, I felt as though I was driving a Ferrari on the freeway without ever having taken a single lesson. Sure, I knew how to make the thing go but without someone to teach me the rules, I was hurtling into oncoming traffic with my brakes cut. All this magic, all these abilities, and I was in freefall.

A rosebud swayed close to caress my face, wiping away the single tear of frustration that rolled down my cheek. The flowers didn't want me to feel bad. They just didn't want to do what I asked. Plants, like people, were sometimes rebellious. Relaxing into their sweet softness, I let a trail of ivy wind itself up around my wrist, and allowed my thoughts to roam, not the slightest bit surprised when they ended up in the same place they always did: replaying every last moment I'd shared with Wyn. I sighed and the flowers bloomed even brighter than before.

Then something in me shifted. Panic, fear, shortness of breath. I sat bolt upright, the flowers closest to me shirking away.

'Emily, help!'

Half a heartbeat before I heard Ashley's cry, a throb of terror passed through our home and into me. My feet scarcely touched the floor as I scrambled upright, racing out of the parlour and up the grand, curving staircase to the second floor, my aunt's terrified voice carrying all the way through Bell House. The floorboards creaked in protest at my hurry, but there was no time to coddle the house if Ashley was in danger. Who or what could've broken through our wards? Ghosts? Witches? Wolves?

Throwing open her bedroom door, I steeled myself for whatever horrors awaited me, but the reality was so much worse than anything I could've imagined.

A half-naked Ashley Bell wailed at me from inside a neon orange cocoon, her arms flailing wildly against its constraints. Only, it wasn't a cocoon, it was . . . a dress? Skin-tight, long-sleeved and half yanked up around her head, the garment squeezed her shoulders like sausage casing, her restricted hands flapping helplessly like an angry little T-Rex.

'About time,' Ashley said, her words muffled by a mouthful of traffic-cone-coloured fabric. 'What took you so long? The zipper is stuck and I can't get the damn thing off. A little help before I dislocate my shoulder?'

The house and I both gave a sigh of relief at the same time. No ghosts. No witches. No wolves.

'You scared me half to death,' I said as my heart rate

skittered back down to something nearer normal. 'I thought you were in trouble.'

She stared at me with big green eyes.

'How is this not trouble? Why do people even wear stuff like this? It's not a dress, it's a torture device.'

'You tell me,' I said. 'You're the one who bought it.'

Along with half of Broughton Street from the look of the endless shopping bags scattered around her room. I grabbed the hem of the dress and she sucked in a deep breath, squeezing her eyes shut in the hope that it might somehow make her significantly smaller. It hadn't worked when she drove her brand-new Mini Cooper through an ultra-narrow 'shortcut', as the scratches up the side of the car would attest, and it wasn't going to work now. She grunted impatiently and I shifted my attention to a tiny concealed zipper, fabric snarled up between the teeth, and did my best not to pinch her skin as I wiggled it loose.

'What's going on back there?' Ashley said. 'Can't you just magic it off of me, oh super-mega magic witch?'

With a stern look and a sharp tug, I felt the zipper give and yanked the dress-slash-straitjacket up and over her head, my aunt yelping with joy as her arms were released, and spinning in a semi-clad circle to celebrate her freedom.

'For a minute there, I thought you were going to have to bury me in that thing.' She snatched the dress out of my hands and tossed it in the general direction of her wastepaper basket. 'I think I pulled something in my neck. I should sue the store.'

'Did you try it on before you bought it?' I asked.

She replied with a glare, an Ashley Bell special.

'Sorry, what I meant to say was, you must absolutely call a lawyer,' I said. 'How dare a clothing store exchange goods and services for money? They must be stopped.'

'Sarcasm doesn't suit you,' Ashley informed me as I crossed

the room, retrieved the dress from the trash and gave it a shake. 'You're not good at it.'

I answered her with a glare of my own.

'Then thank goodness I'm learning from the best.'

Laying the straightened-out dress on the bed, I ignored her as she pulled on an oversized blue shirt, then glanced towards the door, her nose twitching as she sniffed.

'What is that smell?' she asked. 'Did you spill perfume or something?'

'Um, something like that.'

With one eye on the door, I willed the flowers and trees that still filled the parlour to return to the earth. As pretty as they were, a field of flowers in the parlour wasn't exactly practical, especially when non-magical company came calling. A blanket of living plants underfoot was the sort of thing people tended to notice.

'Are you hungry?' I asked, quickly changing the subject. The last thing I needed was another lecture from Ashley about controlling my magic. 'I thought maybe we could go out for dinner tonight. I don't know why, but I'm totally craving barbecue.'

'While I would bite your arm off for a half-rack of ribs, I can't.'

My disappointed face only earned a huff of frustration.

'Since Catherine is still "visiting friends overseas", I have to show my face at the historical society meeting,' she explained with air quotes and a look of distaste. 'Unless you want to conjure my mother up from whatever godforsaken magical hole she's hiding in before six p.m., in which case, ribs are on me.'

While I had spent the last four weeks getting to grips with my new reality as a witch, Ashley had spent it getting to grips with reality altogether. For eleven long years, Catherine kept her magic-less daughter tethered to Bell House, unable to leave the enchanted grounds without permission. At twenty-seven, she was free to stray, and shop, as she pleased for the first time in her life, but Catherine's absence came with a price. Someone had to take over all the responsibilities that came with belonging to one of the most prominent families in Savannah and, super-mega witch or not, I was still only seventeen, which meant most of the dull day-to-day stuff fell on Ashley's shoulders. I felt terrible. The blessing only visited every other generation; so Catherine and I were witches, but Ashley was not. Instead of enjoying her new-found freedom, her days were taken up with Catherine's business interests, her volunteer groups, council meetings, and the historical society. Not quite the stuff dreams were made of, but there was no way around it.

'Oh gosh, why didn't I think of that before?' I exclaimed in my very best Georgia peach accent. 'Let me just snap my fingers and bring her on back – I sure would hate for you to be inconvenienced in any way, Miss Ashley.'

'No need to be so touchy,' she said with a smirk. 'It was only a suggestion.'

I attempted a smile but my reply came out as a rough-edged whisper. 'You know I've tried. I want to know where she is as much as you do.'

It was the truth. Catherine wasn't just Ashley's mother, my grandmother and a grand dame of Savannah society. No, first and foremost, she was a Bell witch. Just like me but at some point, she had decided magic was more important than the lives of people she was supposed to love. She killed my mother and my father, her own son, but when she tried to siphon off my abilities for herself, it was one transgression too many for our ancestors to forgive. Even when she offered up her own life to save mine, it wasn't enough to appease them. One moment we were together in our family crypt, surrounded by every Bell witch to have ever lived, the next she was gone. Whatever plane of existence Catherine found herself on now, she was lost to me and Ashley until our foremothers decided otherwise.

'Maybe she doesn't want to be found. Or maybe she really is . . .' My aunt's eyes drifted over to the window. 'Maybe she really is gone.'

I didn't reply because I didn't know what to say. Like Ashley, I felt conflicted about Catherine. The woman was a manipulator and a murderer; she'd taken the lives of both my parents and had been ready to sacrifice my friends and my love in order to control my magic. Yet despite all the horrific things she had done, there was still a part of me that missed her.

When I was alone in the world, my grandmother had given me a home, made me feel I belonged. When I woke up screaming from a nightmare, it was Catherine I hoped to find sitting by my bed, telling me I was safe. Without her intervention, I might never have found my magic – a fate I couldn't begin to comprehend now. And I knew that, even in her darkest moments, she'd truly believed she was doing the right thing. In her eyes, she wasn't stealing my magic but defending the Bell legacy from someone she saw as unworthy.

Ashley flipped her long brown braid over her shoulder, letting it slice through the tension in the room.

'You'd think those ancestral ghosties might be more helpful,' she said. 'Not that I don't appreciate them saving your life and all, but it's bad manners to swoop in and spirit Catherine away without giving me a chance to ask where she keeps the credit cards.'

'Typical long-lost relatives,' I replied. 'Show up for your birthday party then vanish into thin air when it's time to clean up.'

'Speaking of polter-gran, still no sign of her?'

I shook my head.

'No sign of any of them.'

Pressing her lips together into a tight line, Ashley's chest swelled with a deep breath, as though she was preparing herself for something unpleasant.

'I'm going to suggest something but, before I do, I would ask that you don't punch me in the face,' she said, holding her hands out to defend herself.

I nodded for her to go on.

'Maybe the formerly-alive members of the family might feel more chatty if you took a trip down to Bonaventure to visit?'

Something fragile snapped in my chest, letting loose that dark sequence of images. Bonaventure Cemetery, Catherine, the archway, a wolf, the moon, black sky, red-haired women and so much blood . . .

'Really?' I replied, taut and tense and forcing the scenes to the edges of my mind. 'You want me to go back to the place where I almost died to ask a ghost where Catherine keeps her Mastercard?'

Ashley sighed theatrically and turned to sift through the assortment of brightly coloured T-shirts and tanks piled on her bed.

'I don't know what this world is coming to,' she said. 'If you can't trust the ghost of your three-hundred-year-old original witch ancestor, who can you trust? But honestly, if it's a choice between risking my life in the cemetery or spending another day bartering with those fools down at the bank, I'd happily choose the cemetery – ghosts, gremlins, wolves and all.'

'And you could pick up Randy's BBQ on your way back,' I said, a half-hearted joke. 'If you come back.'

Softening slightly, Ashley abandoned the pile of clothes and smoothed my hair away from my face. We'd come a long way in the last few weeks. It felt like only two minutes since I'd been dumped into her life, the aunt I didn't know existed, the niece she'd never asked for. Now I couldn't imagine my life without her.

'You're spending altogether too much time cooped up in this house,' she said. 'Trust me, I should know. Why don't you call Lydia? Surely that little monster will find the time to come over and keep you company while I'm out at this dumb meeting.'

'Really?' I replied with wonder. 'You're really suggesting I invite Lydia Powell into this house?'

'As long as she's gone by the time I get back.'

Former enemies, my aunt and my best friend had forged an unspoken truce, finding a way to tolerate each other ever since Lydia and her twin brother, Jackson, had been dragged into our family drama. And by 'dragged into', I did mean 'were almost killed by'.

'As much as I know you would love to see her, Lyds has something planned with her grandmother,' I said, pretending not to notice when she let out a small exhale of relief. 'Don't worry about me, I'm fine.'

'A likely story,' she replied. 'What about Wyn, have you heard from him?'

I bit into my bottom lip, pressing down until I tasted blood. I had not heard from Wyn.

'That's it, you're coming to the meeting with me,' Ashley declared. 'And don't you try to talk your way out of it because if I have to sit through another debate about whether or not Mr Ellison can paint the front of his townhouse fluorescent pink, then you should suffer too. And I just know Mr Chisholm would love to educate you on the history of the Farewell Ball at City Market. I swear, if that man tries to show me the photos of his grandmother dressed as a slice of cantaloupe one more time—'

'While that sounds incredible,' I said, interrupting her and backing away towards the door, 'I have way too much to do around here. This place is a mess. There's laundry to take care of, my bed needs to be made – just so much stuff.'

Ashley stood scrutinizing me as I spoke. The hollows under my eyes, the lank red waves that fell around my face, the grey shirt I'd been wearing for the last two, maybe three, days.

'Em, you need to take a pause,' she said, firm and decisive. 'If you carry on like this, you're going to burn out – and no one in this family wants to hear the word "witch" and "burn" in the same sentence.'

The room seemed to sway around me and I rested one hand on her bed to steady myself.

'I'm fine,' I said. It was a lie and not a convincing one. 'I have to keep going.'

She clucked her tongue dismissively.

'Last time I checked, it's a good idea to stay sharp when there's an apocalypse scheduled.'

'But that's half the problem – it isn't scheduled. We don't know when it's coming, only that it is.' Gnawing on the edge of my thumbnail, I pressed my ten toes into her floorboards, connecting with the house. 'I don't want to put anyone in danger,' I whispered. 'Not again.'

The words were barely out my mouth when Ashley pulled me into a hug, squeezing me tighter when I instinctively flinched.

'*You* weren't the one who put us in danger,' she said, sounding frustrated and empathetic in equal measure. 'You can't blame yourself for Catherine's actions, Emily. None of it was your fault.'

'If I hadn't come to Savannah, none of this would've happened.'

'And if a frog had wings, he wouldn't bump his ass when he hopped.'

The Witch and the Wolf

She released the hug and I replaced her arms with my own, wrapping them tightly around myself.

'You can't say that every time you want to get out of a difficult conversation,' I told her, smiling in spite of myself.

'Watch me. Hey, before you go.' Reaching into the pile of new clothes, she produced a pair of white jeans and a tiny hot pink tube top, holding them up for my approval. 'What do you think? Does this work for an evening of octogenarian company?'

'Only if you're planning to give Mr Chisholm a heart attack.'

Across the room, she considered the potential outfit in her freestanding mirror.

'That would probably get me home in time to enjoy some barbecue.'

'I'd laugh if I thought you were joking,' I said, rummaging in the pile and tossing her a black and white striped T-shirt instead. 'Ribs can wait until tomorrow and Mr Chisholm lives to see another day.'

Most of the walls of Bell House were covered with exquisite hand-painted silk wallpaper, every room setting a different scene. The parlour reminded me of Forsyth Park with its grand old oaks, while my bedroom felt more like the little park outside my window, birds and squirrels playing hide and seek among the eternally flowering azaleas, but entering the upstairs hallway was like losing yourself in Georgia's marshlands. Tall grasses swayed softly and dozens of tiny critters darted in and out among the reeds, all day and all night. When I left Ashley to change, ranting to herself about meeting agendas and historic landmark by-laws, the gentle breeze that always blew through, no matter the weather outside, had become a bitter wind, and an unexpected chill picked its way down my spine. There wasn't so much as a periwinkle snail to be seen. Even the cordgrass seemed to pull away from me. I pressed my hand against the wall but it trembled under my palm. Something was off and the house wanted me to know.

There were only three rooms on the second floor: mine, Ashley's and, at the end of the hall, Catherine's, which had been sealed shut ever since she failed to return home after my Becoming. Sealed not by magic but by choice. Neither Ashley nor myself had any interest in stepping foot inside. Beyond my grandmother's room, the staircase looped around, climbing up to the third floor of Bell House. Catherine had forbidden me to go up there. It was dangerous, she said, structurally unsound. But how could I trust anything she'd told me? Whatever had sent the marshland creatures scrambling had nothing to do with an unsafe roofing situation.

Without realizing I'd moved, I found myself at the foot of the stairs. The midnight blue ceiling was directly above me, so dense it looked like velvet with every constellation picked out in silver paint. Beneath my feet, brass runners held down a lush maroon carpet that led up the stairs to an ornately carved mahogany door. My parents' old rooms. The rooms where I'd spent the first months of my life. For four long weeks, I'd almost forgotten about it. Too much going on to worry about attic rooms full of lost memories. But now . . .

A sudden beating of wings broke through the quiet and I spun around to see a stork rising from the marshes, taking to the air on the wall behind me and flying into nothingness. With one last glance upstairs, I turned and sprinted back along the hallway and all the way down the stairs to the ground floor.

Hanging on the banister, panting, I looked up at the midnight fresco above me. With my grandmother gone, the house belonged to me, the sole surviving Bell witch. There was literally nothing to stop me walking right back up there, opening the door to the third floor and finding out what secrets lay inside for myself.

But I didn't. I couldn't. I literally could not move. My feet were glued to the ground and I wasn't holding onto the banister anymore, the banister was holding onto me. It was only when I let go of the notion to visit the third floor that Bell House released me, allowing me back into the parlour to work on my orchid.

It wasn't Catherine who didn't want me up there after all.

It was the house.

Chapter Two

Before he died, my dad and I travelled all the time. In sixteen years, I'd lived in more than a dozen countries, unpacking my single suitcase everywhere from exciting, overcrowded cities to sleepy little villages where our nearest neighbours were sheep. I'd always found something to love about the place we lived, but there was nowhere on earth quite like Savannah.

After waving Ashley off to her meeting, I stayed outside, lounging on the front steps until the fuzzy humidity of the early evening swallowed me whole. I'd thought it was hot when I arrived back in May. Then June came and I realized we were just starting. Now, the oppressive July temperatures made my memories of May seem practically arctic. The air was so thick it felt like a tangible thing, something I could take hold of and wrap around myself like a blanket. Too close, too sweaty, and absolutely perfect. Every day, I felt closer to my magic and, as our connection grew stronger, I became more attuned to the harmony of the natural world. This weather wasn't exactly pleasant, but it was exactly as it should be and when Mother Nature was happy, I was happy. She adored the scorching days and sweaty nights. The people of Savannah? Not so much.

The Witch and the Wolf

Settling on the sun-warm stone steps, I wrapped my arms around my shins and rested my chin on my knees, watching as my city passed by. People walking their dogs, others taking their nightly stroll, the masochistic runners attempting a not-so-speedy jog, all passed through Lafayette Square, and I liked to daydream about where they were going. Down to River Street to watch the enormous container ships pass under Talmadge Bridge? Up to the park to lap the fountain? Or maybe they had nowhere in particular to be. Wandering aimlessly around the city used to be one of my favourite things to do. I loved getting lost in the historic district, zigzagging around Savannah's squares, studying the beautiful old houses and dodging the tourist-laden horse-drawn carriages, before inevitably ending up at Leopold's Ice Cream Parlour for a double scoop of caramel swirl and butter pecan. Lately, I'd found myself sticking closer to Bell House. Or to be more accurate, I did not leave. Ever since my birthday, I hadn't been in the mood to do much of anything but sit in my room and stare out the window. Even making it out as far as the front steps felt like an achievement. But when I stayed home, Savannah stayed safe. Seemed like a fair trade to me.

The sweltering weather didn't let up as evening approached. We still had another good couple of hours of daylight, the sunset a long way off, but when I turned my gaze to the sky, the moon was already peeking out from behind the spire of the cathedral, a pale shadow of itself, almost transparent against the fading blue. Four weeks since the last full moon. I couldn't help but wonder what this one would bring.

My fingertips tingled as I traced abstract shapes on the ground beside me and pictured Wyn, somewhere out there, waiting to phase. As much as it hurt, the radio silence between us wasn't unexpected. Before he went quiet he told me his mother and his grandfather, both senior members of his pack, were taking him out of town to some sort of secret Were camp, and I could tell from the tone of his voice they weren't going to be making s'mores and singing around the campfire. No phones, no computers, no communication with the outside world whatsoever. Only, Wyn's mom and grandpa hadn't reckoned on the fact I didn't need a strong WiFi connection to check on my love.

Turning my longing outward, I searched for him across the miles. It was something I'd got better at, locating people across long distances. Before my Becoming, I was able to latch on to a general sense of someone; provided I'd met them before and knew who to look for, it was simple enough to get a broad idea of their whereabouts, whether they were safe or in trouble, alive or dead. Now it was clearer, like someone had boosted the signal. Hidden away in the mountains of North Carolina, surrounded by magic ancient as mine, Wyn still shone as brightly as the North Star. There was a golden string wrapped around our hearts, long enough to span any distance and strong enough to survive any threat. Nothing could sever our connection. I wouldn't allow it.

He appeared to me as soon as I closed my eyes. So tall and handsome, with chameleon eyes of green and grey and bronze, I still couldn't believe he was mine. He was running along the side of a lake, his hair curling against the nape of his neck in dark ash waves, shirtless in the early evening sun, his body glowing in the golden hour. Full lips blew out long and even breaths, powering his lean muscles as he pounded the brush and bracken beneath his feet. There was no sense of fear, he was running to, not running from. His nerves felt easy, excited, and he smiled as he jumped over a fallen log. It was the kind of smile that could make me lose my breath. I was a walking encyclopaedia of his facial expressions. A tentative tilt at the corners of his mouth that came with soft, uncertain eyes, the half-cocked grin, always chased by his rich, warm laugh, and the broad, beaming happiness that forced his cheeks upwards into a joy he could not contain. I knew Wyn the way I knew my favourite song and my memories of him sang like lyrics. His strong arm wrapped around my shoulders, calloused fingertips tracing my cheekbones, full, firm lips pressing against my own. Wyn only ever looked for the good in things, only saw the good in me, and I missed him so much that when I looked down at the step where I sat, a chunk of stone had ground away into dust in my fist.

Things weren't going to be easy for us, we both knew that. Witches and Weres weren't exactly enemies but, as far as I could tell, we didn't count each other as friends either. A fact that was all the more true in my case since I was responsible for the death of his brother, Cole. At the time, I'd had no idea the wolf I'd slain to save my grandmother's life was a Were, but I couldn't envisage a scenario in which the pack would accept that as a defence for my actions. So Wyn hadn't told them. Not yet. They knew Cole was dead but they didn't know exactly how. They knew there was a powerful witch in Savannah but they didn't know exactly who. The two of us had been lied to our whole lives and we'd promised never to keep the truth from one another but that didn't mean we had to share it with everyone else. Yes, our love was complicated, probably reckless, definitely dangerous, but I couldn't change the way I felt, and I knew I would do whatever it took to protect it.

Opening my eyes, I let go of the golden thread and left Wyn to his run, allowing my gaze to wander. A magnificent magnolia tree took pride of place in the front garden of Bell House, rising all the way up to the wrought-iron balcony outside my bedroom window, armed with glossy green leaves, its huge white flowers, bigger than my fist, gone for the summer. I breathed in deeply and allowed the scent of the blossoms to conjure up recently acquired memories: the view from the window on my first night; Lydia climbing the tree to call on me without Ashley knowing; watching a meteor shower on the balcony with Wyn.

I missed him. I missed him so much.

Directly across the street in Lafayette Square, another tree waited patiently for my attention. Another living marker of my time here. The place where we'd exchanged our first words. A live oak with low-hanging branches, each and every one of them draped in swathes of grey-green Spanish moss.

'Only it ain't Spanish and it ain't moss,' I said to myself and the bright pink bobblehead of a zinnia planted beside the steps drooped onto my shoulder to console me.

'Spoken like a true Savannahian.'

I whipped around to see who was there and the zinnias shot up straight, as though they'd been caught doing something they shouldn't. There was no need for concern. Leaning against the front gate, a friendly look on his handsome face, was exactly the right person to pull me out my own head.

'Jackson!' I said, returning his easy, comfortable smile. 'Hey!'

'Em,' he replied with a nod, one hand hovering over the latch on the gate. 'Are y'all open for visitors or is it too late to come calling?'

'You know you're welcome any time.'

Hopping to my feet, I dusted off the back of my shorts as he let himself in the gate. 'What can I get you to drink? We've got everything.'

He laughed and waved away my offer.

'Nothing for me, thank you. And congratulations, your southern training is coming on strong. A true hostess from the hostess city – my grandmother would be proud.'

'Now that's a real compliment,' I said, my cheeks flushing a warm pink.

The Witch and the Wolf

It was to be expected when my best friend's brother was around. The boy was born to make you blush. He always seemed to know exactly what to say with charm to spare, and he hadn't exactly missed out on his fair share of good looks either. His long, muscular legs stretched out from a pair of baggy basketball shorts and his deep brown skin positively glowed as he joined me on the steps, dropping down to the ground and propping himself up on his elbows.

'How's it going?' he asked with genuine interest. 'Haven't seen you in a while.'

I tried to remember the last time and realized he was right, it had been a minute.

'I'm OK,' I said, joining him on the step. 'How about you? Lyds said you were at basketball camp?'

'Finished up yesterday.' He ruffled the loose curls on the top of his head then smoothed down the fade at the side, his subtly expensive cologne wafting my way. 'Now I have two whole weeks of summer vacation to myself.'

'Any big plans?'

'Oh yeah,' he said, lighting up with enthusiasm. 'There's a lecture at the historical society tonight, this guy who grew up here in the 1940s. Gonna be fire.'

I stared at him and he grinned back.

'Seriously? You're voluntarily going to the historical society? On purpose?'

'Hey, dumb jocks can take an interest in history too. Sometimes a guy has layers.'

'You're not dumb,' I corrected right away, nudging his knee with mine. 'Even if you are a jock.'

'Guilty as charged. For real though, it's gonna be fascinating. Mr Moore was involved with the civil rights movement, ran with W.W. Law back in the day. Just think about all the changes he's seen, the stories he must have. Real history is way more interesting than those weird fairy books you and Lyds are so obsessed with.'

'Agree to disagree,' I said archly, earning another laugh. 'Wait, didn't the meeting start already? Ashley left a while ago.'

Jackson shook his head. 'Guest speakers don't go on until seven, before that it's all business and I really don't care who wants to paint their front door an unauthorized shade of pink.'

'Mr Ellison?'

'Mr Ellison,' he repeated with the same groan I'd heard from Ashley. 'No, thank you, I just want to hear the good stuff. I reckon I've learned something new about my family every time I've been to one of these things. Savannah is pretty fascinating, even if you aren't the descendant of a centuries' long line of all-powerful witches.'

'Technically, you are the descendant of a long line of all-powerful witches,' I reminded him. 'Only your line got cut.'

'Thank God.' He looked down at his feet. 'Nothing against witches in general, but can you imagine Lydia with magic? No one would be safe.'

Chewing on the inside of my cheek, I nodded. Once they'd been pulled into the Bell family mess, it hadn't felt right to keep the truth about their own family from the Powells. Their ancestors had been witches, just like mine, but somewhere over the years, their connection to the blessing was lost.

Jackson rubbed a hand over the scruff on his chin. He hadn't shaved in a couple of days and he looked older than he did when he was clean-shaven, more rough around the edges. It suited him.

'She's obsessed, you know? Convinced you must have a way to bring it back.'

I did know. Lydia asked me about reviving her family's lost magic at least once a day, every day.

'My grandmother told me once the blessing is gone from a

line, there's no way to find it again,' I said softly. 'So don't worry too much. Lyds won't be levitating down your street any time soon. There's nothing I can do to change that.'

'Good.'

His eyes hardened and the word fell from his lips like a stone. I couldn't blame him. After what he'd seen, after what Catherine had done, it made sense. Magic was dangerous and who would want to put someone they love in danger? Not Jackson. Not me.

'Full moon tomorrow.'

I looked over at him, surprised.

'No need to look so shocked, Em,' he said, finding his easy smile again. 'When you find out there are giant magical murder wolves masquerading as people twenty-seven days out of the month, keeping an eye on the lunar calendar seems like a pretty sensible thing to do.'

'True,' I admitted, more than a little uneasy at his definition of a Were. 'You really do have a wild selection of hobbies.'

'Basketball, local history, defence against the dark arts. Colleges like to see a diverse mix of extracurriculars.'

He hopped up to his feet, shifting his weight from foot to foot, his hands deep in his pockets. Discomfort rolled off him in waves and I prickled at the unease in his posture. What was this? I didn't think it was humanly possible for Jackson to look this uncomfortable.

'I should get going, this was only meant to be a quick detour on my way to the meeting,' he said, poking at the step with the toe of his sneaker. 'I wanted to ask if you might do me a favour.'

'Of course, anything.'

His eyes lit up.

'Oglethorpe Country Day has its annual varsity fundraiser tomorrow night – kind of a getting-ready-for-the-new-school-year thing? It's basically a dance. They have a band, a photo-booth, killer food. All my friends are going. We get to hang out while the school tries to screw our families for money.'

'Sounds . . . fun?'

The rising inflection at the end of my sentence was intentional. Did it sound fun? I wasn't sure. Jackson stretched his arms up over his head and wrung his hands together as though he didn't know quite what else to do with them.

'So much fun,' he said. 'Only problem is, my date cancelled on me.'

'Someone cancelled on *you*?' I couldn't believe it. If Lydia was to be believed, no one turned down a date with Jackson Powell. Well, there was one exception to the rule.

Me.

'Want me to put a curse on them?' I said, joking. 'Pretty sure I'm not supposed to, but I'll give it a go if you like.'

'Are you sure you didn't already? She texted me from the hospital: she has appendicitis. She's OK but not in much of a dancing mood.'

'You want me to try to heal her?' I asked, not quite following. 'Because if she's in the hospital—'

'No, Em,' Jackson cut in. 'I was thinking, if you're not busy, if you wanted to, you could come to the dance with me.'

My eyes widened and a breeze rustled through the zinnias, their heads bobbing together as though they were debating this development.

'Pretty sure you owe me a date,' he added.

He was right. On my birthday, the two of us had sat in his car outside Bonaventure, Jackson doing his best to take my mind off the terror of what lay ahead, and me agreeing to a rain check even though I didn't know whether I'd still be alive the next day.

'A totally platonic date.' He held his hands out in front of him, fingers splayed wide. 'I'm not trying to step on anyone's toes. Although, if we dance, I might have to take that back. Two left feet over here – don't wear open-toe sandals.'

The look on his face was so genuine and so hopeful, when I opened my mouth to politely turn him down, nothing came out.

'Where is it?' I heard myself ask instead.

'The DeSoto Hotel. If you hate it, you can totally ditch me and be home in under two minutes.'

'Is Lydia going?'

Her brother pulled a sour face at the very thought.

'When I asked if I should get her a ticket she said she'd rather poke out both her eyes with a rusty spoon. Lydia isn't much for school spirit.'

Stifling a smile, I looked at my friend, kind, clever Jackson, picturing him in a suit instead of his late summer uniform of baggy shorts and basketball jersey, and me in the kind of pretty dress I most certainly did not own. I'd never been to a high school dance. The last four weeks had been nothing but study and stress and waiting for Wyn. I thought back to him, running around the lake, content and carefree. Tomorrow was the full moon. If I stayed home, I'd spend the entire night worrying about him when there was no need. He was safe with his family, with his pack. Wyn wouldn't want me alone and unhappy when I could be having fun with my friends.

'I swear we'll have a good time.'

The corners of Jackson's mouth tilted upwards and I realized I didn't want to say no. I wanted to go to the dance with him.

'OK,' I said, a flurry of excitement in my chest. 'I'm in.'

'Really?' He sounded more surprised than I'd expected and I couldn't stop myself from laughing. 'I mean, great! Uh, it's semi-formal but you can pretty much wear whatever you like and, um, I'll pick you up at seven?'

'Seven it is,' I said, watching as he dashed down the path and out the gate before I could change my mind. 'See you then.'

'Everything is going to be perfect, I already know it,' he yelled over his shoulder. 'Don't worry about a thing, we'll have the best time, I promise.'

And for once in my life, I really wanted a prophecy to come true.

Chapter Three

The city was ablaze. Black flames incinerated everything they touched, racing faster than any fire I had ever known, and filling the air with an overwhelming smell of sulphur that made it hard to breathe as I darted through the streets, trying to outrun the scorching heat that hunted me down with as much ferocity as the wolves at my heels.

Past the Olde Pink House, across Bay Street, hurtling down the steep cobblestoned street to Factors Walk, they didn't trip or stumble the same way I did. Grey fur, golden eyes, claws sharp enough to tear a soul in two, the wolves gave chase, howling louder than the end of the world. My bare and bloody feet left a bold trail, as if they couldn't follow the scent of my panic alone. But there was no time to check for injuries, no time to search for a weapon. I'd been sentenced to death by the pack, declaring themselves judge, jury and executioner all in one. If I could get back Bell House I'd be safe, but there was no way I was going to make it that far, not even with my magic. One hundred wolves and one witch, what chance did I have?

Over the roar of the pack, I heard terrible screaming, true

mortal fear made manifest. Someone, something, was feeding on it. Not wolves, not witches but another entity entirely, darker and more devious. Whatever it was, it was expecting me, having waited centuries for this moment. And if the wolves had their way, I would be delivered right on time. The Savannah River roared at my side as I took off down River Street, following the disused streetcar tracks, and I felt the charge of the water, surging forward, pushing me on. Not far now, just a little further. Something sharp sliced into the bottom of my foot, embedding itself in the tender arch, and I gasped, falling to my knees. Before I could recover myself, they were on me, fangs and claws, red hair and red blood in front of my eyes as I held my arms up to defend myself. The scream that tore from my lungs blasted through the city like an explosion, black fire filling the sky, and in the near distance, as the wolves tore into my flesh, I heard someone laughing . . .

I woke with a start, tethered to my mattress by bedsheets turned into ropes. Covered in cold sweat, I disentangled myself, peeling away the damp fabric to free my arms and legs. It was just a dream. I was home, I was in my room. I was safe.

But I wasn't alone.

Between the bookcase and the bathroom I saw a shuddering in the shadows. A shape, a hunched figure, faced the wall. Long strings of matted hair fell down its back as it clawed at the wallpaper, emaciated arms stretching up, jagged, yellow nails leaving scars on the walls. I tried to call for help but couldn't, all the air suddenly sucked from my lungs, silencing my cries. It was so much worse than the wolves, so much more terrible than the invisible threat, only I didn't know why. As the figure slowly turned to face me, its face bone white and hollow, I finally snatched in a breath and screamed so loud it tore up my throat as the thing flew out of the corner and across the room towards me, screeching a single word.

The Witch and the Wolf

'*Onginnan.*'

My eyes snapped open.

I was still anchored to the bed by my sweaty sheets. A dream within a dream, a nightmare wrapped up in a nightmare.

Panting for breath, I tore off the bedclothes and slid to the edge of my four-poster bed, uninjured feet finding the soft rug. Safe and unharmed. At least until my knee collided with the open drawer of my nightstand. Rubbing the injury with one hand and cursing myself under my breath, I switched on my bedside lamp and inspected the contents of the open drawer. The silver filigree pin with its glowing moonstone centre, the smooth pebble of glinting black arfvedsonite, my ice-blue cell phone, and a pouch of protective herbs; lavender, bay laurel, mugwort and yarrow. I flicked off the lamp, somehow safer in the dark, and pulled out the pouch, nursing it to my chest. If these were the dreams I had with protection, I hated to think what my mind might conjure up without it.

Across the room, my window seat called to me, drawing me away from my bed to leave the nightmares behind. It was a beautiful night and the all-but-full moon lit up Lafayette Square and cast a milky luminescence over the sleeping fountain at its heart. The quiet was unnerving, so, almost without thinking, I encouraged the pipes that ran beneath the square to ignore the settings on their timer and spring to life a few hours early. I stared blankly out my window as water began to burble from the fountain, the soothing sound calming my frayed nerves. The window seat was one of my favourite spots in Bell House, somewhere that felt wholly mine. I loved to sit and watch passers-by or stare up at the stars. Wrapping a strand of wavy red hair around my forefinger, I looked up. It helped to know I wasn't alone, not really. Wherever Wyn might be, he was under the same moon, maybe even counting the same stars. I reached out for him, my search featherlight, and found his calm, restful energy. He was sleeping, like I should be.

It was nothing, just a nightmare, my own mind playing tricks on me, no reason to think it was anything more. I hadn't experienced a vision in weeks, that soft fall backwards into velvet black, a scene from the past or future waiting for me on the other side. It was difficult to explain, even to myself, why they didn't feel quite the same. My visions were crystal clear, all of them brought about by something specific, induced by a herb, a ritual. This dark dream was more chaotic, an ugly blend of fears and feelings. My dad had always told me facts are the enemy of fear, seek out the truth and you'll see there's nothing to be afraid of. Of course, he was talking about political and societal unrest rather than waking up in the middle of the night to freak out about being chased by a pack of vengeful, bloodthirsty Weres. But it still applied, kind of. The not knowing of it all was the thing that scared me the most. I'd been raised by a historian, a man in search of the truth, and research was second nature to me, every source and first-hand account checked, double-checked and verified. Problem was, my ancestors hadn't left me much to go on.

Witches, Catherine had told me, were forbidden to write down anything that might give our enemies power over us, and that included a list of our abilities and a detailed account of our history. There were journals in the Bell House library, diaries, but they were full of day-to-day musings rather than thorough accounts of the lives and times of the Bell witches. Once, I found an ancient book containing details of a binding spell but, true to Catherine's promise, it caused more problems than it solved, and after I confronted my grandmother with it, I never saw that book again. All of our history, our knowledge, was handed down from grandmother to granddaughter, shared over a lifetime. Except Catherine and I only had a few weeks together, not decades, and I couldn't be sure the things she'd told me were the truth.

And so I kept records for myself, reciting a litany of my abilities when I lay awake in bed at night, adding new ones whenever they expressed themselves. Some abilities were common to us all, according to my grandmother. I was stronger than I had been before my Becoming, faster too. All witches were closer to the natural world than the average person, attuned to Nature's messages. Beyond that, each of us was gifted with a single special connection to the blessing, a distinct ability, something that would assist our world in its time of need. Catherine was able to manipulate the elements: water, earth, air and fire. The first Emma Catherine Bell, who crossed the Atlantic in 1733, was an English apothecary. She intuitively understood herbs and plants and used them to help the earliest Savannah settlers survive in their new home. Catherine's grandmother had been a conduit, able to move through people's dreams and communicate with those who'd passed over. Her grandmother's grandmother was a healer who saved endless lives in the early twentieth century when the Spanish flu came to the United States.

I was different. I was an apothecary who could see into the past and see visions of the future. I could influence the weather, manipulate the elements, slow my perception of time, heal injuries, sense the location of my loved ones, and I could talk to ghosts – when ghosts wanted to talk to me. According to my grandmother, I was the witch spoken of in a prophecy passed down through our family for centuries. A witch who is born and Becomes under a full moon and a king tide, who will know every gift ever bestowed on her family line and awaken her sleeping sisters and their dormant magic. A witch who must decide whether to save the world or end it. And that was all I knew. I had no idea where the prophecy came from, no clue how I was supposed to find these sleeping witches or revive their magic. Worst of all, there was no ETA on the incoming apocalypse, no explanation of the part I was meant to play. And there was no one to turn to for help, not even in the form of a written record of our history, a guide to our powers. I couldn't even keep track of my own thoughts by documenting them in my Notes app.

Turning my hands over, palms down, I stretched out my fingers and stared at my fingertips. Lyds had given me a manicure on her last visit and every nail was painted a different colour. The pink, purple and blue polishes were already chipped, but the silver glitter on my ring fingers held fast. These were not the hands of a woman destined to end the world. No one with a Sharpie-drawn heart on her thumbnail could be expected to bear that burden. Which was why I needed answers, needed to understand my magic better. Which was why I needed Wyn. Everything seemed to make more sense when he was close by.

A creaking noise across the room revived the memory of my nightmare.

'There's nothing there,' I told myself. 'It's just a dream. Nothing can hurt you inside Bell House.'

But the darker corners of my room called me a liar and demanded proof. My eyes fell on a scented candle sitting on my desk. A belated birthday gift from Ashley, the same kind they used at her new favourite restaurant. With barely any effort, I brought it to life, a spark igniting the paper wick, a flickering flame to illuminate the empty corners of my room. Nothing there. The tiny birds in the tree branches painted on my wallpaper flocked towards the candle. They chirped among themselves, used to being woken in the middle of the night but not in the least amused by it. *We should all be asleep*, they seemed to say, *we should pay no heed to tricks of the mind.*

The Witch and the Wolf

They were right.

Closing the window and lowering the blind, I sloped back to bed and shook out the soft cotton sheet before slipping underneath it. All was quiet, all was well.

Until it wasn't.

A shadow, a cold threat against the warm candlelight, moved between the bookcase and the bathroom, just like it had in my dream. I sat up to see my breath clouding in front of my mouth, the air all at once bitterly cold as a low, sibilant hiss filled the room.

When the dead fight back. When the earth consumes. A lie becomes the truth. She will return.

The flame of the candle exploded into a burning orange fireball when I screamed, exposing the creature. It was tall and slender with long, matted hair that fell in front of greyish white skin, and the empty hollows of its eye sockets seemed to be trained on me. With one swipe of my arm, I sent the flaming candle towards the dark thing, but it was already gone. All the painted birds shrieked at once, feathers flying as they took to the air. My room was empty and my wastepaper basket on fire. Leaping from the bed, I grabbed a forgotten glass of water from my desk and dumped it into the trash, extinguishing the flames, if not the fear that gripped me by the throat.

This time I hadn't been asleep. The creature, whatever it was, had freed itself from my nightmare and found a way into my home, my sanctuary. The one place I truly believed I was safe.

The water glass in my hand cracked and split into three pieces, slicing into my palm, but I felt nothing.

'Em?'

Bleary-eyed and wielding a pair of hair straighteners like a baseball bat, Ashley stumbled into my room.

'Em, is everything OK?'

'I saw – I had a bad dream,' I said shakily, eyes fixed on the spot between the old mahogany wardrobe and the open bathroom door as blood dripped from my hand onto the rug.

Pressing the heels of her hands into her eyes, my aunt let out a frustrated sigh.

'A dream? Great. Stay there, I'll get the whiskey.'

I shook my head.

'I don't want a drink,' I told her. 'I'm fine.'

'Good, because I didn't say I was getting it for you.'

She left the door open, the hallway light spilling in and illuminating the darkest corners of my room. Completely empty. No one here but me. The birds settled back on their branches, a little higher than they'd been before, and all of them on the opposite side of the room to the bathroom door.

'It's gone,' I said aloud, the words making the facts real as the cut on my hand sealed itself shut. 'It's gone and you're safe.'

But I knew better than to lie, even to myself.

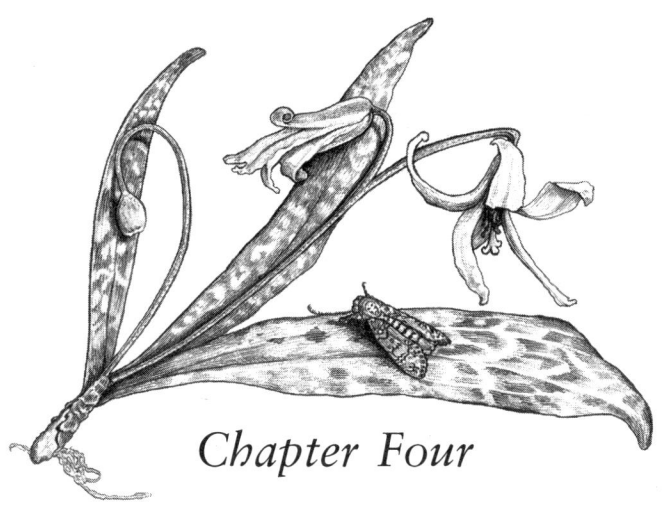

Chapter Four

'Let me get this straight,' Lydia said, peering at me from over the top of her heart-shaped sunglasses. 'Out of all the places we could spend this beautiful day, you want to hang out in a cemetery?'

'Just in case you're not feeling it,' I said, holding out a white paper bag, already beginning to turn transparent from the greasy goodness inside. 'I brought a bribe.'

My best friend's eyes popped open and she snatched the bag from my hand, sticking her nose in and inhaling deeply.

'Em, you know I would follow you through the gates of hell for a fried chicken biscuit,' she declared. 'But please don't hold me to that.'

The Colonial Park Cemetery was busy. No matter how high the temperature soared, Savannah's tourists never failed to ignore the memo about staying out of the heat, continuing to bop around town in their belted chino shorts and slip-on Skechers, damp patches appearing on the back of their popped-collar polos. I had slathered myself in sunscreen and put on a flowing blue slip dress that touched as little of my body as possible, my hair clamped in a claw clip on the top of my head.

As with everything else, Lydia managed the sun in her own vibrant way; her fluffy black curls were held back from her face with a stretchy fabric headband that matched her neon pink tube top and bike shorts.

After the incident in my room, I'd spent the rest of the night in the parlour, staring out the window and willing the sun to rise. But even magic as deep as mine couldn't hasten the dawn. While Ashley dozed on the sofa, insisting she was awake every time her snoring woke her up, I kept my eyes on the sky, impatiently waiting for the hazy pinks and lavenders of dawn. Candles burned out. Electric lights failed. I needed the safety of sunlight to chase away the shadows, and anything or anyone who might be lurking within.

I messaged Lydia before the sun rose and as soon as the two little blue checkmarks appeared next to my message, I was up and out the house, banging on her front door ten minutes later.

'It is too darn hot,' she said, turning her face up to the sun to bask in its savage rays. 'I'm sweating worse than a hooker in church on a Sunday.'

'Can't think why my dad never shared such a pretty southern saying with me,' I said. 'To think your grandmother wanted you to be a debutante.'

'My grandmother wanted me to be a lot of things,' she returned with a dark look. 'She's learned to live with the disappointment.'

With the sun directly overhead, we walked across the grass towards an elm tree and Lydia flopped down to the floor, melting under its leaves and branches. I knelt beside her, pressed my palms into the earth and blew a gentle breath out through pursed lips. The softest of breezes sprang up around us, brushing against my skin before ruffling her curls.

'Does that help?'

She relaxed against the grass and exhaled a blissful sigh.

The Witch and the Wolf

'My own portable air conditioner. How did I ever survive without you?'

'Pretty well, as I recall. One hundred per cent fewer Sleeping Beauty moments in your pre-Emily past.'

Ignoring my comment, she tore into the bag I'd given her, pulling out the wax-paper-wrapped chicken biscuit sandwich. A couple in matching Georgia Tech T-shirts shot us filthy looks as they hurried by, the sounds coming out of Lydia's mouth not entirely suitable for a public audience.

'You know it causes me physical pain to say anything nice about your aunt,' she said, her huge brown eyes rolling in ecstasy. 'But she should really think about opening a restaurant. This biscuit is even better than Virginia's.'

It was high praise. Lydia's grandmother was almost as famous for her baked goods as she was for her old-fashioned southern manners and perpetual state of hypochondria.

'She's been trying to teach me how to make them but mine never turn out as good as hers,' I said as I started on my own sandwich. 'She says my hands are too hot.'

Lydia clucked in response.

'Makes sense that hers would be ice-cold. Seriously, Em, you couldn't find another single soul in this city to save my life? Not that I'm not grateful but she's going to hold it over me forever, which is, not to exaggerate, almost worse than spending the rest of my days in a catatonic state.'

'And there I was thinking how well the two of you have been getting along lately.'

She looked at me as though I'd suggested the sun was green.

'Last time I came calling, she was watching some old movie and I was trying to be nice, so I said she looked just like the leading actress. And she told me that I reminded her of one of the cast of *Dune*.'

'That's hardly an insult.'

'She meant the worm.'

A piece of chicken caught in my throat as my laughter turned into a coughing fit, Lydia banging me between my shoulder blades as I swallowed it down.

'I still think it's a big step up from where you were before,' I said, swiping at my wet eyes with a napkin. 'The two of you will be besties by Christmas.'

'I'd say stranger things have happened but, knowing everything I do, that would be a lie.' She popped the tab on a can of Coke and settled down with her back against the tree, looking out over the cemetery. 'You know we were never allowed to hang out here when we were kids. Virginia calls this place "the Devil's Sandbox".'

'Well, that's not creepy at all. Any specific reason?'

'It's haunted.'

I had to smile.

'Everywhere in Savannah is haunted.'

'Yeah, but the cemetery is haunted by some dude named Rene Rondolier.'

She pronounced his name with a forced, spooky intonation, her eyebrows creeping up her forehead as she spoke.

'And what did Rene do?' I asked, not sure I wanted to know the answer.

'Depends who you ask,' she said. 'Some folks say he was the innocent victim of an angry mob. Others say he was a supernaturally strong giant covered in fur who murdered kids for kicks from beyond the grave.'

For the first time in a month, I was pleased the ghosts of Savannah were playing hard to get. Rene did not sound like the kind of person I wanted to share my lunch with.

'According to the stories, he tortured and killed a bunch of people's pets, so the townsfolk demanded his family keep him in their house, which was right over' – Lydia twisted at the waist, searching over her shoulder then pointing at a tall, red-brick house on the eastern boundary of the cemetery – 'there. His folks, who were filthy rich by the way, built this crazy tall wall to keep him in, but the dude was, like, seven feet tall and strong as an ox, so naturally he got out. The same night, a couple of kids were killed so the townspeople came together to overpower him. And that' – a croaking sound scratched the back of her throat as she drew a finger across her neck and stuck out her tongue, her eyes rolling back in her head – 'was the end of Rene Rondolier.'

'When you say a couple of kids "got killed",' I said, my gut twisting at her casual turn of phrase, 'do you mean they were murdered?'

'Two died before they got him but then two more died in the exact same way afterwards, plus a woman. So who knows? Maybe he had unfinished business to complete, or maybe he had nothing to do with the murders in the first place. Guess we'll never know.'

'So they killed a man without any evidence then blamed his ghost for three more deaths?' I said, eyes bugging out of my head.

Lydia shrugged and picked at her sandwich.

'Wouldn't you rather blame a ghost than admit you unalived the wrong man? It was the nineteenth century, things were very kill-first-ask-questions-later. Much quicker than going through the courts. The folks in charge decided he did it so they cancelled him. Off the planet.' She paused to lick hot honey from her fingers. 'There was no legit proof Rondolier did it but, you know how it is; he was different to everyone else and people don't like different.'

It wasn't the first time I'd heard those exact words. More than two hundred years after Rene lost his life and we witches, Weres, and whatever else was out there, all stayed hidden for the same reason. Sliding the rest of my sandwich back into its paper bag, I tucked it away in the canvas tote at my side. Strangely enough, my appetite had disappeared.

Lydia continued to inhale her lunch and I leaned back in the grass, quietly checking for any ghostly goings on among the gravestones and monuments. My first ever encounter with a ghost had taken place in Colonial Park. This was where I'd seen the original Emma Catherine Bell. Perhaps Ashley was right: I wasn't ready to set foot back in Bonaventure just yet. All the same, I kept hoping she might decide to show herself. It was a strange feeling, being ghosted by every ghost in the city. The perennial new kid wherever I went, I was used to being shunned by the cool kids, but being shunned by ghosts was truly a new low in the popularity stakes. One of the privileges of being dead, it seemed, was the ability to decide whether or not you wanted to interact with the living. And right now it seemed no one wanted anything to do with me. As the only witch in the entire city, it was hard not to feel just a little offended.

Other than myself and Lydia, there was no one else around save a handful of tourists, electronic fans hanging around their necks and golf visors dipped low over pink faces. Most sensible people were inside, as close to an air conditioning unit as humanly possible. Even as a relative newcomer to the city, I found it easy to discern locals from visitors here in the park. Out of towners tended not to linger in the cemetery. They wandered in, read a couple of the historical markers, snapped a picture of Button Gwinnett's grave, then they found themselves back out on the street at the other end of the block, keen to move onto the next sightseeing opportunity. Savannahians, on the other hand, were in no rush. They strolled, they sat, while their kids scrambled over the climbing frame in the playground at the southern end of the cemetery, separated from

The Witch and the Wolf

the grave markers by nothing more than a set of open iron railings.

Savannah's citizens were far less squeamish about spending time with the dead than most people and it wasn't difficult to understand why. They were practically everywhere. So many of the city's historic homes and landmarks were built on top of burial grounds. Just last week, Ashley had come home from some city planning meeting, desperate to tell me how Mr Preston on Bull Street had dug up a complete human skeleton while prepping his backyard for a new koi pond. Mr Preston and his very expensive fish were currently waiting for the Georgia Bureau of Investigation to clarify what, or rather who, was squatting on his property. Or was it the other way around?

'OK, enough murder ghost chat, on to something way scarier,' Lydia said as she screwed her empty sandwich bag into a tiny ball. 'I know why you asked me to come here today.'

'You do?'

'I do,' she said with confidence. 'You wanted to soften me up before confessing that you're going on a date with my brother.'

'It's not a date!' I protested loudly as Lydia clapped her hands together in delight at my reaction.

'Sure. Whatever you say.'

'It is not a date,' I said again. 'I am nothing but a last-minute platonic stand-in for the girl who cancelled.'

'A girl cancelled on *my* brother?'

'Yes.'

'The day before the dance?'

'That is correct.'

'Huh.'

'You're going to feel terrible in a minute,' I told her. 'She's in the hospital.'

'Who is?'

'His date!'

I knew she was messing with me but I still fell for it. Lydia paused to bounce her pointer finger against the tip of her nose. 'And what terrible ailment struck down this alleged date?'

'Appendicitis.'

'Ri-i-i-i-i-i-i-ight.'

She stretched the word out just long enough to make it clear she didn't believe me.

'It's not a date,' I said, my voice hot. 'I'm doing him a favour, don't make it weird.'

'One question. Did he happen to mention this supposed date's name?'

I bit my lip, racking my brains. He had not.

'Because I hadn't heard anything about a date or a girl with a burst appendix, and that kind of news travels weirdly fast,' she said. 'And if I was trying to get someone to go on a date with me who definitely was not inclined to agree to go on a date with me, inventing a hospitalized hottie wouldn't be the furthest thought from my mind.'

'That's because you're a terrible person,' I said, and she laughed. 'No one would make up something like that.'

Propping herself up on her elbows, exactly the way Jackson had the night before, Lydia grinned. 'Sure, babe.'

'Besides,' I added, picking at a few strands of sun-scorched grass by my side. 'He knows I'm in love with Wyn.'

'He also knows Wyn hasn't been around lately.'

I flashed a warning look in her direction.

'Which means nothing and I'm not reading into that at all, and Jackson definitely won't be either, and I can see from the look on your face that you're completely chill about it so I won't mention it again ever as long as I live.'

'Appreciated,' I replied with a nod.

'I know!' She sat up, suddenly excited. 'Why don't we cast

a truth spell? You make the potion and I can sneak it into his gross post-workout smoothie, then we'd know for sure.'

'You really think the answer is to drug your brother?'

'Almost always.'

She reached for the necklace that hung from her neck, the silver twin of the gold locket hanging around mine, her eyes wandering across the cemetery. 'Although, if I were a witch, I could make the potion on my own . . .'

This again. A variation on the same conversation we'd had a hundred times since I told the twins about their magical ancestors. It wasn't a total surprise; if there was any chance she had a magical legacy, it made sense that Lydia would want it restored. That much made sense. But the thought of willingly putting her in danger? That was something else entirely.

'That's not why we're here,' I said, attempting to steer the conversation in a different direction. 'I was hoping Emma Catherine might make an appearance.'

'The OG?'

I nodded. 'Tomorrow is the full moon and I have so many questions. I figured, maybe, if we came to the cemetery . . .'

'Well, did you bring a chicken biscuit for her too?' she asked with a kind smile. 'No sign of her, huh?'

'No sign,' I confirmed. 'It's frustrating. What's the point in having all these abilities if I can't use them?'

'I wonder what kind of abilities I would have had.' Lydia looked contemplative, elbows digging into her thighs, chin resting on her fists. 'Something cool, for sure. Can witches fly? I would be very open to flying.'

'Lyds,' I started slowly, rubbing my locket between my finger and thumb. 'I wish there was something I could do but—'

'But once the magic is gone from a family, it's gone for good. Yeah, I know.'

The July heat weighed down on me, pressing my bones into

the hard ground. Lydia batted the scrunched-up paper bag back and forth in front of her like a kitten with a ball. All that was missing was the tinkle of a bell.

'Only, it's part of your prophecy, isn't it?' she said after a moment. 'To awaken your sisters, to revive dormant magic? That could be me.'

'Funny how you're super keen for the prophecy to be accurate when it might concern you but not so much when it talks about defeating enemies and ending the world,' I said, one eyebrow raised.

'Not that funny. My part sounds badass.'

'Then you must not have been paying attention over the last few weeks,' I said. 'I'm sorry, I really am, but I'm sure Catherine would've told me if there was a chance of bringing your family's magic back. Your grandmother was – *is* – her best friend.'

'Catherine said a lot of things, including but not limited to, I'm going to kill your parents and your friends, and I'll get you, my pretty, and your little werewolf too.'

'I don't think they were her exact words,' I replied with a frown.

But Lydia wasn't about to give up that easy.

'If it's not written anywhere, how can you be so sure? You said it yourself: according to your ghosties, nothing is set in stone. There must be a test I can take. Can't you prick my finger and drop my blood in the cauldron, see if the smoke turns white?'

'Lyds, that's the Pope.'

'Then put me through the *Survivor* trials you did with Catherine,' she insisted, refusing to let the matter drop. 'Let's me and you go for a midnight stroll around Wormsloe, tiptoe through the headstones of Bonaventure or whatever. Just witch me up already.'

'Being a witch isn't exactly fun,' I said, still hoping to change her mind in spite of the fact I was well aware that had never, ever happened in the almost-seventeen years she'd been on this planet. 'Besides, I have no idea how to even conduct the rituals. If I got something wrong and anything happened to you . . .' I rested a hand on my friend's knee. 'I'd never be able to forgive myself.'

Lydia curled her hand around mine. 'I know you would never put my life in danger on purpose, but don't you have Witchipedia plugged right into your brain now? Can't you press a button and pull it all up?'

'It doesn't work like that,' I said with a wry smile. 'Some things are meant to be passed down generation to generation.'

She was right in a way. All the knowledge of every Bell witch who went before existed within me, but accessing it wasn't quite so straightforward. I wasn't a walking encyclopaedia, it wasn't like turning on my laptop and opening a search engine; more like chasing down a memory. Sometimes crystal-clear, sometimes fading away or just out of reach. There were things I knew instinctively, like which herbs to blend for a good night's sleep, how to start a fire or summon the wind, but there were plenty of others that remained a mystery. Where the blessing came from, why had I been chosen and, most frustratingly right now, how was I supposed to awaken my sisters.

Lydia twisted a chunky silver ring around and around on her pointer finger and I had to stop myself from telling her it would all be OK, because I didn't know if that was true.

'It's not only about the magic,' she said, looking over at me with her head cocked to one side. 'I want to help. You have no idea what it's like, to know about all this stuff and feel so powerless. If there's a way to get my family's magic back, I want it. I want something to belong to.'

She hid it well, but the queer, mixed race girl twin who'd

never known her father, whose mother left her behind to live with her new husband, whose grandmother didn't know quite what to do with her, longed to belong. Even her twin, who she loved more than anyone, made her feel like an outsider. Not intentionally; it was just that Jackson was all easy charm and inviting charisma, while she kept people at a distance. For all her bright colours, bravery and bluster, underneath it all, Lydia was just as lost as I was. We were two outsiders who never quite fit in, until my Becoming made me part of a magical tradition that, from Lydia's perspective, I was refusing to share.

'You do belong,' I said, squeezing her hand tightly. 'You don't need magic to matter, not to me.'

'But I want it,' she whispered back. 'Em, I want it so bad.'

'I know,' I said. 'But your seventeenth is so soon and, from everything Catherine told me, if you had abilities, they would have manifested by now.'

'Again with the unreliable narrator.'

She huffed and tossed her balled-up paper bag into the open mouth of my tote. 'Just say you'll help me. I'll do all the research myself if you tell me where to look.'

And though I'd assured Jackson there was nothing I could do to connect Lydia to the blessing, there was a selfish part of me that wanted her to be my sister in magic. Against my better judgement, I nodded and her face brightened like the sun on a cloudy day.

'I will,' I said, guilty and relieved all at the same time. 'I'll check the books in Bell House again, and you keep digging for any information you can find on your ancestors. Anything could be helpful: family tree stuff, weird stories about the women in your family, that sort of thing.'

'The *only* stories we have in my family are weird stories,' she said with a snort. 'I asked Virginia if she knew any good ones and she told me about a distant cousin of hers who ran away to join the circus. I thought that was just a thing people said, not something anyone would actually do.'

'And you think she was a witch?'

Lydia shook her head.

'Trapeze artist. Only she wasn't so great at it – broke both her legs her first week on the road. Came crawling back to Savannah. Literally. Anyway, Virginia was a bust, but my mom gets in tomorrow. Maybe she'll have some useful info.'

My head snapped around so sharply I felt a twinge in my neck. 'Your mom is coming to town?'

Alexandra Powell wasn't a witch but she definitely knew a thing or two about keeping secrets. My father's childhood best friend, Alex had been close to both my parents. The matching lockets Lydia and I wore had once belonged to Alex and my mom. She'd even managed to stay in touch with my dad during his self-imposed sixteen-year exile. Ever since I found out how close our parents had been, I'd been pestering Lydia to introduce us, but Alex hadn't been anywhere near Savannah in months, and their mother–daughter relationship wasn't without its own complications.

'Yeah, I know I told you,' Lydia said, giving me a gentle kick. 'Every year we go to Hilton Head for the last week of summer vacation. One of Virginia's fancy friends loans us their fancy house. You said you'd come with, remember?'

'I did?' I replied. 'When?'

'Before or after you found out you were a witch, fell in love with a werewolf, almost got trapped in an underground crypt and had to fight your psycho grandmother, you mean?'

I nodded.

'Somewhere in the middle,' she said with a shrug. 'Either way, you're not leaving me with my mother, Jackson, Virginia and *Jeremy*, so don't even think about trying to get out of it.'

'Wouldn't dream of it,' I replied, parking that problem for future me.

'So, this non-date of yours,' Lydia said, changing the subject. 'What are you wearing?'

'The only formal dress I own is the one Catherine had made for my Becoming,' I said, thinking about the gorgeous white gown that had been hanging in the back of my closet for the last four weeks, unworn. 'Will that do?'

'Way too dressy for a party like this. I suffered through one a couple of years ago. It's more fun-formal-fancy than debutante-formal-fancy.'

My face flattened with confusion.

'I literally have no idea what you just said.'

'Don't sweat it.' She picked up her can of Coke, took a sip and smacked her lips together. 'You can wear something of mine.'

'You own fun-formal-fancy party dresses?'

'I contain multitudes. Let's go take a look.'

'Thank you,' I said, pulling myself to my feet and wrapping my arms around her in a hug. 'You're the best, you know that?'

'Sure do,' she replied with a grin. 'But it's nice to be reminded every now and then.'

I draped my arm around her shoulders and she wrapped hers around my waist as we walked and talked. Not much had gone smoothly over the last few months, but as we strolled out of the cemetery and back up Abercorn in the direction of the Powell House, I was beyond grateful for her existence. Lydia was the best friend I'd ever had and I would do everything in my power to protect her.

Chapter Five

'Will you please stop fidgeting?' Ashley said as I fussed with my borrowed dress. 'If you're not comfortable, go get changed.'

'Changed into what?' I pulled up my left shoulder strap for the tenth time in the last sixty seconds. 'Do you have something I could wear?'

'Absolutely not.'

As helpful as ever.

Lydia had me try on every dress in her vast collection, declaring me a lost cause when I vetoed her first ten picks for being too short, too tight or both. By the time she was done, my arms ached from raising them up and down as she dressed me up like a Barbie doll, I was left with one vaguely wearable option, and no time or energy to shop for an alternative. Ashley rolled her eyes when I tugged at the lipstick-red hemline of the only dress that wouldn't bring my father back from the dead just so he could say 'There's no way you're leaving the house in that, missy.'

'Just relax, would you?' Ashley said. 'There's no reason to feel so self-conscious, I see kids wearing that kind of thing all the time.'

'You don't wear this kind of thing.'

She gave an offended snort. 'That's because I have no desire to walk around looking like a busted can of biscuits, thank you very much.'

'I don't understand what you just said but I know it didn't make me feel better.' I glanced at the clock; Jackson would be here in five minutes. No time to start from scratch. 'Maybe I'd feel better if I put something over it, like a wrap or a sweater?'

'Or a trash bag. We have some of those scented Hefty bags in the kitchen. They smell better than whatever perfume you're wearing.'

She placed her romance novel face down on the sofa, pages splayed open as I let out a howl of despair.

'Calm down, you're going to a party not marching out to your death. Unless you've had a vision of marching out to your death at the party?'

'The last time I marched out to my death, I felt better about my outfit,' I said, gloomy grey clouds assembling on the ceiling of the parlour. Ashley cast her eyes upwards, and pursed her lips, displeased.

'If you make it rain in here, I'll kill you. I just got a blowout.'

I looked longingly at my aunt, legs up, book beside her, an icy glass of lemonade on the coffee table next to a plate of freshly baked cookies. A perfect evening ahead of her. Why on earth had I agreed to go to this dance in the first place?

Ashley folded her arms over her tie-dye tank top, an article of clothing Catherine would never have allowed – which I guessed was the point of it – and zeroed in on me with a glare.

'You look fine, you smell fine and you're being a fool,' she said. 'There is no need to be so anxious. Anyone would think you've never been to a party before.'

'But I haven't,' I said, allowing myself a delicate, self-pitying sniff. 'At least, not a party like this.'

The Witch and the Wolf

My planned seventeenth birthday celebration had been understandably postponed after the whole disappearing grandmother, Lydia-in-a-coma, me and Wyn nearly dying thing. Before that, I'd been home-schooled my entire teenage life. This was officially my first ever formal dance and I was almost as stressed out about it as I was about the 4 a.m. incident in my room.

'It feels wrong,' I said, throwing my arms out wide then letting them flop to my sides.

'The dress? It should.'

'Going to a party,' I corrected her, scowling when she yawned. 'I ought to be looking for Catherine and figuring out the prophecy, not hanging around at a dumb dance.'

'You were planning to figure all of that out this evening? Impressive. I guess you've been sitting on your ass doing nothing for the last month.'

My lips pulled together in a pout and the hands of the clock ticked forward one more minute.

'Speaking as someone who physically could not leave this house for eleven years,' Ashley said, ignoring my sulky expression, 'locking yourself away in Bell House will not help anyone or anything. What's the point in saving the world if you're not out there living in it? And before you start with me, yes, I know, Fido is your soulmate or fated mate or whatever you crazy kids are calling it these days. But you should still be out there, spending time with other people, having the teensiest, tiniest amount of fun. Since hanging around like a bad smell hasn't improved the situation, why not see if a change of scene will do you some good.'

'But what if something happens while I'm out? What if the prophecy is supposed to happen tonight? Or I cause another earthquake? Or Wyn's pack figure out what really happened to Cole? Or—'

Ashley slammed her book shut with a loud and dusty clap.

'Jeez, are you not capable of doing a single damn thing without overthinking it?'

I paused to consider my answer.

'I guess not,' she said with a sigh. 'Em, I say this with love. You're young, you're new in town, you could end the world at any second. Why wouldn't you want to sample everything it has to offer before you annihilate the city and sentence us all to death?'

Truly, my aunt had a beautiful way with words.

'And if nothing else, get out from under my damn feet for one blissful evening,' she muttered as she went back to her book. 'Watching you mope around with a face like you've been sucking farts out of a possum's butt, it's enough to drive a woman to drink. More than usual.'

As much as I hated to admit it, even to myself, she had a point. Not about the possum's butt, perhaps, but I'd been haunting Bell House like I was already dead. Perhaps it was time to start living.

With a reluctant look in the mirror that hung over the fireplace, I adjusted the spaghetti straps of my dress one last time and straightened my shoulders. I could do this. For one night only, I could be a normal girl at a normal party, talking about normal things.

'You done with your fussing?' Ashley said, her green eyes meeting mine in the mirror.

'Yes,' I replied, fighting the overwhelming urge to tug at my dress again.

'Good, because your date just walked through the gate and will be knocking on the front door in approximately fifteen seconds,' she said, making me break out into a cold sweat all over again. 'I may not agree with all my mother's rules, regulations and homicidal tendencies, but there is still something to be said for good manners. When a lady accepts a date, she does not spend the entire evening looking lower than a bow-legged caterpillar, so find a smile, sunshine.'

Right on cue, the doorbell rang. I glanced up at the storm clouds on the ceiling, chasing them away to leave the parlour walls their pale and proper sky blue. In one languorous movement, Ashley rose from her spot on the sofa while I checked the unchanged contents of my borrowed evening bag just to have something to do with my hands.

'Now, if you're done with your hissy fit, I'll go get the door while you concentrate on not summoning a natural disaster,' she said. 'If it's all the same to you, I would really rather not have my internal organs crushed into tomato paste again.'

'Can't a girl accidentally cause an earthquake one time without having it thrown back in her face forever?' I muttered as she sauntered away into the foyer, the sound of our double doors swinging open and Ashley's gushing tones echoing through the house.

'Why, Mr Powell, I do declare,' I heard her exclaim. 'You look like quite the gentleman.'

'Thank you, Miss Ashley, I do try my best. May I say you're looking radiant this evening.'

Great. Here I was, worrying about the end of the world, and the two of them were cosplaying *Gone with the Wind*.

In the bottom of my bag, I felt my phone vibrate and opened it to take a quick peek. A text from Lydia:

> I am trusting you with my brother's honour
>
> jk he has none
>
> if you even pity make-out with him, I will kill you

Nothing for her to worry about there. When I cleared the notifications, smiling up at me from the lock screen was the selfie I'd snapped of me and Wyn at Tybee Island. The skies were blue, the sun was bright, and Wyn's indescribable eyes crinkled with the same happiness written all over my face. I ran a fingernail over the glass screen, keeping my touch light so as not to disrupt the image, then closed my eyes and cast out a net, searching for him. He was there, somewhere in the mountains, but the connection was quieter than before, out of focus almost. In the murky, unclear depths of my newly acquired magical knowledge, I knew it was because of the full moon. The phase was coming, his bond to the pack growing in strength and pulling him further away from me.

'Holy shit.'

I looked up to see a slack-jawed Jackson Powell in the doorway, hovering as though halted by some invisible forcefield. A smirking Ashley Bell followed closely behind, the look on her face completely contradicting his expression of disbelief. Was it possible to die of embarrassment? We were about to find out.

'I take back the gentleman comment.' Ashley clipped him around the back of the head as I tucked a loose curl behind my ear, blushing such a deep shade of scarlet, my dress looked like camouflage. 'I believe what you meant to say was, "Goodness, Miss Emily, you sure do look as pretty as a picture."'

'Nope,' Jackson said, tugging at the knot of his tie. 'I said holy shit and I meant it. Em, you look incredible. Totally . . .' He flicked his eyes over at Ashley before finishing his sentence. 'Pretty as a picture.'

'You're a fast learner,' she said with approval. 'But her eyes are up top, mister.'

'It's not my usual style,' I muttered, trying to figure out what to do with my arms. They swung around in front of me like a magician trying to distract someone from their trick. Jackson only continued to stare, unabashed, like he'd won some sort of prize.

'You look great yourself,' I added, nodding awkwardly at his sharp lines and crisp fabrics.

My date pulled at the starched collar of his white shirt with one crooked finger, a pretence of discomfort for my benefit. He truly looked born to wear it.

'Not my usual either, but my grandmother would have me in a suit seven days a week if she could,' he said. 'Oh, hey, I have something for you.'

He held out a white cardboard box, small and square, a little larger than his hands.

'Cake?' Ashley enquired hopefully.

'No, but Lyds was cooking up a batch of red velvet cupcakes when I left. Last I heard she didn't have plans, if you wanted to stop by.'

'Or I could open up the garbage and eat whatever I find inside instead,' she grumbled in response, and Jackson winked in my direction.

'I didn't know what colour you were wearing so I went with white,' he said as he peeled back a sticker seal and opened the box. 'The lady in the store said this was a classic beauty, so I figured it would be perfect for you.'

Inside, on a bed of pink tissue paper, was a corsage. The swirling petals of a gardenia blossom, its sweet scent filling the air, grounded by the earthy scent of the fern fronds wrapped around it. Gardenia, known to enhance magical abilities, ward off evil spirits and negative energy, and bring serenity to the wearer. And ferns, often used to enhance the abilities of other plants and flowers. Without realizing it, Jackson had gifted me one of the most beautiful protective talismans I'd ever seen.

'I love it,' I said as he slipped it on my wrist before pinning a matching boutonnière to his jacket. 'Thank you.'

'Y'all look like you were made for each other,' Ashley said, hands clasped to her chest and a mischievous smile on her face. 'I just know your folks would be so happy to see this scene. Let me take a picture.'

Before I could protest, Jackson slid his arm around my waist, grinning at her ancient digital camera like it was his best friend in the whole world. The flash popped brightly and I blinked away circles of light, steadying myself against his sturdy warmth. Ashley took one look at the screen and slipped the camera back into her pocket without sharing the result before exchanging her smirk for a not entirely successful attempt at an authoritative glare.

'You have her back by curfew, you hear me?' she said, and I felt my date stiffen at the side of me.

'What time is curfew?' I asked.

She shrugged and looked to Jackson for an answer.

'No idea,' he said. 'Never had one. Does one a.m. sound about right?'

'It sounds extremely lenient,' I said, a sudden flash of panic at the thought of staying from Bell House for so long.

Ashley gave a shallow bow.

'Then you're welcome. Truthfully, I don't give a flying fuck or a rolling doughnut what time y'all come home, just so long as you wake up in your own beds in the morning.'

She waved us through the parlour door, out of the cool air conditioning of Bell House and into the sweltering evening heat.

'Now, y'all have fun tonight,' she called as I tiptoed carefully down the steps in my low heels. 'And don't do anything I wouldn't do.'

'How much does that leave us with?' he asked me out the side of his mouth.

I grimaced as Ashley traded her wave for a flash of her middle finger as soon as he looked away.

'Unless we get arrested for scaling the Pulaski monument completely naked and under the influence, we should be fine.'

'What if we're naked but not under the influence?'

An unfamiliar sensation rushed over me as I climbed into his car, laughing. A swell of anticipation, the good kind. Something I hadn't experienced in a while.

'Ready to have some fun?' Jackson asked, slipping into the driver's seat and closing the door.

I nodded and smiled.

'So ready.'

And as he gunned the engine, much to my surprise, I realized it was true.

By the time I'd fastened my seatbelt without flashing my bra and worked out how to hold my bag over my skirt in a way that would not reveal my underwear, we were already pulling into a parking bay. A man dressed in a dark blue polo shirt waited impatiently to open my door as Jackson hopped out, the car engine still turning over.

'That wasn't even two minutes,' I said, looking back the way we came. 'It would've been quicker to walk.'

He accepted a parking receipt from the valet with a manly nod.

'My grandmother would disinherit me if I invited a lady to a dance then expected her to walk in this heat,' he replied.

'But your grandmother would never know.'

'That's what you think. My grandmother has spies everywhere.' He lowered his voice, eyes darting around. 'Seriously, nothing in this town happens without Virginia Powell knowing about it. Come to think of it, are you sure she isn't a witch?'

'Sure as I can be,' I said, an edge of nerves cutting into my choked laugh.

All around us, people were pouring out of their cars, hugging one another and admiring each other's outfits. As usual, Ashley had been right. My dress was not the least bit out of place. In defiance of the heat, everyone was gussied up in either classic black tuxedos, patterned dinner jackets, or shiny, colourful, strappy dresses. Jackson and I fit right in.

'Is this your first time?' Jackson asked.

I stared at him in surprise and he tilted his head towards the hotel in front of us.

'At the DeSoto?'

'Oh, yes,' I said, squeezing my purse until I felt the beads bite into the flesh of my palm. 'I mean, I've walked by it a million times but I've never been inside. Have you been here before?'

'Feels like we were here every weekend last year. Weddings, birthdays, bar mitzvahs, quinceañeras.' He reeled off occasions as we walked up the steps and into the hotel lobby. 'So many sweet sixteens.'

'Think yourself lucky,' I said, grinning at the look of despair on his face, like they were punishments and not parties. 'There weren't many social events in the Welsh countryside. Not unless you wanted to celebrate the sheep anyway.'

'Trust me, I would trade,' Jackson said. 'Sometimes when I close my eyes at night, I can still hear Pitbull's voice in my brain. Chilling with a bunch of sheep would be an upgrade.'

'You wouldn't know what to do with yourself. I know y'all like to say Savannah is a sleepy town, but we had to drive thirty minutes just to get to the closest grocery store.'

He stopped short in the hotel foyer and grabbed my arm. I halted beside him in a panic, people flowing around us like water flowing around a tree sticking up in the middle of a river.

'What's wrong?' I asked.

'Emily James Bell,' he said with a gasp. 'Did you just drop your first "y'all" on me?'

Shaking off the unwelcome hit of anxiety, I gasped.

'Jackson Powell, I do believe I did.'

He held up his hand for a high five and I met it with a resounding slap, smile firmly fixed to my face when his fingers meshed with mine.

'I do believe we'll make a southern belle out of you yet,' he said, clasping my hand tightly in his as we rejoined the mass of people moving through the hotel. 'Come on, let's go celebrate.'

The DeSoto was a beautiful hotel. I'd lived in some beautiful locations when I was younger, most of my travel experiences were a long way from luxurious. The university housing offered to my historian father was basic to say the least. Our Welsh cottage, charming as it was, could have been politely described as 'rustic'. But just like everywhere else I'd been in Savannah, the DeSoto was warm and welcoming and perfectly polished, with one eye and its whole heart set on its heritage. This place knew it came from good stock and wanted you to know it too.

'The original hotel was knocked down in the Sixties, but one way or another, it's been here since 1834,' Jackson said as we passed under an enormous crystal chandelier. 'A bunch of people tried to save it, but there's only so much you can do when money is involved. It's a real shame. From the photos I've seen, the original building was an amazing example of Romanesque architecture. What?'

'Nothing,' I said, my hand warm in his. 'Nothing at all.'

This Jackson Powell was so different to the version I'd first met. That Jackson was so slick, it felt as though you'd slide right off if you tried to touch him. Irresponsibly handsome, impossibly charming, and incapable of uttering a word that wasn't dripping with honey, he was altogether too smooth for my liking. This new and unimproved version was far superior. Still handsome and charming but genuine and natural, passionate about his secret historical hobby. I didn't feel as though my foot was quite so firmly stuck in my mouth every time we spoke.

'You think I'm a nerd,' he said, a flicker of self-consciousness passing over his face.

'I do, but only in the best way. I think it's cool how much you love the city's history.'

'Then you're the only girl I ever met who does.'

He ducked his head to hide his embarrassment but he couldn't erase the enthusiasm from his voice and I couldn't help but share it.

'Learning about our history, knowing what came before, feels important to me,' he said, the sound of our shoes clicking against a marble floor as we walked. 'Folks are always complaining about the way the world is today but maybe if we paid a little more attention to the past, it would be easier to see how we ended up here and try to change things for the better. Instead of repeating the same mistakes and wondering why.'

'My dad used to say something similar,' I said softly. 'Understanding our past is the best way to make sense of the present.'

'Your dad was a historian, right?' He offered me a bittersweet smile when I nodded, chewing on the inside of my lip to tamp down the unexpected swell of sadness. 'I'm sorry he isn't here anymore, Em. I wish I could have met him.'

My words came out soft and cautious. I was determined not to cry.

'Me too,' I said. 'I think you would have liked him.'

'You think he would've liked me?'

'No doubt about it,' I answered. 'He got along with just about anyone, but someone who would willingly listen to him talk about history? Forget about it. One time, in Germany, we were asked to leave a production of *Hamilton* because he was fact-checking the show in real time and the people behind us complained.'

'The musical is great and everything, but they really did miss out a lot of important stuff,' Jackson said, suffused with the same kind of excitement I remembered in my dad. 'Did you know Hamilton proposed senators should be appointed for lifelong terms?'

'OK, confirmed: my dad would've loved you.'

'Confirmed he must've been a cool guy,' he said happily. 'Had to be, what with raising such a cool daughter and all.'

'Me? Cool?' The snort that exploded out of me was anything but. 'Trust me, I have never been cool in my life, and that's fine by me.'

He met my snort with a scoff. 'I'm not calling you a liar, but I don't believe you.'

'If you're a nerd, I'm queen of the nerds and you are only one of my minions. Until I moved here, my idea of cool was begging my dad to take me to visit Stonehenge for my thirteenth birthday.'

'What I'm hearing is thirteen-year-old Emily was cool beyond her years.' Jackson's head rolled back and he held a hand against his heart in a faux swoon. 'What about now? Let's say I'm the one with the magic and I can wave my wand and take you anywhere you want, past, present or future. Where are we going?'

I started to laugh but the sound fell apart, escaping more like a panicked gasp. Anything, anywhere, past, present or future. A past built on a lie, a present I didn't understand and a future I was afraid of. It was too hard to see past the prophecy. Planning for a tomorrow that might never come felt like a trap.

'Wasn't supposed to be a tough question,' Jackson said gently.

'I know,' I said with an apologetic wince. 'Most people probably have an answer ready.'

'Most people's lives aren't as complicated as yours. Sorry, Em, it was a dumb question.'

'It was a great question,' I argued. 'I just need a little longer to come up with a good answer. You go first, what would you do?'

'Wake up early, play some ball, head home for grandmother's fried chicken steak then get in my time machine and head back to June fourth 1976. Courtside seats at the NBA finals game five, Boston Celtics, Phoenix Suns, triple overtime, Celtics win 128 to 126 and go on to win the series. Go Celtics. You're coming with me, obviously.'

'Yes to lunch, no to the game. People who sit in courtside seats are asking to get a basketball in the face. But I am impressed at how fast you answered. How come you're a Boston fan?'

The awkward weight of a complicated answer shifted off my shoulders and onto his.

'One time, a few years ago, Mom mentioned our dad grew up in Massachusetts.'

The twins never, ever mentioned their father and I knew his confession was a precious gift. He tugged at the cuff of his shirt, eyes darting away, but vulnerability looked good on him.

'I don't know what I'd do because I'm not even sure who I am anymore,' I admitted, a return offering of honesty. 'Anything in the past would hurt too much, the present is not what I thought it would be, and the future I thought I'd have seems kind of impossible now.'

The Witch and the Wolf

'Not everyone knows what they want to do with their life at seventeen,' Jackson said, adjusting the corsage on my wrist. 'How about we start with tonight and go from there?'

'Deal,' I replied, slapping my hand into his, content that my future, at least for tonight, was something to look forward to.

Chapter Six

'Welcome to the Oglethorpe Country Day Co-Ed Varsity Fundraiser,' Jackson announced as we passed into a huge ballroom, already packed full of teachers, kids and parents, each and every one of them dressed to the nines. I pulled back slightly from the sea of bodies in front of us. I wasn't used to this many people in such an enclosed space and I felt an unwelcome tingling all over my skin, magical self-defence.

'Good luck fitting all of that on one banner,' I said, exhaling slowly until the feeling settled. 'Who or what is an Oglethorpe?'

'James Oglethorpe, the founder of Savannah. He came over on the HMS *Anne* with your ancestors but he ditched and sailed back to England in 1734. He thought Savannah was going to be a kind of utopia but it didn't quite turn out that way.'

'Ten points for optimism, I guess.'

'Wild to think he would've known our ancestors.'

'Isn't it?' I replied, unable to stop myself from wondering if Mr Oglethorpe was a friend to the Bell and Powell women or . . . not.

I looked around the party, bass already thumping through the floor, a bar set up on either side of the room, all the kids crowding one, the adults swarming the other. It was easy to guess which side had the alcohol.

'What do you want to do first?' Jackson asked. 'Get something to eat, grab a drink, dance? There are a million people I want you to meet, everyone is dying to say hello.'

It was one thing to feel at ease with Jackson but the thought of meeting his super-cool basketball buddies made my stomach churn and my tongue twist until just the idea of talking to them was an impossible feat. Still, talking to strangers had to be easier than dancing. Sure, on a good day I could see into the past, present and future, but move my hands, feet and body in rhythm at the same time? Simply asking too much.

'Eat?' I said, choosing the option with the least potential for humiliation.

'I really hoped you were going to say that, I am starving.'

Jackson slapped his flat stomach before practically dragging me across the room towards a huge buffet station covered in silver dishes and bowls, some of them on ice, some of them steaming, and all of them manned by very serious-looking men and women in white jackets and chef's hats.

'This place has some of the best food in town but you have to attack it with a plan.' He picked up a large dinner plate from one end of the table and handed it to me. 'With all those parties last year, I got pretty up close and personal with the catering here. Forget about the vegetables, not worth it. Bread is a waste of time, you'll fill up and miss out on the good stuff. The mini pimento grilled cheese and the crab cakes are god tier, and if you see a server go by with shrimp skewers, grab as many as you can. Forget about good manners, we do not mess around when it comes to appetizers.'

'Shrimp skewers, got it,' I repeated as Jackson turned his attention to a large man with an even larger carving knife, standing behind the biggest turkey I had ever seen.

'I'm actually not that hungry just yet,' I said, quietly setting my plate back on the pile, my date mesmerized as he watched the chef sharpen his carving knife. 'Why don't I find us somewhere to sit while you load up?'

'Sure,' he said, eyes glazing over at the sight of a massive side of ham. 'I'll come find you.'

Caught in the lure of the buffet's siren song, Jackson drifted away to pile his plate high. Fully aware nothing and no one could compete with the call of a sixteen-year-old boy's empty stomach, I took myself off to one of the tables at the edge of the dance floor to wait for him. If there was one thing I was good at, it was hiding in plain sight. I'd been the new girl more times than I could count and blending into the background had been my super power long before I discovered I was a witch. Moving every couple of years, combined with my dad's strict no-cell-phone-and-no-social-media-until-you're-seventeen rule meant long-lasting friendships were a struggle, and while I was a pro when it came to making small talk with my dad's co-workers, I was far less talented at conquering conversations with people my own age.

Living in the countryside sounds romantic until you realize you're the only teenager for miles around, especially if you happen to be in a European country where no one your age speaks English. We never stayed in one place long enough for me to learn the local language and make real friends. By the time we moved to Wales, I was fourteen; and when Dad decided to teach me at home rather than send me to the local school, I was relieved. There was nothing more awkward than trying to fit in with a bunch of kids who had known each other their whole lives. And that was exactly how I felt in the ballroom of the DeSoto Hotel.

As he stood in line waiting for his cut of prime rib, Jackson was bombarded by friends, teammates, teachers, coaches, and even, judging by the occasional blank look in his eyes, complete strangers. Everyone wanted to talk to him, be near him. Lydia once told me I shouldn't look directly at her brother, that he was like the sun, one glance and he'd be burned into your retinas forever. It felt true. Everyone at the party wanted to be in his orbit, circling him impatiently until they got their chance to bask in the warm glow of his attention.

For sixteen years it was just me and my dad. Then it was me and Catherine. Now, my world had expanded to include Wyn, Ashley, Lydia and Jackson, but I couldn't imagine what it would be like to walk into a room as crowded as this one and have everyone know everything about you. These people had a lifetime of shared memories and experiences. First days and field trips, long summer breaks and holiday parties. The only people I knew that well were the characters in my favourite books, and that was a pretty one-sided relationship. I couldn't really expect the Ilyrians, the Cullen family or a ragtag bunch of hobbits, elves and dwarves to care about my wellbeing.

Very slowly, I melted away from the crowd until I found a wall to lean against, and took my phone out of my purse, adopting the official 'I'm totally OK no need to look at me' stance of twenty-first century human beings everywhere. Usually, I had an emotional support book with me at all times but not even my slimmest paperback would fit in the tiny beaded evening bag I'd borrowed from Lydia (and I knew that because I'd tried to shove my dad's old copy of *Franny and Zooey* in there). I scrolled though the photo albums on my phone instead, keeping my expression neutral. Not too sad in case someone stopped to ask what's the matter, not too happy in case they wanted to know what I was smiling at. It helped. Right away I felt better and was quietly, calmly marvelling at the freckles scattered across Wyn's nose when I realized his weren't the only pair of eyes locked on me.

'Miss Bell, isn't it?'

The woman standing in front of me was petite, at least three or four inches shorter than I was, but she held herself in a way that made her seem much taller. There wasn't so much as a hair out of place on her highlighted head and the fine lines that gathered around her eyes and mouth had been pulled taut by a very severe up-do, a tight, tucked-in braid that made my scalp sore just to look at it.

'You must be Catherine's granddaughter,' she said, a declaration rather than a question. She extended a hand in my direction. 'Why, you're the very image of her.'

I shook her hand, recovering my manners a moment too late according to the frown on her face. Jackson would have to take back my newly acquired southern belle status.

'That's right, I'm Emily. James. Emily James Bell. Still getting used to the new last name – or rather, my old last name. Well, I'm sure you know the whole story.'

Her static smile remained frozen in place as I babbled, making no attempt to help me out of the verbal hole I was digging for myself. When I let go of her hand, she glanced down at her palm, as though touching me might have somehow left a stain.

'You're a friend of Cath— of my grandmother's?' I asked.

'Ileen Stovell. I'm sure she must have mentioned me.'

'Not *the* Ileen Stovell?!' I said, feigning the surprise she seemed to expect. 'She talks about you all the time. Constantly, in fact.'

Catherine had not uttered this woman's name even once in my presence.

Fingertips fluttering at her exposed collarbone, Ileen Stovell continued to stare at me with hawkish blue eyes. Her dress was a matronly ballgown with a sweetheart neckline, small pink flowers printed on a powder blue background. My grandmother wouldn't have been caught dead in it.

'We were so sorry to miss her at the historical society meeting last night,' she said. 'It's so unlike Catherine to miss out, especially when we are graced with a guest speaker.'

I nodded with understanding. 'I'm sure she was devastated to miss it but, as you know, she's travelling right now.'

'So your aunt said. She's in Europe? Paying her respects to your father?'

That was the official story Ashley and I had agreed on. Something people would accept without question and invited very little follow-up.

'That's right,' I confirmed. 'She's spending some time in Wales.'

An indefinite amount of time, I added to myself.

'A shame he was laid to rest so far from home.' Ileen's gaze sharpened. 'Quite peculiar.'

'He really loved Wales,' I said with a shrug, sweating under her interrogation. 'Who knows why people make the decisions they do?'

After a long pause, she tilted her head to one side with grudging acceptance; not a strand of her hair moved, her whole head was lacquered into some sort of hair helmet.

'Truer words never spoken,' she said as she finally broke eye contact to examine her flawless fingernails. I felt my shoulders sag with relief. 'I do hope she's having a marvellous time, in spite of the sad circumstances. I have never been to Wales myself but I just know she'll adore Paris.'

'Paris?'

My eyes popped wide. Who said anything about Paris?

'I personally would never choose Paris this late in the summer,' she went on, thankfully oblivious to my surprise. 'It's more of a spring destination, but who could begrudge Catherine a European adventure after all she's been through.'

My face tightened as I silently cursed Ashley for going off script without telling me.

'Odd that Catherine would choose to undertake such a journey after all these years without travelling at all,' Ileen said, flicking her gaze back to me, her eyelids weighed down with too much mascara and just the right amount of suspicion. 'And to go alone when you have so recently arrived in Savannah. It seems to me you and Ashley might've accompanied her.'

'She wanted to say goodbye to my dad in her own way,' I replied, reciting my side of the story perfectly. No need to add any more layers to an already precarious house of cards. 'And Ashley and I have a lot going on.'

'Such as?'

I could not think of a single thing. The left corner of Ileen's mouth quirked upwards, cracking her mask of foundation.

'All these years, the ladies and I have been trying to drag her out of town on a real vacation. She gave us every excuse in the book until we simply stopped asking,' she said. Then, leaning in towards me, she added, 'Not that I would ever spread gossip, but with the way she took off without telling anyone, Margaret Seiler wondered if there might be some sort of family trouble?'

'Trouble?' I echoed nervously.

She lowered her voice, eyes widening with meaning.

'Perhaps with the IRS?'

'The IRS?'

'That's right,' she said. 'It's not unthinkable for a woman in Catherine's position to find herself in trouble with the tax man, especially after managing her own finances for so long. Without a man to guide her, I mean. Is that the case?'

She held her breath, giving me a whole second to confirm

or deny, then sighed with disappointment when I shook my head. This was beginning to get annoying.

'There's no trouble with our taxes and Catherine doesn't need a man to manage her finances. She's just gone away, nothing weird about it.'

'If you say so,' Ileen said with a sniff. 'But the whole endeavour seems very strange, very peculiar. Disappearing without telling her closest friends, this bizarre refusal of hers to use a cell phone. But I'm not one to gossip.'

'Not even a little,' I said, looking around for Jackson or one of his friends, or literally anyone else, dead or alive, who might want to talk to me. I'd probably take a werewolf if it was the only offer on the table. Where was a distraction when I needed one? Unfortunately, Ileen Stovell was not finished.

'And of course, I wanted to officially welcome you to Savannah.'

'Thank you, I—'

'Since Catherine didn't feel it necessary to arrange a formal introduction for you before running off on her grand European tour.'

'That's entirely my fault.' I spotted the back of my non-date's head and silently begged him to turn around and save me. 'Catherine was desperate to arrange something but I asked for more time to settle in.'

'It would be my honour to introduce you at the August meeting of the historical society,' she suggested readily. 'Or perhaps the next parents' association meeting at Oglethorpe Country Day. I hear you graduated early, but I'm sure you'll still want to show support for your local school, especially since your father was an alumnus, and, dare I say it, your beau is our star basketball player? Well done, by the way, you have the most excellent taste. My granddaughter tells me Jackson Powell is quite the popular young man, and here you come, swanning into town after sixteen years away, to snatch him on up.'

And just like that, any reserves of politeness I had vanished.

'You can dare say anything you like but that doesn't make it real.' I pulled back my shoulders as I spoke, drawing myself up to my full height and ignoring the gasp that escaped her pink-painted lips. 'Jackson is just a friend, so feel free to tell your granddaughter she's still in with a shot.'

Ileen Stovell blinked at me with vacant surprise, as though she needed to be turned on and off again at the mains. I ignored my father's voice in my head, telling me to apologize, and instead listened to a new voice, one that insisted I stand my ground, that I was a member of the Bell family, and we were a force to be reckoned with.

That voice, I realized with some surprise, belonged to Catherine.

'Thank you for the kind offer,' I said with a civil dip of my chin. 'But I'm sure Catherine will introduce me to anyone she considers important enough when she gets back.'

Without waiting for a reply, I stepped around Ileen, head held high as I sailed across the room to meet Jackson, blood burning in my ears and pride flaming in my chest. Catherine would be proud of me, I was sure of it.

But since when was that a good thing?

The party was a success.

Time seemed to speed up when I was with Jackson, every minute passing twice as quickly as the hours I spent wallowing around Bell House. He was the perfect date, proudly introducing me to all of his friends, bragging about the places I'd lived, the countries I'd visited, and telling everyone who would listen how incredibly cool and smart I was. It was beyond awkward, at least at first. I'd never been someone to take compliments well and I couldn't refute his claims quickly enough, but Jackson wouldn't hear of it and the look on his face every time he showed me off to someone new filled me with a warm sense of belonging. Very, very slowly, I started to shed the first few layers of social anxiety, letting everyone else talk and joke around until I felt safe enough to join in. Contrary to Lydia's broad summation that her brother exclusively enjoyed the company of jocks, dummies and the kind of girls who already had coaches helping to make sure they were accepted to the best sororities in the south, his friends seemed nice, sweet even. But there was one thing I couldn't stop thinking about. Did any of these people know the true depths of Jackson's inner history nerd?

My guess was no. He hadn't mentioned a single historical fact since taking me to see what he assured me was a historic fountain at the back of the hotel. His cheeks had been flushed with excitement as he told me all about its storied past, until an enormous boy, who was either a football player or part rhino, came over. Jackson immediately pretended we had got lost looking for the bathrooms. I didn't say anything and he didn't offer an explanation. He didn't need to, we all had things we preferred to keep hidden. Lydia kept her desire to belong buried deep and Ashley would rather die than have people know about the girl she'd loved and lost more than a decade ago. My secrets were a little less common than most, but the theory still held. Jackson's life was complicated. I hadn't really thought about it until tonight, watching him work the room, all things to all people. His friends wanted the good-natured, easy-going, all-American guy. The teachers and the parents saw an all-conquering sports hero and that's what he gave them. His grandmother wanted a charming, polite young gentleman, so that's what she got. For Lydia, he was the pain-in-the-ass older-by-twelve-minutes brother, always looking out for her whether she liked it or not; and although she would never admit it, that was exactly what she needed. But who was he to himself? I couldn't stop wondering which version was closest to the truth.

'Having fun?' he asked, his eyes bright as his head bobbed along in time with the music.

'I am,' I said, delighted to discover it was the truth.

The band was loud, the lights were low and after a few short speeches all the attending adults had disappeared to another room, leaving us the dance floor and the dessert bar. I couldn't have asked for more from my first school dance.

Jackson moved to the beat, tugging his bow tie loose before unbuttoning his collar.

'I wish they'd turn up the AC,' he yelled. 'It's hot as blue blazes in here. Probably cooler outside than inside right about now.'

'You want to go see?'

I gestured toward the sliding glass doors at the end of the ballroom and he held out his arm, grinning like he'd won the lottery. I hooked my arm through the crook of his elbow and we slipped around the edge of the room, fresh air dead ahead. Everything was normal, everything was nice.

Until it wasn't.

It happened so suddenly, I wasn't prepared. Only Jackson's firm grip kept me upright when the shockwaves hit and I stumbled forward, reaching out for the wall. My footsteps faltered as the room shuddered, quaking so violently that pictures leapt from walls and the chandeliers fell from the ceiling, a cascade of crystal crushing the people below. I looked on helpless as a chorus of a hundred screams pierced my soul.

'Em?' I heard Jackson say. 'You good?'

The quaking stopped and I leaned into his body, panting and shaking.

The Witch and the Wolf

The ballroom was perfectly fine.

My fingers curled around the fabric of his shirt as I scoured my surroundings, searching for the injured people and broken glass, but there was nothing. No one screaming in fear, no one running for the exits. Everything was exactly as it had been two seconds earlier.

'You didn't feel it?' I said, still clinging tightly to his side. 'The earthquake?'

Jackson wrapped a protective arm around my shoulders and held me close, resting his chin on top of my head.

'Em, there was nothing to feel, there was no earthquake.' His voice dropped an octave when I started to shake. 'What happened? Do we need to leave?'

'No,' I said, still not quite ready to believe him or my own eyes. 'It was nothing. I must've tripped or something.'

He looked about as convinced as I sounded.

'If you're worried, we can leave. Say the word and I'll hit the fire alarm, we'll have this whole place evacuated in five minutes flat.'

'Honestly, everything is fine,' I insisted, looking back at all the happy faces, searching for some clue as to what had just happened. 'I need fresh air, that's all. You're right, it's super hot in here. No need to ruin everyone's night because I'm a klutz.'

'But I'm not worried about everyone,' Jackson said. 'I'm worried about you.'

Locked onto his huge brown eyes, I felt my bottom lip begin to tremble. The slight pursing of his lips, the frown that pulled his eyebrows together, it was enough to tip two fat tears over my lashes and down my cheeks.

'I don't know what it was but it's gone now.'

He took a deep breath in through his nose then exhaled steadily.

'This way,' he said, steering me towards the glass doors.

His arm was still around my shoulders, holding me close enough to feel his heart pounding against his ribs. Without resisting, I let him lead me out to the terrace, only looking back once. Until I had a clearer idea of what just happened, there was no reason to alarm anyone else, but there was no denying that something was wrong. It wasn't a vision or a nightmare, and as far as I knew a ghost couldn't cause that kind of illusion.

Someone at this party was capable of wielding powerful, brutal magic.

Someone other than me.

Chapter Seven

As soon as we stepped outside, I felt the humidity on my skin, tendrils of my hair curling up at the nape of my neck like a fortune-telling fish. All around us, people were leaning against the hotel walls, lounging on metal chairs, or resting on the railings that guarded the edge of the terrace. The change in energy was tangible. Inside was loud, music, happiness and excitement. Outside was soft, tentative voices and gentle touches. The sun had already disappeared, leaving the party unchaperoned. Only the moon watched over the city now, bathing us in tender twilight and looking the other way as couples made the most of the moment.

I rested my forearms on the railings and looked down onto the street. The oak trees nodded their acknowledgement, swathes of Spanish moss drifting towards me on a non-existent wind. We're here, they seemed to say, nothing will harm you, remember who you are. Rolling my shoulders as if to push the weight of the unfamiliar magic away, I closed my eyes and let the heavy evening air cover me, clearing my head and my heart. The eddies of unwelcome energy ebbed away, the tide washing in and out again until the natural flow of things was restored.

'You don't have to talk about it if you don't want to,' I heard Jackson say softly. 'Just tell me, are we safe?'

'I think so,' I said, grateful for his calm presence.

He clucked his tongue against the roof of his mouth and took his position, standing sentry beside me, not quite touching. In one fluid move, he snaked the bow tie from around his neck and stuffed it in the pocket of his pants, jacket long since abandoned.

'Do you want to leave?'

'No,' I told him. 'I should stay, just in case.'

'So there is something—'

There was an anxious question in his voice but he stopped himself, raising his chin with confidence.

'I'm not worried, I know you can handle it, whatever it is.'

His words made me feel both better and worse. It was nice to know he was so certain but what if his confidence was misplaced?

'There's something – someone – here,' I said, keeping my voice as soft and unbothered as I could. 'Someone with magic. It took me by surprise, is all.'

'Your grandmother?' he suggested.

'No. Definitely not. But if I can sense them, they can almost certainly sense me.'

Now the shock had worn off, I was more curious than anything. It was strange, an unknown energy, nothing I'd ever felt before, but the thought of meeting another witch or magical creature was beyond exciting. I'd seen what they could do, not what they *would* do. There was every chance they would be ten times more afraid of me than I was of them. And not without reason.

'No one is going to mess with Savannah's legendary super witch.' Jackson's lips twitched with a smile. 'Even if they did, they'd have to get through her useless but dedicated sidekick first.'

'You're no one's sidekick, useless or otherwise,' I told him, meaning every word. 'You're the definition of main character.'

'Hmm, I don't know about that,' he replied. 'Doesn't the main character usually get the girl?'

His shoulder blades squeezed together under the thin fabric of his shirt; the white cotton contrasted against his gorgeous brown skin. When he dipped his head to let the looser curls on top fall forward, I noticed how much his hair had grown out in the last month; the colour at the ends had been lifted by the relentless sun, but the sides were still tight in a flawless fade that looked freshly done. Jackson definitely wasn't letting his sister cut his hair. Unlike me. He tilted his head to squint in my direction.

'I'm joking, I'm joking,' he said when I didn't reply. 'I know you and Wyn are fated mates or whatever.'

'Fated mates? Have you been raiding Lydia's fantasy bookshelf?'

'No, but she introduced me to the concept. Didn't shoot my shot when I had the chance, wasn't meant to be. I might not know much about magic, but I do know you can't fight fate.'

'That's what I hear,' I said, too brightly. 'Although, whoever the Fates are, I would like to have a word with them.'

'He's doing OK, though?' Jackson asked, looking at me through squinting eyes. 'Wyn, I mean?'

The smile on my face did not match the tumble of emotion I felt in the pit of my stomach.

'Doing great. Fantastic actually.'

'That's good.' He pinched his shoulders up around his ears and my too-big smile faded by a fraction. 'Only, Lyds said you hadn't heard from him in a while. I figured he'd have been back by now.'

I didn't have an answer. Lydia was correct and to be honest, I'd figured the same. Jackson looked down at the ground while I raised my eyes to the sky to see the full moon peering down, quietly keeping an eye on us. Spying. I felt a tug around my heart and a small gasp slipped through my lips. The invisible string that kept me connected to Wyn, the one that had nothing to do with magic and everything to do with love. I clutched the railing to keep myself upright as the sensation rolled through, sweeping me hundreds of miles away from Savannah to where he was, out in the woods, lost in the smell of earth, moss and mud, bowed down on hands and knees. He was thinking of me right as his phase took hold, sharing the moment with me, the apprehension and the anticipation. When he lifted his head, I saw through his eyes. Wolves. Wolves everywhere. But I wasn't afraid. Wyn wasn't afraid. Any fear in his heart melted away, replaced by a sense of purpose and exhilaration. Suddenly, he threw his head back to release an ear-splitting howl as the wolf took over.

And then he disappeared.

'Emily?'

Jackson grabbed my forearms as I returned to myself, to the DeSoto. I looked over at him, dazed, displaced. It was the first time I'd lost track of Wyn since he left Savannah and I was completely unmoored.

'It's OK—' I started, but he wasn't going to take my word for it this time.

'So help me, if you say you're fine one more time, I think I'm going to scream,' he said. 'Tell me what you saw.'

He truly looked as though he wanted to help, just like his sister, only Lydia wanted to run toward the magic, while Jackson wanted to run away from it.

'Wyn.' I nodded up toward the sky. 'The moon just peaked. His pack is in its phase.'

The Witch and the Wolf

'You can feel that?' he asked.

'I can feel him,' I answered. 'Or at least, I could.'

'You can't sense the wolf?'

'Can we talk about something else?' The wolf was racing further and further away from me, leaving an unbearable emptiness where my heart should've been. 'Anything, really. School, sports. College? Do you know where you want to go yet?'

'There's a shortlist,' he replied. 'What about you? You already graduated, right?'

'Thanks to the wonder of homeschooling,' I confirmed. 'I was planning to travel for a year, visit some schools on the East Coast then enrol next fall. Dad wasn't crazy about the idea of sending me off to college at seventeen.'

'But?'

I attempted to block out the loss of Wyn and shook my head. 'For a family without magic, you sure are good at reading minds.'

The corners of his eyes crinkled in response.

'Just good at reading people. What's stopping you following through on the plan?'

'Oh, I don't know,' I said. 'Missing family members, mystical threats, that sort of thing. Not that being the subject of an ancient prophecy wouldn't make for a killer personal essay, but what am I supposed to do, major in English and minor in apocalypse avoidance?'

'Maybe the other way around. Just to be safe.'

'Metaphysical poetry at nine, astral projection 101 at ten?' I sighed and stood up straight, rubbing the indentations of the railings out of my forearms. 'It might be easier to plan a future if someone had bothered to put together some sort of schedule, but there's nothing. No instructions, no QR code, batteries not included.'

'This does feel like an ancient-scroll-type situation,' he agreed.

'Or at least a stone tablet written in an archaic language we could translate as a summer project.'

The laugh that rattled out of me took me by surprise.

'See?' Jackson said with a sly grin. 'I make you laugh – key sidekick trait.'

'Key friend trait,' I corrected. 'And don't think I don't appreciate it.'

With a roll of his eyes, he brushed off the compliment. 'Like we said, you can't fight fate. You were always going to be stuck with me, one way or another.'

My eyes found his, a genuine, grateful smile playing on my lips.

'This whole prophecy thing,' he said. 'It's a whole lot of pressure to put on one person.'

The smile faltered.

'Agreed,' I said. 'The powers that be could've shared out the responsibilities a little. Why do prophecies always pick one person? Why can't it be a team?'

Jackson reached for my hand, his skin warm and soft as he squeezed it between both of his.

'But there is a team. You're not on your own, you know.'

Behind us, the doors to the terrace slid open and stayed open, a slow song echoing out from the dance floor.

'Miss Emily James Bell.' Jackson took a step back and bowed at the waist. 'As your fated friend, may I have this dance?'

'Mr Jackson Powell, you may,' I said, accepting his arm and following him back inside, the sharp shift from the humid night to the chill of the air conditioning prickling my skin into goosebumps.

No one looked at us as we snuck onto the floor and Jackson expertly pulled me into a dancing position. I felt the careful weight of his hand on my waist as I placed mine on his shoulder, our two joined hands starting somewhere in the air around my shoulder until I rested them against his chest. The corners of his mouth turned upwards, his eyes soft, as we shifted our weight from foot to foot without really going anywhere. Silently, I let the energy of the room wash over me, all the fast-beating hearts, the excitement and disappointment that was to be expected when you put a bunch of teenagers together, turned down the lights and played slow songs. But whatever magic was here before was gone now. It was only us.

Dancing with Jackson was so comfortable, so easy. I leaned in to tuck my head under his chin and heard him sigh contentedly. He meant what he said. He was on my team. But putting my loved ones in danger was something I could not allow. Pain was a warning. You only touched the hot oven once. According to the prophecy, there was much more pain in my future but I would protect them from it if I could. I would be the only one to suffer the flames, I would not hold my friends' hands to the fire.

'You ever think how different things would be if you'd grown up here?'

Jackson's voice was so soft I could barely hear him over the music.

'All the time,' I said, a quiet admission. 'I wonder who I'd be if we'd stayed.'

'You would still be entirely you,' he said with absolute certainty. 'Only you'd be dropping those y'alls more often, I reckon.'

'And my biscuits might be better. And we would've grown up together.'

'Our folks would've spent every holiday together,' he said, adding colour to my loosely sketched fantasy. 'You and I learned to ride our bikes together in Forsyth Park, ran around the neighbourhood trick-or-treating every Halloween, spent every Fourth of July at the beach watching the fireworks.'

'I was going to say I'd have kept Lydia out of trouble, but more likely she'd have gotten me into it.'

His chin nudged the top of my head when he nodded in agreement.

'And my mom and dad would still be alive,' I added. 'Ashley would have been free to do as she pleased and Catherine would never have gone off the deep end. We'd all be one big happy family.'

Jackson's fingers tightened around mine.

'Only one complication, I guess,' he said. 'If trouble never came to town, neither would Wyn.'

There was another version of my life, even if I didn't want to admit it. One where I grew up with a crush on the boy down the street, where he was my first kiss and my first love, and we strolled through the halls of our high school, holding hands, his letterman jacket around my shoulders. It would be easy to fall in love with Jackson.

If I hadn't already met Wyn.

'We would've found each other another way,' I said. 'He used to come here when he was younger, with his grandfather. I think all four of us would've met somehow, you, me, Lydia and Wyn. I think we were all meant to be friends.'

Jackson didn't reply, just carried on dancing, holding me close, and I was suddenly too aware of his body, the hint of cologne on his skin, a dime-sized birthmark behind his ear I'd never noticed before. It was only a couple of shades darker than his skin and almost a perfect circle. My eyelashes grazed his cheek and I heard a sharp intake of breath pass through his lips.

'You're probably right,' he said, pushing me away, only very slightly but enough to put clear space between our bodies. 'But, as your friend, I wish he was here with you now, when you need him. You deserve to be with someone who can be with you all the time, the kind of person who yells about you from the rooftops.'

And doesn't have to live with the guilt of lying to his family because the girl he loves killed his only brother.

'It's complicated,' I said, for what felt like the millionth time, before looking up to meet Jackson's eyes, deep, dark brown with flecks of gold.

'It doesn't have to be,' he replied.

I hadn't realized we'd stopped dancing until a couple bumped into my shoulder, mumbling their apologies before shuffling around us.

'It's getting kind of late and I'm pretty tired.' I raised my wrist without actually looking at my watch, an obvious excuse. 'I think I'm going to head on out. But you should stay.'

'Not an option,' Jackson said. 'A gentleman always sees his date to the door. Anyway, you can't walk home in this weather. It's raining cats and dogs out there.'

'It is?' I replied, turning to look back out onto the terrace.

It was. Not the kind of quick shower to cut through the humidity and freshen the night, but an out-and-out downpour, dark skies filled with heavy clouds, thunder and lightning surely close behind. And then I felt it. Standing still in the room full of swaying couples, a shudder struck against my senses, the ground trembling under my feet. The magic I'd felt earlier had returned, ten times stronger than it was before, and streaked with malicious intent. It knew I was here and it did not care. This time I could not promise we were safe.

'My jacket is over here somewhere,' Jackson said, leading me away from the dance floor, his back to the look of terror on my face. 'Those guys downstairs are assholes about releasing your car without the valet ticket, even though I have known pretty much every one of them for my whole entire life and—'

'Jackson, don't move.'

He turned to face me, confusion shifting swiftly into fear when he saw the expression on my face and, as though he couldn't stop himself, he looked over his shoulder to see what I was staring at. Behind my friend, just beyond the open glass doors, an enormous grey wolf leapt from the street and up onto the terrace in one graceful bound, a cacophony of car horns heralding its arrival, accompanied by screaming pedestrians and barking dogs. It paused to shake off the rain, silver droplets flying from its fur like liquid mercury, before it turned towards the open glass doors of the DeSoto Hotel ballroom, its ravenous eyes set on me.

Chapter Eight

'Do not cross that line.'

Words I'd heard Catherine say, spilling forth from my lips.

The wolf, the Were, looked unmoved by my threat. It paced back and forth as the rain thrashed down, a live action blur between us. Behind me, in the hotel ballroom, there was only screaming. Half the party ran for the doors, the other half were locked in place, too afraid to move a muscle.

'Do not cross that line,' I said again, stepping in front of Jackson and rolling my shoulders as a fast-flowing river of magic washed over me. It covered my skin and filled my veins, consuming me. No prickling in my fingertips, no gentle tingles, just straight fire, burning me up. I knew the words to say without thinking. The wolf had to be challenged, this was *my* place, these were *my* friends and I would protect them no matter the cost.

'Turn around and leave right now.' I widened my stance, steadying myself. 'And you might survive the night.'

The wolf wasn't listening. Instead of obeying my commands, it continued to prowl up and down the terrace, daring me to come outside. A risky move. Who knew if either of us would survive if I did? Stalking closer to the doors, my feet barely leaving the ground, I held my breath against the rising heat inside me. A fingertip's distance from the threshold, I heard an alarm blaring, screeching through the background noise. Then, without warning, it began to rain inside as well as out. I looked up, momentarily confused.

'Emily!'

Across the room, standing next to a bright red lever on the wall, I saw Jackson staring at me. The fire alarm. He'd hit the fire alarm to clear the room.

'Em, let's go!'

Jacket in hand, he jerked his head towards the exit as his friends flooded from the room, but I couldn't. I couldn't back down. And when I didn't make a move to join him, he was at my side, standing shoulder to shoulder with me.

'Don't think about touching her,' he yelled when the wolf drew back its lips and snarled, vicious teeth on display. Sharp enough to tear through flesh like freshly baked bread.

Since arriving in Savannah, I'd encountered two Weres in phase and neither had shown the slightest suggestion of fear. Cole's attack had been relentless, even in the face of death. His jaws snapped at my throat until every ounce of life was drained from him. Dosed with wolfsbane and torn up by silver barbs, Wyn had had continued to fight Catherine, in spite of the excruciating pain. This wolf certainly wasn't scared of Jackson. It didn't even seem afraid of me. But it should've been. Magic flared as the knowledge of my ancestors swirled inside me. Ways to kill a wolf; a silver blade, a silver bullet, decapitation, suffocation. If I could get it into the ballroom, if I could suck the air out of the room . . .

I would be no better than Catherine.

Guilt knocked me backwards and blunted the edge of my threats. Weres preferred to stay hidden, like witches. There was only one reason I could think of for this wolf's appearance in such a public place. It had come for the witch who killed one of its kind only two moons ago and my first reaction was to kill again. End the life of another living being to save myself when I was the guilty one.

There wasn't time to battle with my conscience. Having waited long enough, the wolf lunged at me, slicing through the rain with terrifying agility for a beast its size. But if it wasn't afraid, neither was I. A wolf had tried to kill me before and I'd lived to tell the tale. Holding my ground, I unclenched my fists and prepared for the fight, to stop the wolf but not kill it. But instead of tearing teeth and matted fur, I felt a pair of strong hands grabbing at my waist to hurl me out of the way. As I tumbled to the floor, I saw Jackson stumble forward onto the terrace and throw himself in the wolf's path.

'No!' I screamed as its claws sliced his belly open. I saw the dark red stain of blood glistening against his skin and staining his white shirt red, then he fell to his knees. There was no look of pain on his face, only surprise – a reaction I remembered all too well.

'Jackson!' I scurried towards him, scraping my wet hair out of my face as the wolf regrouped. 'You're going to be OK, just breathe. Can you keep your hand pressed down here for me?'

I grabbed his jacket from the floor and placed it over his injury, pressing his hand over the top.

'Em,' he muttered, paling as the wolf reared for a second attack. 'You need to run.'

'No.' I rose to my feet, any trace of confusion gone now. 'It's the wolf who needs to run.'

Catherine warned me never to think of my magic as power. Our abilities were a gift, a connection to the blessing, something freely given and gratefully received. Power was sought by people who wanted control, but as the pink orchid in Bell House had reminded me, control was an illusion. We could only ask for what nature was prepared to offer. If you took more than you were entitled to . . . Well, I had seen what happened to my grandmother.

But it was hard to keep that in mind when my friend lay bleeding on the ground beside me.

Filled with rage, I raised my hands and focused my attention on the wolf. The water streaming from the ceiling swirled up into a tornado that twisted in the air, sucking up plates, glasses, chairs and tables. I took one step towards the wolf, then another, my anger surging, changing into something like anticipation, and with every moment, my desire to keep the beast alive dissipated. I wanted it to attack me. I wanted a reason to strike back.

'Do it,' I said, flicking my wrist to drag a concrete fire pit across the terrace as if it weighed nothing at all, and raising it above the wolf's fragile skull. 'I want you to.'

The Were wasn't afraid but it wasn't stupid. It lowered into a crouch, head lowered, hind legs ready to spring.

Suddenly, new sirens joined the chorus howling through the ballroom, growing louder as they approached the hotel from the street outside. The wolf pricked its ears, its stance shifted. With the rain still beating down, it gave one last gnash of its jaws and leapt over the edge of the terrace, bounding off down the street with unnatural speed and disappearing into the night.

'Em?'

Jackson's voice was too weak.

Panting, I dropped the fire pit and it landed with an almighty thud, splitting in two and cracking the concrete slabs beneath it. The plates and glasses, chairs and tables, all of it clattered to the ground as the tornado died down. I squeezed my eyes tightly shut and, willing the overwhelming rage inside me to calm, I dropped to his side and cradled his head in my lap, removing his hands from his stomach to check the wound.

'It's gone.' I winced at the ugly gash as I peeled away the sodden fabric of his jacket. 'Everyone is safe now, because of you.'

He was still bleeding, the flesh of his stomach visible as blood pumped out with every shallow breath, but if he felt any pain, it didn't show.

'Because of you,' Jackson said, his lids fluttering shut, the words barely a whisper. 'Because of you.'

'Oh no you don't,' I said, summoning all the fire in my blood. 'You keep those eyes open. I need you to stay with me. Keep breathing – please don't go.'

The blessing could heal most wounds, no matter how severe, but there was one thing it could not do and that was bring anything or anyone back from the dead. From the state of his stilted breathing and fading heartbeat, I could feel Jackson fading, teetering over the edge. Outside, the rain was still pouring down, fresh water full of the energy I sorely needed. Laying my hands flat on the ground, I begged the blessing for help, offering myself to save him; whatever it might take, I would do it. Almost at once, the water running down my face stopped; then, as my skin scorched with magic, the droplets began to run backwards. The rain outside defied gravity, rushing towards me instead of falling straight down to earth. Rivulets turned into rivers, flowing up my arms and legs, winding their way around my body, a conduit for its fresh, healing energy.

I placed my hands over Jackson's stomach, covering the five clean gashes from the wolf's claws, the fire within me, the rain without. Warmth and water brought life. A pulse rose up through the floor and I closed my eyes to steady myself, saw Jackson's flesh knitting itself back together, believed he would be healed. Knowing what I could do was half the battle. A pained gargling sound emitted from his throat and I opened my eyes to see his eyes roll back in his head.

'Hold on,' I begged, watching the hard muscles of his stomach repair themselves, his soft, unblemished skin coming back together. 'One more minute and we're out of here.'

A sharp inhale filled his lungs with fresh air and he jerked upright. I collapsed back on my heels as he pressed his palms to the five tiny silver lines that marred his torso. He was alive. He was scarred but he was here. With a silent thank you, I let go of my magic and slumped backwards, exhausted.

'We need to leave,' I said, staring up at the ceiling. 'Can you walk?'

'Can you?' Jackson climbed to his feet and reached out two hands to pull me up as though he hadn't suffered so much as a scratch.

Beyond the ballroom, there were raised voices, ordered and commanding, either police or paramedics. Neither would be helpful. I really did not feel like sitting down to give a witness statement with my hands stained by my friend's blood. Yes, officer, I saw the wolf. No, officer, I don't think it was just a very large dog. Why, officer? Because I'm a witch and the wolf was a Were and I suspect it was here to kill me because it knows I killed its packmate. Any more questions? Who is my legal guardian? Well, I'm so glad you asked . . .

'You're sure we shouldn't stay and tell them what happened?' Jackson asked, nodding at the uniformed officers just outside the door. 'Maybe they can help. Or at least warn animal control?'

If I'd had the energy to laugh, I would've been hysterical. It was only two months since I'd said the exact same thing to my grandmother.

'There's nothing they can do,' I said, forcing one foot in front of the other. 'Unless you want to explain why we're both covered in blood but neither of us are injured, we should probably leave now.'

But leaving was easier said than done. The police were already at the door, looking into the ballroom, and I knew there would be more outside, guarding the terrace.

'How do we get out without anyone seeing us?'

With a grim smile, I reached out once more and in the same moment the thought passed through my mind, a flash of lightning lit up the sky. The world slowed down until it seemed to stop. All the loud voices quieted and the droplets of water falling from the sprinklers lingered in midair, as if waiting on me. Beyond the terrace, I saw cars paused in the middle of the road, people stopped mid-stride on the sidewalk. The whole world had come to a complete standstill. Jackson gazed at me with something like awe.

'Are you doing this?' he asked, looking back out at his static city.

I grabbed his arm and dragged him out of the ballroom and through the hallway, past his friends, his coaches, and more men in uniform than I could count.

'I'll explain later,' I said. 'Keep moving. Don't stop until I say so.'

With blind determination, I pushed through the frozen crowds, across the marble foyer, down the front steps. Raindrops burst like water balloons on my hot skin as we wove our way through the living statues on Liberty Street. By the time I stopped and took a deep breath, we were safely hidden around the corner, both of us leaning against a low brick wall on Drayton Street as the rain began to fall again.

'I didn't know you could do that,' Jackson said quietly, eyes on me as his bloodstained shirt flapped open at his stomach.

Flushed with fear, relief and the unwelcome reminder of my otherness, I felt tears well up in my eyes.

'Heal wounds or slow down time?'

He didn't reply. Instead he just swallowed hard.

The rain began to slow around us, naturally this time. The worst of the storm was over and through the yelling and sobbing that still rang out all around the block, I could feel the pull of Bell House, summoning me home. She wanted me where she could see me, where she could keep me safe. We both knew this wouldn't be an isolated incident. The Were would return and any dream I might have nursed of escaping the consequences of Cole's death had just been extinguished. But that wasn't why my hands were shaking at my side. The thought of another attack didn't frighten me nearly as much as the rush I'd felt when standing face to face with the wolf, willing it to attack so I could surrender to the seductive strength of my magic.

'Hey,' a voice said. 'Come back.'

A strong hand cupped my face, long fingers brushing my wet hair away from my face.

'Where did you go?' Jackson appeared in front of me as my eyes refocused on the here and now. 'You looked like you were miles away.'

The rough finish of the bricks behind me sawed into my skin, reminding me of what was real.

'Just tired,' I said. 'I'm here, I swear.'

'Good. Because I need to thank you. For saving my life.'

I chewed the inside of my cheek as I looked away.

'Don't thank me. You never should've been in danger in the first place.'

'Are you kidding me?' He gently turned my face back towards his. 'Those dances are known to be vicious. Getting out alive was only ever a fifty-fifty possibility, and that was without the threat of a giant magic murder wolf.'

Jackson gave me half a smile, working his own kind of magic, distracting me from my darkest thoughts.

The Witch and the Wolf

'Not sure how I'm going to explain to my grandmother what happened to this shirt,' he said, pawing at the stained and shredded white cotton. It was hanging from his body by the only two buttons still fastened, just below his throat. 'You don't happen to have a mending spell?'

'Not that I know of.'

But that didn't stop my fingertips from trembling as though they might like to try. With shaky hands, he undid the last two buttons and balled the shirt up before tossing it into a trash can on the street corner.

'Where do you reckon this falls on Ashley's spectrum of behaviour?' he asked.

'Mortal peril should balance out the shirtless part,' I said. 'How do you think Lyds will feel about the water damage to her dry clean only dress?'

'Oh, certain death. Wolf attack or no wolf attack, you're toast.'

He gave me a once-over, from the top of my wet-through head to the soles of my now bare feet. I couldn't remember when I'd lost my shoes, but now the pavement felt hot, wet and sharp against my soles.

'Come on,' he said. 'Better get you home.'

We turned away from the hotel, Jackson leading the way. I managed a few steps before a roaring wave of exhaustion overwhelmed me and I stumbled over my own feet, careening into the window of a neighbourhood dive bar. Before I could protest, he had slipped his head underneath my arm and scooped me up off my feet, light as a feather.

'You don't have to carry me,' I said as he started down the street, picking up his pace when a police car rolled by. 'I can walk two blocks.'

He cast me a sideways glance.

'I could crawl two blocks,' I corrected myself as we turned

onto Harris Street and the world seemed to pull away from me, everything zooming out of perspective as my head lolled back against his chest. 'Or maybe I can't.'

Two blocks from home and I could see the edge of Lafayette Square. Being carried back to the house was embarrassing but it was better than crawling. I relaxed into my friend's arms and saw his mouth curve upwards out the corner of my eye.

'You might not believe this,' he said. 'But I gotta say, that was still not my worst date ever.'

'Really?'

'Alison Worthy, eighth grade Valentine's dance. She ditched me halfway through the night so she could slow dance with Julian Lopez. I never got over it.'

'So much worse than almost being mauled by a Were,' I agreed. 'Why are male egos so fragile?'

'Hey, isn't that Ms Stovell?' Jackson said instead of answering my question.

Across the street, I saw the woman I'd met at the dance stumbling down the sidewalk, her arms stretched out in front as if to keep her from running into something that wasn't there.

'Ms Stovell?' I called out, but she did not stop or look back.

'She looks like she's in shock or something,' Jackson commented when she kept going, stumbling on.

All the trees around us quivered with dark anticipation. A cherry blossom that should've shed its petals months ago shook until every last pastel pink petal was on the ground, as though it had been saving them for this moment. My stomach twisted with an unpleasant flash of familiar magic that was not my own. I slipped out of Jackson's arms, still holding onto him as I found my feet. Ileen Stovell stopped in the middle of the crosswalk then turned slowly until she was facing us, silently mouthing words I couldn't make out. I walked towards her, ignoring the sharp stones digging into my feet, only a fingertip's

The Witch and the Wolf

distance away. I didn't see the car coming, didn't hear the rumble of its engine, until it was almost on top of us, yellow headlights blinding me.

'Em, watch out!'

A rope of Spanish moss wrapped itself around me and dragged me out of the path of the car right as I shoved Ms Stovell into the safety of Lafayette Square. Dazed but safe, she stared at me as though she'd seen a ghost, the Spanish moss lying slack at her feet.

'What just happened?' she asked, still upright somehow, bracing herself against the live oak that sat at the corner of the square. 'You silly children. Don't you know not to distract someone when they're crossing the road? I could've been killed.'

'We're so sorry, Ms Stovell,' Jackson said, eyes cutting over in my direction as I clutched the rope of Spanish moss like a safety blanket. 'You think you can get home OK or do you need some help?'

She was not amused.

'I should think you've helped quite enough already,' she said. 'First the chaos at the DeSoto and now this. I swear, this town is going straight to hell.'

Pausing to look me up and down, she gave an audible tut, the slightest hint of a smirk colouring her disapproval.

'I'm glad your grandmother isn't here to see this.'

I opened my mouth to reply but before I could say anything, a rush of someone else's magic swept me off my feet and sent me stumbling into the tree. It was back. It was back and here and so strong, and I couldn't do anything to stop it as Jackson's terrified face disappeared and the whole world crumbled into darkness around me.

Chapter Nine

It was dark in my dreams again.

The howl of the wolves at my heels, the leaves and branches crunching underfoot as I ran, the smell of burning buildings and bodies poisoning the air. The screaming I'd heard the night before grew louder, more desperate, as I ran. It was a woman's voice, her agony clawing at my soul like nails down a chalkboard. I had to get to her, I had to save her. It was only when I paused, hesitated for just a second, that I understood where I was. The archway up ahead, the silver dagger in my hand. A figure dressed in white waiting for me at an altar. This was a witch's Becoming ceremony.

'Lydia?' I said as the woman came into focus. 'Lyds, is that you?'

She couldn't answer. Lydia Powell was too busy fighting off what looked like a legion of wolves, dozens if not hundreds, emerging from the woods and all of them racing right past me to lunge at my friend, staining her beautiful white gown scarlet.

'Lydia, no!' I screamed. 'Get away from her!'

I fought blindly, attacking anyone who would do her harm,

blasts of wind, wild rains, sheer force of will, the knife in my hand. It found unwilling flesh over and over until my arm ached with the effort but it was still too late. By the time I fell to my knees beside her, drenched in Were blood, my best friend's eyes were vacant and soulless, evidence of the wolves' claws and teeth everywhere on her mauled body.

'End it.'

Her lips formed the words but there wasn't enough air in her lungs to make a sound.

'Please, Emily, kill me. End it all.'

Two tears cut a stark path through the ripe red gore on my cheeks. With a scream, I raised the dagger above my head and plunged it down with all the strength left in me. As my best friend's last breath left her body, a huge silver wolf with green-grey eyes the colour of Spanish moss appeared in front of me. It was a wolf I'd seen before. In Bonaventure Cemetery. Wyn's brother, Cole.

'Kill him again,' a guttural female voice commanded as he approached, pressed low to the ground. 'You've done it once before.'

'I didn't know,' I said, my hands trembling. 'I couldn't have killed him if I'd known.'

'Then you'll die,' the voice replied. 'And if you die, so goes the world.'

Dropping the knife, I held my arms out wide, eyes closed, accepting my fate as it lunged at my throat and everything went black.

When I shot upright, eyes wide open and panting hard, it took a long moment for me to realize where I was. Then, it took an even longer moment to understand why Jackson Powell was curled up in a nest of blankets and pillows at the side of my bed. I sat up slowly, doing my best to piece together exactly how we had got here. Reality chased the dream away, almost equally as chilling. The party. The wolf. The blood.

'Can't wait to spend the rest of my life lying about how I got these.'

Jackson was awake. He lay on the floor, tracing the five new silvery lines that sliced across his bare torso.

'If you come up with a good one, let me know.'

I raised my shirt to display evidence of my own werewolf encounter on my belly. 'Snap.'

His nostrils flared with recognition.

'Matching werewolf scars. So much cooler than matching tattoos.'

Rolling up into a sitting position, he pressed the heels of his hands into his eyes then pulled his hands away, blinking once, twice, as though he was making sure they still worked properly.

'How do you feel?' I asked.

'Surprisingly good, considering.'

The blanket fell away from his body and I saw he was only wearing boxer briefs, the black elastic waistband tight against his washboard stomach.

'I wish I could say it's all a blur, but the whole night is altogether too clear. How about you?'

'Not great.' I rubbed at a tender spot on my forehead. 'I don't remember anything after leaving the hotel.'

'That old excuse.'

Ashley sailed through the door without knocking, hair clipped up on the top of her head and wearing a baggy blue T-shirt and a pair of grey sweatpants that would've killed Catherine on sight. In her arms was a huge wooden tray full of food: freshly baked biscuits, pancakes, bacon and sausage gravy.

'For crying out loud, Powell, could you put your pants back on already,' she said, kicking the edge of Jackson's makeshift bed. 'I'm gay and she's taken, no one here wants to see what you're packing.'

'I couldn't sleep in them, they were wet.'

Jackson grabbed a pile of black fabric that turned out to be his dress pants, protesting his innocence as she carefully unloaded a pot of coffee and pitcher of freshly squeezed orange juice onto my desk. 'From the rain and the sprinklers and, oh yeah, *my own blood.*'

'Men.' Ashley clucked her tongue as she rested the tray on my desk then helped herself to a piece of bacon. 'Y'all are nasty.'

'I'll have you know I shower twice daily,' he said, standing with his back to the pair of us to quickly pull on his pants and fasten the zipper. 'Except on nights when I'm being pursued by werewolves or making sure my unconscious friend survives the night.'

'I was unconscious?' I asked, poking the sore spot on my forehead again.

'Yes,' they both replied.

'Did I black out?'

'You fell,' Jackson said, 'in the square. Right after you pulled Ms Stovell out of the path of that truck.'

'And we'll debate the merits of that decision later,' Ashley said sternly. 'You were completely out of it when he brought you home. I asked if y'all were doing drugs but he assures me it was good old-fashioned violence.'

'Ashley!'

'Ain't one answer better than the other.'

Her eyes narrowed, aimed in Jackson's direction. 'I said he didn't have to stay but he would not budge. Bedded down at the side of you like Old Yeller. You sure there ain't any wolf in you?'

'Most assuredly not,' Jackson said.

Standing in front of my fireplace, he carefully stretched his hands up over his head, testing his scars.

'Don't worry, it wasn't an entirely selfless offer, I was pretty freaked out last night.'

My aunt turned her inquisitive gaze on me.

'He said there was a wolf. Was it a Were?'

'Yes,' I replied. 'I'm sure of it.'

'Then we'll thank the universe you're alive and leave it at that.'

'You might leave it at that,' Jackson said, absently stroking his new scars, 'but I don't know how I'm going to explain any of this to my grandmother.'

I blanched at the thought. His missing shirt and ruined jacket would be enough to send the fragile Virginia Powell to her bed for the rest of the month. The fact he'd stayed out all night might put her in the hospital.

'No shirt, no shoes, no service,' Ashley said, slapping his hand away when he reached for a pancake, but he managed to dodge the attack, grabbing two and stuffing one straight into his mouth. 'Speaking of shoes, any idea where yours might be?'

Kicking away my bedclothes, I ran a hand over the bottoms of my feet. All cut up and filthy like I'd been running in the woods. Just like in my dream.

'No idea,' I said weakly, glad to be already lying down.

'I don't want Virginia Powell banging on my door, asking questions, any more than you two, so this is what you're going to tell her,' Ashley said. Planting one hand on her hip, she pointed at Jackson with the other. 'First up, the scar. I'm fostering a rescue dog and it gave you a little scratch when you came by to collect Emily – nothing to worry about, hardly broke the skin. You left the car at the hotel because you and your sportsball buddies were drinking underage, like everyone else at those stupid Country Day parties. You lost your shirt during a quick game of shirts versus skins, and you stayed out all night because you two dummies hooked up.'

The Witch and the Wolf

Suddenly I was very much awake.

'Ashley!' I yelled. 'No way!'

'It's the most logical explanation,' she replied coolly, splitting one of her biscuits into two equal pieces. 'Or do you have a better one?'

'She'll be furious,' I said, my too-slow brain trying and failing to come up with an alternative. 'You want Jackson to tell his grandmother he was drinking? That he, that we . . .? No way. I'd call you an idiot but that would be an insult to idiots.'

'Well, actually . . .'

My eyes shot across the room to where Jackson had cupped his chin with his hand, one eyebrow arched as he considered her proposal.

'I think Ashley's right.'

'As always,' she said, giving a little curtsey.

'If Lydia stayed out all night and told your grandmother she'd been drinking and hooking up, she would be sent to a nunnery,' I said, a red rash of mortification spreading across my chest and throat. 'She would literally never be allowed to leave the house again.'

Ashley and Jackson glanced at each other, my aunt's expression irritated, Jackson's bemused, before speaking in perfect unison.

'It's different for boys,' they said together.

I buried my face in my hands.

'Boys get away with more, that's just how it is,' Ashley said when Jackson snorted out a laugh. 'A night of drinking and partying won't ruin young Master Powell's reputation, but if it was Miss Powell? That would be another matter entirely.'

'And what about my reputation?' I said, utterly indignant.

'I'm sorry, did you want the town to think you were saving yourself for marriage?'

Ashley spoke to me but stared daggers at Jackson. 'I know

it's giving nineteenth century but the reality is, things have not changed nearly as much as we like to think they have. Besides, no one else will ever know. Jackson here will not breathe a word and I dare say Virginia Powell will be low-key thrilled. She has been praying for the two of you to get together since the first day your mamas missed their periods. I'd be surprised if she doesn't throw a damn party to celebrate.'

'Hate to make a habit of admitting it, but she's right again,' Jackson said when I looked to him for a rebuttal. 'You want to get out of this situation with as few questions asked as possible? This is the way.'

I sank back against my pillows, staring at the two of them as they accepted the proposal on my behalf and went back to bickering over biscuits and bacon. It was scary how quickly someone could adjust to this life. He'd been attacked, almost died, and Jackson hadn't even lost his appetite. If it wasn't for the sound of the doorbell echoing through Bell House, I might've started crying.

'I'll get it,' I offered before anyone else could, clambering from my bed to stagger out of the room.

The marshland on the hallway wallpaper swayed in the breeze, back to itself again. Bell House was at peace, at least. If only I could say the same. There was no time to worry about what Virginia Powell thought about my virtue or lack thereof, I needed to focus on the bigger picture. The wolf. As I stumbled downstairs, I tried to remember everything I could, how big it was, the shade of its fur, the colour of its eyes, but so much of it was a blur, the bump on my head stealing away the finer details. It probably didn't matter too much, I thought, as my feet found the foyer floor.

But I knew I hadn't seen the last of that wolf.

Chapter Ten

'Lydia!'

I threw open the front door with one hand and bundled my best friend into a hug with the other, holding her as tightly as humanly possible. I couldn't recall a time I'd ever been so happy to see anyone in my whole life.

The sentiment, however, was not returned.

'Oh, so you are alive, good to know.'

She broke away from my hug and stomped past me into the foyer. Her furious face was makeup free and it looked like she was still wearing her pyjamas, along with a pair of baby pink Converse. Lydia had been in a rush to get over here and did not wait to be invited inside.

'Lyd?' I said as she poked her head in the parlour, cast a filthy look back at me, then began a purposeful march up the stairs. 'Lydia, wait.'

'Why? To give you time to hide my brother?'

She didn't even stop to turn around and look at me. 'Jackson Charles David Powell, I know you're here, get your ass out here right now.'

Jackson Charles David Powell did not get his ass out

anywhere. He didn't get the chance. Instead, Lydia stormed into my bedroom, flinging the door open with a vindicated yell.

'Ah-ha!' She jabbed her pointer finger into her brother's chest with an accusatory glare. 'I was right!'

'Lydia Virginia Sarah Powell,' Jackson replied with a shallow bow. 'I guess there's a first time for everything.'

'It's not what you think,' I said, following her into the room, just in time to see my best friend punch her brother in the arm as hard as she could.

'Really?'

'Really,' I replied.

Lydia turned on her heel and glared at me.

'You mean the Oglethorpe Country Dumb fundraiser wasn't attacked by a werewolf?'

'OK,' I said, taking a surprised step backwards. 'It's exactly what you think.'

'How did you know?' Ashley asked as Jackson massaged his newly injured arm. 'Is this some kind of twin telepathy thing?'

'No, it's an I-woke-up-to-one-thousand-messages-about-a-wolf-escaping-from-Oatland-Island-wildlife-refuge-and-crashing-the-dance thing,' Lydia replied. 'Last night was a full moon. Jackson didn't come home, neither of you are answering your phones. Didn't take a genius to work out y'all had to be mixed up in it somehow.'

She shook her head at Ashley in disgust. 'Twin telepathy? You really are as stupid as you look.'

'Please don't,' I held Ashley back with one arm as she rolled her sleeves up to the elbows, ready to fight. 'Lyds, start from the top. Who is saying what about a wolf?'

'Depends who you ask,' she replied, eyeing the biscuits on my desk. 'There's the official report that's on the news, wolf escaped from the refuge, but obviously the refuge is denying it because it's not true. If you look at social media, Kayleigh Cavanaugh is crying about a rabid dog on Instagram, Maxon Jones is all over TikTok claiming he punched a wolf in the face, and Jennifer Vance texted me to say no one saw the two of you leave the ballroom, which naturally meant the wolf must've eaten y'all, and I know you can't believe a word she says most times, but this time I had a bad feeling. And then—'

'I think we've got it,' Ashley cut her off, earning a bitter glare for her trouble. 'Thanks for the "he said, she said".'

'*And then*,' Lydia said again, louder this time, 'I went to the DeSoto and found—' She fished around in a tote bag hanging from her shoulder and pulled out several items, presenting them one at a time before laying them on the bed. 'Em's shoes, purse, and my idiot brother's phone and valet ticket. I know Jackson doesn't abandon his car overnight without good reason, so there were only three possible answers.'

'Can't wait to hear 'em,' Jackson said.

She held her hands out and, without her having to say a word, Jackson grabbed a biscuit and tossed it to her. Ashley and I exchanged a look but neither of us said a thing.

'One, y'all really were eaten by the wolf,' she said, splitting the biscuit in half. 'Two, y'all hooked up – and we both know that's less likely than reason number one. Or, number three, one or both of y'all got hurt and came back to Bell House to heal. So, on a scale of one to absolutely, how extremely correct am I?'

'Very nearly absolutely,' I told her, jumping in before her brother could. 'Jackson tried to stop the wolf attacking me and got cut up for his effort.'

'I knew it,' she said, squinting in triumph before turning to her brother. 'You really tried to fight a wolf?'

He nodded.

'You are so stupid.'

'I think you mean brave.'

She raised an eyebrow, a perfect mirror of the expression I'd seen on his face a few moments before.

'You couldn't find your butt with your hands in your back pockets. Here—'

She passed me my evening bag and I immediately opened it to find my phone. The screen was blank.

'Probably waterlogged,' Jackson said when I pressed every possible button over and over. 'Put it in a jar of rice to dry out, we'll have it working by tomorrow.'

'Don't panic,' Lydia said. 'You can message Wyn on my phone.'

Jackson held up his own phone, a picture of a baseball field on the lockscreen.

'I can text him,' he said. 'I have his number.'

'You do?'

He nodded at my surprised look.

'Gave it to me when I drove him home. In case of emergencies.'

Ashley cleared her throat.

'Speaking of Wyn and his wolfie brethren,' she said, her voice loaded with caution. 'I know no one wants to say it, but someone has to. The Were that attacked the party, was it from his pack?'

'No idea.' I reluctantly replayed the dark energy I'd felt all around us at the party. 'Whoever it was, they were beyond strong and definitely not in town to see the sights.'

'You think they know about Cole?' Lydia asked.

'I think we should assume they do. And I think we should assume this wasn't a one-and-done attack.'

'Meaning we have a month to figure this out before the next full moon,' she replied.

I nodded, then turned to Jackson, who was busy tapping away at his phone.

'My memory is still kind of foggy,' I said. 'Did you notice anything in particular? Colour of its eyes, any distinctive markings?'

Tucking his phone in his back pocket, he gave a shrug.

'Not that I can recollect. Eyes could've been green, could've been yellow, rain made it hard to see. Coat was grey but I couldn't pick it out of a line-up, I was more concerned with the teeth and the claws, if I'm being honest.'

A line-up of wolves. He had no idea how terrifying that thought was.

'So, you're not entirely stupid,' Ashley said with a heavy sigh. 'But you are mostly useless.'

'For real, I don't get any points for getting Em home in one piece?' he said, throwing up his arms in frustration.

'A million points,' I said.

'Minus the million you lose for taking her out in the first place,' Lydia said.

'And we're done.' Ashley clapped her hands together and ushered the twins towards the door. 'I get a trillion points for tolerating both of y'all so early in the morning. Go on, scat, my little super witch needs a nap.'

The pair of them looked to me and I returned a rueful smile. I wasn't exactly clamouring to be on my own but I needed space to concentrate and the twins weren't exactly a calming influence.

'I can't go home like this.' Jackson waved a hand at his bare chest as Lydia bent down to squint at his new scars before giving them an exploratory poke. 'Lyds, go home and grab me a shirt.'

Without asking, she opened the drawer of my dresser and took out a powder puff pink baby tee. 'You can wear this, I'm not your servant.'

He pulled the comically small T-shirt over his head. Within

seconds it was ruined, stretched irrevocably out shape, but it was worth it to see the matching grins on Ashley and Lydia's faces.

'Can I speak with Em for a second, please?' he said, beseeching eyes turned to Ashley.

'Nuh-uh, you got her all last night,' Lydia said, hip-checking her brother out of the way. 'I need to speak to her.'

'So in demand.' Ashley looked from twin to twin to me, rolling her eyes at the slight inclination of my head. 'Fine. Jackson, you're with me. I have something big and heavy that needs moving in the kitchen.'

'What?'

'I don't know,' she said, clipping him around the back of the head then directing him out of my bedroom. 'I'll think of something when we get there. Just walk your ass down those stairs before I push you down.'

Lydia closed the door behind them, hovering by it until she'd decided they were all the way out of earshot. Then she turned to me with the most serious look I had ever seen on her face.

'What's wrong?' I asked, prickling with concern.

'I'm only going to ask you once,' she replied. 'But did you bang my brother?'

'Lydia!'

'Did you make out with him?'

'We both almost died and you're asking if we kissed?'

'Gonna need verbal confirmation,' she said, arms folded across her chest. 'You forget, I know him. He can be very charming when he wants to be.'

'Not that charming,' I assured her. 'No, I didn't bang your brother. No, we did not make out. We went to the party, we talked, we danced, we battled a mystical creature, and all the way through, he was a perfect gentleman.'

The Witch and the Wolf

I poked at a piece of extra crispy bacon, knowing Ashley had cooked it just the way I liked, but my appetite was completely MIA.

'I'm sorry,' I said. 'I should've called you or messaged as soon as I woke up, but I don't even remember going to bed.'

Lydia frowned. 'The bed you shared with my brother.'

'He slept on the floor.' I pointed at the pile of pillows and blankets. 'Lyds, listen to me, I would never.'

After one very long moment, her eyes searing into me, she relented.

'Fine, I believe you,' she said, stuffing his jacket into her tote. 'Thanks for saving his life, I guess. I might need that kidney someday. How dumb does a boy have to be to leap in front of a werewolf?'

'If anyone is to blame here, it's me,' I replied. 'He was only trying to help.'

'He was only trying to get into your pants,' she muttered under her breath, and for a second it looked as though she was going to say something else but changed her mind.

'Well, while you were running around not banging my brother, I was going through a bunch of family records and ancestry stuff,' she said. 'And I'm pretty sure I found the last Powell witch.'

My breath caught in my throat. Lydia in a white gown, begging me to end her life, the dagger in my hand. I fought to keep my face neutral.

'Really?'

'Really. I have a few more things I want to check out, but can we get together and look at it?'

'Sure,' I managed to say, the smell of the food in my room suddenly making me nauseous.

'Awesome.'

She shoved everything down into the bottom of her tote bag

and flashed me a smile. 'Our mom should be arriving soon. She'll probably want to catch up with me and Jackson, get dinner or something. You should come over tomorrow morning and meet her, we can talk after.'

I nodded, following her out of my room and down the stairs, the foyer floor cool under my injured feet, my bare legs prickling. The silk walls shifted from a pale pink to a soft coral and the front door opened without waiting for Lydia to reach for the handle.

'I'm glad you're both OK.'

She hugged me tight, the throbbing pulse in her neck pressed against mine, and the sight of her throat torn open, blood gushing, assaulted me once again.

'And I'm so glad you didn't bang Jackson.'

'Said the classiest girl who ever lived.'

Her brother leaned against the staircase, his forehead creased with disapproval.

Lydia replied with a sweet smile and a middle finger held aloft.

'See you back at the house,' she called as she skipped out the front door. 'No way I'm walking down the street with you in that shirt.'

The door closed itself and I turned back to him, inviting Jackson into the parlour with a tilt of my head. In my too tight T-shirt, six-pack peeking out the bottom, fabric straining over his biceps and triceps, he looked just as comfortable as he had in a tux.

'She's only kidding,' I said, settling against the back of the sofa with my arms folded. 'She doesn't mean anything by it.'

He cupped the back of his neck and gave me a cockeyed grin.

'Yeah, she does. She loves you, Em, she doesn't want to share. Trust me, I get it.'

The Witch and the Wolf

I made myself laugh, though it didn't feel like an especially funny statement.

'Well, she'll just have to learn,' I said. 'You're allowed to love more than one person.'

'I'm glad we agree on that.'

A light breeze rustled the leaves of the tree painted on the wall behind him and a flock of tiny bluebirds alighted on its tallest branch, eyeing us with interest, but if Jackson noticed, I couldn't tell.

'Because, you know, it's important to have friends,' he said, bringing his arm across his chest to squeeze a tense muscle in his shoulder. 'You wouldn't limit yourself to one friend, right? Especially not at our age, especially not when you've just moved here and you haven't even had a chance to meet everyone yet. How else would you know you've made the right friends?'

The smooth, confident Jackson was gone and he was babbling again, the same as when he stopped by to ask me to the dance. He was anxious and we could all feel it, me, the birds and the trees.

'Jeez, Ashley's coffee is strong enough to send a man to the moon.' He turned his eyes up to the ceiling. 'What I'm trying to say is, I heard what Lyds said.'

'About what?'

'About me,' he replied. 'And you.'

'And she isn't entirely wrong.'

Even the wisdom and knowledge of two hundred years of witches could not have prepared me for this conversation.

'Last night was the most fun I've had in forever,' Jackson said, shaking his head as though he'd tried to convince himself otherwise. 'At least it was until a werewolf tried to rip out my guts, but honestly, it still wasn't the worse night of my life.'

'I know.' I laughed nervously. 'Alison Worthy, eighth grade Valentine's dance.'

He threw up his hands as though I'd proved his point. I'd never noticed how huge they were before, easily big enough to palm a basketball. No wonder he was so good at it.

'See?' he said. 'You listen, you get me. I've never felt more myself with anyone, ever.'

'Yes, because I'm your friend.'

He took a step towards me and I snatched in a breath. Somehow I was more tense standing in front of Jackson Powell in my own home than I was facing off against a wolf three times my size.

'It's not just the way you make me feel about myself, Em, it's everything about you.'

Not once did he break eye contact. It was brutal, like someone holding my hand to a flame and refusing to let me pull it away.

'You're smart, you're genuine, you make me laugh. Do you have any idea how damn funny you are? And yes, you're a witch, which I happen to think is very cool, but that's only one part of this incredible person standing in front of me. Anyone alive would be lucky, so damned lucky, to get to stand beside you and say, "That's my girl."'

The flock of bluebirds twittered excitedly among themselves, terrible gossips that they were.

'Thank you?' I said when he stopped talking.

Thank you? Really? I cringed, the words echoing through my mind. I squeezed my eyes shut, wondering if there was a way to take them back.

'And you're the most beautiful girl I ever saw in my life.'

Jackson's voice was so husky and low it made me shiver. I opened my eyes to see he was even closer now. 'I could've lost my life last night. Worse still, I could've lost you. If I walked out this door today without telling you the truth, I'd be a coward.'

The caps of his shiny leather dress shoes were almost touching my toes and I gripped the back of the sofa behind me, no words to speak, nothing to add. Not that it was time for me to talk. Jackson wasn't finished.

'Wyn and I got to know each other pretty well when I drove him back to Asheville. He's a good guy, I guess, as far as werewolves go, and I'm not the kind of person who goes around trying to steal someone else's girl—'

'No, you're not,' I said, doing my best not to look directly into his soulful brown eyes. Instead I studied the stubble on his chin, the healed-over mark of an old piercing in his left earlobe, silver ring on the middle finger of his right hand.

'But Wyn's not here and I am.'

The words settled on the ground around us like freshly fallen snow in the middle of July, so unexpected they stole my breath away.

'I'm not asking you to make a choice,' Jackson said, a hint of self-restraint tightening throat. 'Only to hear me out. I am your friend, Emily, I always will be. Whatever you need from me, it's yours, but after what happened last night, I don't want to waste time wondering what if, so just think about it. You and me.'

It sang to me again, that sweet life I might've lived if I'd never left Savannah. But it was like he said, no point in wondering what if.

'Jackson, you are so special to me,' I said eventually, forcing myself to meet his eyes. 'Beyond special. But I love Wyn and that isn't going to change.'

He leaned in towards me and gripped the sofa, one hand on either side of my hips.

'I don't need you to stop loving Wyn. I just need you to love me more.'

The kiss he pressed to my cheek was so soft, I barely felt it. Lighter than the beat of a butterfly's wings, there one heartbeat and gone the next. But when he pulled away, I was breathless. The look on his face was determined. He had hope.

He turned to leave, almost out the door when I remembered how to use my voice.

'Jackson,' I called and he stopped in his tracks.

'When Wyn messages you back, will you please let me know right away?'

His shoulders sagged but he held his head high.

'Will do,' he replied.

'Thank you.'

Our eyes locked and I saw a reflection of myself in him. Emily James Bell, Jackson's version. She was confident, proud and capable. An Emily who laughed more easily and lived a life not quite so full of worry and angst. She looked happy and I realized I was envious of her. She was loved and she knew it. I wiped away a tear that came out of nowhere, half of me desperate for him to leave, half of me wondering what might happen if he stayed.

'I don't mind waiting,' he said with a wistful smile. 'I've been waiting on you since before you knew I existed.'

And then he was gone.

Chapter Eleven

I was in the library when Ashley found me hours later, once again carrying food.

'Since you didn't touch anything at breakfast.'

She placed her tray directly on top of my work, covering the yellow legal pads and Post-its and pencils. 'Starving yourself isn't going to help you fight your enemies.'

'Might save some money on the grocery budget,' I said as she opened a bag of chips and dumped them on a plate next to a turkey sandwich.

I fished out one small chip and took a bite, making a face as the salt crystals cracked on my tongue. She'd changed her clothes from this morning, her sweatpants replaced by tight flared jeans and a pretty floral shirt, her long brown hair braided over one shoulder.

'What time is it?' I asked.

'Almost two.'

She pulled one of the yellow legal pads out from under the tray and squinted at my list.

'Your penmanship is almost as bad as your biscuits. What's

this? "How can I convince Lydia she doesn't want to be a bitch?" Good luck with that.'

'It says witch, as you well know,' I said as she scanned the rest of it. 'I thought if I wrote down everything I need to figure out, it might not seem so overwhelming.'

'And?'

'And I was wrong.'

Pushing the plate to one side, I dropped my head into my hands and groaned. Ashley walked around the desk, took a seat in the chair opposite mine and kicked up her feet, resting them inches away from my nose.

'Thought you weren't allowed to write this stuff down. Witchy by-laws and all.'

'I'm not documenting anything.' I spoke louder than necessary, just in case any ancestral ghosts happened to be passing by and felt the need to police my list. 'It's just a list, nothing incriminating, and I'll burn it when I'm done.'

'Hmm,' Ashley said before reading my list out loud. '"Wolf attack, Catherine missing, why can't I see the ghosts, how can I convince Lydia she doesn't want to be a bitch—"'

'*Witch*.'

'I stand by my interpretation. Prophecy, where does blessing come from, and, oh, interesting, this last one is underlined, one, two, three, *four* times? Jackson. Tell me, darling niece of mine, whyever would you need to underline Jackson Powell's name four times when your honey, Wyn, didn't make the list at all?'

'Wyn isn't on the list because I'm not worried about him,' I said, although it wasn't entirely true.

Wyn wasn't on the list because every time I thought about him, I was overcome with guilt I did not have the emotional bandwidth to entertain. I allowed myself one self-indulgent sigh and rocked back against my leather chair.

'Why is nothing ever easy?' I said. 'With everything else that's going on, wouldn't you think the universe would at least give me a pass on boy trouble?'

Ashley leaned forward to steal a handful of my chips. 'It's only trouble if you have feelings for him. Which you don't. Right?'

'Right,' I said, sounding way more sure than I felt. 'I mean, I like him as a friend. Do I think he's attractive? Sure. Do I like spending time with him? Sure. If I had never met Wyn, would things be different? Who knows.'

'Not so shabby for a runner-up prize.'

'Jackson doesn't come in second to anyone,' I said too quickly, looking away when she raised an eyebrow.

'But you love Wyn.'

'I love Wyn,' I confirmed. 'And only Wyn.'

'Not to make myself unpopular but . . .' She nudged my plate towards me and I obediently picked up half the sandwich and took a bite. 'Can I ask why?'

I looked back at her, confused.

'Why do I love Wyn?'

She nodded, waiting for my answer while I chewed and swallowed. It was absurd to me, the thought of having to justify our connection. Wasn't it clear to everyone? Wasn't it as obvious as the sun in the sky? According to the look on Ashley's face, it was not, and when I searched for the right words to describe it, I struggled.

'Because we're part of each other,' I said finally. 'It's like we're woven together. If you pulled on one thread, we would both unravel.'

'Deep.' Ashley's eyebrows flashed up her forehead. 'Also he's stupid hot.'

'Doesn't hurt his case, but that's not why I love him.'

I paused again, looking for words that didn't exist.

'I don't know how else to explain it,' I said, 'other than to say we're the same. Not two pieces that fit together but one whole that should never have been separated. He is me and I am him. I know we're meant to be together the same way I know I have to keep breathing.'

'Same person, huh? So I only have to buy y'all one Christmas gift?' She opened her mouth and tossed in another chip. 'Then there isn't much of a problem here, is there? Jackson likes you. You like Wyn. Wyn likes you. Too bad, Jackson. Why are you so vexed?'

It was something I'd been wondering since he left and I didn't like the answer I'd come up with.

'Because,' I said, dropping my voice as though afraid the books might hear me. 'What if I'm wrong?'

'About what?'

'About Wyn's feelings,' I made myself say, grimacing at another stab of guilt. 'About mine.'

'Oh, brother.'

She grabbed the glass of lemonade and took a swig.

'Should've thrown some bourbon in here,' she muttered before wiping the palm of her hand over her face. 'OK, let's go at this from the top. As for whether or not you're wrong about Wyn, honey, there's no way to be sure about that. Smarter women than you have done dumber things than fall for the first pretty boy to bat his eyes in her direction. For what it's worth, I believe he loves you.'

'I know he does,' I said, as certain as it was possible to be. 'But people who love me have hurt me before. How am I supposed to know if that's enough?'

She didn't speak for a long while. Instead, she sipped her drink and went on eating my chips until they were all gone. I ate my sandwich in silence. We were thinking of the same people. People who loved us but still made choices that hurt us all. Her mother, her brother, my grandmother, my father.

'Since I can't read those boys' minds, let's go back to you,'

The Witch and the Wolf

Ashley said when the plate was completely clear. 'Pretend you were meeting them both brand new. Jackson is the easier option on paper. Good kid from a good family, got great prospects, and yes, even as someone with a lifelong preference for the ladies, I can see he's a looker. Doesn't hurt that he thinks the sun comes up every day just to hear you crow, and even better, his family doesn't want you dead.'

'As far as we know,' I said.

'Even if they did, I'd rather take on Virginia and Alex Powell than a whole pack of werewolves,' she pointed out. 'The most vicious thing the Powells can do is have you barred from the Savannah ladies bridge club. Social suicide, yes, but would you rather be excluded from society holiday parties or have your guts ripped out by a pack of wolves?'

'First one,' I replied, gulping down what was left of my unspiked lemonade. 'I'd very much like to keep my guts intact.'

She inclined her head in agreement.

'And then we have Wyn,' she said. 'Also missed every branch of the ugly tree, also eyeballs to entrails in love with you. Polite, which I appreciate, but also a Were. Which might not be quite as big of a deal if you hadn't, you know . . .' she dragged her hand across her throat and made a croaking sound. 'Offed his brother. Things like that make holiday parties a little complicated.'

'Especially if his pack knows,' I replied, eyes on the pressed tin ceiling.

'They were going to find out eventually. You know you can't live a life built on lies.'

'If that's right, how come so many people try?'

When I looked back to my aunt, her gaze had turned steely. She picked up a pencil and tapped it against the legal pad.

'I once told you not to be a fool for love and I stand by that. One way or another, people always show you who they are eventually. It's up to you to decide whether you want to wait around to see it or make the call yourself.'

The list swam in front of my eyes, my own handwriting, the familiar loops and swirls, turning into incomprehensible scribbles on the page.

'I just don't know what to do,' I said. 'I thought coming into my full magic would make things easier, not more difficult.'

'You can put wheels on your grandma but it won't make her a wagon,' Ashley replied. 'You have the tools but you don't know how to use them.'

Flicking her legs down from the desk, she stood slowly, picking up the empty chip packet and folding it three times into a small square.

'Stop looking for answers in the library and start searching in the right place. You're not studying for a test, you're studying yourself.'

'If only we had a room for that,' I said with a sigh.

'We do.'

Slipping the foil square into the back pocket of her jeans, she gave me a pointed look.

'It's time to stop pretending it doesn't exist. You've tried everything else, done all that you can on your own and nothing has changed. A strong woman knows when it's time to ask for help.'

I knew exactly what she was talking about.

'I don't want to,' I said, quiet but certain. 'Not after what she did in there.'

'We don't always have the privilege of having everything the way we want it,' Ashley said with a soft touch on my shoulder. 'You've got to be stronger than your fear, Em. You're not just a Bell witch, you know, you're my niece as well. Don't let me down.'

When she left the room, tray in hand, she didn't bother to

close the door. An invitation for me to follow. To go somewhere I'd been avoiding for a whole month.

Bell House was a mansion, four floors and more rooms than I could count on both hands, and there was more than one we left alone. As well as the library, the kitchen and the parlour, there was a study, a formal dining room and a breakfast room we never used. Behind the door opposite the library, a staircase led down to the garden level and three closed-up guest suites that had been untouched for decades. And upstairs, beyond mine, Ashley's and Catherine's rooms, the third floor, my parents' old suite. But that wasn't what Ashley was talking about. There was another room I'd deemed off limits, one I'd entered just once before and only then in the most dire of circumstances.

I found myself on my feet, walking towards the blue-painted door at the end of the hallway, ignoring the anxious reverberations of the house.

Catherine's craft room.

The place she went to work her darkest magic, hide her secrets, cast curses and spells. The place she had offered up her own blood to take the lives of others.

If Bell House was a living thing, that room was its beating heart.

And like it or not, it was time for me to step inside.

Chapter Twelve

When Catherine called it a craft room, I assumed she was talking about sewing or scrapbooking, and it took me far too long to discover the truth. Now, the thought of her hiding away with a glass of wine, a fun podcast and a bag full of goodies from Target made me choke. The things she had done in this room defied belief. While I was upstairs, in the same house, she'd been in there, plotting.

Standing before the sky blue door, the air turned frigid, blasting down on me, even as the brass doorknob twisted all on its own and the door creaked open. The room wanted me to enter, but the house did not.

'You don't need to worry,' I told it, one hand on the now grey-tinged wallpaper. 'Whatever it was she did in there, that's not what I'm looking for.'

When my grandmother ran Bell House, the hallway walls were a cool sage green. Now they changed every day, depending on the house's mood. Or mine. We were linked in ways I didn't understand just yet but I knew in my bones it was right and good. Unlike the acts Catherine committed in this room.

The Witch and the Wolf

'She's gone,' I reminded us both. 'She can't hurt us now.'

Unless she wasn't. Unless she was waiting just a few feet away on the other side of the door. There was only one way to find out.

Without another second's hesitation, I pushed myself over the threshold before I came up with any more reasons not to, and once inside, I couldn't believe my eyes.

'What the heck?'

I turned to make sure I was in the right room, in the right house. Sure enough, I saw the hallway behind me and beyond that, the foyer, as it always was. But this wasn't the same room I'd stepped foot in before.

The last time I was in here, the small, dimly lit, windowless space was a mess. Covered in half-burned black candles, leather-bound journals, and every kind of crystal, from the tiniest shard of black garnet to giant hunks of smoky quartz. There were bundles of dried herbs and piles of bloody feathers everywhere I looked, with a twin-sized bed pushed up against the wall, laden with more of the same. That was the place where Catherine had recuperated after almost killing herself in order to take my father's life.

Today it was completely different.

It was still the same size but other than that, utterly changed in every possible way. The walls gleamed as though made from mother of pearl and the iridescence shifted with the flicker of white candles that sparked into life when I closed the door behind me. The pale wood shelves were well stocked with untouched notebooks and books I'd never seen before, some of them written in languages I didn't recognize and all of them singing to me in a beautiful, harmonious tune. All of Catherine's uncut crystals had been replaced with tumbled rocks and polished stones, the largest piece of amethyst I'd ever seen sat on what looked like an altar, and white roses and pink carnations grew from nowhere, sweetly scenting the air. Every trace of Catherine and her darkness was gone.

I knew the layout of Bell House like the back of my hand. The craft room sat right beneath the curving staircase that led from the foyer up to the bedrooms yet somehow, the ceiling of this tiny space reached up to the sky. I sank into a cream-coloured armchair in front of the built-in desk that ran along one side of the room, my legs weak as I watched a flock of doves pass overhead. All the bitter, insidious energy I'd felt in here before was gone, replaced with only light. A clean slate. Was this how the room started for Catherine? I wiped away a stray tear at the thought.

'Thank you,' I whispered, wiping my face with the back of my hands. 'It's beautiful.'

A pair of crystals rolled off the desk and under the bed. Dropping to my hands and knees, I pulled them out, weighing one in each hand. Clear quartz and selenite. Clear quartz I already knew but the selenite whispered its name to me, the same way all the plants in the garden had introduced themselves when I first arrived. I returned to the desk and laid my list out on the white oak surface, feeling so close to my magic and my ancestors, tears welling up behind my eyes.

Wolf attack
Catherine missing
Why can't I see the ghosts?
How can I convince Lydia she doesn't want to be a
  witch?
Prophecy
Where does the blessing come from?
Jackson

The Witch and the Wolf

I stared at the piece of paper and felt my mouth twist at the order of my concerns. Three months ago, my worries ran to which colleges to apply to, how long it would take to get my driver's licence and what kind of mascara could actually hold a curl. Things had changed.

With Ashley's words still ringing in my ears, I reluctantly picked up a pen and added another item. There was no point leaving anything out.

How can I be sure Wyn loves me?

Reaching out for him, I found the connection peaceful and still. It had been that way all morning. His phase was over, I could feel that much, but he was still so far away from me. It was a relief, in a way. As desperate as I was to hear his voice, I knew telling him about the attack would only add to our mounting pile of problems. And that was before I attempted to explain the Jackson situation.

The blessing announced itself with a tingling sensation, the very tips of my fingers sparking ever so slightly, as if it didn't want to scare me. Priorities, it seemed to say, stay on track. I inhaled as it spread through my body, seeping into my blood and amplifying my senses. This was new. It felt like slipping into a bath that was just slightly too hot, snatching my breath away, relaxing and invigorating in equal measure. The room was a crucible, everything was intensified, my sense of touch, of smell, and I understood at once why Catherine had chosen to spend so much time in here. It was like being reborn and the closest I had ever felt to the blessing. What I couldn't understand was how she could take all this light and still turn to the dark.

Heightened intuition directed my hands to a tall white candle, a box of matches and a shallow silver bowl, all resting on the desk, and told me to add pinches of dried mugwort, valerian and yarrow to the bowl. Instinctively, I took my list and folded it in half, towards me. I turned it once, clockwise, and folded it towards me again before placing it in the bowl with the herbs and striking a match. A white flame caught the yellow paper, burning it slowly and consuming the lines of black ink one line at a time. As each item on the list disappeared, a sense of calm built inside me, until my eyelids grew so heavy, I could hardly keep them open. The thin mattress on the bed was so much more comfortable than it looked. It accepted my weight easily as I rolled from the chair to the bed, sinking deeper and deeper, the sky above seeming to move further and further away. I looked over at the desk and saw the list was gone, reduced to a small pile of canary-coloured ash. With the scent of burning herbs, roses and carnations in the air, the clear quartz in one hand and selenite in the other, I closed my eyes and let my magic take over.

The gardens of Bell House were beautiful, lush and green and full of life. I walked barefoot over the earth, a white gossamer gown brushing against the ground, my hair long and loose, and all I felt was peace. The blessing, the world and my magic were all in precious harmony and it felt as though every living thing was celebrating the fact. When I touched a fingertip to the delicate petals of a blossoming azalea, I noticed a ring on the third finger of my left hand. A dainty gold band that wrapped around three stones, a diamond, a sapphire and an emerald.

At the far end of the garden was a copper arch, wrapped in honeysuckle and Spanish moss, and beneath it stood a beautiful woman with long red hair. The first Emma Catherine Bell. She smiled when she saw me and I smiled back, comforted by the sight of her. My ancestor, my ghost, a piece of my heart. To her left stood Ashley and Lydia, and to her right, Jackson and

The Witch and the Wolf

Wyn. All four of them were dressed in clothes I'd never seen before, Lydia in a pretty yellow dress, Ashley in a lavender tuxedo and Jackson and Wyn in matching blue suits so dark they were almost black. Ashley and Lydia looked ecstatic, a miracle given the fact they were standing so close together. The same could not be said of Jackson and Wyn. I sensed sadness and regret woven through with love. All their feelings were stitched together in a complicated tapestry.

'Emily?' I heard a voice say. 'Are you ready?'

A couple emerged from Bell House. A tall man with dark hair and a beard, and beside him, a petite, pale haired woman. His face was serious, a permanent frown line carved between his eyebrows. She was his opposite. Sunshine and light, the promise of laughter never far from her lips.

'Mom? Dad?'

I took a step back, so surprised as they came towards me and gathered me in their embrace.

'Are you ready?' my father asked again.

'Ready for what?'

My mother handed me a bouquet of gardenias and ferns wrapped with Spanish moss, then leaned forward to whisper in my ear.

'Ready for what comes next.'

Standing behind me, she covered my eyes with her hands and the garden disappeared.

'Are you ready, Emily?'

The same words. A different voice. Another time, the same place.

When my eyes were uncovered, my parents were no longer beside me. Instead, Catherine took their place, dressed in black silk, her expression defiant. Behind her, Bell House stood in ruins, the roof caved in, every window smashed and black smoke billowing up into a green sky. The garden was a wasteland. Instead of waiting for me with anticipation, Ashley lay on the floor, arms and legs jutting out from her torso at impossible angles, her unseeing eyes staring straight to the sky. Beside her, Lydia shrieked as barbed vines crawled out of the earth to wrap themselves around her arms and legs, draining her life until all that was left was a pale, dusty corpse. My parents clutched at each other, screaming as a tornado of fire consumed them both, leaving effigies in ash, standing until the slightest breeze picked up and blew them into nothingness. Wyn and Jackson stood right where they were, side by side, their faces etched with regret, but made no move to help. The first Emma Catherine was gone. Beyond the walls of the garden, I heard screams that tore up the unnatural night as my nightmare reality bled out into the rest of the world.

'What do I do?' I said, turning back to my grandmother in panic. 'Help me, what do I do?'

'Don't you think you've done enough?'

She brushed my hair back from my face, her expression impassive. 'This is the choice you made.'

Pushing her away, I ran, tearing out of the garden and around to the front of the house, just in time to watch a wall of black flame racing toward Lafayette Square, consuming the trees, incinerating my beloved Spanish moss. Behind the inferno, the howls of hunters closed in, not just the wolves but the other thing, the worse thing.

'If this is my choice then I'll unmake it,' I told Catherine when she appeared at my side. 'Tell me, how do I stop this from happening?'

Opening my fists, I saw the black arfvedsonite crystal in one hand and my silver brooch with its glinting moonstone in the other.

'Who's to say the decision that leads us here hasn't already been made?' she said. 'Who's to say this isn't for the best?'

The Witch and the Wolf

Her gentle hand caressed my cheek for a brief moment then caught my chin and squeezed until her nails dug into my flesh. Ignoring my protestations, she twisted my head, forcing me to look at my fallen family.

'I tried to stop this,' she said with a hiss. 'Don't you dare look away.'

'I can still change it,' I sobbed, reeling at the sight of the broken bodies, Jackson and Wyn unmoved, still staring blankly in my direction. 'I can still fix it.'

The pointed tips of my grandmother's nails dug into my cheeks, deeper and deeper until I cried out in pain. Wrenching my face from her hands, I turned back to her but Catherine was gone. Bell House was gone. The full moon shone down on Bonaventure Cemetery, my family's monument lying shattered before me, the staircase to the underground chapel smothered by rubble, and under the rubble, Jackson's mauled body.

Wyn emerged from behind an oak tree, his green-grey eyes full of tears and razor-sharp claws at the end of his fingers.

'It's your choice, Emily,' he said, voice breaking as he spoke. 'It's your choice to make.'

Blood ran down my cheeks as his claws pierced my skin, but instead of pushing him away, I pulled him closer, meeting his lips with an urgency I couldn't begin to understand. His claws retracted and his hands knotted themselves in my hair, drawing me in as if I could never be close enough.

'I'm sorry.'

A whisper on the wind, a voice I couldn't place.

Wyn seized up in my arms. His chameleon eyes widened until I could see the whites, then he collapsed against me, sliding down to his knees as I struggled to keep him upright, a dead weight in my arms.

'Help!' I screamed into the night as his head lolled back, the gold string that tied us together unspooling. 'Someone, anyone, please help us!'

Seven figures stepped out from the shadows wearing grey robes. Forming a circle around me, they pulled back their hoods to reveal their faces one by one. Ashley, Lydia and Jackson, resurrected, Catherine, Wyn's brother Cole, and two others. A man and a woman I didn't quite recognize but somehow knew.

'You're not ready,' sang a high-pitched voice, as sweet and southern as a magnolia blossom.

Still in her party dress and pretty shoes, the little girl's hair curled against her pale cheek as she skipped into the centre of the circle. We'd met before, she and I, here in this graveyard, on the way to my Becoming.

'Someone gave me a gift,' she said. 'But I don't like it. You should take it away and keep it safe.'

She placed something cold into my hand and, leaning into its weight, I brought it up to my face, the ornate gold handle, the sickening serrated silver blade shaped like a tree branch and crusted with Wyn's blood. It was a sword, and when I curled my hand around the hilt, my fingers fit perfectly into the grooves as though it had been made for me.

A dozen or more images shot through my mind. A burning pile of wolves, Wyn's body on top. Lydia writhing on the ground, screaming. Jackson surrounded by sapphire flames. Ashley brought to her knees, clutching at her throat. Catherine with her head thrown back and her feet floating off the floor. Crystals, herbs, black fire, green skies, skyscraper tides, and Bell House wrapped in thorns, being pulled down into the earth.

'You're not ready but you will be. You have to be,' the little girl said.

The seven figures replaced their hoods and stepped back into the darkness. And as they vanished out of sight, the ground beneath my feet crumbled away and I was falling through the inky black, a haunting voice whispering in my ear.

When the dead fight back. When the earth consumes. A lie becomes the truth. She will return.

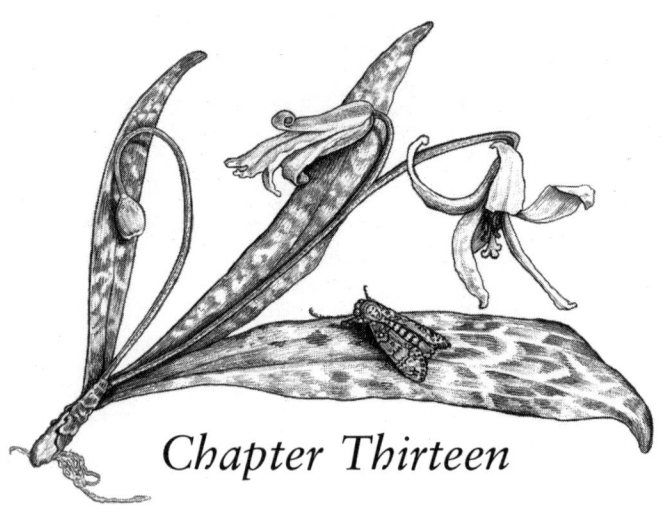

Chapter Thirteen

It was dark when I came to, no longer in the craft room but lying in Lafayette Square underneath the oak tree that was mine and Wyn's. The moon sat high above in a velvet sky, still almost full, only the slightest sliver chiselled away, and I stared up at it from the cold, hard ground, my throat raw from screaming or sobbing or both. All my nails were broken from scratching at something I couldn't name. In the distance, Bell House glowed, her white walls reflecting the moonlight, shining just for me.

'Emily. I'm sorry.'

Turning away from my home, I watched as the first Emma Catherine came into view, emerging from behind the fountain at the heart of the square.

'Sorry for what?' I replied, relieved and afraid and infuriated all at the same time. 'Disappearing the whole month or what I just saw?'

I forced my aching body into a sitting position, leaning against the tree trunk for support. A single strand of Spanish moss came down to rest on my shoulder, gently brushing back and forth against my cheek. *She will return.* The repeated refrain from my vision. And here she was.

The Witch and the Wolf

Emma Catherine knelt down at my side, lifting my hands to inspect the jagged remains of my nails. The last time we'd met, our hair was the exact same shade of deep, shining red. Now hers was back to its ghostly white, matching her translucent gown. She held out her hands for the moss and it moved towards her, allowing the ghost to wind it around my bloody, injured hands.

'For what has happened and what is to come. None of us want this for you.'

As angry as I was, the sight of her was beyond reassuring. She was here, I hadn't been abandoned.

'But there's no way around it,' I said as the soft, soothing moss whispered away the pain in my palms. 'Because someone, somewhere came up with a prophecy and determined the course of my life for me.'

'Not someone,' she replied simply. 'Me.'

I blinked at her surprisingly straight response.

'You?'

Emma Catherine showed me a sombre smile and nodded. The ground was hot and hard beneath me but I felt like I was floating on an uncertain tide.

'You're the witch who made the prophecy?' I said. 'Why didn't Catherine tell me it was you?'

'Because she didn't know. There were witches who held the knowledge but it was lost over time. Whoever spoke the words hardly mattered compared to the message itself.'

The moss that had woven itself between my fingers fell away, leaving me fully healed and full of new questions.

'Please, you have to tell me everything you can,' I begged. I wanted the truth. I would not leave room for doubt. 'How do you know? When did it happen? How can you be sure it's me?'

She gazed over at Bell House, her once emerald eyes cool and distant. 'There was no one moment, no mystical event. All my life, I bore knowledge I could not explain and never once sought it out. This is a different gift to your visions, Emily, this knowing. It doesn't come wrapped in fancy language or trapped in a crystal ball. It's closer to a feeling, like being tired or hungry or thirsty. One moment you aren't, the next, you are. The knowledge simply is and there is no disputing it.'

Like my love for Wyn. I didn't ask for it, couldn't explain it, but I was beyond certain. Of my feelings, at least.

'So, it's like intuition, a gut instinct,' I said, searching myself for any new awareness. Nothing. Just more confusion than ever.

'One that leaves no room for doubt,' the ghost replied. 'The things I knew took me to the places I needed to be, showed me the people I needed to help. I had to leave my family when I was fourteen years old, I had to travel across England to meet my husband in Wales. I knew he would love me truly, that I would love him in return, and we would travel to the new world together but he would not survive the voyage.'

'Did you tell him he wouldn't make it?'

'No.' A flicker of sadness passed over her serene visage. 'It couldn't be helped and knowing in advance wouldn't have lessened his pain, only increased his suffering.'

I tried to imagine the burden of knowing the person you loved, the person who loved you, was going to die. Somehow, it felt much worse than wondering whether or not you might end the entire world. My hands were shaking now and the wounds healed by the Spanish moss threatened to open once more.

'I thought I would understand the blessing better after my Becoming,' I told her as another layer of uncertainty draped itself around my shoulders, 'but every day there's something else, something new to deal with. Catherine said my connection to the blessing would be stronger and I'd understand everything, but the more I learn, the more I realize I don't know a thing.'

'Some would say that is the definition of wisdom: admitting what you do not know.'

'Wow,' I gasped. 'I must be so wise.'

Two men walking a corgi passed by without so much as glancing in our direction but the dog's head turned sharply towards us and gave a short, sharp bark. I pulled back, holding my breath, but my companion merely watched then held out her hand when the dog came forward with an inquisitive sniff.

'Oh, Millicent,' one of the men said, letting go of his partner to tug on the leash with both hands. 'Why did we spend all that money on obedience training if you're going to bark at nothing?'

'The men can't see us,' I said in a whisper, my back pressed against the tree.

'They don't want to see us,' Emma Catherine replied. 'We don't want to be seen. The blessing obliges us all.'

'And the dog?'

'Who wouldn't want to be seen by a dog?'

Millicent growled happily as a ghostly hand passed over her fur, then barked once more and raced away, running after her owners with her tongue hanging out.

'There are so many things I need to know,' I said. 'If I ask you direct questions, will you give me straight answers?'

She inclined her head in agreement. 'I will speak to the things I can, but please know that it does more harm than good, expecting quick and easy answers.'

'Well, I'm pretty used to getting them instantly,' I said, instinctively reaching for my phone but it wasn't in my pocket. No, it was still drying out in a bag of rice in the kitchen.

My ancestor tilted her head towards the moon, her

translucent profile etched in pale and milky light. 'Answers, yes, but not the truth. One is more easily obtained than the other.'

I studied her face as she moonbathed, the fine, delicate features I saw softened in my own reflection, echoed in Catherine and Ashley and even my father. Where to start? What to ask? I had a million questions and I knew she wouldn't, couldn't, answer them all.

'Why me?' I said eventually, settling on the one thing I truly couldn't make sense of. 'Why is this happening to me and not any of the witches before or after?'

'Why not?'

OK, perhaps not the best place to start.

'Why is one person a talented artist and another good with numbers?' Emma Catherine said, oblivious or indifferent to my frustration. 'One person is a natural leader, another a born caregiver, the next a problem solver. No one asks for the gifts they are born with, all have a choice as to whether or not they will honour them.'

'But I don't have a choice,' I pointed out. 'This is happening to me whether I like it or not.'

'Everything is a choice. Talking to me now is a choice. Walking into the craft room was a choice. What you do next, it will all be your choice, Emily. Sadly, our choices aren't always as simple as deciding between something we want or something we don't. Sometimes it's what's best for us or best for others. Oftentimes, we must select what we consider to be the lesser of two evils. The idea that the right decision is always the one that makes you happy is an optimistic fantasy.'

Strangely enough, I did not feel better.

'Do you have another question?' she asked, casting her eyes upwards to the sky, and though I couldn't see it, I could feel dawn beyond the horizon.

'Why can't I see ghosts anymore?'

She cocked her head a little, a bemused, upward tilt to the corner of her mouth.

'Obviously I can see you right now,' I added for clarification. 'But ever since my Becoming I haven't seen any others. Did they leave Savannah or did they leave me?'

'No one left anyplace,' she replied, her eyes roaming the square as though she could see things I could not. 'Ghosts are still the people they were before they passed and sometimes people do not wish to be perceived. The whispers of your destiny are louder where we are. Until the ghosts are certain of your intentions, they may not consider you a friend. Try not to take it personally.'

'What about you?' I pushed. 'Where were you?'

'I've been here.'

'If that's true, why couldn't I see you?'

'Because you didn't need me.'

'Of all the absurd things I've heard in the last few months that might be the craziest,' I replied, uncontrollable laughter bubbling up out of me. 'No, I think you'll find I definitely needed you.'

'You needed time,' she corrected me kindly, 'to find your own feet and your own feelings. There comes a day when we all have to learn to fly.'

'So you kicked me out the nest and hoped I wouldn't come crashing to the ground?'

Crouching down in front of me, her white gown billowing around her, she nodded.

'And look at you. You're soaring.'

Nothing about the past few weeks felt like a success to me. No Wyn, no Catherine, no closer to understanding the prophecy or interpreting my visions and nightmares, and every day it felt as though the danger around us grew.

'There's only so much I can do without guidance,' I said,

terrified she would vanish again if I so much as blinked. 'And I have no one to guide me. Do you know how frightening it is to go through this alone?'

'Very much so.'

It was a clear statement of fact. I stared, shamefaced, at the ground, thinking of how much she must've suffered. The first witch in our line, no grandmother to guide her, no ancestors to turn to.

'You worry too much about the past and hold too much fear of the future,' she said when I eventually found the strength to look at her again. 'When you tear yourself in two, it becomes impossible to exist in the present.'

'To be honest, these aren't the answers I was hoping for,' I said, pressing my pointer fingers into my temples and making small circles that did nothing to help the headache that throbbed there. 'Can we take this inside? I need an ibuprofen or a cyanide pill or something.'

An unfamiliar look of alarm upset her usually placid expression.

'This is as close as I can come to Bell House. I can visit the square but no further.'

'Why not?' I asked. 'Wasn't it your home too?'

'It was,' she said. 'But it does the dead no good to cross onto the ground where their lives were taken.'

My head jolted backwards as though someone had slapped me hard across the face. One by one, the buildings on Lafayette Square faded away, the homes, the houses, the cathedral, all the centuries-old buildings, replaced by a moment from the distant past. Where Bell House stood, I saw a wooden dwelling, a bonfire and a little girl running after a pig as her redheaded mother watched.

'Decades before your Bell House was built, my second husband owned this land,' Emma Catherine's gentle voice intoned over the scene. 'We had a house, little more than a shack really, but it was our home. We grew crops, raised animals to eat. My daughter played under different trees. After that man passed away, it was decided that I would be allowed to keep the plot. Not everyone was happy about the decision. Some didn't like the way I helped the women in the community with my apothecary skills, some resented my refusal to marry for a third time. Others simply disliked me for what I was.'

'A witch?' I said.

'A woman,' she replied.

The echo of my ancestor and her child walked into the house and outside, the fire died down to its embers. When the door opened again, the daughter walked out, older now and hand in hand with a kind-looking man. Emma Catherine waved them off, watching them go from the doorway before returning inside. As soon as she was alone, shadowy figures emerged from all corners of the memory, surrounding the house, each of them carrying a different weapon.

'There are too many ways for a woman to make enemies,' she said. 'A fact that remains as true today as it was back then. They came in the night, not long after my daughter was wed, a dozen of them or more. I never saw another sunrise.'

'But I thought Bell House was supposed to protect us,' I said, my jaw clenched at the violence. I felt a sudden grief that cut so sharp I could hardly tolerate it. 'Catherine said nothing could hurt a Bell in Savannah.'

'You must remember, sometimes Catherine spoke with the tongue of a loving grandmother and not a witch,' the ghost replied. 'Bell House will protect you. My last gift to my line.'

The men entered the house and the scene faded away, returning Lafayette Square to all its present-day glory.

'Tell me you killed them,' I demanded, hot tears spilling from the corners of my eyes. 'Tell me their names. Do their descendants still live in Savannah?'

A cool hand rested on my shoulder, tempering my rage but not subduing it entirely.

'Revenge is never worth the price you pay for it. Today, those men are all dead, gone and forgotten, they took my life but not my story. And no, I didn't fight. I knew it was my time; I knew my blood would run through the bones of Bell House. I live on in her, and in you.'

She touched a finger to the ground between us and drew a circle. Slowly at first then all at once, a flurry of tiny white flowers with golden hearts pushed their way up through the grass.

'Daisies are my favourite flowers,' she said contentedly. 'Isn't it wonderful that something so perfect can grow just about everywhere you look? Everything feels right with the world when I see their pretty faces.'

'Everything?' I replied, still reeling from the violence she'd endured.

The flowers shivered with delight as she stroked their petals and something sharp poked at the back of my neck, scratching at my skin. I pulled a white feather from my messy braid and laid it on the ground beside her flowers.

'A feather from a dove,' she said. 'See? There is hope.'

Using the tree to pull myself up, every part of my body in pain, I struggled to my feet. Emma Catherine rose with graceful ease. We stood face to face, the same height, the same hair, the same eyes. My ancestor. My beginning.

She raised an opalescent hand and instinctively, I did the same, reaching towards her until we were touching, whatever she was made of cool against my warm flesh. An electric thrill ran through me and the door inside my mind cracked open, the good and the bad all fighting to escape at once. All our knowledge, there inside of me.

'I want to get things right, make you proud,' I said, still marvelling at her touch when she pulled her hand away and the door slammed shut. I staggered back into the tree, immediately grieving the loss. 'But I'm afraid. All the things I saw, everything I knew when we were together in the chapel, it's gone. Half of what I've experienced contradicts most of what I've been told. How am I supposed to make the right choices if I don't know what's true and what isn't? If I can't control the magic?'

'The pursuit of control is a dangerous waste of time.' She was calm again, as though my rising panic was all for nothing. 'Your grandmother sought to control the blessing and look what happened.'

'Which means?'

'Our magic does not give us what we want but what we need,' Emma Catherine said. 'When your sisters come, the messages will be clearer.'

'And when will that be?' I asked, stepping towards her at the exact same moment she took a step back. 'Why can't you just tell me what's going to happen, *when* it's going to happen?'

'Because answers are easily obtained, the truth less so.'

An echo of her own words.

'If nothing else, I have to protect my friends,' I said, pleading with her though I knew there was no point. 'At least tell me how to keep them all alive.'

'I cannot.'

'Because you don't want to or because you don't know how?'

'Because I do not know if they are meant to live.'

It was a punch to the gut. In spite of everything, all the fear, the nightmares, the dark visions. I'd felt sure she would say something consoling, even something vague, what was meant to be would be, the blessing would take care of them, my sacrifice would be enough to save them. But no. There was a very real chance my friends would not survive whatever was to come.

Emma Catherine traced a finger around one of the late-blooming azaleas by the fountain, her expression indifferent. She didn't look regretful or apologetic. She looked accepting.

'The prophecy says you will make the choice, Emily, not me. How could I know the outcome?'

'My dad taught me not to make any kind of decision until I had all the information possible,' I said softly, trying to find the same kind of peace but acceptance without hope felt a lot like defeat. 'If you don't know, how will I know the right choice to make?'

Emma Catherine only smiled and shook her head.

'There are no right or wrong decisions,' she replied. 'No good or bad. There will only be a before and an after.'

'Then I choose to save the world,' I said fiercely. 'Now and forever, that will be my choice.'

My magic thrummed under my skin, rising up to meet my declaration as I looked at the world around me. The square, my home, my friends, my family, the whole world. How could there be any other?

My ancestor cocked her head to one side, as though she heard something, though the night was eerily quiet to my ear.

'It's time for you to go inside,' she said, a breeze picking up out of nowhere and pushing me in the direction of Bell House. 'Quickly now, he mustn't know you saw him.'

'Who?'

I spun in a circle to check the square for signs of life.

'There's no one there,' I said, but when I looked back to the ghost, she was gone.

'Two steps forward, one step back,' I whispered to myself as I started for home, walking quickly across the street and opening the gate. The second my feet were back on Bell

The Witch and the Wolf

property, I felt infinitely more at ease. Emma Catherine's sacrifice. Her first gift to her descendants.

The front door opened without a key, swinging on silent hinges, but something made me pause. Hiding behind a pillar, I peered back to the square and watched with wide eyes. A tall boy with dark ash hair was stalking away beneath the trees. Jeans, a grey T-shirt, a familiar graceful, loping gait. I held my breath until he disappeared completely then exhaled a choked sob. I'd followed Emma Catherine's instructions: he hadn't seen me.

But I had seen Wyn.

Chapter Fourteen

It wasn't yet 9 a.m. when I held down Lydia's doorbell the next morning. Far too early to call on anyone but she had said to come over and meet her mom, and I was sure she wouldn't mind. At least, I hoped she wouldn't.

Sleep had evaded me all night long, my body, mind and soul racing after I crept back into Bell House. Nothing helped bring me down, not the warm shower, the hot tea or my soft feather bed. I was full to bursting with all the things I had seen, the words Emma Catherine had spoken and the sight of Wyn walking away in the shadows. The sun was barely over the horizon when I gave up on sleep altogether and took myself downstairs to make an admittedly terrible breakfast for Ashley and me, never eating a single bite. I'd half-expected Wyn to be waiting for me on the doorstep but there was no sign of him and I'd had no word from Jackson to say that they'd been in touch. Perhaps he got Jackson's message and drove straight here to make sure I was OK. Perhaps he thought it was too late to call by the time he got into town. It was wishful thinking. Wyn could've flown in on the wings of an eagle at four in the morning and he still would've climbed right up the magnolia tree outside my room and knocked on my window. Whatever reason he had for not letting me know he was back in Savannah, it was known to him and him alone. For now.

The girl reflected back at me in the Powells' front door was far from a proper little lady, come calling on her friend. My hair was a matted mess from where I'd attempted to sleep on it wet, and my meagre makeup skills were no match for the dark circles under my eyes. Possibly I could've chosen a nicer outfit than a baggy T-shirt and running shorts, but fashion wasn't super high on my current list of priorities. Perhaps Emma Catherine was right and answers only led to more questions, but today I was determined to cross at least a few queries off my list.

As I pressed the doorbell one more time, all the things I wanted to ask Alexandra Powell ran through my head at once, tumbling around like bingo balls. I truly didn't know which one would escape from my mouth first. Had she been in touch with my dad all the years we'd been away? What could she tell me about my mom? Did she know about my family's magic? Did she know about *her* family's magic? A blurry figure appeared in the glass pane of the door and a shred of my anxiety escaped in a little high-pitched squeak.

'Good morning—' I started to say as soon as the door opened but Virginia Powell cut me off before I could finish.

'I'm sorry,' she said, half hidden behind the door, eyes downcast. 'This is not a good time for visitors. I shall let Lydia know you stopped by.'

'But she told me to come,' I said, trying to jam my arm into the sliver of space between the door and the wall.

Not once did her eyes meet mine, rather they stayed on the ground then skirted up to the sky, looking anywhere other than at me.

'I know it's still early,' I said, though she was already dressed. 'But Lydia said I should stop by and meet her mom.'

'Then she misspoke.' Virginia's words were as cool as her manners. 'Both Alexandra and Lydia are otherwise occupied.'

'Otherwise occupied?' I repeated. 'Do you know what time they'll be free? Is Lyds here? Can I just see her for a moment?'

If I sounded desperate it was because I was.

Finally, Virginia's eyes found mine, a watery blue that complemented her greying blonde hair, but her usual fragile composure had been replaced with a steely determination I'd never seen on her before.

'No.'

'No?'

'No,' she said again. 'Miss Bell, neither my daughter nor my granddaughter will be home to you today or tomorrow or the day after that. Neither will my grandson, for that matter. So I would ask that you stay away from my house.'

'Stay away?' I couldn't believe what I was hearing. 'But why?'

'Because,' she replied, 'you are a bad influence.'

I stared at the door when it slammed shut, the genteel Savannahian equivalent of a slap in the face. Too shocked to move and half expecting Lyds to throw open the door and declare the whole thing a hilarious Powell family inside joke, I stayed right where I was. No one was coming. No one was laughing. In no uncertain terms, the Powell matriarch had told me to get lost.

Above me, a flurry of clouds covered the sun as my mood darkened. There was only one rational explanation I could come up with. Virginia Powell wasn't nearly so taken with the idea of me and Jackson going to a party, getting drunk and staying out all night as he and Ashley had led me to believe.

'You're not going to say I told you so,' I muttered to myself, retreating from the front door before Virginia came out and

The Witch and the Wolf

threw a bucket of cold water over me. 'You are not going to say I told you so.'

I was absolutely going to say I told you so.

My bad mood cooled the streets by a few comfortable degrees and I watched as people scurried out of their cars into their jobs with one eye on the sky, in fear of a sudden shower, but my righteous indignation kept one hand on the wheel of the weather. I should be sitting in the Powells' dining room, eating biscuits and gravy, listening to stories about my parents right now. Instead, I was prowling the streets with tangled hair and, I realized when I looked down at myself, a back-to-front T-shirt, hearing nothing but the frustrated voices in my head. I took a long route back to Bell House, marching down Bull Street, overtired, overstressed and with no idea what to do with myself. My arms and legs ached with a frustrating energy, like an elastic band pulled too tight, ready to fly but unable to work themselves loose. Without my phone, I couldn't text Lydia to ask what was going on and, while I wasn't exactly a tech expert, I didn't like the look of the blank grey screen when I'd retrieved it from its bag of rice and plugged it in before leaving the house.

Monterey Square was always busy, day and night. The tour buses hadn't arrived yet, but there was no shortage of sightseers, all with their cameras out in front of the Mercer Williams House. Some just snapped a quick pic and moved on, but other posed out in front, smiling and throwing up peace signs, and sending a chill down my spine. It was a house that demanded attention, not nearly as beautiful as Bell House, at least not in my opinion. The square red brick mansion couldn't compare with our Victorian elegance but there was something beyond bricks and mortar that drew the eye. Too many people had died in this house in unpleasant ways and too many people wanted to know all about it.

I leaned against an oak tree, absently running a hand over the bark and smiling at a friendly bundle of moss when it landed on my shoulder. In the beginning, the plants would tell me what they were, what they could do. Now I realized with no small measure of delight, they had so much more to share. The Spanish moss was full of news, idle gossip mostly, which flowers were blooming out of season, which trees couldn't keep hold of their leaves, but then another whisper slipped into my ear. A wolf. There was a wolf in Savannah, it had set foot in this very square. My smile faded away at once. Was it Wyn? Was it the wolf who attacked me at the party? The moss didn't know. Only that this wolf was shrouded in magic.

I felt a sudden prickle, not so magical, more like the feeling I was being watched. Sure enough, when I casually glanced over my shoulder, I spotted someone sitting on a low bench across the square, not so subtly spying on me from behind a newspaper. Turning to get a better look, the newspaper shot upwards to obscure the person's face but I already knew who it was.

'Ms Stovell?' I said, as pleasant an expression as I could muster on my face as I approached her. 'It's Emily, Emily Bell. We met at the DeSoto.'

'Oh, is that you, Miss Emily? I didn't see you there.'

Cheeks flooding with colour, she attempted to fold her newspaper in half but it was not in the mood to cooperate, fighting her every step of the way.

'I hope you're feeling better after the other night,' I said as she karate-chopped the Style section and shoved the bundle into her bag. When she looked back up at me, her embarrassment shifted into something more bitter, the fine lines around her mouth puckering into a sour pout.

'I'm feeling just fine today, and was feeling just fine at the party until you and the Powell boy almost had me run down in the street. As I recall, you're the one who had to be carried home.'

'All the excitement was a little much for me,' I replied, and she smirked, thrilled to have the upper hand.

'Has there been any word from your grandmother? While I completely understand her desire to live beyond the beck and call of a cell phone, it feels a little foolhardy to travel without one. What if there was an emergency?'

'There's no emergency,' I reassured her. 'And I really wouldn't worry about it; Catherine is fine.'

'Yes,' she said with a pointed stare. 'Catherine always is.'

I tugged at the hem of my T-shirt and pouted. Something about this woman put me so on edge, not least her laser-like focus that burned through me.

'Is your shirt on back to front?'

'Yes,' I replied as she touched one hand to her perfectly coiffed hair. 'It's how people are wearing them now—'

'Oh, honey.'

With her eyes closed, she turned away as if she could not bear to watch. 'First the party and now this? As your grandmother's closest confidante, I feel it is my duty to step in and offer my help.'

'Help for what?' I asked. 'What are you talking about?'

'Acknowledging the problem is the first step to a solution.' Ileen held up a serious hand, as if to swear an oath. 'I would never forgive myself if something terrible happened to you while Catherine is away.'

Above us, the clouds darkened by a noticeable fraction.

'You really don't need to worry,' I said. 'Nothing terrible is going to happen. Not to me.'

She stood, her ladylike leather handbag hanging from the crook of her arm, an unreadable expression in her pale eyes.

'You are so like her,' she said softly. 'And you sound so sure.'

An unexpected jolt of magic shot through me. A warning. My fingers flexed instinctively but I kept control. Just. With a Cheshire Cat smile, Ileen Stovell clucked her tongue loudly and slapped the side of her purse.

'I must be going, I have house guests and it wouldn't do to leave them alone all day,' she said. 'How lovely to catch up with you, Miss Emily, we must do it again very soon.'

As I watched her slinking away through the square, the lingering threat of something I couldn't name scratched at my skin like the papery tag of a cheap shirt. I'd felt the same way on Sunday. This woman brought out the absolute worst in me and my magic, but I wasn't about to ruin the whole city's day with an unnecessary storm just to mess up her blowout, as tempting as it was.

Desperate to shake off the feeling, I breathed out slowly, sending the dark clouds on their way and stalked off in the opposite direction to Ms Stovell, not stopping until I reached the edge of the historic district at Broad Street. I needed the river.

Oceans were a problem for witches, unpredictable, uncontrollable, and too vast to manage. Magic didn't cross large bodies of water well, and neither did we. Just being near the ocean or the sea could play havoc with our abilities, amplifying or diminishing or altogether drowning our senses when they were most needed. I could only imagine how painful the first Emma Catherine's crossing had been, surviving on a cramped wooden boat for weeks on end. Leaving the open waters and sailing up the Savannah River must've felt like coming back to life. Rivers were our friend. The constant flow of the current refreshed a witch's energy, the old and the new, a reminder that nothing stays the same for too long.

The water was almost in sight when I noticed him standing in front of the Pirates' House restaurant, I knew right away this man had long since left the land of the living. The half-mast trousers, a blousy shirt that was white once upon a time but now a dirty beige, a scarlet scarf tied around his head and a matching sash at his waist. When he caught my eye, he nodded towards the restaurant, a slight gesture I might've missed if I wasn't watching so closely. He disappeared into the wood-clad building with its Haint blue shutters and proudly flying flags, and I crossed the road quickly, darting between moving cars rather than using the crosswalk, and followed the ghost of the pirate inside.

The Pirates' House was one of the few popular places in town I still hadn't visited. According to Lydia, it was too touristy to be worth her time, and even though Jackson would happily share lurid stories of the sailors and pirates who passed through this place over the decades, it wasn't one of his favoured destinations either. I had no idea what to expect as I passed through the rickety doors into a dimly lit but wildly decorated entryway, plenty of evidence of its past life as a haven for scoundrels on display. The brick walls and wooden trim looked their age and, standing in the doorway, the whole place felt like a maze. There were staircases going up and down, and narrow, uneven hallways leading off to who knew where. I was lost before I could even begin.

'Can I help you, hon?' a kind voice asked from behind the hostess stand.

A woman in a full green skirt, white shirt and wide black leather belt blinked at me, one hand hovering over a digital screen. Not a ghost but a very committed hostess. I had to applaud her commitment to the bit.

'Um, yes, I'm meeting my family,' I said brightly, looking past her to search for my guide. 'Is it OK if I go look for them?'

'You know where they're at?'

'Oh, I sure do.' I leaned into my best Savannah accent, hoping to pass myself off as a local who knew her way around and definitely didn't need to be accompanied. 'I reckon they're at our usual table, I can find them.'

'Sure thing,' she replied, handing me a menu. 'Just holler at your server when you're ready to order.'

I gave her a grateful smile, taking the menu and holding it in front of me like a shield. My guide waited just beyond with visible impatience.

'Are you in some kind of rush?' I asked under my breath.

He said nothing, only continued to lead the way, passing easily through tables and chairs without a care for the people sitting in them. It was early, but the place was packed, a tourist-heavy brunch crowd, and it took me more time to navigate around the diners, struggling to keep up with him as he sailed directly through someone's shrimp and grits. Three dining rooms later, he stopped in front of a door, old and dark with a black iron ring for a handle. I raised one hand to the wood, soft and solid at the same time.

'Don't bother, it's sealed shut.'

A young server dressed in almost exactly the same outfit as my ghost guide, only with Nikes on his feet and an absurd parrot perched on his left shoulder, appeared beside me.

'Been that way for years,' he said as I pulled my hand away. 'The boss says it led down to a pantry back in the day, but they sealed it up when the floor caved in after a flood.'

'Right,' I replied. My fingers trembled as magic sparked under my skin. He was wrong. There was no pantry behind this door.

'You want the tour?' he asked, a hopeful look in his eye. 'I'm on my break. I can take you around, if you'd like.'

'Thanks, but my food is waiting,' I replied as the ghost disappeared, walking straight through the wooden door. 'I just went to the bathroom. To wash up. Before my food.'

The Witch and the Wolf

It was too much information. The hopeful glint in his eye shifted into something more suspicious.

'Why d'you have your menu?'

'Oh, you know,' I said airily. 'I like to have something to read.'

That did it. Hope became suspicion became a complete lack of interest.

'Uh, OK. I'll let you go.'

I waited until he was out of sight before I tried the door. It was beyond heavy and the server was right, it was sealed shut, but not because of any flood and not by anyone who had worked in that restaurant in the last hundred years. Taking a deep breath, I clutched the iron ring in one hand and pressed my other palm against the wood. It had swollen after so many years, lodging itself against its frame, but the wood and the iron were both open to negotiation. I silently cajoled them, whispering to the trees that gave their lives to make the door, to retake their original form. Asking the iron to return its rust to the elements that created it in the first place. On the first tug, there was no give at all and I grimaced as my shoulder pulled against its socket. If brute strength was needed here, I was in trouble. Without my magic, I was hardly the world's strongest girl – I couldn't get the lid off a jar of peanut butter without Ashley loosening it for me. But I wasn't without my magic. Closing my eyes, I shut out the world around me and concentrated on the door, picturing it wide open, seeing myself walking through, until I felt it give. Just an inch. An inch was enough.

The happy laughter of families dining in the restaurant shifted into something more raucous. The smell coming from the kitchens changed too, fried fish and fresh bread still in the mix but blended with something far less pleasant and altogether more rancid. Unwashed human bodies and sweet spilled rum stung my nose and when I opened my eyes, the hand grasping the iron ring tightened and I pressed myself against the door. I was still in the Pirates' House but I was not in the twenty-first century anymore.

'This is new,' I whispered, still gripping the door tightly, all my senses on high alert.

The carefully laid tables with their China plates and linen napkins had vanished, replaced by smaller tables all crammed together and surrounded by stools, each and every one taken by the kind of person you wouldn't want to meet in a dark alley. Some tall, some short, all of them weathered, and very few had a full complement of teeth. *Pirates of the Caribbean* it was not. The only light came from torches burning on the walls, but even in the gloaming I could see this was not the kind of place any reasonable person would want to be in for one minute more than absolutely necessary, least of all the young man I watched ambling through the door. He stuck out almost as much as I would if anyone could see me, but they could not. When I held out my hand, it had the same eerie translucent quality as my ancestor.

'WhereamI?' the man asked, his words bleeding into one long slur of a sound. 'This isn't Habersham's house.'

'It is, it is,' hissed a one-armed man who drew him deeper into the tavern, much to the amusement of his cohort. 'You haven't been in this room before, that's all. This spot here is only for friends.'

'Only the most entertaining company,' agreed a loud voice from the back corner of the room.

His black hat and black coat rendered him almost invisible, the torchlight only reflecting the gold coin he flicked up and down on the back of his knuckles.

'Will you sup with us, John Stiles, or are you too fine to drink with we friends of Habersham?'

The Witch and the Wolf

The assembled all roared with laughter.

'I'll drink,' the first man said, loosening his blue coat. As soon as the final button was undone, it slipped off his shoulders, passing from person to person until it disappeared through the door.

'Don't worry about me,' he said, trying to disguise a hiccup with a belch. 'I can drink with the best of them.'

'Unlucky for you then,' the man in black replied. 'We're the worst of them.'

When he stood and stepped into the light, I saw the marks on his face. Five deep red gashes on his left cheek. Scratch marks. But not from a supernatural being. Those wounds had been inflicted by a woman.

'What do you think of this?' he asked, handing John Stiles the gold coin. 'Ever seen anything like it?'

'Coin's a coin,' Stiles replied blindly without looking at the token in his hand. 'Where's the gin?'

'We're rum drinkers,' grunted the man in black, taking the coin and slipping it into Stiles's pocket. 'And so are you from now on.'

In one swift move, he produced a club from behind his back and slugged John Stiles in the back of the head. I let out a terrified gasp and the menu I was holding slipped from my fingers and floated to the floor, disappearing into thin air before it could meet the flagstones beneath my feet. Stiles tottered forwards as the room cheered, several men rising at once to hoist his unconscious body above their heads and carry him from the room. I dodged out of their way before they could pass straight through, the leader yanking the previously stuck door wide open, and all of them singing an ugly song as they marched down a long sloping tunnel that led off into the darkness.

'You all saw, Stiles took my gold,' announced the man in

black as he took his seat at the table. 'He works for me now. Everyone back to the ship, we raise anchor at dawn.'

Despite a chorus of moans, every man in the room stood, reluctantly following John Stiles and the rest of their shipmates through the door and down the tunnel.

'And next time his father tries to cheat me at cards, he'll think twice,' the man grunted into his silver flagon, a self-satisfied smirk on his face.

'Only there won't be a next time.'

It was a promise and a threat, spoken by a woman I hadn't seen enter the room. She stood tall in a blue brocade gown, heavily embroidered with bronze thread. Her green eyes burned and long, fiery red hair spilled down her back.

'Back for more already?'

The pirate stood, slamming his flagon on the table and moving into the light, his huge body primed to intimidate. The blood on the woman's right hand was as red as her hair, her nails sharp but broken and, I realized, a perfect match for the gouges on his face.

'No man lays his hands on me and walks away,' she said, raising her bloody hand to make a fist. 'You've done enough damage here, Laffitte. Few will mourn your end.'

He stalked towards her, murder in his black eyes.

'And fewer still will know how you met yours.'

He knocked a table out of his way, lunging towards her. His body took up too much space in the room, crossing the floor in less than one stride, but the woman didn't care. She didn't need to be bigger or faster or stronger than him. She squeezed her fist tightly until drops of blood, hers and his, mingled together and fell to the floor. Without laying a hand on him, she held him exactly where he was, wide-eyed and ashen-faced.

'Witch!'

The Witch and the Wolf

The accusation dragged itself out of him as he grabbed at his throat, bubbles of spit issuing from his mouth.

'I'll have you burned at the stake,' he said, gargling the words as he choked on his own blood. 'I'll have your bones ground to dust.'

'No, I don't think you will.'

The woman squeezed her fist so tight her knuckles turned white and the man fell to his knees, slumping face-first and striking the flagstones.

'Or else how would my descendant be here to observe your ugly passing?'

She turned to me, her emerald eyes full of triumph as blood began to pour from his mouth, his nose, his eyes and ears, limbs convulsing on the floor.

'You've seen all you needed to see,' she said, looking me right in the eye. 'Go, while you still can.'

With her unblemished left hand, she gave me a short, sharp shove and I tumbled backwards through the open door. With a cry of surprise, the back of my head struck hard wood. Several diners turned to see what was happening as the past melted into the present and I stumbled sideways into a chair, almost skidding on the menu I'd dropped on the floor two hundred years ago.

'I'm fine,' I said loudly, raising both hands above my head to prove the point. 'Just slipped. Very clumsy, enjoy your dinner.'

Stooping to collect the menu, I stopped halfway, eyes catching on the handle of the door. Tentatively, I grasped it lightly and twisted to the left. It opened without complaint, the locking mechanism clicking open as the previously warped wood gave way. I closed it again, dropped my menu on the nearest table, and sprinted out of the restaurant and all the way home.

Chapter Fifteen

The walk back to Bell House was a slow one. It took me a while to find my feet and I stuck to the side streets as I picked my way home, my mind struggling to play catch-up with my body. The fierce spark of vengeance burning in my ancestor's eyes haunted me even now, when she was more than two centuries away.

What did she mean, I'd seen all I needed? The monstrous actions of the pirates, the threat of Laffitte, the ease with which she took a life. It all frightened me but accidentally stepping into the past was terrifying. I'd slipped back through time so easily, too easily. I had a hard enough time finding the tea in the pantry without having to navigate through unexpected time periods. All I wanted now was my bed, to close the curtains, shut out the world and rest until at least one thing made sense again.

But that was not going to be an option.

Sitting on the front steps of Bell House, idly toying with the shoelace of his brown leather boots, was Wyn. He looked up at me without saying a word, then jumped to his feet, the electric charge that ran through me jolting him into action. My heart stuttered in my chest and my mouth went dry, and when I tried to open the gate, my hand missed the latch. Not once did I take my eyes off him.

He waited patiently as I fumbled with the gate, walked up the path and climbed the stairs. A few short feet that felt like a million miles. Neither of us were smiling, instead we stared at each other, dazed. Looking at him was like laying eyes on something otherworldly and I lost all capacity for speech. Finally, I was in front of him, face to face, inches away and I opened my mouth, hoping something smart or funny or meaningful would come out, but before I had the chance to utter a single word, Wyn's lips were on mine. His hands cupped my face, his thumbs pressed against my cheekbones, fingertips in my hair. It was a ferocious kiss, full of need, that I met and matched at once. We stumbled, the pair of us, into one of the colonnades that supported the portico over the front door, the back of my head bouncing off plaster and stone. I didn't feel it. I didn't feel anything other than Wyn, his touch, his hard body, hot and wanting, in my cool and welcoming embrace, and so deliriously happy when I lost my footing, only to be lifted off the ground as he pulled me ever closer, making me his.

'You're here,' I murmured against his mouth as I looped my arms around his neck. 'You're really here.'

'Had to be.'

He pulled back from me, just far enough to stare at my face in happy astonishment.

'You know what today is?'

'Tuesday,' I breathed, dazzled.

Wyn smiled.

'Three months to the day since we met. I left home at dawn, didn't stop once the whole way. Could not get to you soon enough, Emily James.'

'You left home at dawn?'

My breath hitched when he kissed me again, his mouth drawn to mine like a magnet. How was that possible when I'd seen him in the square, hours before the sunrise?

'We got home yesterday evening,' he said, nuzzling into my neck and sending sweet shivers all through my body. 'If I hadn't been so exhausted, I would have got straight back in the truck and made it here before midnight, but I couldn't keep my eyes open.'

'I thought I saw you last night,' I said, struggling to maintain my line of thought as his hands roamed up and down the sides of my body, as if to check I was exactly as he'd left me.

'Only if you were dreaming. Same way I've been dreaming about you.'

Even though it physically hurt, I tore myself away, taking hold of his hands to keep them where I could see them. My eyes roamed his body, his hair, his indescribably beautiful face.

'We should go inside. You must be starving.'

Wyn's crooked smile lit him up, brightening dark circles under his eyes and the scruff of overnight stubble on his chin.

'For food,' I added, wondering if he had always looked quite so wolfish when he grinned at me that way.

'I'm so hungry, I could eat a horse,' he admitted. 'Not literally, in case you were worried.'

'Good because we're fresh out.'

Using one hand, he yanked his long-sleeved T-shirt back down from where it had ridden up to expose his taut stomach and the blue cotton of the boxers that peeked over the waistband of his jeans. The other gripped mine so tightly, it almost hurt.

'I should probably freshen up first,' he said as we walked inside, giving himself a surreptitious sniff. 'It was a long drive.'

Reluctantly releasing him, I pointed down the hallway.

'Powder room is right through there. I'll be in the kitchen.'

'I'll find you,' he said, a throwaway comment that wrapped itself around my heart and refused to let go.

The wildlife painted on the silken walls of Bell House flourished as I passed through. Flowers blossomed on vines, birds sang in the trees and a handful of tiny rabbits hopped along beside me, twitching their noses with excitement. He was here, he was here, he was here. Wyn was back in Savannah, he was safe and healthy. Everything was good, everything was right and the darkness of my morning disappeared, at least for a moment.

I pulled a jug of lemonade from the fridge and poured two glasses, as well as a tall glass of water, sure he must be parched if he'd driven for five hours straight without taking a break. Although she wouldn't admit it, the full moon had set Ashley off on an anxiety-driven baking spree so there was no shortage of cookies and cake and freshly baked bread in our kitchen. I loaded it all onto the table, adding butter and jam and cheese and anything else I could get my hands on. The only thing I couldn't seem to do was stand still.

'So, Mr Evans, what'll it be?' I said, full of butterflies all over again when he walked through the door. 'We've got pretty much everything.'

'All at once I'm not so hungry.' He stalked around the table to trap me between his arms again. 'It is so good to see you, Emily James.'

'Technically, it's Emily James Bell now,' I told him, smiling against a fresh onslaught of kisses as a vase full of sunflowers that had begun to wilt on the windowsill sprang up with renewed vigour.

'You can call yourself any name you like as long as I can call you mine.'

My mind went blank every time his soft lips touched my

skin, the longing between us as thick and heavy as the July air, so dense I could've cut it with a knife. And if I hadn't reached back to steady myself, knocking over one of the glasses of lemonade in the process, I wasn't entirely sure what might've happened.

'I've got it,' I said, laughing softly, awkwardly, as I reached for a cloth to mop up the sticky liquid.

Wyn took the cue to compose himself and grabbed the untouched glass of water, chugging the whole thing.

'You had me worried,' he said, the tip of his pointer finger trailing up and down the side of the now empty glass. 'When you didn't answer your phone, I kind of panicked. Don't think I took my foot off the gas once after I crossed the state line.'

'It got wet. I'm trying to dry it out but it's taking forever.' I glanced over at my phone, dry and plugged in at the wall but still blank. 'Didn't Jackson message you?'

'No.'

He took out his own phone, checking a bunch of different apps to make sure. 'Haven't heard from Jackson since the day he drove me home.'

I pressed my lips together to stop the torrent of abuse on the tip of my tongue from spilling out. Jackson would be dealt with later. Right now, my sole focus was Wyn.

'Doesn't matter,' he said, his eyes searching my face for something he seemed to find, judging by the smile playing on his lips. 'There's nowhere else on earth I'd rather be right now.'

'You really only just got here?' I asked as he hopped up onto a stool. I took the one next to him, shivering when our knees touched.

'Really.'

The spark that connected us shone so brightly it was blinding. If he said it wasn't him, it wasn't him. I didn't feel like he was lying, nothing about the look on his face or the light in his eyes said he was being untruthful. And what was more likely, Wyn lying about when he arrived or me making a mistake in the dark after waking up in the square without knowing how I got there?

'What did you tell your parents?'

'The truth,' he replied and I felt a surge of magic over my skin. 'At least part of it. That I had a girl waiting on me in Savannah and needed to get back to her. As long as I'm back before the pack leaves for the crynhoad, it's all good.'

'Crynhoad?'

We were in my kitchen, just the two of us but Wyn glanced over both shoulders, as though checking to make sure no one was listening.

'It's a Were term, it's what we call our full moon gathering. Hey . . .' He brushed his fingers against my cheek. 'Something's wrong. What's happening here?'

'What isn't?' I replied, but he didn't return my sardonic smile and so it melted away like summer snow. 'Last night, I was outside in the square and I really thought I saw you.'

He took my hand and held it against his steadily beating heart.

'If I'd been in Savannah last night, I wouldn't have been hanging around in any square. I'd have been here with you.'

And just as surely as I knew how to breathe, I knew he was telling the truth.

'Maybe it was part of the vision,' I said, shaking my head as I tucked my hair behind my ears. 'It's hard to know what's real and what isn't right now.'

'Vision?' he replied, fresh concern on his face. 'I don't like the sound of that. And I don't like the sound of someone lurking around Bell House in the middle of the night. Y'all don't have security cameras?'

When I couldn't stop myself from laughing out loud, his lips twitched upwards.

'Yeah, OK, that was pretty dumb,' he conceded. 'Even if you weren't a witch, I would pity the poor soul who tried to break in and found Ashley waiting for him.'

'Exactly,' I said, placing my hand on his chest. At the gentle thud of his heart beating against my palm, all my fears were replaced by hope.

'Well, well, well, look who it is.'

Ashley entered through the back door, gardening gloves tucked into the waistband of her denim shorts and an unimpressed scowl on her face.

'Emily, I thought I warned you about letting the dog on the furniture.'

She dumped a pair of gleaming, sharp secateurs on the table and picked up my glass of lemonade, taking a long and thirsty sip.

'That is so good,' she said, smacking her lips with delight. 'Oh right, because I made it. So, how's tricks, Rover? Made it through the full moon without destroying any chew toys?'

'Good to see you too, Miss Ashley,' he said, his smile steady and strong. 'I hope you've been well.'

'Still alive. Can't complain.'

'OK, let's go,' I grabbed Wyn's wrist, pulling him from his stool. 'This has been fun, so glad the two of you had a chance to catch up.'

Ashley's smirk grew as I hauled him away. We had too much to talk about to make time for her constant quips. Plus it was at least two minutes since he'd last kissed me and I didn't know if I could go two minutes more.

'Y'all leave that bedroom door open,' she called as she refilled her glass.

I stopped at the kitchen door, looking back at her in disbelief.

'Seriously?'

The Witch and the Wolf

'No. You know I don't care what y'all do but try to be safe at least. I'm not fixing to be a great-aunt any time soon.'

Wyn grinned when I coloured up, the tops of my ears burning with embarrassment.

'I swear, Emily, keeping track of your gentleman callers is a full-time job,' Ashley said with a sigh. 'We need to get a calendar, stick it to the fridge. I'll colour code it for you, if you'd like?'

Wyn's grin disappeared.

'Gentleman callers?'

'You didn't know?' Ashley asked with mock surprise. 'Interesting.'

'Ignore her,' I said, dragging him down the hallway, the roses on the windowsill wilting as we went.

Chapter Sixteen

The door to my room wasn't even all the way closed when Wyn's body crashed against mine. His strong, hard chest pressed against my back, lips on my neck and hands on my hips, while his soft moans sent me flying out of my body. There was something different about his kisses, more confidence, more certainty, but it was still blissful just to be in his arms. All the hours I'd spent dreaming about this didn't compare in the slightest.

'I missed you,' he said, his teeth nipping at my ear in between the words. 'I missed you so much.'

'I missed you too,' I replied, twisting in his arms until our mouths found each other. Just for a second, I pulled back, taking a beat to return to myself. We'd both been through a lot in the last forty-eight hours, I wanted to savour every moment with him. Who knew how long we had together this time.

'Are you OK?' I said, lips already chafed and sore. 'Do you need to rest? Is this OK?'

'*You're* asking *me*?' He held my face in his hands, light dancing in his eyes. 'Yes, I'm OK, I'm more than OK, and if it's fine by you, I can't think of anything else I'd rather be doing right now.'

'I don't know, Leopold's has a couple of new flavours you haven't tried yet,' I told him, curling my fingers through his thick, wavy hair. 'There's a chocolate raspberry swirl that's to die for.'

'Only one thing I'd die for,' he replied. 'She's standing right in front of me.'

He held me in his gaze and I let him guide me backwards across the room, only stopping when the backs of my legs met my bed. I stumbled onto the mattress, safe in his arms, a rush of desire shooting through me as my shoulders met my pillows. When I pulled him to me, green vines rose up from the floorboards to entwine themselves around the posts of my bed, deep red roses coming into full bloom as my hands travelled down his body, tracing out the new pronounced muscles in his shoulders, his back. He met my touch in kind, exploring me tenderly and everywhere he touched sang, as though I too was discovering that part of my body for the very first time. One hand on my waist, one in my hair, his lips on my collarbone, the flutter of his eyelashes against my jaw. It felt like he was colouring me in, bringing a black-and-white outline to life.

Every part of me craved more. My breath became ragged and my lips bruised, however close he was, it just wasn't close enough. I hooked a leg around the back of his, holding him in place and as his hand just barely grazed the side of my breast on its way back down to my hip, I melted into the mattress. It was maddening and terrifying, too close and not close enough, too much and not enough. But Wyn didn't force me to make the impossible decision of when to say when. He broke away before I knew I needed to, holding his head above mine, our lips so close I could still feel them, his face a blur of golden skin and green-grey eyes.

'You missed me, huh?' He placed one last careful and considered kiss on my swollen lips before rolling over to the other side of the bed. I straightened my shirt, pretending not to notice as he adjusted his jeans and rolled carefully onto his front.

'Almost as much as you missed me.'

My voice was light and teasing but when I reached for the glass of water on my bedside table, my hands were shaking. He stretched out an arm to trace the petals of a rose, then plucked the flower and handed it to me.

'Look at you,' he said with wonder. 'You are incredible.'

We'd spoken every day until he left for the phase, but I still wanted to hear about every detail of every second of every day we'd been apart, no matter how mundane. What he ate, what he wore, how he'd slept, the silliest, most random thoughts that had crossed his mind. And then there were the things we hadn't discussed, darker, deeper matters that weren't meant for phone calls. I wanted it all.

'Tell me everything I missed,' he said, reading my mind and mirroring it back. 'Any new magic stuff? You read anything good? Lydia still in love with that girl who works at Blicks?'

The way he threw my magic in with Lydia's ever-changing crushes and my insatiable reading habits made me smile. He accepted me in a way no one else could. Wyn understood.

'Yes, yes and no, she's moved on to the new ticket-taker at the Lucas theatre but they're already spoken for so she's sworn off love forever. Or at least this week.'

'And still no sign of Catherine?'

I sniffed the rose, its sweet sparkling fragrance filling the room.

'No sign,' I replied, impatient to get to my turn. 'What about you? How was your phase? And the gathering, what was it you called it? The *crynhoad*? Were there other new wolves? Did they ask about your brother?'

The Witch and the Wolf

Mentioning Cole was a mistake and I knew it at once.

'All you need to know is, I'm back in one piece.'

'That's it?' I said as Wyn's blissful expression clouded over. 'Your first pack phase and that's all I'm going to get?'

He moved away, the delicious weight of his body gone, leaving me unanchored. While I watched, he shuffled backwards until his head hit my pillows, then he lay gazing upwards at the canopy over our heads. It was filled with roses, occasional petals fluttering down to frame his exquisite face.

'You know I trust you completely,' he began, legs crossed at the ankle, one foot tapping insistently against the other. 'If I could, I would answer every question you have, tell you every last little thing, but with the wolves . . . Em, they're not my secrets to share.'

'I understand,' I said right away. Too quickly. I did understand but I wasn't satisfied. We'd said no secrets. 'I'm sorry.'

'Please don't apologize, I'm glad you asked, I *want* to tell you,' he insisted. 'There's still so much about it I don't completely understand myself, and I know talking to you would help, but truthfully, I already shared more than I should. Just telling you the name of the *crynhoad* could be enough to get me in trouble. Our words, our rituals, they're sacred to the Weres and definitely—'

He stopped himself just in time but I knew what he was going to say.

'Definitely not meant to be shared with witches,' I said.

Wyn ducked his head, looking ashamed of the accuracy of my assessment as I sat in my own discomfort. There was so much we didn't know about each other, not only me and Wyn, but the wolves and the witches, and because of those mysteries, there would probably always be secrets between us. I didn't like it.

'It wasn't anything like I imagined,' he said after a long

moment, deciding what he could and couldn't share in real time. I could feel the conflict in him as he worked it through in his mind. 'I didn't realize how big the pack would be. There were people from all over the south, Mississippi, Tennessee, Kentucky, some folks over from Florida. I wasn't expecting for there to be so many families. So many Weres. And yes,' he added, some of the anguish draining away and replaced by something closer to joy. 'There were other new wolves.'

'Sounds like you made some new friends,' I replied lightly. 'Probably not that keen on witches.'

It was petty but I couldn't stop myself.

So many Weres, he said. And here I was, a lone witch.

'It doesn't matter what they think, not to me,' Wyn announced with defiance, and I hoped that would be enough.

He sat up to move closer to me again, as though the slightest distance between us was still too much.

'Were you there?' he asked. 'When I phased, I thought I felt you.'

'Just wanted to make sure you were safe.' I peered at him from behind my hair and covered his hands with mine. They were so warm. 'Is that OK?'

'More than. It's not like you could shoot me a text, I'm glad you were with me.'

'I always will be.'

As I rubbed my thumb in circles on the back of his hand, more and more flowers blossomed around us.

'Right after the phase, I lost you,' I told him. 'Like you'd fallen off the face of the earth completely.'

'That makes sense,' he reasoned. 'Some kind of natural defence against witches, probably.'

The casual way he dropped his theory made me freeze up, the flowers wound around my bedposts trembling. Our perfect reunion was not going exactly as I'd hoped.

The Witch and the Wolf

'Not against you,' he added hastily. 'I mean witches in general and wolves in general. Because, you know, witches and wolves, they're not exactly . . .'

'It's all right,' I said, cutting him off before he could dig the hole any deeper. 'I know.'

'It was totally different this time.' He spoke in hushed tones even though we couldn't possibly be more safe than we were in my room. 'No pain, no fear. I felt so alive, completely connected to myself. They told me I wouldn't remember much of anything afterwards but I do recollect most of it. The running, the hunt.' He paused, biting his bottom lip as that one specific word settled. 'Mom was kind of shocked but Gramps said it means I'm going to be a strong wolf. Maybe a pack leader someday.'

There was pride in his voice and his posture but I only felt trepidation. A witch and a wolf was unlikely enough. A pack leader and a witch destined to revive her sisters, to save or end the world? These weren't the regular problems couples our age had to overcome. But when I looked away, Wyn crooked his finger and lifted my chin so that my eyes met his.

'This might not be easy,' he said, his words echoing my thoughts. 'But that doesn't make it wrong. Remember, we only belong to us, no one else.'

When I closed my eyes, I could hear his heartbeat. It was stronger than I remembered, his pulse a little slower than mine, a gently thudding reminder that yes, he was different now. But so was I. Craving his closeness, I rested my head on his chest and sighed as his arms folded me into him.

'Your turn,' he said in a soft and husky voice, more suited to the middle of the night than the middle of the day. 'I want to know everything. Where've you been? Who'd you see? What in the heck happened to your phone?'

'That one is a long story,' I replied, not a lie at all.

'My favourite kind.'

As he spoke, he fought back a yawn, burying his face in his shoulder rather than releasing me from his embrace.

'You must be exhausted,' I said, swooning at the sight of his sleepy-eyed smile. 'Why don't you take a nap?'

'Because I don't want to take a nap,' he replied but the way his eyelids flickered as though his lashes weighed more than they could bear said differently. 'I want to hear the sound of your voice. Tell me anything, I don't care what: the weather report, the latest with Lydia, what you had for breakfast.'

It was only when my stomach rumbled to answer the question for me I realized I hadn't eaten at all. Where to begin? The situation with Jackson, the wolf at the party, Lydia's grandmother? My conversation with Emma Catherine? None of those seemed like good conversation starters.

'It's been a crazy couple of days,' I said. 'But it can wait until you're rested, there's no rush. Is there?'

'No,' he replied, a dreamy murmur. 'We have forever.'

Forever. It wasn't nearly long enough.

'But you're OK?' Wyn asked. 'I hated being so far away. I never stopped worrying about you, Emily.'

Slowly, I drew myself up to rest on one elbow and lightly stroke his hair. Wyn's breathing slowed, his chest rising and falling as he fought his own exhaustion.

'You don't have to worry about me now,' I promised. 'You're here, we're both safe. You can rest.'

And it felt true, at least for as long as we remained here, in my bedroom, inside Bell House. Wyn surrendered to sleep, his eyes closed and his lips slightly parted. I stayed by his side, watching him sleep, listening to the gentle catches of his breath, the inaudible murmurs that escaped his dreams, and luxuriating in the peace of the moment. No fears, no threats, just me and him, alone together. When he woke, I would have to tell him

The Witch and the Wolf

about the wolf at the DeSoto, my latest visions. Eventually he would have to tell me what the pack knew about Cole's death and my part in the act. But for now, we could simply be.

Only when I was sure he was fully lost in his dreams did I slip out of his embrace, sliding off the bed on unreliable legs and reaching for one of the rose-wrapped wooden posts to secure my balance. With a sharp intake of breath, I pulled my hand away, a lightning flash of pain disturbing the tranquil moment. I'd forgotten roses had thorns. When I turned my hand over, a single pinprick of ruby red blood bloomed above my heart line. It quivered, fighting gravity in order to decide its own path and trickling down to where my life line met the fate line. Slowly, the droplet split in two, bleeding into both lines. I stared at my hand until the blood ran all the way down my wrist and along my forearm, when I snapped to my senses and wiped it off with the back of my sleeve.

It didn't mean anything.

While Wyn slept, I blew on the climbing roses, casting the petals all around the room and watching sadly as they disappeared back beneath the floorboards.

'You're here, you're safe,' I swore to him as his eyelids flickered, dreaming of something I could not see. 'And we have forever.'

Chapter Seventeen

Wyn was still sleeping when I felt Lydia crossing Lafayette Square, on the march towards Bell House.

'What, no Fido?'

Ashley lowered her tattered paperback to observe me tearing down the stairs and past the parlour door, in an attempt to beat my best friend to the door before she could ring the bell.

'He needs to rest,' I replied, backtracking three breathless steps. 'So if you could be quiet?'

'Got it,' she replied with a thumbs up. 'Let sleeping dogs lie.'

It didn't deserve a response, which was just as well since I had no time to come up with one.

'Aggressive,' Lydia said with a grunt as I threw the door open and tackled her across the porch. 'Some might even say unnecessary.'

'Sorry,' I winced as she rubbed her ribs. Sometimes I forgot I was stronger than I used to be. 'Wyn is upstairs asleep, I didn't want the doorbell to wake him.'

'Wyn's here?' Her eyes widened at the scent of scandal. 'In your bedroom? Asleep? Girl, did you tire him out already?'

'He's tired because he drove down overnight,' I told her,

slipping my arm through hers and leading her around to the back garden. 'Don't get excited, nothing happened.'

'Tell that to the stubble rash on your chin.'

She pointed at my face and cackled when I looked away.

'Thanks for answering my questions anyways,' she said, arms folded over her cropped blue button-down, one eyebrow quirked upward. 'I was going to ask where you'd gotten to, but I know I can't compete with his wolfiness up there.'

'What are you talking about? I came by earlier,' I told her. 'Your grandmother said you were busy, told me to leave.'

'*Virginia* told you to *leave?*'

She looked and sounded as though it was the most scandalous thing she had ever heard and I confirmed with a grim nod.

'I think her exact words were neither her daughter, granddaughter or grandson wanted to see me ever again because I'm a bad influence.'

'Damn.'

She dropped into a wrought-iron chair and swatted at a mosquito as it flew by her bare midriff. Mosquitoes loved Lydia.

'That's practically my grandmother's version of spitting in someone's face. Why didn't she just slap you and have done with it?'

'That's what it felt like,' I replied, perching on the edge of the seat across from her, our knees touching under the table. 'Looks like she wasn't nearly as impressed with Jackson's overnight cover story as everyone thought she would be.'

I pulled a couple of leaves from a nearby lemon verbena plant, massaging them between my finger and thumb to release the oils for extra protection against the mosquitoes, then handed them to my friend.

Suddenly another horrifying thought occurred to me.

'Oh God,' I gasped, crushing another leaf in my palm. 'Lyds, what if she told your mom?'

'Oh, yeah. She probably did.'

I dropped my head to the table, mortified in advance but Lydia just laughed. 'Don't sweat it. Even if she did, Mom hasn't blacklisted you. She's the reason I'm here.'

Raising my head very slightly off the table, I gave her a quizzical look.

'She wants to meet you,' Lydia explained, sticking out her tongue to taste one of the leaves. 'I told her you were stopping by this morning and when you didn't show, she suggested we get a late lunch. Don't think she'd invite you out to eat if she was mad at you for whatever you did or did not do with my brother. Unless she wants to know your intentions towards him.'

'Lunch? With your mom?'

Alex Powell. My dad's best friend. The one person I knew for sure he'd been in touch with for all the years we'd lived in hiding.

'I know, what a drag.' She half-rose out of her chair, pulled a tube of mango lip balm from her pocket and passed it across the table into my hand. 'She's cool though. Most of the time. At least, she's not an old-fashioned nag like Virginia.'

Dabbing the balm onto my chapped lips, I asked what I hoped was a very breezy question.

'Is it just us or will Jackson be there too?'

'Why?'

Apparently not nearly as breezy as I'd intended.

'No reason,' I replied. 'Just wondering.'

'Any reason why he shouldn't be?'

'No.'

She stood up and came around to stand behind me, freeing my hair from the claw clip I'd grabbed on my way downstairs.

'Are you avoiding him?'

I was absolutely avoiding him but I did not want to talk about it.

The Witch and the Wolf

'Why would I be avoiding him?'

She yanked on my hair a little harder than necessary and I scowled straight ahead.

'You tell me.'

'Nothing to tell.'

'If I were a less trusting woman, I might think you're not telling me the whole truth,' she said, loosening some of the strands and tightening others then fastening it with an elastic band retrieved from her sling bag. 'But I'm hungry so I'm letting it go for now.'

She flicked her eyes over my baggy T-shirt and bike shorts when I stood up and turned to face her. 'But not so hungry you don't have time to go change. My name is Lydia Powell and I do not approve this message.'

'Give me two minutes.'

She appraised my outfit once more.

'I'll give you five.'

Rolling my eyes, I slipped back inside the house. Everything else might be changing but at least Lydia was always going to be Lydia.

'Then I said, you're so wrong you don't even know how wrong you are, literally do not come to me with your theories until you've read every book in the series because you don't know the characters, you don't know their motivations, you can't spell the dragon's name right! Like, you are showing your whole ass and I'm embarrassed for you.'

Lydia's arms flew around in the air, gesticulating wildly as we waited to cross Gaston Street to Forsyth Park.

'Then what happened?' I asked, anxiously tugging at the hem of my white linen tank. It was creased. I should've ironed it but Lydia had insisted there was no time and it was parental approved.

'He deleted his account. The romantasy subreddit is no place for amateurs. Hey, did you finish the book I loaned you?'

'I'm kind of avoiding romantasy right now,' I admitted, studying the don't walk sign, every second stretching out into an eternity. 'Feels a little too much like homework.'

'Does that mean fae are real?' she asked, her eyes bugging out of her head. 'And dragons and direwolves and selkies and—'

'I hope not,' I cut her off before she could really get going. 'But who knows?'

When the light changed, Lyds strolled easily on as I bounced along on pins and needles. What would Alex be like? Would she think I looked more like my mom or my dad? What if she didn't like me? What if she thought I would be a disappointment to my parents?

'Em?'

'Lyds.'

'Does Wyn have a knot?'

'Oh my God,' I howled, wrenched out of my panic spiral by my best friend's wild laughter. 'Please never ask me that again.'

'Gotta admit it's a maybe,' she said with a note of caution. 'Like you said, who knows?'

Forsyth Park was packed, teeming with Savannahians and visitors of all ages. Lydia danced around a pair of bubble wand-toting toddlers while I smiled politely at an older couple, watching the world go by from one of the benches that lined the main footpath leading from Gaston Street to the fountain. The trees were happy here, surrounded by life and love. The live oaks, the sycamores, the cedars and the gingkos, they all grew tall and proud, and I heard whispers on the Spanish moss as I passed by, my skin tingling all over.

'I know we can't talk about this in front of my mom but I've been doing some more digging into the family tree,' Lydia said, pushing her curls away from her face and holding them back with a stretchy hairband she'd had wrapped around her wrist. 'There's definitely a bunch of weird stuff going on.'

'Such as?' I asked, one eye on the sky above us.

The forecast was for sun all day but the way my panic kept rising and falling, I couldn't be certain we weren't in for an unexpected shower or two.

'You know how old southern families are.' Lydia examined her silver-painted nails as we walked. 'We love to chart that ancestral line. Virginia must have three hundred years of photographs and paperwork, birth certificates, death certificates, marriage licences, graduation diplomas, everything for everyone. Or at least everyone except my great-aunt Juliet.'

'Great-aunt on Virginia's side?'

'Uh-uh. She died when she was sixteen. Virginia was still a baby so she never knew her. There are photographs from when she was born, a few school pictures, some early birthday portraits, but as soon as she hits fifteen, boom, she disappears. It's like she just ceased to exist two years before she actually died.'

'Maybe she was sick and didn't feel like having her photo taken,' I suggested.

'Nope. I asked Virginia and she said Juliet died suddenly, right before her seventeenth birthday. But that could make sense, couldn't it? If Juliet was the last witch and she died before she could go through the rituals, our magic would've been lost.'

'It's possible,' I admitted, tugging on my locket. 'Catherine told me, if a witch misses her Becoming, all the magic in her family dies.'

'And if my great-aunt was supposed to be a witch, her granddaughter would've been the next one. Not me.'

All the sounds of the park were deafening, but all I could hear, all I could feel, was Lydia's disappointment.

'Even if everything lined up and you were supposed to be a witch, I still don't know whether or not I could help bring your magic back,' I said softly, seeking out her hand and holding it tightly. 'The prophecy says I will awaken my sisters' dormant magic. It doesn't say how or when. Could be old magic families, could be new ones. Either way, I know you don't want to hear it now but, Lyds, you're safer without magic.'

She stopped in front of the fountain and the lightest mist hit my hot skin.

'And are you safer without a sister witch?'

Deep down, the darkest, most selfish part of me was just as disappointed as my friend. Ever since discovering the Powells had once been connected to the blessing, with magic of their own, I'd nursed the tiniest hope that Lydia might be the one to share my burden. Now that light was extinguished for good, I could admit it to myself.

'Anyway, it wasn't only the magic,' Lydia said, drawing me on around the curved footpath. 'I'd kinda been hoping, maybe, this would be the thing that made me special. Something that was just mine and not Jackson's. Twins always have to share everything, you know.'

'I'm sorry,' I said, and meant it. 'But you are special. Please don't ever doubt that.'

'And you're a simp,' she said, throwing an arm around my shoulders and tossing off her moment of melancholy. 'Don't matter none anyway. When it's apocalypse o'clock, I'll be right by your side, woman or witch. Come on, I told my mom we'd be there by now and I am dying for an Aussie iced latte.'

Collins Quarter was beyond busy, just like always. White tables and teal umbrellas filled the outside patio but when I searched all the customers for the face my mother had kept in a locket close to her heart, I couldn't see her.

The Witch and the Wolf

'Where is she?' I asked Lydia as she applied another slick of mango balm to my lips. 'Did she leave?'

'What are you talking about?' she replied, pointing to a table only a few feet away. 'She's right there.'

I couldn't believe I'd missed her. More than seventeen years had passed since the photo inside my locket was taken but Alex Powell had hardly aged a day. Her brown hair was shorter, cropped into an elegant bob rather than pulled up in a ponytail, but I would've recognized her anywhere in the world. When her warm brown eyes fell on me, the rush of emotions that overtook me were almost too much. The sunshine overhead seemed to swell as my magic rose up to hold me down, and when Alex stood and opened her arms to me, I fell into them without a second thought.

Home. She felt like home.

'Em,' she exhaled into my hair, her arms clamped around my body as though she were afraid I might float away. 'Oh my goodness, here you are at last.'

She smelled expensive but inviting, some medley of shampoo and perfume and lotion that all came together in a warm, floral bundle. When she let me go and I pulled back to take in her blue jeans and pink button-down, accessorized with delicate jewellery. Clean lines and clear colours, everything about Alex Powell seemed intentional, especially compared to her chaotic-good daughter.

'Look at us, blubbing like a couple of babies,' she said, reaching to wipe away a tear I hadn't felt fall with a clean handkerchief. 'I do not know where to start.'

'You could thank her for saving my life,' Lydia suggested, clearing her throat when I let out an audible squeak. 'By moving to Savannah and saving me from boredom.'

'Thank you for your service to the community,' Alex replied drily, still standing with her hands on my shoulders while Lydia flopped into a chair and ran a finger down the menu until she found what she was looking for. 'My daughter hasn't stopped talking about you since you arrived.'

'How would you know? You've been busy with *Jeremy* in *Charleston*.'

Alex was still staring at me as though I was some sort of long-lost jewel, and I blushed under her close inspection.

'She acts like he's a monster but her stepfather loves her very much. He would just love to have Lydia and Jackson living with us, but we couldn't get them enrolled in the school we wanted.'

'Also we'd rather die,' Lydia declared. 'It's bad enough that *you* live there.'

Jackson and Lydia didn't know their father, from what they'd told me. A touring musician who had given Alex a fake name and a burner phone number that went out of service as soon as he left Savannah and his pregnant girlfriend behind, but I could see more than a little of this petite southern woman in both of her children. The same warm brown eyes, Lydia's pointed chin, Jackson's high cheekbones, and all three of them shared the irritated expression she currently wore all over her face.

'Charleston is a beautiful city,' she assured me. 'Jeremy and I would love to have you out to visit. With or without my ungrateful children.'

'That sounds amazing,' I said, a scratch in my throat as I tamped down my magic, a nascent patch of camellias threatening to force their way into existence in the big concrete planter at the side of us. Alex's eyes followed my gaze and I thought I saw the slightest hint of a frown trouble her face, but it resolved itself immediately when a tattooed server appeared with a handheld device to take our order.

'What can I get you?' they asked, eyes squarely on Lydia.

The Witch and the Wolf

'We'll have three Aussie iced lattes, the French toast, chicken and waffles and a side of bacon,' my best friend replied before giving me a look when I opened my mouth to make my own selection. 'Trust me.'

'Three of my favourites,' the server enthused. 'You've got great taste.'

'My daughter always makes good decisions.'

The tone was unmistakable. There was no confusing the warning edge to her words and no mistaking the fact this woman wasn't just Lydia's mom. She was also Virginia Powell's daughter. The server's head bobbed up and down like a puppet on a string as they walked quickly away.

'Thanks, Mom,' Lydia said, tilting her head to check the server out as they went. 'They were cute.'

'Cute and too old for you.' Alex rummaged around in her fancy black leather purse, not interested in debating the topic. 'Well, I'll be. Lydia, honey, I seem to have forgotten my wallet. Would you be a doll and run back and grab it for me?'

'No. You can pay with your phone.'

'I don't have the right card set up to do that.'

'You really want me to go all the way back home for your wallet?'

'I have my wallet, I can pay,' I offered when the two Powell women locked into an acrimonious stare-down.

'That is very sweet of you, Emily, but I couldn't possibly allow it,' Alex replied before turning directly to her daughter with a meaningful look. 'The house is two minutes away. I would very much appreciate it if you would go get my wallet. Thank you.'

'If it's so close, why don't you go?'

'Lydia.'

Alex was all out of warnings and Lydia all out of comebacks. With a host of complaints muttered under her breath, she pushed back her chair, the legs scraping against the brick patio.

'If the food comes while I'm gone, don't eat all the chicken,' she said before climbing directly over a planter box full of ferns instead of walking around to the exit. 'And tell them to hold my coffee!'

A new server came over to deposit big plastic tumblers of ice water in front of each of us and Alex gave me an exasperated smile.

'I'd love to say I don't know where she gets it from, but I do. Only difference is, I would have never gotten away with speaking to my mother the way she does. Virginia would've grounded me for a month.'

'You would need round-the-clock guards to keep Lydia in the house.' I laughed nervously, picking up my napkin and rolling the edges between my fingers for something to do. 'She really has been an incredible friend to me. I feel like we've known each other forever.'

'In a way, you have. You and your mom were with me when I gave birth.'

'We were?'

She nodded and I seized onto this new piece of information, tucking it away for safekeeping.

'Was my dad there?'

'He was around. Mostly he took care of the snack runs. Paul had no interest in what was happening at the business end. He stayed out of the way until me and the twins were cleaned up and presentable. Your daddy always was a little squeamish.'

'That's so true,' I agreed. 'You should've been there when I got my period for the first time.'

'I know,' Alex said softly. 'I should.'

'Oh, no, that's not what I meant,' I replied quickly. 'I was only joking.'

The Witch and the Wolf

'I wasn't.' She lowered her head, a delicate pink flush colouring her cheeks. 'Your mom and I made a lot of promises to each other when it came to you kids. I swore I would always look out for you if anything happened to her. At the time, I didn't imagine anything ever would, not even for a second. But before I knew it, you and Paul were gone.'

'He didn't tell you he was leaving?'

'He didn't tell anyone. You'd been gone six months before I heard from him. We were all losing our minds.' She picked up her glass of water and took a small sip. 'You must forgive me for not coming to see you before now,' she said. 'Catherine and I have never gotten along well and I couldn't imagine her being too thrilled at my being involved in your life. But when Lydia mentioned she was out of town . . . Do you happen to know when she'll be back?'

I shook my head and she pressed her lips into a thin white line.

'*Will* she be back?'

'I don't know,' I admitted. 'We haven't really been in touch.'

We both sat quietly when our coffees arrived, Alex watching me while I studiously avoided eye contact.

'You really do look like her with that red hair.' Alex's words were whisper soft. 'But I can see your mom in there too. Paul would be so proud of you.'

'Were you in touch with him the whole time?' I asked, so uncomfortable under her gaze, I felt the temperature drop by a few degrees as a heavy cloud blocked out the sun directly overhead.

'More or less. Occasionally there would be gap when y'all were moving around, but I always heard from him eventually. Sometimes emails, mostly with letters, but never anything that came to the house. Paul always used a third-party address and he insisted I keep a PO box at a post office over in Hardeeville.'

'Where's that?'

'Across the state line in South Carolina.'

'Across the river,' I said, more to myself than her. He kept water between Catherine and the letters.

'Your daddy could be a little dramatic when it came to your grandmother.' She picked up a sachet of raw sugar and flicked it three times before tearing the brown paper package open and pouring it into her coffee. 'Said he didn't want anything he had touched in my mother's house, as though Catherine might smell the two of y'all on it, like some Eileen Fisher-wearing bloodhound.'

I spun the straw in my iced latte but said nothing. Alex leaned towards me, one hand hovering beside mine but not quite touching it.

'Emily, I can't pretend I know what happened exactly between your grandmother and your parents,' she said. 'Paul never offered the details so I didn't ask, but I know it ran deeper than simple family disagreement. He went to great lengths to protect you from Catherine.'

'I don't fully understand it myself,' I told her, not entirely untrue. 'But I do know everyone thought they were doing what was right at the time.'

'Surely,' she agreed. 'But like they say, two things can be true at the same time.'

Someone had said that to me once. Ashley.

'Your daddy gave this to me.'

With the utmost care, Alex removed a delicate silver ring from the middle finger of her right hand then held it out for me to take. I hadn't noticed it on her hand but I couldn't believe I'd missed it. The ring wasn't silver but a delicate band of tiny fire opals, each one held in place by tiny platinum prongs. Each stone sparkled in the sunlight, a fiery rainbow held inside each milky white stone, unexpected strength hidden in plain sight. It thrummed with protective energy and not only from the gems. I began to slip it on, just to see if it would fit, but as I slid the ring down my index finger, the metal burned against my skin. What had been ice cold was now red hot. I wrenched it off my finger and dropped it on the table, the tiny circlet dancing on the smooth surface until it came to a stop. The ring had been spelled to protect and conceal, specifically against a witch.

With a strange look, Alex picked it up and slid the ring back on her finger, rotating it once, twice.

'Is something wrong?' she asked, head cocked to one side.

I pursed my lips, wishing I had some aloe or calendula for my irritated skin. She couldn't have known.

Could she?

'Paul could be a superstitious soul. He gave me this ring right after Angelica passed, told me to wear it always.'

'I think that's a good idea,' I said, choosing my words with the utmost care. 'I mean, personally, I just know I would feel horrible if I lost something that was of such sentimental value to me.'

'Like this, you mean?'

She reached across the table and took my locket in her palm. I nodded. 'I never take it off.'

'It is so very strange to see it hanging around someone else's neck,' Alex murmured. 'After we lost your mom, I couldn't stand to look at mine. I can't lie, it was a shock to see Lydia wearing it when I came home.'

'Dad told me my mom wanted me to have it,' I said, covering the golden orb with my hand when she let it go.

'Your mom wanted you to have the world. Angelica gave her life for you.'

She looked away as her words registered on my face, a look of shock I couldn't cover up quickly enough.

'That is, she would've given her life for you,' she corrected, twisting her ring around and around on her finger.

It didn't take a witch to know there was something she wasn't telling me. I couldn't believe I was once again face to face with a woman who knew more about my past than I did but had no intention of sharing the truth with me.

Before I could say anything else, Alex spoke.

'I heard there was a wolf attack at the school dance.'

It caught me off guard. The twins had been adamant about not telling their mother for fear of her using the incident to force them to return to Charleston with her.

'Jackson told you that?'

'No,' she said, her face tightening at my surprise. 'He didn't. Which I'm sure we can both agree is a concern. Secrets are never healthy in a family.'

'Probably didn't want you to worry,' I told her, casual, breezy. 'It wasn't that big a deal.'

I was not casual or breezy enough.

'I'd hate to think the twins were in danger,' she said, fixing me with a level gaze. 'You'd tell me, wouldn't you, Emily? If you thought there was something I should know?'

'If I thought there was something you should know,' I repeated, all at once too hot, my clothes too tight. Alex's eyes burned through me and it was a struggle just to stay in my seat.

'Did they catch the wolf?' she asked.

'No,' I said, looking down at the ground. 'They did not.'

'Do you think they will?'

'I don't know. I hope so.'

I looked up, forcing myself to meet her gaze. Somewhere in the distance I was sure I heard a foreboding rumble. Even without a weather event, the look on her face was thunderous.

'Because I swore to both your parents I would protect you,

The Witch and the Wolf

and I will,' she said. 'But not at the cost of my own children's lives.'

Stunned, I stared back, open-mouthed, as a light, welcome breeze swept the clouds from the sky and it seemed as though all of Savannah gave a sigh of relief.

'Your wallet.'

Lydia appeared out of nowhere, dropping a quilted leather wallet on the wooden tabletop, and I almost jumped out of my seat.

'Oh man, half the ice is already melted in my coffee,' she groaned, stirring up the latte with a paper straw. 'I knew I shouldn't have gone.'

'Thank you. We'll get you another,' her mother said.

Lydia fell into her chair then leaned forward to take a taste. 'No need, it's still good.'

She looked from me to her mom then back again, brown eyes bright and beaming. 'Catch me up, what did I miss?'

'Nothing,' I replied, matching her expression as best I could although, underneath the table, my hands were shaking.

'The usual getting-to-know-you stuff,' Alex agreed. 'Emily and I were getting acquainted.'

Oblivious to the tension between us, Lydia beamed at the pair of us.

'This is cool, right?' she said, folding her legs up underneath her. 'The three of us hanging out together at last?'

'So cool,' I agreed weakly.

'I almost feel as though your mom and dad are with us,' Alex said, never once taking her eyes off me. 'Watching over everything you do.'

Lydia grinned, as though it were a reassuring thing to say, but all I heard was a threat.

Chapter Eighteen

Finding Wyn in the back garden of Bell House felt like winning a prize after surviving lunch. Thankfully I didn't spill anything, break anything or cause a tornado, so I chalked it up as a success, even if I left with more questions than answers.

'You're back,' he said, his face lighting up with delight when I swept through the garden and fell right into his arms. 'Ashley told me you'd run away to join the circus.'

'I considered it,' I replied, before raising my lips to his, happy to forget the last hour and lose myself in his kiss.

Anyone walking past Bell House could see what a grand old home she was but few got to share the beauty of the back garden. High walls had been built to keep our magic in and the world out, flowering vines and climbing roses covering the tabby walls then wending their way around the branches of the trees and scenting the air with jasmine and honeysuckle. In the centre of it all was a small square koi pond, dotted with water lilies and home to a school of happy fish, and every other available inch of space was covered with flowers, shrubs, herbs, bushes – anything that could be planted in the ground, lived and thrived in our garden.

The Witch and the Wolf

Before I arrived, Ashley took care of things, giving it any extra attention it needed, but I knew the plants could take care of themselves. They sang out whenever I passed by, waving to me when I walked by a window, willing me to come outside and be with them. As a natural apothecary, I was never happier than when I was surrounded by the natural world, and so I drew on the strength of some of the most useful herbs as I pulled away from Wyn, borage and yarrow for confidence, spearmint for clarity and wood betony to help me concentrate and not get sidetracked by the freckles on the bridge of his nose or the powerful muscles that stretched out his T-shirt in a way they hadn't before. There were things we needed to discuss and that wasn't going to happen when I could feel his heartbeat right beside my own. He reached over and unclipped my hair, letting the red waves fall around my shoulders. I moved to straighten them but he caught my hand in his, staring at me starry-eyed.

'Leave it,' he murmured, winding a random strand around his finger. The tension as he pulled it lightly triggered tingles up and down my body, sweeter than the tell of my magic.

'We need to talk.'

Before Wyn, my romantic experience was literally zero, but still I knew these were unpopular words.

'I don't love the very serious look on your face right now,' he said, releasing my hair. A shaft of late afternoon sunlight sliced through the branches of a sycamore tree, separating us with an intangible shot of gold. It was still too much of a barrier.

I walked over to the table and chairs and sat, waiting for him to do the same, his apprehensive expression now matching mine.

'There was a Were,' I said, starting slow, remaining calm. 'On the full moon.'

'Here in Savannah? You're sure?'

Now it was me who didn't like the look on his face. More than surprised, he looked as though he didn't believe me.

'Sure I'm sure. We were at the DeSoto Hotel, at a dance, when it attacked. It came straight for me.'

'We?'

'Me and Jackson.' I breathed in the clean, cucumber scent of the borage and the sweet aromatics of the wood betony, a welcome waft of lavender finding me as well. 'It was some school fundraiser thing.'

'Was Lydia there?'

'No, it was a sports fundraiser thing.'

He crossed his arms over his chest, his lips working themselves into a frown.

'Wyn, it attacked us in public, in front of dozens of people. If Jackson hadn't gotten in its way—'

'They,' he interrupted. 'You mean, *they* attacked. If Jackson hadn't gotten in *their* way.'

I stared at him for a moment, completely lost.

'You said "it" but you meant "they". If your wolf was a Were, it's a person, not an animal. They're no more an "it" than I am.'

'I'm sorry,' I said, letting his statement sink in. 'They. They were definitely a Were and I think they were looking for me.'

He considered the information as I pushed my hands under my thighs, holding myself back from rushing him. Wyn was an open book, no good at keeping secrets, and a dozen different emotions churned across his face. I'd expected him to have questions but I hadn't expected him to doubt me. What could he possibly be thinking that he couldn't say out loud? After a very long pause, eyebrows drawn together with consternation, he looked right at me.

'Was it a date?'

Not what I was expecting him to say. I gave him another second, waiting for him to laugh or tell me it was a joke. But no. It was an entirely serious question.

'I just told you I was attacked by a Were in Savannah in front of a hundred people and you're asking if I was on a date?'

'It's OK if it was,' he replied, although the set of his jaw and the way he clenched his fist suggested otherwise. 'I know Jackson likes you and I was gone and everything. People go on dates sometimes, doesn't always mean something.'

'His date got sick. I stepped in at the last minute. It was a friend date.'

'Maybe on your side. Pretty sure Jackson didn't see it that way.'

'It doesn't matter how Jackson saw it.' I reached across the table to entwine my fingers through his, my skin cool and pale against his warm bronzed tones. 'I'm yours, remember?'

'And I'm yours,' he said, sounding as though he'd landed somewhere between ashamed and relieved. 'Jackson's your friend. Hell, he's my friend. I'm sorry, Em, there's nothing to be jealous of, I know.'

And there wasn't. No matter what Jackson had said to me at the dance or in the parlour the morning after, he wasn't a factor when it came to Wyn and me. We had very real problems to solve without worrying about things that were never going to happen anyway.

He sucked in a long deep breath then gave me a half-smile.

'I missed you so much,' Wyn said. 'Can't believe the universe couldn't give us a single day.'

A rush of magic passed over the surface of my skin and I could almost see the golden thread between us, glowing as it tied itself ever tighter around our hearts.

'The universe can have today,' I told him. 'We have forever.'

I leaned forward to seal my promise with a kiss, revelling in the sensation of his eyelashes against my cheek, the clean scent of his deodorant, the warmth of his skin, the taste of him. This was worth fighting for. This was worth living for.

'Tell me everything you remember about the wolf,' Wyn said when we broke apart. 'What size, what colour, anything at all.'

'It's kind of a blur.' I closed my eyes to help me concentrate. It was difficult when all I saw was him. 'Mostly grey, more white around the muzzle, maybe? And it, I mean, they were big. Really big.'

'Bigger than me?'

'Biggest wolf I ever saw.'

'Did it come from inside the hotel?'

'From the street,' I said. 'Jumped right up from the sidewalk onto the terrace of the DeSoto. I told them not to come inside the hotel but they lunged for me and Jackson got in the way, got clawed across the belly for his trouble.'

'The wolf clawed Jackson?' Wyn leapt to his feet, ready to bolt. 'Did he get bitten? Is he OK?'

'He's fine, I healed him, and no, there was no biting,' I replied. 'If he had been bitten, would that mean . . .?'

'He wouldn't turn into a wolf, no.' He drove the heels of his hands into his eyes before pushing his hair back off his face. 'The phase is hereditary but any wound from a Were, teeth or claws, can be fatal to humans if it isn't treated right away. He's lucky you were there.'

'If I hadn't been there, he wouldn't have been in danger.'

'You don't know that.'

It was obvious from the look on his face he didn't believe his own words any more than I did.

'Would a Were bite kill a witch?' I asked, absently running a hand over my scarred abdomen.

He ducked his head.

'I don't know how you survived after I clawed you. I was told a scratch would incapacitate. If it were deep enough, any injury, tooth or claw, would kill a witch instantly.'

'Catherine told me the Weres act as kind of magical law enforcement, that they keep order in the magical world so they won't be discovered,' I said, trying to recall my grandmother's exact words. 'She talked as though Weres considered us to be a threat to their secret existence. But if the witches knew a single Were bite could kill . . .'

'Then the witches would most likely try to eradicate Weres,' Wyn finished for me as he sank back down into his seat. 'It's one of the reasons we all gather where we do, to keep people safe. Em, you have to swear to keep this to yourself.'

'Who would I tell?'

There were no other witches. I was all alone while Wyn was part of a pack that could slaughter an entire city in minutes.

'It doesn't make any sense. Every wolf in the region was with us on the full moon. If there truly was a Were in Savannah on Sunday night, it was a lone wolf.'

'And that's bad?'

'It's not good. Once you've been initiated, the call to gather is so strong, Em, I can't even start to explain it. I could feel the pull hours before the moon rose. If your grandmother hadn't poisoned me, I would've done everything in my power to get to the pack before the first phase. To be part of a pack and not share the experience with them must be excruciating.'

The guilt that would bind the memory of my grandmother's assault to me always pressed down on me and I curled my shoulders inward, cowering from the pain.

'You're saying this wolf ignored that call?' I asked in a whisper.

'You can't ignore the call,' he replied softly. 'A wolf cannot leave its pack by choice, only by exile. It's the most brutal and agonizing thing that can happen to a Were.'

I thought back to the wolf in the hotel ballroom, the waves of pain and rage that rolled off its body, the sickening disconnect between the school party and its violent desires.

'It only happens if a Were commits one of the high crimes,' Wyn went on, pressing his hand against his forehead as though feeling for a fever. 'They're locked in a silver cage the day before the phase, then, when the moon rises, the pack all turn their back on the exiled wolf and run without him. It would be an agony beyond anything you can imagine, enough to make you lose your mind.'

I opened my mouth but had no words, only the taste of ash.

Wyn pulled his cell phone out of his back pocket and swiped through the contacts.

'I need to talk to my mom. If there is a lone wolf running around the south-east, she needs to know.'

'What would a lone wolf want with me?' I asked, every living thing in the garden shuddering as one, Wyn included.

'There's only one way you can return to a pack after exile,' he replied hesitantly.

'And that is?'

'Present a still beating heart of a wolf killer to the pack leader.'

The garden fell silent and he looked at me with more fear in his eyes than I had ever seen before.

'A wolf killer like me,' I replied, my voice as light as air. 'Who's your pack leader?'

Wyn swallowed hard, his Adam's apple bobbing up and down in his throat as he turned his head away from me.

'My mom.'

He placed his phone down on the table, the photo of a strangely familiar woman filling the screen with the word 'mom' underneath. He wasn't the only one of us who was afraid. On his phone, she wore a purple smock and a smile. In my vision, she wore grey. Wyn's mother was one of the strangers I had seen in my vision.

'And what does the pack leader do with the beating heart of a wolf killer?' I asked, my words dancing away on the air like dandelion seeds.

Wyn looked at me as though I was about to be snatched away right in front of him, tears in his eyes and his voice rough-hewn as it scratched out the back of his throat.

'She eats it,' he answered. 'The pack leader has to eat the heart.'

Chapter Nineteen

'Relax,' Ashley said. 'From what I hear, most people have difficult relationships with their in-laws.'

I stared at my aunt as she took a huge lick of her ice cream cone.

'Yeah, about where you'll spend the holidays or whether or not they're spoiling the grandkids. Not whether or not they're going to eat your heart to make up for killing your boyfriend's brother.'

She took another bite and licked her lips.

'When they're eating the hearts of their enemies, are they in human form or wolf form?'

'I don't know.'

'Do you think they'd cook it or eat it raw?'

'Ashley!'

'What?!' She rolled her eyes, a picture of innocence. 'I'm only wondering.'

'Could you wonder about something that doesn't involve me having my internal organs ripped out?' I suggested.

'Well, pardon me for having an inquisitive mind.'

She went back to attacking her ice cream, the two of us side by side on an old wooden bench in Oglethorpe Square. Hours after Wyn left to check in with his family, Ashley found me still sitting in the garden and insisted on dragging me out of the house, more or less literally, but not even the promise of early-evening Leopold's ice cream could brighten my mood. Pointing at the regency-style mansion with what was left of her ice cream cone, she nudged my arm with her elbow.

'You ever see any ghosts over there?'

'No,' I replied, focusing on the pretty buttermilk yellow stone home. 'And from what Jackson told me about that place, I don't know if I want to see any.'

'If you're trying to avoid houses that kept enslaved people, you'll have to walk around the whole city with your eyes closed,' Ashley replied. 'It might not be a pretty part of our history, but it's very real.'

I kicked my legs back and forth, scraping the toes of my sneakers against the dry ground. 'What I don't understand is how the founders banned slavery in Savannah but as soon as their backs were turned, it was happening. Surely everyone must've known it was wrong or it wouldn't have been outlawed in the first place?'

'You sweet summer child,' Ashley said with a sigh. 'You're forgetting that there have always been two kinds of people who take charge. Good people who want to change the world for the better and shitty people who are only looking out for themselves. The shitty people make the biggest threats and they're not afraid to play dirty. Most people just want an easy life. You've got to be real brave to stand up against a bully, even when you know what they're doing is completely wrong.'

'But things can change for the better,' I insisted, wanting to believe it was true. 'Someone always stands up for what's right eventually.'

'Usually after too many lives are lost. Way I see it, the world is like a pendulum, it swings one way and then the other. Sometimes it swings a little harder or a little faster in one direction but it swings back the other way after a spell, for better or worse.'

'Can we go back to how and when Wyn's mom is going to eat my heart?' I asked, utterly miserable.

'If I had to guess, I'd say they're eating it in wolf form,' Ashley replied, far too enthusiastic. 'And let's be real, they're serving it rare.'

'So glad I didn't get ice cream,' I muttered.

Growing up as the only child of a historian, I was well aware of the darker side of human nature. My dad used to say, to love the present, you had to acknowledge the past and want better from the future. I'd always taken that future for granted but now I was a lot more wary of what could be. But I wanted it so badly. I wanted to sit on this bench with Ashley fifty years from now, the pair of us crotchety little old ladies, bickering over silly, inconsequential things rather than whether Wyn's mother would consume my heart bloody or broiled. I wanted to watch the seasons change and the city grow, and I wanted to do it all with Wyn by my side.

When my future was an unwritten book, I hadn't worried too much about the shape it might take. There were certain things I took for granted: college, travelling, falling in love, my dad walking me down the aisle, a family of my own. That was something I wanted. A partner, two kids, maybe three. My childhood was full of love, lousy with it really, my dad never once let me question how proud he was of me and how my mother would have adored me, but growing up with just one parent, no aunts, uncles, siblings or cousins was miserable in its own way. Sometimes it was suffocating with just the two of us. Sometimes his love was smothering, sometimes I was just being a brat. If anything, my dad was too tolerant, always writing off my teenage tantrums as just that, when I wanted him to yell and shout then ground me or take away my screentime, just like the parents I saw on TV. But no. When I acted out, he disappeared into his books and waited for my emotions to blow over. Every now and then I had to wonder if he was afraid of me, scared an outburst might unlock something inside me and unleash my magic. The thought made me ache. But the thought of my future family, the vision I had of kids on a swingset, my heart catching on fire every time I looked at my partner, that was something I cherished. Except now, I had no idea how to make that dream a reality.

The only person I could ever imagine in my future was Wyn. The only person I ever wanted in my future was Wyn. Just the thought of him left me breathless. It was only a few hours since he left Bell House and it already felt as though he'd been gone for a month; the warm buzz that hummed around me had devolved into a low-level hiss, anxiety replacing anticipation. There were so many obstacles for us, so many reasons why the future I'd imagined for myself would be impossible. Could a witch and a Were build a life together? Not if he had to keep me a secret from the pack. And if we did manage to exist as a couple, would we be able to have children? Would they be witches or Weres? I had a duty to continue the line, but any child of mine would be doomed to the magic-less life of a caretaker, just like Ashley. If they chose to be initiated into Wyn's pack, what would that do to their magic? If I didn't find a way to satisfy Emma Catherine's prophecy, none of it would matter anyway.

Even knowing all this, I let myself daydream for a second and saw us years from now, walking together, hand in hand. Wyn's hair was shorter, his jawline more defined, my hair was longer and my body softer, a ring glinting on the third finger of my left hand.

It wasn't a vision, only a fantasy, but that didn't mean it wasn't worth fighting for.

'Am I being naïve?' I asked, cutting into our contented silence. 'Thinking things will work out for me and Wyn?'

'You're not naïve, you're seventeen,' Ashley replied. 'I don't know, maybe? Doesn't mean you shouldn't try, but like I said, it's not always easy to be brave.'

I brushed my hair out of my face, my waves still loose, the way Wyn liked them, and gazed over at the Owens-Thomas House. For a moment, I thought I saw someone standing on the veranda that jutted out from the side of the house, a man in a blue-and-white coat with gold tassels at the shoulders and oddly white hair but when I blinked, he was gone.

'Did I ever tell you how I found out Catherine tethered me to Bell House?'

Ashley was staring straight ahead when I turned back to her.

'No?'

Her mouth made a grim line, an ugly impersonation of a smile.

'It's simple magic, really, all you need is something that connects the subject to the location and something sharp.' Holding out her left hand, Ashley ran a finger along a delicate silver scar that sliced across her palm. 'Catherine told me it was a surprise for my birthday. Not a lie, I guess,' she said, splaying her fingers wide then closing her fist. 'For months I'd been growing sunflowers from seeds and I kept one in a pot in my room, watering it, feeding it, using a heat lamp. It's honestly sick how proud I was of that plant. At the time I didn't realize it, but Catherine was using magic to keep it going, I only realized too late that sunflowers don't usually bloom in November, but I was so pleased with the flower and so wrapped up in Ellie, I didn't think to worry about it.'

The Witch and the Wolf

Ellie. Ashley's lost love and a name I hadn't heard uttered since she first told me the story of how they'd met and how her own mother drove Ellie away.

'My birthday came around, I had plans to meet Ellie and spend the day together, only Catherine wanted to do this birthday ritual first, a spell to keep me safe, she said. Even caretaker generations come of age at seventeen in witch families and she made a big show of wanting to protect me, so I went along with it. Let her take me into the garden, slice open my palm and bleed all over my favourite flower.'

The thought of it made me shudder, imagining Ashley when she was my age, still openhearted and trusting. She didn't often volunteer anecdotes from her life before I arrived; hardly surprising when I considered everything she'd been through, so I kept quiet, holding space for the rest of her story.

'I felt it right away, a stronger connection to the house, but I didn't question it. Catherine said it would protect me, I had no reason to question her until I tried to walk out the front gate and couldn't.'

'Couldn't, you were physically incapable or just couldn't, you didn't want to?' I asked, trying to understand the magic.

Ashley sighed. 'Both. Neither. It wasn't an option. I stood in front of the gate, stared at the damn thing for an hour, but I couldn't move. When I didn't show up, Ellie came looking for me. She was crying, all upset because her dad had been offered a job back in New York and they were leaving right away. I couldn't go to her, couldn't even open the gate to let her in. She didn't wait around long – I guess she thought I was punishing her.'

She didn't want my pity, I knew that, but it was impossible not to listen to her story and feel my own heart break, and I wanted her to know that. I rested my hand on the bench next to her leg, allowing the slightest contact between my pinky finger and her thigh. Ashley allowed it, tossing the briefest hint of a smile my way.

'She was almost out of sight by the time I got the gate open,' Ashley said very softly. 'At first it was like a headache but with a cramp at the same time. It got worse with every step I took away from the house, pressure building in my ears like I was going deeper and deeper underwater. My lungs burned like they were on fire and I was truly afraid my heart was going to explode. I remember falling to my knees, trying to crawl after Ellie, but somewhere between the corner of the block and the front gate, I blacked out. Can't have made it more than a few yards before I quit.'

'You didn't quit,' I told her, actively not noticing when she wiped away an errant tear. 'You survived.'

She shrugged as though the difference wasn't much. 'Slept through the rest of my birthday, woke up two days later to see my sunflower wilting on the windowsill. After Catherine told me what she'd done, told me I was tied to the house for my own good, she took it away and put it in that awful room. I didn't see it again until you broke the tether.'

Oglethorpe Square seemed to honour Ashley's pain, the oak trees bowing their heads, the Spanish moss swaying. Footpaths that had been swarmed only a moment before were now completely empty and even the sun dimmed itself with a cloud out of respect.

'All of that is to say, no, I do not think you're being naïve,' Ashley said. 'I would have happily died for one more moment with Ellie. You and Wyn, you met for a reason. You shouldn't give up on one another, no matter the obstacles.'

'Thank you,' I whispered, surprised when she patted the top of my hand.

'And I'm glad you went into her craft room yesterday,' she added on a deep exhale. 'I didn't want to say anything but, I guess, I'd been a little worried about what might be lurking inside.'

'Me too,' I admitted. 'But it wasn't bad at all. Beautiful, actually. Waking up in the dirt aside. Catherine was the darkness, not the room.'

She leaned forwards and flicked her long brown braid over her shoulder. 'Kind of thought maybe she'd be in there.'

'Yeah,' I said gently. 'I kind of thought it too.'

'We any closer to working out where she is?'

'Nope.'

'And the prophecy?'

I shook my head.

'Just let me know as soon as you find out,' she said. 'I'll be damned if I'm filing taxes if the end of the world is right around the corner. Ain't no audits in hell.' She paused and her ice cream dripped onto the back of her hand. 'Unless that's all there is.'

'Emma Catherine said things would be clearer when the other witches arrive, like they'll amplify my signal or something.'

'More witches?' She groaned before tossing the end of her cone into her mouth, talking while crunching. 'Exhausting. You do know they're not staying with us, right? I'm not running some magic-friendly B&B.'

She scowled and I smiled, leaning forward to rest my forearms on my thighs. I watched a pair of squirrels chase each other around a tree, one tagging the other then racing away in the opposite direction, both of them chattering with delight.

'When I was little, I always wanted a sister,' I said, turning my head to watch Ashley examining an ice cream stain on her shirt. 'I hated being an only child. I used to dream of moments like this.'

'Sitting on a bench, eating ice cream and discussing how

your matriarch went mad with power?' she replied, smirking when I laughed. 'You must've been a weird kid.'

'Takes one to know one.'

This time her nudge was more of a shove and I had to grab hold of the bench to avoid slipping right off. When I righted myself, she put her arm around my shoulders and rested her head against mine. It was a small gesture, but it made my heart swell and all of a sudden I was fighting back tears. It was nice, having a family. It was something worth fighting for.

'You know the Powells used to be witches?'

'I did,' I confirmed. 'Catherine told me.'

'You think Lydia . . .?'

'No.' I tugged on a loose thread on my denim shorts, pulling until it unravelled, adding a millimetre of new light blue fringe to the hem. 'No way to know for sure, but she did some research and it's not promising.'

'Good,' she said with a puckish grin. 'Imagine that little monster with magic. Although if she was a witch, at least I could understand why you might consider ending the world.'

Squinting against the setting sun, I wrinkled my nose at my aunt. 'Do you think Alex Powell knows the truth about our family?' I asked.

Ashley stood up and dusted off her hands, taking her time before she replied.

'Only one thing I'm sure of,' she said, gazing off at the pretty orange-pink sky. 'All the women in this town are very good at keeping secrets.'

Chapter Twenty

It had been the longest day but I still couldn't sleep.

The house attempted to coddle me with the hypnotic sound of the wind rustling leaves in a tree, gentle birdsong from the friends painted on my bedroom walls, all the colours of my room muted, soft and soothing. Nothing worked. When the grandfather clock chimed eleven, I gave up, rolling over to open the drawer in my nightstand and pulling out a sachet of recently harvested lavender. I tucked it into my pillowcase and breathed in deeply, the herbaceous perfume trying its very best to knock me out, but there was only so much one plant could do.

Especially when there was someone opening our front gate and creeping across the lawn. Shooting out of bed, I almost tripped over my own feet as I knelt onto the window seat, throwing open my window to look outside.

'There's no way to surprise you, is there?' Wyn asked with a chuckle as his head popped up in the magnolia tree.

'This is a surprise,' I confirmed happily. The birds in my room switched their song to something more excitable as Wyn moved gracefully from the branches of the tree to my balcony and I hastily ran my fingers through my bedhead, biting colour into my lips.

'A good one I hope.'

'The very best.'

For a moment, I was transported back. Kneeling on my window seat, smiling at my sweetheart, the moon and stars dancing in the night sky behind him. It wasn't so long since the first time he'd climbed the tree to watch the night pass by my side but at the same time it was forever ago. A month and a lifetime all at once. It was too easy and too quick, the way the world changed, and rarely for the better.

'You could've come to the front door,' I said, pulling the oversized Atlanta Braves jersey I loved to sleep in down over my thighs as I climbed out the window to join him.

'And risk waking Ashley?' He chuckled lightly and accepted the pillow I handed to him. 'Besides, this is our tradition.'

Inching along the balcony until my bare legs were touching his denim clad-thighs, I rested my head on his shoulder, sighing with happiness when he draped an arm around me, both of us leaning back against my pillows. Sleep could wait. The warmth of his body and the soft humidity gave me a tender sense of security I hadn't felt in forever.

'Couldn't let the universe steal all of our first day back together,' Wyn said with a sigh that was almost a purr. 'Wouldn't be right.'

'Agreed,' I replied.

'I spoke with my mom.'

His words hung heavy in the air.

'And?'

I felt him shift at the side of me, tense for a second, before he sagged, touching his lips to the top of my head.

'They didn't believe me. Hard to explain how come I'm so certain there was a Were in Savannah when I wasn't around and no one here is supposed to know we exist. This is witch territory, no pack members in the city limits.'

'They couldn't feel it?' I asked, recoiling at the memory of its magic, the shockwaves that almost took me off my feet.

'Magic, yes. A Were, no.'

A shiver of alarm threatened my peace.

'Don't worry,' he said, my head nestled under his chin. 'I said I'd look into it, Mom said OK. Doesn't help us with your lone wolf though.'

But I was still anxious. The Weres had sensed magic rising here before I ever arrived. Catherine was gone but I wasn't. If they came looking for the source, if they sent more of the pack to the city . . . I gripped his thigh, the solid muscle underneath his jeans yielding to my touch.

'Should I be worried? Should I send Ashley out of town for safety? What about—'

'Hey, Em, don't.' He brushed his thumb over my bottom lip. 'I know there are a mountain of problems to figure out, but right now everything is OK. If it's only for tonight, I want to forget about the rest of it and be with you.'

Days that turned into weeks and weeks that felt like decades had passed since we'd last been together like this. Things were more complicated now, perhaps they always would be, but when he carelessly raked his fingers through my hair, twisting the waves at the nape of my neck around his hand, I dissolved, all my worries and fears melting away for another day. There wasn't a fraction of my being that understood how Emma Catherine's prophecy could come to pass. Why would anyone choose to end existence when love this pure existed in the world? Surrendering to his touch, I lay my head against his chest and luxuriated in the steady sound of his heartbeat.

'Can I ask you something?'

'Anything.'

'Do you feel different?' I asked, leaning closer into him, running my hand up and down his arm, from shoulder to wrist, marvelling at the lines of his bicep and triceps, the turn of his forearm. 'Since you phased with the pack?'

'Yes,' Wyn admitted. 'Everything is amplified. I'm stronger, faster. I feel more tuned in, like I'm always on my third coffee, if that makes sense.'

'It sounds familiar.'

He pressed another kiss to the top of my head and I let myself relax deeper into him.

'It's still new. I have a lot to learn, some parts of the phase start slow and get stronger over time, but the connection to the rest of the pack?' His heart began to thud a little faster. 'I always felt like I was on the outside of my family. Now I'm a part of something so much bigger and it's overwhelming, in a good way. Do you know what I mean?'

'Yes and no.'

A frown drew my eyebrows closer together as I tried to put my own experience into words. 'When Catherine was here, things were clearer, but since she disappeared . . . It's just me, no pack to share my experiences, no other witches. I'm all alone.'

'No, you're not,' Wyn whispered, his fingers finding my cheekbone, then my chin, finally turning my face up towards his. 'You'll never be alone, Emily, not while I'm here.'

Words I wanted to hear but still struggled to believe.

'How long *are* you here?' I asked.

'Forever.'

His eyes were fierce, burning in the darkness.

'Even when I'm not in the city, I'm with you, Em, I am yours always.'

The kiss that chased his words was an explosion. A million stars burst into a billion fragments, consuming my body and soul. When our lips met, I transcended. I was locked in my body and hovering outside of it at the same time, fighting to get closer to Wyn, slipping into his lap, my arms around his neck, my legs draped over his. Swathes of plush, night-blooming jasmine unfurled along the walls of Bell House, the tiny white flowers scenting the night with a heady perfume as they wrapped themselves around my balcony, around me, around Wyn. We were tied together, to each other and the house, my magic embracing him as tightly as he embraced me.

He pulled away first, panting for breath, our foreheads still touching and the sliver of air between us hot and hazy.

'I didn't think the way I felt about you could be more intense, but ever since the phase . . .' Wyn's whole body trembled as he huffed out the slightest nervous laugh. 'I'm trying not to scare you.'

'You could never scare me,' I promised, stroking his silky hair, pained by the inches of space between us. He caught my fingers and brought them to his lips.

'Not even on the full moon?'

'You're always you.' I traced the outline of his mouth, his breath hot on my skin. 'I've seen the wolf and I wasn't afraid.'

His gaze was so full of love, I lost my words, tongue-tied and too caught up in his eyes for talk. There on my balcony, surrounded by jasmine, the rest of the world went away. It was just the two of us, him and me, and no one else.

'Sometimes I forget who I was before this all started. I think about the day I got in my truck to come looking for Cole and somehow, I think I was always driving to find you.'

The mention of his brother cast a shadow, it always did, it always would, but Wyn wouldn't let me look away. With his palm flush against my cheek, he held my gaze.

'I think that's why I didn't fit into the world. I was missing the most important piece: you.'

'And your pack.'

'The pack I would never have known about,' he amended delicately. 'If your grandmother hadn't brought you to Savannah.'

It was a strange way to look at things but it was true. If Catherine hadn't caused my father's death, manipulated me into murdering Cole during his phase, Wyn would never have been inducted into the pack in his place.

'There's so much I would change if I could,' I said, unable to keep a tear from my eye. Unknowingly taking Cole's life ate away at me every day.

'Can't change what is, only what could be,' Wyn replied. 'Except when it comes to you. Nothing could change that. I'm a moth to a flame, Em, you burn so bright, even in the darkness. I will always find you.'

My mouth cocked upwards in an uncertain smile. 'I'm not sure I love that analogy for you. Moths don't tend to fare well around flame, at least not for long.'

'You're not afraid of me and I'm not afraid of you.' He plucked a flower from the jasmine vine and tucked it behind my ear. 'I don't care what your grandmother told you or some ancestor decided two hundred years ago, you won't hurt me. Your magic is beautiful, just like you.'

I kissed him again because I wanted to believe him and when he kissed me back, the golden string wound around our hearts pulled me into him, straddling his lap to get closer. My jersey rode up around my waist and his hands found the bare skin of my lower back, drawing a soft moan from me, a sound he echoed, only stronger, more fervent. My jasmine vines surged upwards, weaving themselves around us until I couldn't see the sky, protecting us from the world and keeping us only for each other. All I could hear was the slip of skin on skin and hard, fast breathing, and I couldn't tell if it was coming from me or Wyn.

'Emily,' he murmured my name and magic flooded through

me, swirling in my blood, filling me up to the brim with sensations I'd only dreamed of before. It wasn't possible for me to hold him close enough, there was no connection we could share that would be too deep.

Surrendering to the ferocity of his kisses, I let go, closing my eyes and losing myself to the pressure of Wyn's mouth, tiny sparks flickering on my skin every time his tongue brushed over mine. He stopped to kiss me again, a quick touch that turned into something deeper when my arms caught him around the waist and his hands found my hair, eyes closed, lips throbbing, all common sense evaporating around us. It was Wyn who pulled away first, leaving a longing burning inside me that I wasn't ready for.

'Emily.'

My name fell from his lips again, only this time his voice was full of wonder. I pressed forward to resume the kiss, impatient fists curled in the fabric of his shirt, until something cold and wet landed on the top of my nose.

'It's snowing,' he whispered as sparkling flecks of white settled on the ground around us. 'You made it snow.'

The cradle of jasmine vines unravelled itself, slipping back along the walls of Bell House until Wyn and I were sitting in the middle of the sweetest snowstorm, Lafayette Square turned into our own personal snow globe in the middle of July.

'I should go,' he said, nuzzling into my neck. 'It's late.'

'And snowing,' I replied, flushing as I gathered myself, climbing out of his lap and rearranging my jersey. The curtains at my window fluttered to remind me there was another option. 'You could stay,' I suggested. 'If you want to.'

Wyn's mouth opened, his green-grey eyes darker than I had ever seen them before and shining in a way that made me catch my breath.

'I want to. I really want to.'

Carefully, with one hand on the railing, he rose to his feet, his wavy hair obscuring his face. 'But we have forever, right? I want it to be perfect.'

My response was a barely there nod and I wasn't sure if I was more confused or relieved. There was nothing I wanted more than to fall asleep with my head on Wyn's chest and wake up to his heartbeat in the morning but the part that came in between? That still made me anxious, no matter how certain I was this was meant to be. The snow melted away and I felt it return to the air, drifting back into the clouds, the trees, the atmosphere, still with me, only in another form. Wyn held out a hand to help me to my feet and pulled me in for another kiss, something softer, sweeter.

'Try to get some sleep,' he said, holding my face in his hands, his lips against my forehead. 'I'll see you tomorrow.'

'Tomorrow,' I agreed and I leaned over the balcony, clutching my jersey around my thighs as I watched him climb effortlessly down the magnolia tree.

'I love you, Emily James,' he called up with that sleepy half-smile I'd dreamed about for almost a whole month.

'I love you, Wyn Evans,' I replied. 'There's nothing in this world that could change that.'

He grinned. 'I know. You'd have to kill me to convince me otherwise.'

The words stole my smile but Wyn was too far away to see. Alone on the balcony, I watched him cross Lafayette Square, and shivered in the balmy night.

Chapter Twenty-One

Of all the possible ways to be woken in the morning, the incessant ringing of a never-ending doorbell was not one of my favourites.

When I reached the front door, bleary-eyed and still in my pyjamas, I found Lydia, her finger jammed into the button, a huge grin on her face.

'OK, I'm here,' I said, swiping her hand away from the door. 'Quit it before Ashley comes out here and chops your arms off.'

'I'm on my way to get the axe,' a voice bellowed somewhere in the house. 'She'd better be gone by the time I get down there.'

'There was always a non-zero chance my relationship with your aunt was going to end in violence.'

Past my best friend, I saw Jackson's Audi, the motor still running, double-parked in front of Bell House. While I tried to make sense of the situation, Lydia pushed past me into the house, looking me up and down.

'You're coming like that?'

'Coming where like what?'

She met my nonplussed look with the loudest, heaviest sigh ever to exist.

'Tell me you have not forgotten?' she said, hands planted firmly on her hips. 'Emily James Bell, you are the worst. Hopefully you're a fast packer or we will leave without you.'

'Lyds, it's six a.m.,' I replied. 'I don't know my own name. What are you talking about?'

'Hilton Head? Vacation? With me?'

'Hilton Head,' I repeated with a groan. 'Vacation. With you.'

'Wow, Em, wow.' She clucked her tongue as she marched herself upstairs. 'Way to make a gal feel special.'

Between ghosting ghosts, returning Weres and nightmare visions, I had completely lost track of the calendar.

'I did forget, I'm sorry,' I said when she strolled past me and into the foyer. 'You know I'd love to come but with things as they are, I don't think I can leave town.'

'With things the way they are I can't think of a better time to get out of Savannah,' she countered, already halfway up the stairs. 'What if this is the last chance we ever get to take a vacation together?'

'Thanks for the vote of confidence,' I muttered, following her into my room, but she waved off my offence.

'Even if the world doesn't end, I still have to go back to school in a week. A lot of people might say that's worse than the apocalypse.'

'No,' I replied. 'They wouldn't.'

Undeterred, Lydia opened my closet and began tossing potential outfits onto my bed: shorts, skirts, shirts.

'It's not that I don't want to,' I said, a blue linen sundress slapping me right in the face. 'But things have changed since I saw you yesterday. Wyn thinks the wolf that attacked at the dance might be a lone wolf and—'

She stopped what she was doing and I cut myself off as her eyes flared.

'Is this about Wyn? Are you choosing a guy over your best friend?'

'No!' I exclaimed. Angry Lydia was a scary Lydia. 'Well, not entirely. I can't just up and leave town when so much is in flux, whether Wyn is here or not.'

'Yes, you can.'

Sometimes there was no use in debating with her.

'Em, be reasonable. You could just as easily end the world in Hilton Head as Savannah,' she said, returning to her task. 'And you can bring Wyn. There's heaps of room at the house. The two of you can catch me up on the Lone Ranger in the car.'

'Lone wolf and it's not funny.'

Jumping in front of her, I held out my arms, defending my clothes from her Terminator-like focus. 'I'm only trying to protect you.'

With a caring but condescending tilt of her head, she pushed my arms gently down by my sides.

'I know and I love you for that. But, Em, it's three weeks until the next full moon, Hilton Head is only an hour away if you need to get back quick and it's not as though you've had any creepy premonition that told you not to take a vacation – have you?'

'No,' I admitted. 'Although there isn't an official system where I put in for official leave. I can't guarantee nothing will happen while I'm gone.'

Lydia walked me backwards to my bed until my thighs bumped against the mattress and I knew I was going to cave before she started speaking.

'You need a break, you deserve a break. A tired witch is a sloppy witch, am I right? This is exactly what you need. One week of sun, s'mores and whatever else you choose to do with your time.' She pinched her shoulders together in a theatrical show of a shrug. 'I don't know, maybe it would be nice for you and Wyn to get out of town.'

'You're not helping yourself,' I replied, my heart skipping several beats at her not so subtle implication. 'Wyn might not be able to come with us. Like I said—'

'Lone wolf, I know, got it,' she interrupted. 'But think about it, no parents, no curfews, no *Ashley*. Just the two of you under the same roof. It'll be dreamy.'

'No parents? What about your grandmother? Didn't you say this trip was the whole reason your mom is in town? What about *Jeremy*?'

'Stuck at work, thank the Goddess. Mom is meeting us there on Friday, said she had some things to take care of in town, and Virginia isn't coming at all, she's having another one of her migraines. You and your boy could get some real, quality alone time.'

My mind raced back a few hours. He wanted it to be perfect.

'What if,' Lydia handed me her phone. 'You call and let him decide?'

The cell phone was too heavy in my hand. What if he said no? What if he said yes? The sun was only just over the horizon and I was already sweating.

'I'll call him, just not right now,' I promised, passing the phone back. 'Why don't you go and we'll follow later today or maybe tomorrow? Wyn has his truck, we can drive down together and meet you there.'

The smile on her face froze and I could practically see her brain working behind her eyes.

'Do y'all have any coffee?' she asked sweetly. 'I'm just dying for a cup.'

'Probably?' I replied, thrown by her response. 'Ashley usually has the coffeemaker set to brew around now.'

She brightened at once.

The Witch and the Wolf

'Would you be a doll and grab me a cup? I just need to use your bathroom and I'll text Jackson, let him know the new plan.'

'Great, perfect.'

I was violently relieved and already halfway out the door, but before I made it to the top of the stairs, I saw Ashley in her robe and slippers on her way up carrying two travel mugs and a bulging paper bag.

'What's this?' I asked when she held out the bounty.

'For you and Wyn. Coffee and croissants for the car ride. I could hear her from all the way downstairs.'

'You didn't hear it all – we're not leaving until later.'

She rolled her eyes and pushed me back into my room.

Lydia was not in the bathroom.

Lydia was stuffing all my clothes into my backpack.

'Hate to say it, but she's right,' Ashley said, leaning against the wall. 'Hilton Head isn't far away and I reckon it'll do you some good to get away. Clear your head.'

'Wait, did I hear what I thought I heard?' Lydia stopped what she was doing and looked up, spinning around and searching the ceiling. 'Did the flying pigs come in early this season? Did Ashley Bell just admit I'm right?'

'But I'm not leaving right now,' I insisted to both of them. 'I can't.'

'About that,' Lydia said brightly, back at her task and wrist deep in a pile of my T-shirts. 'I texted Wyn and he was already awake and totally down, so get dressed, baby, we need to hit the road. Now, do you not own a single bathing suit or am I going crazy?'

'I'll see you next week.' Ashley pressed the travel cups into my hands. 'If the Weres declare war, I'll let you know.'

'Thanks,' I replied before taking a very long, very deep drink of coffee. 'Appreciate it.'

* * *

The drive from Bell House to Hilton Head was only an hour, including one stop to pick up Wyn, another to get Starbucks for Jackson and a fifteen-minute backtrack when Lydia realized she'd left her phone in my bedroom. Nestled next to Wyn in the backseat, I let the twins fill the silence for most of the ride, alternating my attention from the pretty scenery outside the car and the beautiful man sitting beside me inside the car. Wyn hadn't said much either, still yawning when we collected him from the carriage house apartment where he stayed in Savannah, but from the moment he fastened his seatbelt, he hadn't let go of my hand once.

'Almost there,' Lydia announced, her bare feet up on the car dash, phone held up to the open window. 'First we need to go to the store then we'll get brunch at Lowcountry Backyard then I want to get ice cream at The Ice Cream Cone then—'

'Lyds, it ain't even eight a.m.,' Jackson said. 'I for one would like to get to the house and relax before you start dragging me all over town. Some of us have been listening to you since five.'

'Happy to drive if you need a break,' Wyn offered helpfully, leaning forward to rest an elbow on the back of his seat. Jackson responded by flooring the gas so hard, Wyn was pushed backwards and my stomach flipped like we were on a rollercoaster.

'Thanks, but nobody drives this car but me.'

'Bullshit,' Lydia scoffed, slapping her brother's arm until he eased off the gas. 'I drive it all the time. So does your buddy, Franklin, half the basketball team, that girl you loaned it to that time who brought it back with a flat tyre . . .'

'And that's why no one drives it but me anymore.'

He put his foot down again and swerved into the exit lane, pulling off the highway and effectively ending the conversation. The rearview mirror reflected a stormy set to his brow, narrowed eyes staring dead ahead, and I felt my insides drop again, nothing to do with the speed of the car.

'Here we are, home sweet home.'

After a slightly tense conversation with a man at the gatehouse of the private community, Jackson finally brought the car to a stop in front of one of the biggest, fanciest houses I had ever seen in my life. It was bigger than many of the hotels I'd stayed in. The house was a pale sage green with white trim and three storeys high with porches that wrapped all the way around on all three floors. Manicured lawns rolled out on all sides and a variety of intentionally planted trees, palmettos, oaks, ash, attempted and failed to hide the mansion from public view.

'This is your friend's idea of a holiday home?' Wyn let go of my hand, his eyes opening wide. 'Where do they spend the rest of the year, Buckingham Palace?'

'I don't know why they don't sell it,' Lydia replied, leaning forward to scrabble under the seat for her flipflops. 'Old Stovell is so afraid of missing a moment of Savannah gossip, I bet she hasn't been out here in a decade.'

'Ms Stovell?' I grabbed onto the back of her seat as Wyn and Jackson both climbed out the car. 'Ileen Stovell?'

She snorted. 'Classic. You don't know the names of your neighbours but you know Ileen Stovell. Don't tell me she's already come calling?'

'We met at the dance. According to her, she's one of Catherine's best friends, but my grandmother never mentioned her as far as I can remember.'

'According to her.' Lydia opened her door and tutted. 'I can't think of anybody in this town clamouring to hang out with that old busybody. Last time she came around to our place, Virginia paid me twenty bucks to say she was out but she kept me talking for so long, I raised my rate to fifty.'

'But you're totally OK staying at her house for free.'

'It's a tradition,' Lydia replied. 'Our families go way back. The Stovells would be offended if we didn't come stay.'

The sun was still shining but there was the sweetest breeze, blowing the scent of saltwater in my direction. We'd crossed over the Savannah River almost as soon as we left the city but I could tell we were closer to the ocean now. My magic prickled, putting me on high alert, and as soon as I was out the car, I found myself pressing two palms against the trunk of a palmetto tree just to ground myself. Everyone here knew about my magic, no one here needed to worry about it while we were away.

'You could fit my entire family in here,' Wyn said with a whistle, cupping a hand over his eyes to take in the sheer size of the Stovell mansion. 'Is there a servant's entrance I can use?'

Jackson opened the trunk of his car and began unloading bags, piling them on the circular driveway. 'If this kind of thing makes you uncomfortable you're rolling with the wrong crowd,' he said offhandedly. 'Emily has to be ten times wealthier than the Stovells, right, Em? Everyone knows the Bells are one of the wealthiest families in Georgia.'

'I haven't really thought about it,' I admitted, immediately uncomfortable. Both of my parents came from money but I'd grown up with only the bare essentials.

'It isn't polite to talk about money,' Lydia chastised her brother, revealing her rarely demonstrated southern training. 'Don't make Em uncomfortable.'

'I assumed we all knew. Never occurred to me to think twice about it.'

'And that's how we know you have money too,' Wyn said with a laugh. 'No worries, I'm sure I'll find a way to earn my keep.'

Jackson heaved his bag from the car, his eyes obscured by designer sunglasses. 'It doesn't make you uncomfortable?' he asked. 'Knowing your girlfriend is a thousand times wealthier than you'll ever be?'

'Jackson!' Lydia admonished again. 'What is wrong with you?'

'If it doesn't bother Em, it doesn't bother me,' Wyn replied, picking up my backpack, his duffle and Lydia's suitcase with ease. 'I might not have as much money as her, but I have plenty else to offer.'

'What a man,' Lydia said with a dramatic sigh, pressing her hands to her heart. 'Also, gross. Now who's ready for the tour? This house is epic, it has everything. You practically need a map.'

Bags on the ground at his feet, Wyn threw an easy arm around my shoulder.

'Only if it's OK with Jackson. I'm more than happy to sleep in the garage.'

'Just messing with you, pal,' Jackson laughed and shot an amiable punch at his arm, only the slightest hint of a grimace showing on his face when he landed it on Wyn's rock-solid bicep.

'Ugh, testosterone,' Lydia said, grabbing the handle of her suitcase then my hand and dragging me away up the garden path. 'You really can't take guys anywhere.'

'Maybe a girls' trip would've been a better idea,' I agreed, leaving the two of them out by the car.

'The great room is that way, there's a home theatre and a gym in the basement, dining room, breakfast room, and allegedly there's a study somewhere but I've never seen it.'

Lydia's tour wasn't quite as comprehensive as advertised. The moment we walked through the frosted glass double front doors, she began stripping off her clothes until she was down to her bikini.

'Kitchen is through there, help yourself to everything.'

The airy entrance hall opened into a double-height foyer, everything sparkling and clean, except for one pair of muddy sneakers tucked away in the corner.

'I thought you said no one was staying here,' I asked, the sight of the shoes jarring against so much grandeur.

She followed my eyes and shrugged.

'Maybe the gardener came in to use the restroom and forgot about them?'

'And drove home in bare feet?'

'How would I know!' she exclaimed, kicking her sweatpants across the room. 'They probably had other people staying here, the Stovells know just about everyone this side of the Mississippi.'

Wyn walked through the door and I shook off a shudder, the same I'd experienced each time I'd met Ms Stovell. That woman had really got under my skin.

'The two primary suites are down here too but we always leave those for my mom and grandmother,' Lydia declared, then gestured towards a dramatic staircase. 'The rest of the bedrooms are upstairs. Mine is the furthest on the left, the rest are up for grabs so y'all run on up there and take your pick.'

I hung back with Wyn by my side, still carrying all the bags.

'And how many bedrooms are there exactly?'

'I don't think I ever counted them all. Six? Seven? Maybe eight, I don't know.'

She looked back at us, registering the tiniest hint of panic in my eyes and clear discomfort in Wyn's.

'Ohhh.' She laughed, delighting in the awkward moment. 'Don't sweat it. There are more than enough rooms to go around, sharing is optional. I'll let y'all work that out for yourselves.'

With that, she sprinted up the stairs, leaving us to follow

slowly behind. Did I want to share a room? Did he? If he suggested it and I said no, surely his feelings would be hurt. But what if I suggested it and he said no? With each silent step up the staircase, I wished I'd had more time to think. I'd slowed down time to make better decisions before but seemingly the blessing didn't think this would be a good use of my magic. Which only went to prove the blessing wasn't always right.

'You want to take a look at this one?'

Wyn stopped in front of the first door on the second floor.

'Sure.'

When it came to the blessing, I had to trust my instincts. A witch shouldn't second-guess herself or try to force her magic, only feel what was right and go with it. But in that moment, my instincts were a maelstrom, my wants, my desires and my fears all fighting with each other, each of them shouting louder than the last. Everything was swirling so fast, I couldn't manage to get a grip on one particular feeling.

'Nice room,' Wyn said, placing my backpack down on the bench at the bottom of an enormous bed, dominated by throw pillows. 'Real nice.'

It was nice. Huge and nice. My brain was too busy trying to process every emotion I had ever experienced to think beyond that.

'Wow, ocean view.'

The ocean.

Sure enough, right outside the windows, the Atlantic Ocean glittered like a sea of sapphires under an aquamarine sky.

'No wonder I can't think straight,' I murmured under my breath, drawn across the room to open the huge French doors onto my very own private terrace. The sea air hit me like a full bottle of tequila. Not that I'd ever drunk a full bottle of tequila but I had to imagine it would feel something like this: light-headed, my thoughts fuzzy, barely able to tell up from down. I backed inside quickly, closing the doors before Wyn could join me.

'Everything OK?' he asked. 'You look kind of pale.'

'I didn't realize how close we would be to the ocean,' I replied, feeling foolish. I could've asked. I could've looked at a map. This was entirely my own fault.

'And that's bad because . . .?'

'The tides don't play well with my magic,' I said. 'Everything feels a little mixed up.'

He raised his eyebrows and nodded, logging the new information, and for a moment I panicked, the Weres might not know witches were weaker around an ocean.

'If you don't want to stay, we can go back,' he offered, reaching for his phone. 'I'll call an Uber, we'll leave right now.'

A rush of shame replaced my worries. This was Wyn. This was about me and him, not a witch and a wolf. I trusted him with my life. Standing there with his messy hair, T-shirt half tucked into the back of his jeans where he'd got dressed in a hurry, just looking at him grounded me.

'We can stay,' I said, steady enough to walk back towards him and place my hands on his hips. 'I want to stay. With you.'

'Any time you change your mind, you say the word and we're out of here,' he replied, and I pushed up onto my tiptoes to meet his lips, already clearer and more focused. He'd definitely got taller in the last month. I had to crane my head back to look up at him.

'I'll take the room next door,' Wyn suggested. 'All you have to do is holler and I'll come running.'

Just like that, he made the decision for both of us. He leaned down to kiss me again then pulled away, taking my breath with him. He was being a gentleman, I was sure of it. If I asked him to stay, he would stay. If told him I wanted him in my room, in my bed. *If* I asked him. Raising my arms to encircle his neck, I opened my mouth, not sure what I was about to say, when the door opened wide.

'Shit, sorry. Didn't know y'all were in here.'

Jackson took one step inside before turning his head away but not before I caught the look on his face and every word he'd said in the parlour of Bell House rushed back to me. Was it really only two days ago? It felt like years had passed since then.

'You're too late,' Wyn said easily, stroking my face before walking over to the door and clapping an ashen-faced Jackson on the back. 'Em already called this one.'

'Unless you want it,' I said quickly. 'I don't really care.'

'It's all good,' he replied, the muscle in his jaw twitching.

With one hand still on Jackson's back, Wyn gently but firmly pushed him out of my room.

'I'll be next door,' he said. 'Remember, holler if you need me.'

With a tense nod, I let him close the door, the two of them leaving side by side, and me, all alone.

Chapter Twenty-Two

Hilton Head was beautiful. At Lydia's insistence, we left Ileen Stovell's house behind, albeit with great reluctance, taking four bikes from the garage and setting off to explore the island. The ocean still pulled at me, tugging at my arm like a persistent child, but things had changed since the last time it tried to steal me away. That was before my Becoming. Now, although it was still dizzying when we got too close to the rippling waves, I was able to resist its tempting call.

Grand homes hidden behind stately oaks gave way to wide, white-sand beaches as we rolled through the town, dotted with navy-blue umbrellas and swarms of people, all of them radiating joy and contentment. Wyn held back, letting Lydia and I ride side by side, her effervescent commentary running at its usual mile-a-minute pace. Jackson rode out ahead of the rest of us, burning off energy I couldn't summon for myself. This place positively demanded a lazy pace and my cute pink bike with its little wicker basket and streamers flying from the handlebars wasn't exactly built for speed.

'And she was in a foul temper for the rest of the day,' Lydia said, sticking her legs out to the side as we coasted down the slightest of hills. 'I asked if there was something wrong with her food but she said it was fine. Probably something Jeremy did.'

'Did to who?'

A crack in the bike path jolted me back into the conversation. I couldn't see Jackson anymore but his black mood hung over me like a raincloud.

'My mom. I just said, she was acting so strange yesterday after we left the park. Did the food upset your stomach at all? Can't think what else it could've been.'

'I was fine.'

I chose not to consider how her mom's bad mood might be related to anything I'd said or done. If Alex was upset with me too, that made three out of four members of the Powell family I'd pissed off without trying. Pretty impressive by anyone's standards.

'Probably coming down with a case of the Virginias,' Lydia said gloomily. 'It was only a matter of time.'

I gave her a sideways grin. 'Does that mean you'll eventually turn into your grandmother too?'

'Wash your mouth out before I feed you to an alligator,' she replied with the greatest indignation.

'Alligators?' I repeated, almost wobbling off the bike path and into the creek that ran alongside us as my best friend cackled. 'Not funny.'

'Not joking. Better watch where you're going.'

'Hey, Em, Lydia!'

Wyn cycled up in between us, his tanned skin glistening, muscles moving under his skin as he turned the pedals.

'I missed a call from my gramps,' he said. 'Y'all go on ahead, I'll catch you up.'

Lydia gave a salute. 'Roger that. We'll be at the Salty Dog, 'bout ten minutes dead ahead.'

He nodded and slowed to a standstill. As Lydia and I rolled on, leaving him behind, I glanced over my shoulder to see him resting his bike against a tree, phone pressed to his ear. I knew it was about the lone wolf. A chill tiptoed down my sun-warmed back.

'You know I would never objectify another human being,' Lydia said, well before we were out of earshot. 'But damn, girl. Was he always so . . .' She scrunched up her face as she searched for the right descriptor. 'Big?'

'No,' I replied, eyes fixed on the path in front. 'No, he was not.'

The last time I'd seen Wyn shirtless, he was recovering from his first phase, bloody and broken in my bed. This was a very different experience. It wasn't like he was skinny or anything a month ago, he'd always had the body of someone who spent a lot of time outdoors, but when he walked into the Stovells' kitchen shirtless, I'd almost tripped over my own feet. While Jackson's muscles were gym-honed, designed for sports and speed, Wyn looked like he could run through a brick wall and smash it into pieces. A set of strong-looking shoulders sat atop a broad chest, his torso tapering into a slender waist that disappeared into a pair of khaki cargo shorts that strained around the top of his tree trunk-sized legs.

'Not that he was a twig or anything, but whatever he's doing, I'm into it. Wish I could get my ass to pop like that.'

'I don't think you'd like the workout regimen,' I said, almost swerving off the path when a cat skipped out from behind a patch of ferns. 'It mostly involves turning into a wolf once every twenty-eight days.'

'Then I'll skip. Waxing is already a chore and I'm enough of a bitch once every twenty-eight days as is – just ask my brother. For real though, you shouldn't let him wear another shirt, like, ever.'

'Not that you would ever objectify another human being.'

'I would rather die,' she declared. 'Except in this one very specific instance.'

'If I see you anywhere near his closet, I will kill you,' I said, her peals of laughter smothered by the tall palmettos that grew up on either side of us.

We cycled on for a half mile without him, me searching for alligators in the undergrowth and Lydia intermittently releasing her handlebars to hold her hands up in the air, just to see if she still could.

Slowing her pace as the trees began to thin out, giving way to homes with big, manicured lawns, a sports field and some tennis courts, Lydia cycled a little closer.

'So,' she said. 'Y'all decided not to share a room?'

'Uh-huh,' I replied. 'It's not a big deal.'

'Sure.'

'It isn't.'

'Didn't say it was.'

'Only . . .'

She pushed her heart-shaped sunglasses onto the top of her head, all eager eyes.

'He was the one who suggested we take separate rooms. Is that weird?'

'Before I make a sweeping statement about boy-kind,' she replied, expertly turning her handlebars to dodge a spilled ice cream cone in the middle of the bike path. 'I have one question.'

'Shoot.'

'Do you want to share a room with Wyn?'

'I don't know,' I replied, somehow riding directly through the slimy mess she had so effortlessly avoided. 'Part of me really wants to and part of me is still a little anxious.'

'Then don't sweat it,' Lydia said. 'This ain't jail, they don't lock you in after lights out. You have free will, Em, you have the power to do this crazy thing I like to call changing your mind.'

'But what if he isn't being polite? What if I ask him to stay and he doesn't want to?'

'Then he will have no choice but to report you to the southern commission for ladylike behaviour and you'll be rapped across the knuckles for your deeply unladylike behaviour.'

She stopped her bike, scuffed-up Converse scraping along the ground on either side of the frame, and I pulled up alongside her. 'Em, aren't you supposed to be busy worrying about the end of the world? Or did I black out and miss the part where you solved that itty-bitty problem?'

'Yes, but—'

'Wasting your energy on wondering whether or not a man who is so obsessed with you he tolerates me, Ashley, and Savannah's 900 per cent humidity, will laugh in your face if you ask him to spend the night in your room makes about as much sense as a one-legged man in an ass-kicking contest. Apocalypse or not, he's still a seventeen-year-old guy, is he not?'

'Yes, ma'am,' I muttered.

'That is the correct answer,' she replied. 'And if by some kind of miracle he *isn't* interested in taking things further, first we put the flags out, and second we commission a statue in his honour. That boy is already one of a kind; the possibility that he might be thinking with his head and his heart instead of his hormones makes me want to cry. We should be throwing a parade and charging every other man alive a thousand dollars a pop to study his forgotten ways.'

Lydia stomped her left foot on the pedal then popped her sunglasses down over her eyes. 'Now get your skinny little butt back on that bike. I should be snout deep into an Oreo-cake batter-cookie dough triple cone by now and stupid questions like these aren't helping none.'

The Witch and the Wolf

'Thanks for the advice,' I said, pushing off from the ground and catching the pedals under my feet. 'Super helpful as always.'

'You don't need my advice, you need your head looking at,' she replied. 'What do I know? I'm a queer sixteen-year-old virgin, pining after a fictional shadow daddy and his fated fae mate. If you want sensible advice, go to a sensible source.'

'And who exactly should a witch go to for sensible advice about dating her Were boyfriend?'

She considered the question for a moment then gave up, pushing out a sigh of surrender.

'Maybe we start with the ice cream and go from there.'

'I've certainly heard worse plans,' I agreed as she picked up her pace and rode on ahead.

When I walked over to the picnic bench where Wyn was waiting, the twins were both at the counter, still sampling flavours though the server had lost patience with them at least six wooden sporks ago. I sat down across from him, knee to knee, nursing a cup of chocolate mint chip.

'How is it?' I asked.

'It's good,' he replied after taking a lick of his strawberry cone. 'But it's no Leopold's.'

'Hard to beat the best.' I nodded in agreement then tasted my ice cream. 'But they're in the game.'

His eyes flicked over my shoulder but I could still hear Lydia and Jackson bickering. There was no need for a visual check on their location.

'None of the other packs in our region have reported a lone wolf,' he said in a low voice. 'Mom might not have believed me but Gramps thought it was worth calling around, just in case.'

'But no one knows anything?'

He shook his head and I frowned.

'Is that good or bad?'

'I don't know. Could be a Were from some other part of the country, up north or out west. If they were exiled by their family, it's possible they'll try to join ours.'

'There are only three packs in the whole country?' I asked, dividing up a map of America in my mind. 'North, south and west?'

'It's a little more complicated than that.' He looked off in the opposite direction, leaving his answer vague. 'Gramps said he'd reach out, find out what he can. He'll call if he has news, but there are still three and a half weeks until the next full moon. At least we don't have to worry about a wolf attack, even if they're tracking you the regular way.'

The thought hadn't occurred to me. Outside of the full moon, I had no way of telling if someone was or wasn't a Were. At least, not as far as I knew.

'They could be anyone,' I said, suddenly on high alert. 'You really think they're following me?'

'I would.'

It was not a reassuring answer.

'Every pack has connections, however loose. It's possible someone heard about Cole and came down to Savannah looking for an explanation.'

'And found one.' I pushed away my dessert, barely touched. 'But how?'

'That's what I can't figure out,' Wyn said grimly. 'There's no way they happened to run into you by chance. No wolf would risk a public confrontation like that unless they were completely sure.'

'But no one knows it was me,' I replied in a small voice. 'No one except you.'

'And I haven't told a soul.'

He rested his ice cream cone in my cup and took my hands

in his, his skin warm and sticky. 'My mom felt your grandmother's power rising and sent Cole to hunt it down, we can't have been the only ones who knew something was happening down here. If they were inside the city limits when they phased, any Were would be drawn to your magic. Could be they figured out the rest for themselves. It's almost impossible to kill a Were if you don't know how. Even if they couldn't confirm you as Cole's killer, the heart of a witch would be considered a nice gift to certain packs.'

'Your pack?'

He flinched but didn't let go of my hand.

'They don't know you,' he said. 'They think all witches are alike.'

It cut deeper than he meant it to. Another reminder that all the important people in his life didn't even know I existed. In the back of my mind, I heard Jackson's words from the dance. Someone who could be with me all the time, someone who yelled about me from the rooftops and didn't have to hide the truth from his family. I could have all those things with almost anyone else in the world but the only one I wanted was Wyn.

Chapter Twenty-Three

'You're sure you don't want to come with?' Jackson asked, smiling at me before shifting to a more suspicious glance at Wyn. 'Someone needs to be on constant Lydia duty otherwise we'll come back with nothing but chips and ice cream.'

'And that's a problem how?' Lydia shoved her brother in the ribs, so hard he almost toppled over. 'We can handle the grocery store by ourselves. Let them alone.'

Letting us alone was what Jackson was afraid of, but he couldn't say it out loud. Lydia grabbed his car keys and held them up high.

'If you're that stressed about going to the store with me, I'm more than happy to take myself.'

'Give me those.' Jackson snatched the key fob out of her hand and stormed off through the kitchen, into the garage. I laughed but Wyn said nothing, a silent observer at my side.

'Y'all behave now,' Lydia sang as she skipped after him. 'I can't prove it but I would not be surprised to find Ms Stovell has those nanny cameras all over this house. If you see a stuffed bear winking at you, flush it.'

'Why do I get the feeling Jackson isn't too crazy about me

being here?' Wyn asked when two car doors slammed shut in quick succession.

'Didn't he say he had to wake up super early?' I suggested. 'Could be he isn't a morning person.'

'Could be he wanted you all to himself.'

'Could be I wanted you all to myself.'

I slipped my arms around his neck and looked around the cavernous kitchen. 'Empty house, me and you, seems silly to waste time trying to guess what Jackson's thinking.'

'I don't need to guess,' Wyn replied as he picked me up off the ground and placed me on the kitchen counter. 'You don't have to be a witch to read his mind.'

'What about mine?' I asked, nose to nose. 'What am I thinking?'

He answered with a kiss, confident and territorial, his teeth grazing my bottom lip when he broke away.

'You're psychic,' I whispered. 'That was exactly it.'

'I've been thinking,' he said, hands planted on the counter at either side of me. 'We should make a list.'

'A list of what?'

'All the things we want to do over the next few weeks.'

My smile soured.

'Before you have to go back to Asheville.'

When I looked away, he tenderly cupped my chin and turned my face back to his. 'After that, we'll start a new list. Everything we want to do in the fall and the winter and the new year, then next spring, next summer. I want to make forever plans with you but forever has to start someplace.'

'It already started,' I said, leaning back in for another kiss. 'It's just hard, knowing we're always on a clock.'

'Then it's up to me to make every moment count,' he murmured against my lips. 'What do you want to do this summer?'

'Besides stay alive, keep my friends out of danger and avoid Armageddon?'

'Besides that.'

The prickling rush of heat that flamed over my skin had nothing to do with my magic and everything to do with the man positioned between my thighs.

'I can't think of anything,' I said, almost dizzy. It was true, I literally couldn't think of a single thing, my brain was just one loud, happy buzz.

'There's a drive-in movie theatre over in Beaufort, could be fun,' Wyn suggested. 'It's only an hour or so from Savannah, we can drive back after the movie. Unless—'

'Unless?'

'Unless you wanted stay in Beaufort for the night. It's a real pretty town. They've got some cute bed and breakfast places by the waterfront.'

Stay in Beaufort. At a bed and breakfast. He'd been thinking about this. It was a sweet possibility, the two of us, cosy in the cab of his cherry-red truck, a short drive back to a quaint hotel, not having to kiss goodnight at the door . . .

'Or we can drive back to Savannah, it's no big deal,' he added hurriedly, his confidence uncertain when I didn't answer right away. 'I only thought—'

'That sounds great,' I pushed the words through my lips and made them real. 'I would love that.'

'The drive-in or . . .'

'All of it,' I said, tiny sparks flicking at my fingertips. 'It all sounds great.'

It didn't sound great, it sounded heavenly. Bell House was my home but it was Ashley's home too. This place was a mansion but with Jackson glooming around like a bitter shadow and the now unshakable threat of Ileen Stovell's spy cameras, we would never truly be alone. But the two of us at a bed and

The Witch and the Wolf

breakfast in another town . . . I could imagine myself waking up in his arms. And everything that came before that too. My skin burned.

'Is it hot in here or is it me?' Wyn muttered, taking a step backwards and walking over to the window. 'Would you look at that pool. I am ready to jump right in. Unless pools aren't safe for you? We could hang out in the AC and watch a movie?'

'Pools are fine,' I said, slipping down from the counter, the tiled floor cool against my hot feet. 'As far as I know. I'm basically a toddler, can't be left by water unsupervised.'

'Good thing I can't take my eyes off of you.'

My teeth bit down into my bottom lip, tempering a smile so big I was afraid it might force every flower on the island into bloom.

'I'm going to go change,' I said as he peeled off his T-shirt, already in swimming shorts. As if I wasn't struggling to contain myself already.

'Don't take too long,' Wyn called as I headed for the stairs. 'We only have forever.'

Whenever the skies were clear and the sun was high, my dad called it a top dollar day. Walking out of the house and into the backyard I wished more than anything he was with me. It was such a top dollar day, the enormous swimming pool sparkling the exact same shade as the sky, it was hard to tell who was reflecting whom.

'You were gone too long,' Wyn chided, breaking the surface of the water and bursting up like some sort of Greek god.

'I was gone five minutes.'

'Like I said, you were gone too long,' he said again.

Grinning so hard it made my face hurt, I hopped onto the blazing hot concrete that surrounded the pool, hastily making my way into the water. The temperature was perfect, cool, not cold, and I walked then swam over to Wyn, testing my front crawl and my magic.

'You're good?' he asked when I reached him, arms sliding back around his neck, where they always wanted to be.

'More than,' I confirmed as my legs locked around his waist. It might've made me nervous on dry land, to be so intimate, but in the water it felt natural.

'Wish we had a pool.' Wyn leaned back, soaking his hair until it was slicked back from his head and almost jet black. 'My gramps had an above ground pool when we were kids, but he never cleaned it right and my mom wouldn't let us swim in it.'

'That's almost as harsh as eating my still-beating heart,' I joked, but he didn't laugh. 'Too soon?'

'Not too soon because it's not going to happen.'

He sounded so sure it was almost easy to believe him.

'I've been thinking of more things we should do,' he said, his cheeks turning slightly pink as I shifted against the waistband of his shorts. 'SCAD has an open day next week, thought we could go check it out.'

'The art school?'

He nodded. 'I know you could go to just about any school you wanted, but we could take a look. It's not just art degrees, they have a bunch of stuff.'

'I hadn't considered it,' I confessed. 'Not so long ago, school was all I could think about. Now it's the last thing on my mind.'

'That's understandable. There's no law that says you have to go next year, but if you do, there's still time. Applications aren't due for a couple of months.'

Water lapped at my skin, blinding sunlight bouncing off its glassy surface.

The Witch and the Wolf

'For years I convinced myself college was going to be the thing that defined me,' I confessed. 'I was so sure I was going to roll up to some ultra-impressive school and they would hand me a personality at orientation, like, a little envelope with my room key, dining hall card and a list of all the proper things you're supposed to like and dislike. Everything I missed out on because of all the years I spent travelling with my dad. Joke's on me, I guess.'

Wyn shook his head in disbelief.

'Emily, that's . . .'

'Tragic?' I suggested. 'Full-on pathetic?'

'Impossible,' he finished. 'As if anything or anyone could define you.'

My legs tightened around his waist and he pulled me closer, foolish flesh and bones the only thing separating my heart from his.

'It kills me to know you don't realize how extraordinary you are,' he said, his nose nudging mine. 'I'm not talking about your magic, I mean you. All the things you've been through and you came out standing on your own two feet, brave and bold and fearless.'

I laughed softly. 'You can't be talking about me. I didn't come through anything yet, I'm still in it.'

'Then I'm right there with you. College applications, drive-in movies, defeating the forces of evil, Savannah Banana games—'

'Sorry,' I cut in. 'What exactly was that last one?'

'Coolest baseball team ever, I've got the tickets already so there's no backing out. It's about time you invested in America's pastime and it's my civic duty to teach you,' he said, planting a kiss on my nose. 'Your skin is turning pink. Let me get the sunscreen.'

Wyn slid out of my arms, swimming over to the deep end. Treading water, I watched him go. Lydia might never objectify a person but . . . if not Wyn, who? And if not now, when? His stroke was smooth and even, muscles working effortlessly under his deeply tanned skin, strong arms, powerful legs. It only took one second for me to forget where I was, lose my footing and dip under the water.

Wyn couldn't see her, I was sure of it. A pale young woman, her blue dress swirling around her and dark hair that floated in front of her face, obscuring the grief-stricken expression and wide-open eyes.

'Don't worry,' she said. 'You won't be alone much longer.'

And then it all went dark.

There were so many wolves gathered together, I could barely see the ground.

When I came to it was late, sometime in the evening, and according to the massive assembly of Weres surrounding me, a full moon. I was shaking, still in my swimsuit and horribly exposed, but the Weres couldn't see me, it wasn't possible they'd allow a witch to wander freely into their gathering. Just like in the Pirates' House, I'd slipped backwards in time. The wolves stood in a clearing, in a forest that would one day be cut down to make way for expensive homes for rich people and they would have to move on. Some of them, including one large grey wolf who stood beside me, to the mountains outside of Asheville. Without seeing him out of phase, I knew it was Wyn's grandfather and I didn't know whether to move closer or run as fast as I could.

'Please,' I heard a woman yell at the head of the crowd. 'Please, listen to me, I didn't do it.'

'We've listened to as much as we need to hear. Hold still before I rip your throat out,' replied another female voice, one that seemed too high-pitched and sweet to deliver such a grim sentence.

The Witch and the Wolf

'But I didn't kill the wolf,' the first woman screamed. 'Why would I?'

I pushed through the crowd, hands sinking into the plush fur of the wolves even though they couldn't feel my touch. As soon as I reached the front, I knew the answer to the condemned woman's question. Hands bound behind her back, red hair, green eyes that stared straight into mine.

'I didn't do it,' my ancestor called to me, screaming until her voice was hoarse. 'There was someone else there, he was trying to kill me, the wolf saved my life.'

'And that's how we know you're lying,' the female Were said, slapping the witch with an open palm. 'Why would a wolf help you?'

'Because he was trying to kill us both!'

'If that were true, he would be standing here today, not you. There isn't a human alive who could kill a Were, and no Were would surrender their life for a witch.'

'My name is Cathy Bell,' the witch went on, ignoring the Weres now, speaking only to me. 'The year is 1814 and I swear it, I swear it on our line, there was a man and he attacked us both, last full moon. I didn't see his face, he was wearing a hood, but he had a sword, a silver sword with a gold hilt, shaped so strangely and—'

The clearing rumbled with the howling of the wolves. They threw back their heads, some crouching down, others rearing up on their hind legs, all of them drowning out the witch's words. I watched, helpless. It was all I could do. Witness her suffering, hear her, believe her.

'You're here,' she said to me as the last remaining female Were slipped back into the crowd and welcomed her phase. 'That means she's safe.'

I nodded, knowing she couldn't say more, wouldn't put her daughter at risk. These were not the reasonable peacekeeper

Weres I'd imagined when Catherine first told me about them. These creatures were vengeful and cruel. Their bloodlust filled the air thicker than the smell of smoke from a nearby bonfire and if there had been any doubt in my mind about Wyn's explanation of what would happen if the lone wolf found me and took me to his pack, it was gone now. This was their idea of a trial: a helpless witch, bound at the ankles and wrists, no Weres left unphased to listen, only furious, ravenous wolves with no interest in the truth. And she was telling the truth, I felt it in my bones.

She forced herself up to her feet, eyes open. Her magic was still close but she was a conduit, she had no violence in her. The blessing gave her the ability to speak to the dead and meet people in their dreams. She had only ever used it to help people but it couldn't help her now.

'I'm not afraid,' she said as the growling wolves nipped at her arms and legs as if to test the statement, not knowing she wasn't talking to them. 'If you're here, I'm not afraid.'

And so I stayed. Even when my magic tugged at my guts, the blessing doing its best to save me from what was about to come, I stayed, bearing witness to the brave, proud, defiant witch.

'Emily?'

Horrified, I turned to see Wyn standing at the back of the clearing.

'Em,' he said as the pack surged forward. 'Where are we?'

'I'm sorry,' I told him, holding out a hand for him to come and stand beside me.

He staggered forward, overcome by what was happening to him or around him or both.

'Can't we help her?' he asked and with tears in my eyes, I shook my head.

'We can't do anything but we need to watch.'

The Witch and the Wolf

Wyn's hand found mine and he stood so close there wasn't a sliver of moonlight between our bodies.

'Find him,' Cathy Bell said to me as the first wolf sank its teeth into her thighs and Wyn disappeared. 'Find him before he finds you.'

They were the last words she spoke before the wolves tore her to pieces. And all I could do was watch.

Chapter Twenty-Four

I woke up in a bed, towels wrapped around my swimsuit, strong arms wrapped around the towels. I was in Wyn's arms. Was it only moments ago I'd been dreaming of this, or was this the dream and the wolves had been real? I could hardly tell.

'You're OK,' Wyn whispered into my hair when I shifted against him. 'You're safe, you're OK.'

We sat up together, his arms never once breaking their hold on me. My hair was a nest of matted tangles, drying too quickly in knots full of swimming pool water and styled by the Stovell family's finest pillows.

'You were there,' I whispered in the smallest possible voice. 'You saw what they did.'

'You went under the water,' he replied in a daze. 'When you didn't come up, I dove in to pull you out, but the pool kept getting deeper and when I came up for air, I came up in the woods. It was a crynhoad but it wasn't my pack. Where were we?'

'Here. But not now.'

He exhaled heavily through his nose.

'When I went back for you, I came back up and everything was normal.'

'Normal.' I smiled at the thought. 'Good one.'

'Whatever that was, a vision, a prophecy,' he said, fire in his voice. 'I won't let it happen.'

'It's already happened. That wasn't my trial, it was another Bell witch. From a long time ago.'

The news didn't seem to make him any happier.

'They wouldn't listen to her. Why wouldn't they listen?' He stopped and bit his lip under a furrowed brow. 'Did you stop them?'

'No.'

What followed after Wyn vanished was so much worse than anything he could imagine. Witches, it transpired, could live far too long without their arms, without their legs. Even when they ripped her heart out of her chest, it kept on beating, and I could almost taste the metallic tang of blood on my tongue here in this room, in this bed, in Wyn's arms.

'The blessing only shows me things I need to know,' I told him, carefully running my hands through my snarled-up hair. 'There has to be something we can learn from what we saw. I know it was terrible but—'

'I learned I'm never letting the pack anywhere near you,' he replied, resolute. 'I know I said we'd find a way to explain everything to them, but there is no way. The more distance between you and my family the better. No arguments, Em.'

I wasn't about to give him one, at least not until I understood what my magic wanted me to learn.

'Do you need anything?' he asked, kissing the top of my head when I tested my limbs, rolling my head and stretching my legs. 'Water, Advil? I'm not sure what's the best cure for unexpected time travel.'

'It's this,' I said, resting against his chest. 'Best possible treatment. At least until the twins get back.'

He didn't move but kept me in his embrace, shifting his weight on the bed. Despite the chuckle that found its way out of his chest, I could see the tight set of his jaw and the grim scowl that marred his beautiful face.

'Maybe we don't tell them,' I suggested through a yawn, suddenly drained. 'Jackson and Lydia, I mean. No need to freak them out.'

'Whatever you want,' Wyn replied. 'I trust you.'

Relaxing into him as I closed my eyes, I clung to those last three words, almost as sweet as an *I love you*.

The next morning finally dawned after a difficult night. Wyn wasn't nearly as good at playing the everything-is-fine game as I'd hoped and even though Lydia marched us through the rest of the day without stopping to ask what had brought on his reflective mood, her brother didn't miss a beat. All afternoon and all evening, he'd kept his eyes on me and Wyn, hurt, maybe, suspicious, definitely.

When I padded downstairs, the sun was only just up but already chasing the moon out of the sky and I was glad of it. I didn't want to see the moon after it stood so idly by, watching what happened to my ancestor, doing nothing to change her fate.

'Didn't have you down as a morning person.'

Jackson stood in the middle of the kitchen, sipping a glass of something green. There was a bullet blender on the counter, alongside leftover parts of assorted fruits and vegetables.

'Juice?' He nodded to the upturned blender cup. 'It's fresh.'

'I'm thinking coffee,' I replied, sloping over to the other side of the room and wishing I'd thrown something over, or under, my Braves jersey. Jackson only wore a pair of low-slung sweatpants and they clung to his chiselled hips like they were hanging on for dear life.

'Didn't get much sleep, huh?'

I shook my head, fighting with the lid of the coffee grinder. Of course the Stovells had a fancy barista-type machine, of course there was no instant coffee in this house.

'In a good way or a bad way?' he asked.

'There's a good way?'

'At least one I can think of.'

It took me too long to catch his meaning and when the realization dawned on my embarrassed face, he laughed.

'It's a joke, Em,' he said, strolling across to take over my poor attempt at coffee making, expertly filling the machine to pull a shot of espresso. 'You really aren't a morning person, huh?'

'I'm really not,' I agreed.

After the incident in the pool, Wyn had stuck to my side like glue, wearing the kind of expression that would make anyone think he'd received the worst possible news. All afternoon, at dinner, around the firepit afterwards, while Lydia handed out chunks of chocolate, marshmallows and graham crackers for s'mores, he had one hand on me at all times, a protective talisman, as though he could stop anything bad from happening to me by sheer force of will. But I drew a line at sharing my bed. This wasn't how I wanted to wake up with him for the first time.

'Good thing you're done with school,' Jackson said as I moved over to the fridge, relieved Ashley wasn't here to judge me for how sweet and milky I took my coffee for a change. 'Class starts at eight fifteen.'

'I would fail everything,' I replied, placing a huge cup in the microwave.

He gave me a disappointed look, removed the mug and started up the steamer on the coffee maker. I made no move to stop him, I was not in the right frame of mind to be messing around with a steamer; third-degree burns were not the thing missing from this vacation.

'Only two more years to go,' he said loudly over the sound of the frothing milk, moving the cup up and down until it was thick and foamy, then he poured the shot of espresso into the milk, a pretty coffee-coloured heart sitting on the surface.

'Impressive,' I said when he presented it with a flourish and a bow.

'It's easy once you know how. Work in enough coffeeshops and you soon figure it out.'

'How come you've had a bunch of different hobbies and jobs and Lydia's only extracurricular is fighting people on Reddit?'

Jackson smiled into his juice glass while I added an obscene amount of sugar to my coffee. 'I love my sister but she doesn't pay attention to boring old things like finances. Sports and things like the historical society go a long way with a lot of colleges, part-time jobs go a long way with living expenses. I'm hoping to get a scholarship but, if I don't, I want to be able to pay my way.'

'Oh,' I said, wrapping my hands around my perfect cup of coffee. 'Right.'

Lydia wasn't the only one who didn't pay attention to finances. Before coming to Savannah, I didn't think about money because I believed we didn't have any. Now I didn't think about it because, in theory, we had more than anyone could ever spend in a lifetime. Even if Ashley was having trouble prising it out of the bank.

'Wyn's going into senior year, right?'

My anxiety prickled at the sound of the name on Jackson's lips.

'Right.'

'Guess he'll be heading back home soon. For school.'

'His classes don't start until the end of August,' I replied, simultaneously wishing he would get to the point and hoping he never would. 'We have heaps of time.'

'Couple of weeks.'

'A lot can happen in a couple of weeks.'

Upstairs I heard the heavy thundering of feet crashing above our heads.

'And so it begins,' Jackson intoned in an ominous voice. 'T-minus two minutes to hurricane Lydia.'

'Couldn't be quiet to save her life,' I agreed, sipping my coffee, hating the discomfort between us. Why couldn't things be the way they were before the DeSoto?

'So, I guess I'm sorry if I acted like an ass yesterday,' he said, a similar regret colouring his voice and his cheeks. 'I wasn't expecting Wyn to be here.'

'Lydia should've cleared it with you,' I replied. 'But yeah, you've been known to be friendlier.'

'Yeah, well. The thing is, I know I said I could wait—'

'Please don't,' I interrupted before he could say something he couldn't take back. 'It doesn't matter if Wyn is in Savannah or Asheville or the next room – nothing's going to change. But I hate when things are weird between you and me.'

'Me too,' he replied. 'But I don't like it, Em.'

'Yeah, he can tell,' I said, impatient for Lydia to come crashing in the room. 'We all can.'

'I don't like the situation,' Jackson clarified. 'It's not him, it's what he is. I don't like having a Were around you. I don't trust him.'

'Do you trust me?' I asked.

'Completely.'

'Then you can trust Wyn, because whatever is happening, he isn't part of it.'

'Only he is,' he said. 'Whether you like it or not, he is involved in this and not on our side. This isn't about my feelings, Emily, this is about your safety.'

'Is it?' I pressed. 'Really?'

'Morning, y'all!' Lydia flew into the room, a brightly coloured silk scarf wrapped around her hair, old-fashioned men's pyjamas on her body. 'Do I smell coffee? Because if I don't, I should.'

'I was just heading out for a run,' Jackson said, setting his juice down on the counter, only for his sister to pick it right back up and take a long drink. 'You should be able to work the Gaggia between the two of you.'

'I think we all know that's not true,' Lydia groaned. 'Looks like we're ordering Starbucks. Unless you want to pick it up on your way back, oh dearest brother of mine?'

Leaning over to lace up his running shoes, Jackson glanced up, his troubled brown eyes meeting mine.

'No,' he replied. 'I don't.'

His sister sighed, then brightened half a second later.

'Maybe Wyn will go!' she suggested.

Jackson's only response was the sound of the door closing loudly behind him.

'He definitely won't be asleep now,' Lydia commented, taking another drink of juice and pulling a face. 'What is in this? It's foul.'

'That's because it's healthy,' I replied, watching Jackson's head bobbing past the kitchen window, his face still stormy. 'Why don't we go out for breakfast. On me?'

'Girls' trip? There are a few stores I've been wanting to check out and I want to pick up a new bathing suit.'

'I've spent half my life sitting outside changing rooms.' Wyn strolled into the kitchen, T-shirt, shorts and hair sleep rumpled. 'I have four female cousins, Lyds, I've seen things in Zara you wouldn't believe.'

'That's what you get for shopping at Zara,' she pouted. 'You're not invited.'

The Witch and the Wolf

'You forced me out of my bed at six a.m. to come on vacation with you, and twenty-four hours later you're dragging my girlfriend away and I'm not allowed to come with?'

'Nailed it.'

'Cold,' he said, pouring a tall glass of water from the refrigerator. 'Ice cold.'

'We won't be long,' I told him, trying to reassure him without sounding Lydia's alarms at the same time. 'We could all meet up for lunch maybe?'

'Maybe,' Lydia cautioned. '*Maybe.*'

'You sure you're good?' he asked quietly when Lydia turned her attention to her phone, muttering to herself under her breath.

'If I need you, I'll let you know,' I said, drifting closer to him, irresistibly drawn as ever.

'I know you won't need me.' Wyn gently brushed away a speck of sleep still clinging to the corner of my eye. 'But let me know if you want me.'

'Always.'

'Jeez you sap.' Rolling her eyes, Lydia shook her head. 'Honestly, anyone would think you hadn't seen each other for a month or something.'

I gave her a look.

'We haven't.'

She gagged and clapped her hands twice.

'That was two days ago. Come on, let's get out of here before he changes his mind and I have to surgically separate the two of you. You've got five minutes to get dressed and we're out of here.'

On her way back upstairs, she swiped Jackson's car keys from the kitchen counter.

'We're taking Jackson's car?' I said, alarm bells ringing in my ears.

'We shared a uterus, we can share an Audi. Besides, he isn't here to stop us.' Lydia said with a quick glance out of the window. 'But we should probably make a move in case he comes back.'

'Lyds, we've passed three different boutiques and you haven't looked in a single one,' I said, following my friend past yet another beachy apparel store in South Shore without pausing to check out the goods in the window. 'If I didn't know better, I'd say you were on a secret mission.'

'There's one place I want to check out first, then we can do whatever.'

'I'm guessing it isn't a bathing suit store?'

Lydia checked a map on her phone and continued marching onwards.

'Why didn't you tell me you had a plan?' I asked. 'What are you up to?'

'Because if I'd told you where I wanted to go, you would've said no.'

With a self-satisfied smile, she stopped in front of a tiny storefront, dark and dimly lit compared to its light and airy neighbours. Their wares were displayed in the small window on a black velvet cloth: crystals, precious stones, herbs, candles, journals, rare feathers. Above the closed front door hung a wooden sign that read *Arcandum*.

'I don't want to go in there,' I said, taking a large step backwards until I blocked her way to the door. The whole shop was vibrating, and not in a good way. 'And I don't think you should either.'

'Well, that's too bad because I am going in,' Lydia replied. 'You can wait outside if you want.'

Her eyes glittered, defiant, as though there was something inside her desperate to get out. Whatever it was, she couldn't possibly be as desperate to poke around some knock-off magic shop as I was to get away from the place. Something about the situation felt incredibly off but I couldn't say what.

'Whoever is running this place is a scam artist,' I told her, searching through the window for signs of life. 'There's no way they could be a real witch. It's just some charlatan selling overpriced junk to tourists. You don't need anything they have.'

'Easy for you to say.'

The look on her face was one I'd seen before, stubborn and determined, otherwise known as textbook Lydia Powell.

'I've been reading a bunch of Wicca subreddits and everyone says this is one of the best magic shops in America. You might be the only *natural* super-mega witch around but that doesn't mean you're the only person practising witchcraft, you know. There are plenty of folks out there who dedicate their whole lives to attain a fraction of the magic you have and they need places like this.'

'For what?' I challenged her. 'To buy overpriced candles and fake crystals? Whoever is peddling this stuff is taking advantage of those people.'

'This is why I didn't tell you where we were going,' Lydia replied, distinctly disappointed. 'I knew you'd look down on it. Just because I'm not destined to inherit the same magic as you, it doesn't mean I can't learn some tricks to help you out.'

Behind her determination and the sullen tilt of her head, I knew she truly wanted to help. And there was something else, not just a genuine desire to be by my side when I needed her the most but an equally urgent need to find a place she felt like she fit in. That was something I understood only too well. I didn't like the idea of anyone taking advantage of people who were curious about magic but I wasn't about to make my best friend feel as though she was anything other than essential either.

I quickly scanned the contents of the window. Chunks of quartz, leather-bound journals, vases filled with dried flowers. Nothing sinister.

'You know I'm only worried about you,' I said, stepping out of her way.

'You know I'm almost seventeen and perfectly capable of looking after myself?'

It didn't feel like the right time to point out exactly how much evidence I had that was very much to the contrary.

'It's just a store,' she said, her tone coaxing as she slipped her hand through my arm. 'I only want to take a quick look around. We'll be in and out in two minutes.'

'Two minutes,' I replied. 'And if anything weird happens, we're gone.'

'Em, it's just a store.' She laughed and as she opened the door, a tiny brass bell tinkled above our heads. 'What exactly do you think is going to happen?'

As soon as she said it, I wished that she hadn't.

Inside was pure cliché. Purple textured wallpaper, endless racks of candles, tarot cards printed in China by the thousand and glass display cases full of cheap crystals marked up to match the deep pockets of their Hilton Head clientele. My magic and my morals bristled as I walked around, inspecting bookcases and poking at conveniently prepackaged love spells to-go. Right by the door, someone had set a small table with cards and a crystal ball covered with a thin black shawl. I had to fight the urge to gag. Every second we spent inside the store made me more uncomfortable, my skin irritated as though I'd brushed by a patch of stinging nettles, my magic bristling with every step.

Although we were the only browsers, the small space still felt overcrowded. I hovered by the window, remaining as close to the door as possible, and watched dozens of happy holidaymakers pass by without so much as glancing our way. It seemed odd, almost as though the store didn't register, like it wasn't there. Surely someone would stop in, just out of curiosity? This place definitely wasn't covering what had to be exorbitant rent on the occasional tarot reading and twenty-dollar candle.

'Oh, I'm sorry,' I said, startled by the sudden appearance of more customers, a couple, a man and a woman around my dad's age. It was only when Lydia walked right through the woman I realized they weren't here to shop.

'Can I help you, ladies?'

A tall, dark-haired woman appeared behind the glass cash desk and the ghosts disappeared. She held a beaded curtain open as she stepped out of a back room steeped in shadows and when she took a step forward into the low light of the store, the irritation in my skin flared, shifting into an all-out burn. Her skin was even paler than mine and her eyes an alarming shade of violet. When I looked down at my forearms, peeking out from the rolled-up sleeves of my shirt, they were mottled red and white, the rash bright and bold.

'Thank you so much, we're doing great,' Lydia cooed, flipping through a stack of Wicca-themed cookbooks. 'I'll holler if we need anything.'

'You do that, I am here to help,' the woman replied in an unusual accent. While she spoke to Lydia, she seemed fixated on me. 'Where are you all visiting from?'

'We're just down from—'

'Is that the time?' I cut Lydia off without even pretending to look at my watch. 'Hey, Jenny, we need to get going, don't want to keep my mom waiting.'

'Your mom?' She frowned when I took hold of her hand, dragging her away from the cookbooks without looking back at the strange shopkeeper. 'Jenny? What is the matter with you?'

'That woman is the matter,' I said once we were out the door. When I glanced up, the welcoming bell was shimmying back and forth but it didn't make a sound. 'We need to get back to the car right now.'

Lydia pulled out the car keys without question. 'No worries, we'll be home in five minutes.' She glanced back and I knew that if I followed her gaze, I would see the woman watching us. 'Who is she?'

'I don't know who she is,' I replied as we melted into the crowd, black clouds gathering overhead. 'But I do know she's a Were.'

Chapter Twenty-Five

'I wish I had better news but no one knows who she is,' Wyn said, emerging from the house with his cell phone still in his hand. 'There's no record of a Were living or working in Hilton Head. You're absolutely sure she was a wolf?'

'I'm absolutely sure,' I replied, holding myself in a tight ball on the sofa, legs huddled up underneath my chin. 'No question about it.'

'Then she's our lone wolf,' he said grimly. 'All but confirmed.'

Her violet eyes had haunted me all afternoon and now it was well into the evening, the sun gone but the skies still overcast, echoing my mood, a darkness I could not shake off.

'Can't you find out more about her?' Lydia suggested, her face flickering in the orange light of the firepit all four of us were crowded around. 'Go sniff her out or something?'

'Not before she could sniff me out,' Wyn replied. 'Were senses get stronger over time. I only have two moons, we have no idea how experienced she is, and if she sensed there was another Were in town, she'd most likely try to find me out.'

'And?'

Jackson looked understandably concerned, leaning protectively over the back of his sister's wooden Adirondak chair. Wyn stuck his phone in the back pocket of his jeans and sat next to me on the sofa, pulling a striped throw blanket over my shivering legs.

'Best-case scenario, she knows I'm a Were and presents herself.'

'And the worst?'

His eyes flickered towards me, the line where he ended and I began blurring under the blanket, our palms pressed so tightly together I could feel his heartbeat in his hand.

'No way a Were wouldn't be able to scent a witch on me. If she is the lone wolf and she's already identified Em, she'd be able to connect the two of us.'

'She's seen Lydia,' I said, unable to keep the fear out of my voice when I looked at her.

'Then she's got your scent too, which, not to weird anyone out, is almost identical to Jackson's,' Wyn added. 'None of us are safe.'

'We need to leave.' I pushed away the blanket but kept Wyn's hand in mine. 'We should go back to Bell House right now.'

'You really think we're in danger?'

Jackson's expression was as grave as his tone of voice. When I nodded, he did the same. 'OK then, we're gone. Lyds, go pack your bag.'

'It's getting late, shouldn't we wait until morning?' she asked, an uncharacteristic tremor shaking the ends of her words.

Jackson was firm.

'If you'd seen what I saw at the DeSoto, you wouldn't be asking that.'

'I'll call Ashley, let her know we're on our way.' I stood, already dreading my aunt's response when I informed her that we were in fact about to become a B&B. 'I'm sorry we have to cut the trip short but we'll all be so much safer at Bell

House. Plenty of time for bonfires on the beach once we've got this thing figured out.'

'Bonfire?' Jackson repeated.

I gestured off into the distance, the general direction of where I felt the fire had to be.

'Bonfire,' I said again. 'You can't smell it?'

He straightened abruptly, sniffing the air then walking over to the edge of the property to peer over the wall. 'Beach bonfires are illegal in Hilton Head. As in thousands of dollars in fines *and* jail time illegal. There's usually a bunch of security guards patrolling to make sure no one accidentally sets the town on fire.'

'Then something isn't right.' Wyn rose to his feet, joining Jackson at the end of the garden. 'We should go check it out.'

'No offence, fellas,' Lydia drawled, staying right where she was. 'I know you're both super strong musclebound boys but only one person here has actual magical powers all month long. Maybe let her check it out?'

I followed Jackson and Wyn, climbing up onto an overturned planter to get a better look. Sure enough, a huge bonfire was burning a short distance away, thick plumes of white-grey smoke winding into the sky in an unnatural spiral. It looked like a signal but a signal for whom?

'It's probably nothing,' Jackson said when I started for the gate, the one that led right out onto the sand. 'Just kids who don't know better.'

Wyn glanced over at him then at me, clearly desperate for Jackson to be right but, just like me, he knew something was amiss.

'What do you think?' he asked, following me to the gate and lowering his voice. 'It's not right, is it?'

No.' I wrapped my arms tightly around myself, wishing I had something to help keep me calm, some lavender or valerian, or even some juniper to give my intuition a boost. 'Will you stay here and make sure they're OK?'

'I'll do what I can.' He caught my face in his hands and kissed me as though Jackson and Lydia were not standing a few feet behind us. 'Be careful.'

'It's probably nothing,' I said, repeating Jackson's statement and willing it into reality as I swallowed hard and let myself out the gate.

The first sign that something was wrong wasn't the fire but the beach. It was completely deserted in every direction as far as the eye could see. As I walked along the pathway, sticking close to the houses and away from the water, I saw lights turning on and off in the windows of mansions and cottages, people living their lives up and down the island, but not a single one of them was out for an evening stroll on the sand. The reddest of flags. Mid-July in one of the most popular tourist spots in the whole country and not one person felt like coming outside to take in the sea air. No. They were being kept away. I knew this magic, I'd used this magic, a compulsion that played into fear. I don't want you to see me, you don't want to see me.

Only I didn't need to burn a six-foot high pile of live oak and Spanish moss to make the spell stick.

My feet touched the sand and the trees screamed, black flames licking up and down their trunks and tearing my heart in two. These weren't any old trees, they had been chopped down in Lafayette Square, the oaks closest to my home. It was dark magic, brutal and unnecessary. To chop down a tree with the sole intent of causing harm was counterintuitive to everything I knew about the blessing and I was in almost as much pain as the trees. I raced towards the fire, searching for a way to put it out. Sand maybe, water too, but the thought of getting any closer to the waves than I already was filled me with another kind of dread.

On the other side of the bonfire, the Atlantic Ocean lapped at the shore, the tide rising as the waning moon pulled higher into the sky. Every push and pull called me on, urging me to leave the bonfire behind, kick off my shoes and feel the fresh, sparkling water on my skin. It would feel so good, the water promised, it would hold me close and take away the pain, the panic would only last for a second then there would be peace. At the same time, the Lafayette Square oaks shrieked as they smoked and between their deafening cries and the insistent song of the ocean, I couldn't even tell who was screaming the loudest, them or me.

The beach seemed to spin, slowing me down, and as I approached the heart of the fire, everything faded into greyscale as I struggled to stay upright. There was something else in the flames, something that caused the serpent-like columns of smoke that had stopped rising into the air and instead directed themselves straight at me. Inhaling deeply for one long, dangerous moment, I waited for the newcomer to announce itself.

'Henbane,' I choked out, trying to anchor myself to the sound of my own voice. Delirium, vision problems, palpitations, drowsiness, the sensation of flying, overheating, and in cases of overdose, death. None of my knowledge of the herb was reassuring.

In the far distance, I thought I heard someone call my name but the sound was swallowed up by the crackling of the fire and the roar of the ocean, and as I fell to my knees, my eyesight began to blur. I shouldn't have come this close. White smoke choked my lungs as I crawled; closer or further away, I couldn't tell anymore, it was only when my hand struck something hard and sharp I realized I was at the edge of the blaze. Tears streamed down my face, trying to wash away the tainted smoke.

The fire was held in place by a ring of stones, huge chunks of clear quartz, each piece touching the next to make a perfect circle. Positioned inside the quartz was a second, smaller circle made of malachite. Alone, it was a beautiful crystal with healing properties but combined with the amplifying effects of the clear quartz, it would work alongside the henbane to overwhelm and disorient someone. Oaks from my home. Henbane, clear quartz and malachite.

I should've let Wyn and Jackson investigate. Instead I had run straight into a trap. This fire had been set for me and me alone.

'What do you want?' I asked no one, the words spitting from my chest as I forced myself to focus. I had to stay present, I had to rise out of this moment, even as it tried to drag me under. 'Who are you? Why are you doing this?'

There was no answer, only the spitting of the flames and another flourish of smoke. Rolling onto my back, I reached deep into myself, seeking the source of my magic. All my ancestors, all the witches who went before me, surely there was something I could do. I couldn't summon a wind or settle the elements, no ghosts rushed to my defence, and knowing what herbs were currently poisoning me did nothing to help me survive. I had no idea how I'd slipped into the past at the Pirates' House and every time I tried to heal myself, drawing energy from the sea and the sand, the henbane seeped deeper into my skin.

'Help,' I whispered as the sky above me disappeared, my eyes watering until I could not see. 'Someone please help me.'

I wasn't sure what I hoped to find when I opened my eyes again but standing over me, growling with menace, was the last thing I could've imagined.

The wolf prowled through the smoke and even with my vision impaired, I could see the size of it, feel the power emanating from its enormous body. It was a Were. Somehow, though the moon was four days past full, I was being hunted by a Were.

'You can't be real?' I croaked, pulling up the hem of my shirt to swipe at my eyes. 'It isn't possible.'

The wolf responded with a snarl that came from deep within its belly. It was very real and entirely possible and I had willingly walked right into their ambush. The henbane leached out of the smoke and into my body, filling my head with silver spirals as it lolled from side to side on my shoulders. Between the agony of the trees and the despair of the moss, I was overwhelmed. The siren song of the ocean was beginning to sound beautiful as the henbane seeped into my blood, burning me from the inside out. I stretched out one hand and began to inch my way towards the water, but my arms buckled under my own weight. I didn't even have the strength I needed to drown myself.

Pacing in a figure of eight, the wolf circled me and then the bonfire, watching us both closely. It was a blur, grey and white, with flashes of red and yellow, teeth and eyes and tongue. I knew it must be a trick of my sore, raw eyes, but for a moment, it looked like there were two wolves, one standing beside the other. As my eyes rolled back in my skull I looked up at the sky, all the stars blacked out to me, and wondered how it would feel to finally see my parents again. One small moment of peace amid all the pain.

The wolf howled up at the same sky but for what? To brag? To scare me? As if I was any kind of threat to it now. Curled up in the sand, I couldn't be less dangerous. I couldn't call my ancestors, I couldn't speak any ancient curses or summon the elements or even think. I couldn't feel my magic at all.

'Please don't hurt my friends,' I begged as the wolf, or wolves, advanced, keeping their forelegs close to the ground, heads lowered and ready to strike.

With a growl that could never be mistaken for a promise, a claw swiped at me, a test blow. I felt my skin split under my shirt but there wasn't any pain. At least it wouldn't hurt too much, I told myself, at least the burning oaks could offer me that much. The wolf was on top of me and the first spittle from its gaping maw dropped onto my forehead, warm like a kiss. With my eyes closed, I prepared myself to join the rest of the Bell witches in the world beyond this but, as I held my breath and waited, the savage clash of its jaws never came.

But the lightning did.

Using every ounce of strength left in me, I forced my eyes open, the world still smeared with henbane, and saw the clouds, a moody grey instead of the malevolent black from only moments ago. Then the beach lit up with a split second of ghostly white light, the sand, sea and sky all the same colour. Single, solitary raindrops turned into something more insistent, the bonfire hissed, spitting at me and the wolf. When it looked away, turning its head upwards as though it was as surprised by the rain as I was, I grabbed at one of the chunks of quartz and broke the sacred circle. The fire leapt out of confinement and lunged at the wolf, punishment for the violent act against nature. The flames licked at its side, and I heard a yowling sound, watching it drop to the sand, the smell of singed fur joining immolated wood.

The fire shrank back as the rain kept coming, a shower turning into a storm, turning into a torrential nightmare, the heavens opening with the most unholy downpour I had ever seen. Torrents of water fell from the sky, washing out my eyes, my mouth, the wound on my back. I exhaled long, hard breaths, pushing out the henbane and breathing in the energy of the storm, bathing in its offering. My clothes were nothing but wet rags, clinging to my body as I crawled, one inch at a time and always waiting for the wolf to strike, over to the edge of the ring of quartz and malachite. Swiping through the downpour, I pushed the stones out of sequence, breaking up the circle and quelling the fire.

'Emily! Emily?!'

Strong arms wrapped around me and I leaned into a solid chest.

'I've got you, I've got you,' Jackson whispered over and over as he crashed to the wet sand beside me. 'You're good, I've got you.'

'*Run.*' I panted into his neck, offering no protest when he picked me up from the ground. 'There's a wolf.'

He pulled me closer, his head on a swivel.

'I don't see it?' he said after a moment. 'Did you get it?'

'No. It nearly got me.'

My body was cold but my blood was warm as it ran down my back, staining Jackson's shirt. I was too weak from the henbane and malachite to try to heal myself.

'Let's get out of here,' he said, holding me like a piece of fragile glass, about to break.

'Where's Wyn? Is he OK?'

'He ran right out after you. You didn't see him?'

I tried to shake my head but my neck was too stiff.

'And Lydia?'

'Right over there.'

He pointed off beyond the edge of the ocean, a familiar silhouette staring out to sea. 'Props on putting out the fire, but jeez, Em, did you have to flood the entire island?'

'I'm not doing this,' I told him, my hair plastered to my head, the rain stinging my eyes as I clung to him, feet slowly moving one in front of the other.

'Good old Mother Nature then. Her timing never misses.'

'Be careful what you wish for,' I said in a whisper. 'Look.'

I slipped out of Jackson's arms, still leaning back against his chest to stay upright, and turned towards the ocean. Wiping the water from my face as best I could, I squinted at the silhouette of the girl I thought I knew, arms raised to the sky as the storm crashed around her. She turned to face me, her brown eyes were golden, sparking like the lightning itself as she brought down the saltwater storm, and when she lowered her arms, lightning bolts danced on her palms.

'What the hell . . .' Jackson whispered, now leaning on me as much as I was leaning on him. The rain stopped, the skies cleared, the silhouette came into focus.

'There you are.'

Wyn almost knocked Jackson off his feet when he rushed me, swooping in from the other side of the bonfire's skeleton, but I pushed him away, all my attention on the swirl of magic at the water's edge.

You won't be alone much longer.

I hadn't caused the storm, Lydia had.

Because Lydia was a witch.

Chapter Twenty-Six

No one said a word on the way back to Bell House.

The four of us bundled ourselves into the car, still soaked through, Jackson blasting the heat in mid-July. Wyn took the passenger seat, leaving me and Lydia in the back.

Once the storm was over, she had walked back from the beach in a daze, allowing us to direct her to the car and strap her in but ignoring our questions, mine and Jackson's. Wyn kept quiet, one concerned hand on my shoulder at all times until we were safely in the back of the car and on the road home to Savannah. Everyone was afraid, everyone was confused. Jackson concentrated on driving while Lydia slept, twisted up in her seatbelt, her head in my lap. Wyn spent the entire drive turned around in his seat, eyes on me, leg bouncing up and down and anxiety rolling off him.

When we pulled up outside Bell House, he leapt out the car before it came to a stop, bolting to my side to help me out while Jackson pulled his sister out of the backseat and carried her sleeping body up to the house.

'Just when I thought I was getting a week to myself,' Ashley said, ushering the four of us inside, scanning the square before closing the door behind us and turning the lock. I hadn't realized the front door to Bell House had a lock. It couldn't be a good sign.

She surveyed the damage as we staggered into the parlour, four messed-up teenagers barefooted, bloody and bedraggled, still wearing our damp clothes and stunned expressions. My ruined shirt was smeared pink with washed-out blood, Jackson's too, and Lydia's crocheted cover-up was ruined, ripped to pieces by the lightning she'd channelled.

'Well, you all look like shit. Anyone care to tell me what the hell is going on?'

I didn't. Instead, I collapsed onto the sofa while Wyn stood guard behind me and Jackson laid Lydia down on the chaise longue before allowing himself to crumple onto the floor. Just being under the roof of Bell House felt like slipping into a warm bath. I arched my back as the gashes left by the wolf began to knit themselves back together, my home healing me as only it knew how.

'Never was one for the silent treatment,' Ashley said. 'Please tell me y'all got drunk and burned down the Stovells' house?'

'Lydia is a witch,' said Jackson.

'There was another Were,' said Wyn.

'Someone chopped down a bunch of live oaks from the square to spell me,' I finished up, gesturing towards the window.

'But no one burned down the house?'

We all shook our heads, no.

'OK, that's something, I guess.'

Ashley was at the window in five long steps, opening the shutters to peer out into Lafayette Square. Her eyes widened and her mouth fell open. I didn't need to see the stumps to know five trees were missing from the north-west corner of the square.

'I didn't hear a damn thing,' she said softly. 'How did they take out whole trees without anyone noticing a thing?'

'Because they're using magic.'

I covered my face with my hands, trying to pull out the facts, something solid I could cling to, but no matter how many times I turned it over in my mind, I still felt adrift.

'A Were without a full moon, magic without a witch and the blessing manifests in Lydia. None of it makes sense.'

'Remind me never to go on vacation with any of you,' Ashley replied. 'What a day to be out of whiskey.'

'It can't have been a Were,' Wyn muttered, more to himself than anyone. 'It isn't possible.'

'Didn't you see it?' I leaned back my head to look at him as he peeled off his plaid shirt and placed it around my shoulders. 'You must've seen it if you followed me out the gate.'

'All I saw was the smoke. I couldn't even see you.'

'What about the gashes in her back?' Jackson's words were barbed and baited. 'Did you see those? Did you hear her screaming? Because I did.'

Wyn lifted his chin to meet the challenge in Jackson's voice. 'I heard it. That's why I ran out to help her while you were still in the yard.'

'Boys,' Ashley chided, a one-word warning. 'We don't stand for dick-swinging contests in this house, if you don't mind.'

Jackson pushed up to his knees and then his feet, one arm on the back of our sofa for support. 'Seems to me you should've been able to tell if there was another wolf out there. Can't y'all sniff out your own?'

'Whoever it was, they aren't one of my own,' Wyn replied, ignoring the edge in his voice this time and turning to me. 'Em, this changes things. I need to—'

'Talk to your pack,' I nodded, completing his sentence for him. 'I figured. Go call them.'

He shook his head at himself.

'They're already suspicious. If I call to say there's a Were running around the low country who can change outside of the full moon, the entire pack is going to be here by sunrise, and they're going to want to talk to all of you.'

'You're going back to Asheville?'

The soft blue tones of the parlour walls turned grey.

'I'm going back to Hilton Head,' he replied. 'Alone.'

Jackson snorted.

'Convenient.'

'That's enough from you.' Ashley grabbed him by the scruff of the neck and directed him towards the door. 'Come help me make tea before I let him rip you a new one. This ain't the time to be making matters worse.'

'I don't want any tea.' He grunted, shaking her off and standing firm, but Ashley wasn't going to be so easily dismissed.

'Cute that you think I give a shit what you want,' she said, giving him a shove. 'Get your ass into the kitchen and hush up.'

As their voices faded away down the hallway, the parlour slipped into near silence, only Lydia's heavy but even breathing audible.

'It's not safe for you to go back on your own,' I said uselessly. I knew he was already as good as gone. 'She'll know you're there.'

'She?' He raised a questioning eyebrow. 'You know who it is?'

'It has to be the woman I met this afternoon, the one from the magic store. There can't be many Weres who understand the blessing well enough to use it to disarm a witch.'

'Weres don't use any magic other than the gifts we have. It's one of our fundamental laws. Breaking it would be a high crime.'

'The kind of crime that might get a wolf expelled from their pack?'

Wyn stood in front of me in his blue jeans and grey T-shirt, the toes of his desert boots darkened with a sea salt stain. I pulled my shredded shirt closer to my body and the walls of the parlour shifted almost imperceptibly from pale blue to pale grey.

'I can't tell you.'

The string that tied me to him pulled tight, straining with the weight of secrecy. Necessary, or so he thought, but I couldn't help but worry about what it meant for us.

'You can't go back on your own,' I said, my body fully healed and my mind clearer than ever. 'Either call your pack and get them down here or take me with you. One way or another, I'll have to face them eventually. The longer we keep it a secret, the more it looks like a lie.'

Falling to his knees, he rested his hands on my thighs, staring up at me with pleading grey-green eyes.

'You don't understand,' he said, words written on his face he was struggling to say. 'If they find out you're a witch, they won't let us be together. If they find out you killed Cole, they'll kill you. I can't live with either of those outcomes.'

'Then what's the plan?' I dropped to the floor beside him, clutching at his hands. 'How does this work after the summer? You're going to lie to your pack for the rest of your life? Keep me hidden in Savannah while you live a double life in Asheville? We can't spend forever counting down the days until we have to say goodbye again, Wyn, it doesn't make sense.'

'I don't know,' he admitted, falling back onto his heels and pulling his hands away, knotting them up in his own tangled, damp hair. 'I don't have an answer yet, but there's no way I'm going to let them take you away from me. There has to be a way I can fix this.'

'Find it,' I said, snatching him back, pressing his hands to my heart and holding his gaze in mine. 'Do whatever you have to do, because I'm not letting go of us.'

The determination that flared in his eyes reflected the passion in mine and when he kissed me, I kissed him back harder, staking my claim.

'Em?'

On the chaise longue, Lydia's eyelids flickered open, her gold-white irises returned to their natural deep brown.

'I'll go help Ashley with the tea,' Wyn said, rising to his feet and squeezing Lydia's shoulder on his way past. 'Good to see you back in the land of the living.'

'Yeah, sure, can you get me a Diet Coke?' she replied without missing a beat.

'It's almost midnight.'

'Which is why you should hurry up and get it while we're still young.'

I felt my shoulders drop in relief. If nothing else, she was still herself.

'So,' she said to me, holding out her hands to examine her fingertips as Wyn slipped out of the parlour. 'I'm a witch.'

'Looks like.'

I sat down at her side, inspecting her palms when she turned them over for me. There was nothing to see but I could feel the same thing she could, the tingling in her fingertips, the prickling sensation on her skin.

'It came out of nowhere,' she said, gazing at her hands with wonder. 'One minute I was in the backyard with Jackson, the next I was walking out to the beach, no idea what I was doing. I saw the fire but something told me to go in the opposite direction, like I needed to get to the water.'

'You were lucky. Manifesting right by the ocean like that could've been so dangerous.'

'It didn't feel dangerous.'

She fingered her silver locket and I automatically reached for its twin around my neck. 'I stood at the edge of the ocean and the waves kind of went around me. Then I heard you screaming and everything went white. The next thing I remember is waking up here.'

'Good news, you saved my life.'

'Fuck, yeah.' She pumped her fist through a yawn. 'Bad news?'

'Nothing that can't wait.' I waved away the things she didn't need to worry about until morning. 'How do you feel?'

Her face softened as she stared off into the middle distance and the corners of her mouth tilted upwards in the smallest smile.

'Amazing.'

Lydia looked around the parlour like she was seeing it for the first time and I watched the clouds pass overhead, songbirds flitting from branch to branch and the leaves of the trees swaying with a breeze only she and I could feel.

'How do *you* feel?' she asked. 'Now you're officially my magical mentor. My supernatural sherpa. My—'

'Yeah, I think I've got it,' I cut in, smiling as I laced my fingers through hers. My best friend. My sister. 'I feel proud to know you, same as ever.'

'Good, because I'm going to need your help. Unless Virginia has been holding out on me, I don't think she has quite so much knowledge about all this stuff as Catherine had.'

My mouth puckered into a pout but I said nothing. Her grandmother might not be a witch but I was certain the Powell family knew more than they were letting on. Lydia squeezed my hand and it felt like a tiny electric shock.

'We'll get to the bottom of it,' I promised. 'I can't pretend I understand what's happening but, even though I didn't expect this, it does feel—'

'Right?' Lydia cut in, her wide eyes meeting mine.

'Right,' I agreed. 'I feel stronger than I did. More connected to the blessing.'

And I did. There was a new clarity in my mind, a new depth to my awareness.

When I looked around the room, the paintings on the walls looked sharper, new details revealing themselves to me, their colours more vivid, the brushstrokes finer than ever before.

'Em, did those birds always move?'

I had to suppress a laugh when a flock of watercolour bluebirds fluttered over to investigate the new witch.

'You're going to be noticing a lot of new things,' I advised my friend. 'Not just in Bell House, everywhere. It can be overwhelming but I'm here, I'll help you.'

A current passed between us, something crackling and alive, not quite like the invisible string that tied me to Wyn but something more fundamental. Wyn and I were bound together. Lydia and I were sisters. I wasn't alone in my magic anymore.

'I don't know about you but I am destroyed,' she declared, stretching as an enormous yawn possessed her entire body. 'I'm too tired to go home and deal with all of that. Can I sleep here?'

'You are sleeping here,' I replied, also in no rush to explain this to her mother and grandmother. 'Let's get you up to bed.'

'No, I mean here-here.'

She curled up into a ball, positioning a throw pillow under her head in place of a pillow. 'As in, get your ass out of this and turn off the lights because I love you but I'm about thirty seconds away from complete lack of consciousness.'

'Understood.'

I hopped to my feet as the lights turned themselves down low, the house listening in on our conversation and acknowledging the new witch in the family. It muffled the closing of the door when I stepped out into the hallway, meeting Jackson, a full glass of fizzing soda in his hand, complete with ice and a slice of lemon.

'She's sleeping,' I said, blocking the door. 'Sorry.'

He held the soda out to me, but I declined.

'This feels like a dumb question, but is she going to be all right?'

'She's a witch,' I replied, leading him back down to the kitchen where Ashley was searching through the pantry for the perfect herbal tea blend. 'That's all I can tell you.'

Looking every inch exhausted and defeated, he placed the glass of soda on the kitchen table and wiped a palm across his tired face.

'Em, you said—'

'I know what I said,' I replied. 'I was wrong.'

He considered my statement in silence then slowly shook his head as though he could see no point in arguing. There really wasn't anything else I could say.

'Don't take this the wrong way, but I don't feel great about it,' he replied. 'So far, this magic stuff hasn't exactly been kind to us and regular Lydia is already enough to worry about without her suddenly turning into a witch.'

'Nothing sudden about it.' Ashley opened a jar of pungent culantro leaves that made him gag. 'If Lydia is manifesting magic then she was already a witch. Her abilities may have been dormant but they were there.'

'And there's no way to stop it?'

'Maybe you should ask her if she wants it stopped,' I suggested lightly.

'And while you're at it, ask your mom and your grandmother why they never mentioned any of this to y'all before,' Ashley added over the sound of the tea kettle whistling on the stove. 'They're going to have a whole lot of questions to answer tomorrow morning.'

He groaned, rubbing his eyes with both hands.

'Twelve hours ago I was on vacation,' he said, sliding off the stool and stretching tall. 'Now I'm covered in my friend's blood, running away from werewolves and my sister's a witch.'

'Just an average Thursday night in Savannah,' Ashley commented. 'Go to bed. You can have the couch in my room, Lydia can have the bed. I'll bunk up with Em.'

'Lydia's already out for the count in the parlour,' I replied. 'But you're stuck with me anyway. It's too late to make up the guestrooms, Wyn and Jackson will have to fight over who gets your bed and who gets the couch.'

Ashley and Jackson exchanged a look.

'What?' I darted a glance between the two. 'Did I miss something?'

As soon as the words were out of my mouth, I realized what was wrong with this scene. A very vital piece of our puzzle was missing and I couldn't feel him anywhere in the house.

'Where's Wyn?' I said, scrunching up my hands inside the cuffs of his shirt.

'He didn't tell you?' Jackson asked innocently.

'Tell me what?'

'Wyn went back to Hilton Head to hunt the wolf,' he replied. 'He's gone.'

Chapter Twenty-Seven

'So,' Ashley stared straight ahead as we drove onto the Talmadge Bridge, 'Lydia is a witch.'

'Lydia is a witch,' I confirmed. 'Her mom is going to kill me.'

'It's not like you got her drunk on wine coolers and then went joyriding together. Unless . . .' She glanced across at me. 'You didn't do it on purpose, did you?'

'No!' I tugged against the seatbelt that held me in the passenger seat of Ashley's Mini Cooper, too tight, too restrictive, but knowing Ashley's driving, not optional. 'If there was a choice, I would never have put her at risk.'

Ashley stared dead ahead, driving along the empty road into the darkness.

'She's going to be insufferable.'

'She's going to be incredible.'

'You think it's a good thing?' she asked. 'Not for my blood pressure clearly, but in general?'

'I already feel stronger,' I admitted. 'Sharper. Like the signal is coming in clearer or something.'

'First time we've seen two witch families in Savannah in

decades. Maybe since her great-great-grandmother. This is going to change things.'

'Hopefully for the better,' I replied, but Ashley didn't respond, just reached over and turned on the radio as I burrowed down in my seat, the image of Lydia standing at the edge of the ocean burned into my mind.

With Lydia sleeping so deeply an earthquake wouldn't have woken her, Jackson was nominated to stay at Bell House and make sure she was safe, leaving me and Ashley to go looking for Wyn. None of us were especially happy with the situation but Jackson couldn't very well leave his twin, and the thought of driving around Hilton Head searching for my AWOL boyfriend with him by my side didn't fill me with joy. Which meant Ashley was my only option because I couldn't drive and, unlike my grandmother, I couldn't bring myself to drag Barnett, our family driver, out of bed in the middle of the night. I couldn't bear to drag him anywhere ever – having a driver on call still felt absurd to me – but he'd done Catherine's bidding without knowing for decades and as far as I was concerned, he had a job for the rest of his life if he wanted it.

The car pulled forward, Ashley hitting the accelerator as we left Savannah behind, making our way onto the open road.

'Any idea where your boy's at?'

'Your guess is as good as mine,' I admitted unhappily. 'He's in Hilton Head but I don't know where.'

'I thought you had your special witchy GPS?'

Without asking permission, I turned off the radio; pop songs were too cheerful, slow jams too depressing. In the darkened window of the passenger side, I saw an outline of myself, ghostly and glum.

'Can't see him.'

The Witch and the Wolf

'Can't see anyone or can't see him?'

Back at Bell House, I could feel Jackson's anxiety spiking every time Lydia murmured in her sleep but he needn't have worried. Her energy was golden and bright, even as she slept.

'Just Wyn,' I replied.

'Has that ever happened before?'

'Only once.'

'Em, I appreciate you're going through something but I just crossed state lines in my pyjamas so it would be great to get a little more clarity without having to prise every damn word from your mouth.'

'I couldn't feel him during his phase,' I told her. 'After he turned.'

'But tonight isn't a full moon.'

'Sure isn't.'

'Jeez,' Ashley muttered, slamming her foot down to the floor. 'Wish I hadn't asked.'

Not knowing where to start, I directed Ashley to the Stovells' beach house, peaceful and still, half the lights still on from where we'd run out in such a hurry.

'You're telling me Ileen lets people come stay here all the time? Without charging them a penny?' She gave a low whistle, closing her car door almost silently as she surveyed the front of the property. 'Note to self, be nicer to her at the next historical society meeting.'

If Wyn had come back to the beach house, it wouldn't be to hang out in the den, it would be to investigate the bonfire, but how could he do that without me? He wouldn't understand the crystals or the herbs; running off without me only put him at risk.

'Maybe he's on the beach,' I suggested, directing Ashley to the backyard, too preoccupied to hear her running commentary on the house's finest features. 'Unless you'd rather I leave you with the hot tub?'

'I'd rather you left me in bed,' she replied, following dutifully through the gate. 'But here we are.'

A trace of magic still lingered along the boardwalk. It wasn't so very late, so the beach shouldn't have been deserted. Ashley, with the blessing in her blood, resisted when I pulled her along toward the soaked and smouldering mess down by the water.

'This does not make me want to pull out a guitar and start singing "Kumbaya",' she stated, holding herself back from the stack of wood and ashes, the disjointed ring of crystals still dotting the sand where they had fallen.

'Our oaks.' Ashley laid a hand on one of the blackened tree trunks, her usually dry eyes full of tears. 'This is a nasty business, Em. I really hope Wyn isn't caught up in it.'

'He is caught up in it, because of me,' I told her, slipping one of the larger pieces of quartz and smaller chunks of malachite into the tote bag I'd brought along for that purpose. Crystals used against a witch could be incredibly useful if she survived them.

'And what if he's caught up in it some other way?'

I lifted my head and watched the black waves push and pull each other away from the shore. My mood was so dark, they didn't try to play with me.

'Such as?'

'He is a Were, you are a witch, can I make it any more obvious?' She crouched down beside me, pyjama pants blowing in the night breeze. 'It all seems a little suspect is all.'

'I get it,' I replied, swiping hair out of my face. 'You've been talking to Jackson.'

'More like he was talking at me but I picked up some of what he was putting down, against my will.'

'He isn't exactly an objective observer, you know.'

'Oh, I know.' Ashley gagged, two fingers in her mouth. 'You don't need witchy powers to see what that boy is thinking when it comes to you. I was there when he came to pick you up for the dance, remember? The thing is, just because he's biased doesn't mean he shouldn't be suspicious.'

'No, the fact he's wrong is why he shouldn't be suspicious,' I snapped back. 'I can't believe you're saying this.'

A wave of something ugly passed through me. The henbane still hanging in the air.

'We should get out of here,' I said, holding my arm over my nose and mouth, breathing through the thick fabric of Wyn's plaid shirt. 'This place is still all wrong. I can't think straight.'

'That's the problem though,' Ashley said as kindly as she knew how. 'When it comes to Wyn, I'm not sure you can think straight. Even if he or his pack aren't involved with this lone-wolf Were whatever, do you really want a life this complicated?'

'I want him,' I said, a plaintive statement. 'I'm a Bell witch, aren't I? Born complicated. This is part of the deal.'

'This isn't part of the deal, this is part of being with Wyn. And sometimes I worry you're signing up for more heartache than you'll be able to stand.'

A lighthouse blinked on and off in the distance and I remembered another time at another beach, what seemed like a lifetime ago.

'How come you can't feel him?' Ashley pressed. 'You said yourself the only other time this happened was during his phase, and there's already a Were out there wolfing it up off schedule. You ever hear the saying if you hear hooves in Central Park, don't turn around expecting to see a zebra?'

'Did you ever hear the saying fuck off?'

It took a lot to earn a look of surprise from Ashley but that did it.

'I do believe that is the first time you've ever said that to me. What a date for the diary.'

'I'm sorry, I'm sorry.' I scampered across the beach after her when she turned on her heel and marched away, kicking up sand in her wake. 'I didn't mean it. it's this place and everything that's happening and I'm so tired and—'

'And you don't want it to be true,' Ashley said, a fierce light in her eyes. 'Trust me, honey, I know a thing or two about a thing or two when it comes to convincing yourself of pretty stories. How do you think I managed to keep myself together all these years with Catherine?'

'I am sorry but I do trust him. And I need you to trust me.'

'You stand there talking like you're asking something easy.'

'I know it isn't,' I replied when her eyes filled with phantoms of her past. 'You're all I have, Ash, I need you on my side.'

'Pssh!' She swiped the back of her hand at her face, looking away so I wouldn't see the tears she brushed away. 'You've got Wyn, you've got Lydia, you've definitely got Jackson, whether you want him or not.'

'But you're my only family.'

'Good job I'm the best one,' she said. 'Come on, your boy ain't here.' She put her hand on the small of my back and pushed me towards the Stovells' yard. 'You want to go look someplace else or head home? You look like someone set fire to your hair and tried to put it out with a brick.'

'We could drive around some, check the magic store?'

'When a man doesn't want to be found, you won't find him. Magic or no magic,' she said, practically jumping off the sand and back on to the boardwalk. 'Whatever made him run off like that, I'm sure you're right. He must have his reasons.'

'If I could just know he was OK.'

Reaching deep inside, I tried to see our connection, trust the blessing, know it was there. All the things Catherine and the ancestors told me to do. Still nothing. Without our golden string tying me down, I didn't know what to do, which direction to turn. Something or someone had pulled on our thread and the whole tapestry was unravelling faster than I could stitch it back together.

'A more cynical person might suggest it's not real trust if you've always got to have eyes on him,' Ashley said. 'Eyes, magical connection, an AirTag – same difference. And you do trust him, right? Completely and utterly beyond a shadow of a doubt and I'll never ever ask you this again I swear it on my own life?'

I thought of the second wolf I'd imagined on the beach. Of the ash-haired shadow walking across Lafayette Square in the dead of night. And then I nodded and smiled, allowing Ashley to turn into the Stovells' backyard in silence because anything I did say would be a lie.

Chapter Twenty-Eight

'What is in these biscuits?' Lydia asked as she grabbed for her third helping of breakfast the next morning. Just like she always did in times of trouble, Ashley had turned to baking to soothe her soul, filling the kitchen with so much food, we'd been forced to eat at the dining table just to find room for our plates.

'They're regular biscuits,' my aunt replied, watching on while Lydia smothered honey butter all over both halves then sandwiched it back together before taking an enormous bite. 'They haven't changed.'

'It's your magic,' I explained, wiping sleep from my eyes, still exhausted.

We hadn't found Wyn in Hilton Head, we hadn't found anything save a couple of white-tailed deer and an all-night doughnut shop on the way back to Savannah, and the couple of hours I'd spent tossing and turning in bed weren't nearly enough to prepare me to deal with my newly minted witch.

'While everything is in flux, your senses might be more overpowering than usual,' I told her. 'It'll settle in a day or so, or at least it did for me.'

'It better not. You can't give a girl turbo-charged tastebuds then threaten to take them away.' She piled her already crowded plate with more food: pancakes, waffles, bacon, sausage patties. 'How are you not eating constantly? I have never tasted anything so good. Jackson, you gotta try it.'

'It's a biscuit,' he replied, sullen-faced. 'How good can it be?'

His sister waited impatiently, holding out her breakfast and waiting for him to take a bite. With a disgruntled sigh, he opened his mouth and she shoved it in, making him splutter and cough.

'See?!' she exclaimed. 'Isn't it the best damn thing you ever tasted?'

'It's a biscuit,' he said again, napkin held over his full mouth. 'Excuse me.'

When he stood to leave the table, none of us made any attempt to stop him.

'He'll be fine,' Lydia said, pouring maple syrup all over her plate. 'He was exactly the same when I got my driver's licence before he did.'

'Sure,' Ashley snorted. 'Exactly the same.'

Lydia smiled at her sweetly. 'I'd tell you to shut up but these biscuits may have changed our relationship forever.'

'Good luck ever getting me to make them again.'

'When you've finished eating and bickering,' I started to say, wondering if that moment would ever come to pass. 'We need to figure out how we're going to tell your mom and your grandmother about all of this.'

Lydia dismissed my concerns with a carefree wave. 'Don't sweat it, I know exactly how to do it. I intend to broach the subject with the utmost tact and diplomacy.'

With an uncertain frown, I broke a biscuit in two and swiped on a smear of honey butter.

'Really?'

'Really!' she replied, loud and reassuring. 'One less thing for you to worry about.'

'Hey y'all, did you know I'm a witch?'

Alex Powell went still and Virginia dropped her coffee cup, the precious antique rolling off the breakfast table and onto the floor where it smashed into a dozen pieces.

Hovering behind Lydia, I held up a hand as a hello but kept my mouth firmly shut.

'Mmm, even this toast tastes amazing,' Lydia gushed, grabbing a slice from her mother's plate and taking a bite. 'Em, you want some?'

'I'm fine, thank you,' I said, flashing my eyes at her. It was my own fault. I should've known better than to let it go when she said she knew what she was doing.

'Like I was saying,' she went on as I rushed over to pick up the pieces of Virginia's broken cup. 'I'm a witch. Did y'all know or what?'

'Lydia Virginia Sarah Powell, that's enough.'

Virginia stood, speaking to her granddaughter but staring straight at me and if looks really could kill, I'd have been six feet under the earth in less time than it took to blink.

'It's too early in the day for your nonsense, now please sit down at the table if you're intending to eat. Miss Emily, I'm sure you have somewhere better to be right now.'

'Not nonsense and Emily stays.'

Lydia pulled two chairs out from under the table, one for me and one for her. I took mine reluctantly, really not sure where to look.

'I'm a witch, she's a witch so you're a witch.' She pointed to herself, to me and to Virginia. 'Witches all the way down.'

'This is absurd.' Virginia stood, clutching at the stiff starched

The Witch and the Wolf

collar of her shirt as though it were suddenly choking her. 'This is absurd and I won't listen to it.'

'Anything we can do about that cup? Can you whizz up some magical Gorilla Glue?' Lydia asked as I assembled all the pieces in front of me.

'In theory,' I said, hands hovering over the pieces. 'It's only clay, stone and bone ash.'

'Bone ash?'

'Animal bones.'

'That is so not vegan,' she replied, grimacing. 'Who knew cups could be so gross?'

Virginia pressed her fingertips into her temples, her face pale and drawn. 'Excuse me, I feel my migraine coming on. I'm going to my room, please do not disturb me.'

Lydia gave me a look and without moving, I closed the dining room door.

'So cool,' she said on a sigh. 'Can't wait until I can do that stuff too – and I'll be doing it soon because, like I said before, I am a witch.'

When she raised her voice at the end of the sentence, her grandmother sank slowly back into her chair. Alex, who had not moved since we walked in, picked up her napkin and I saw her dab a single tear away from her eye, just before it fell.

'Who wants to start?' Lydia asked, glancing from family member to family member. 'Mom? Grandmother? Or do you want to let Em take it from the top and y'all can put your pieces in the puzzle after you hear her story?'

'Lydia, stop,' her mother said forcefully. 'You don't know what you're saying.'

'I know I summoned a lightning storm last night. I know I drew water out of the ocean and turned it into rain to put out a fire set by a demon werewolf.'

A tiny gasp escaped Virginia's throat as she touched her hand to her chest.

'Not a demon,' I whispered. 'A regular werewolf. As far as we know.'

'How did this happen?' the oldest Powell woman asked, fingers fluttering at her collarbone.

'Which part?' Lydia replied through a mouthful of toast.

Understandably, her grandmother looked as though she didn't know where to begin.

'I understand if this all feels like a lot to accept,' I told her, no more certain myself. 'It's true, I am a witch, so is Lydia. Your family and mine have a history of magic going back centuries. It's been dormant in the Powell line for years, decades maybe, but there is a prophecy in my family that says a witch will awaken the dormant magic of her sisters—'

'Not only in your family.'

Virginia Powell sat up straight and rested her hands on the table, cool and composed. The frail little old lady who'd existed up until one minute ago disappeared, nothing but a lifelong act.

'So it's you, is it?' She stared at me as though she was seeing me for the first time. 'No wonder Catherine was always so desperate to get you back. You're the one.'

The slice of toast slipped from Lydia's fingers and across the table. Tears flowed freely down her mother's face.

'You knew?' I said, stunned. 'About all of it?'

'Knowing isn't the same as believing,' Virginia replied. 'When Catherine disappeared so very suddenly after your seventeenth birthday, I remembered the stories and the thought began to prey on my mind.'

'You've always known I was a witch?' Lydia slammed a fist on the tabletop, making me and the flatware jump. 'Why didn't you tell me? Doesn't that seem like the kind of thing you'd casually drop into conversation, oh, I don't know, from birth?'

'Please do not raise your voice in my house,' her grandmother chastised, not entirely removed from the woman she was five minutes ago. 'To the best of my knowledge the blessing was dead in our line, but I was concerned enough to encourage some separation between the two of you.'

My turn to ask a question.

'Why? You've been close with Catherine your whole life.'

'Because,' she replied. 'If you were to Become when Lydia could not, I did not want her to spend her life in the shadow of a witch. I know that pain all too well.'

We all sat for a moment, no one sure what to say next. Eventually, it was Virginia who broke the quiet.

'Not for one minute did I ever suspect I would need to explain any of this, or myself, to any of you,' she said, addressing the three of us. Alex remained speechless at her side, worrying the opal ring on the middle finger of her right hand.

'The Powell witches were once almost as strong as the Bells. We have been sisters for centuries, ever since we arrived in Savannah. If a Bell witch died before she could instruct her granddaughter in her ways, a Powell witch stepped in, and vice versa. We have always been close in that way. This friendship,' she gestured across the table to me and Lydia, 'is not a surprise. It's fated.'

'But you don't have magic,' Lydia said, and I could tell by the yearning in her voice, she desperately wanted to be wrong.

'Because people do terrible things to protect those they love.'

Virginia tented her fingers under her chin and stared straight ahead.

'Since before I was born, my existence has been based on a lie,' she began, absently patting her daughter's hand, tears still streaming down Alex's face. 'My mother, Juliet, was only fifteen when she fell pregnant.'

'Juliet?' Lydia interrupted. 'I thought that was your sister's name.'

Despite the wistful smile on her face, Virginia looked so sad, I thought I heard her heart break.

'In 1963, an unwed teenage mother was considered a very shameful thing in polite society. Juliet and her mother, my grandmother, Sarah, left Savannah before she started to show. When Sarah returned, she brought back her daughter's baby and passed me off as her own. People believed Juliet died in childbirth, a tragedy that invited no questions about the authenticity of my parentage.'

'People believed she died in childbirth,' I said, overwhelmed by the rush of revelation coming from the Powell matriarch. 'but it wasn't true.'

'If Sarah had lived longer, there's a chance everything might have been different for me, but she died three years later, leaving me with my great-grandmother, Edwina,' Virginia replied. 'Edwina's mother was a witch, she was a caretaker, but almost all of those she was destined to care for were murdered. Her mother, her daughter and her granddaughter.'

Outside, I heard a rumble of thunder and placed a steadying hand on Lydia's shoulder until the sudden storm passed.

'Her mother was killed in the street on the way home from the theatre, everyone assumed thieves but nothing was taken. Sarah slipped on the staircase of a department store on Broughton Street, hit her head, died instantly. Juliet's death was the ugliest of all. Days away from giving birth, her throat was slit on the porch of the house they were staying in. Her life was taken to prevent mine from ever coming to be but there was a doctor in the house next door. He could not save my mother, he was able to deliver me safely enough.'

'They were all murdered,' I said quietly. 'By whom?'

'I don't know,' Virginia said, before taking a steadying sip from her juice glass. 'She wouldn't speak on it. But Edwina didn't blame the people who slew her family, she blamed the magic that put them in a murderer's crosshairs. And she was determined not to let the same thing happen to me.'

No wonder Virginia was always so sick, carrying the weight of these secrets for so long.

'How could she stop it?'

'Simply enough. A little while before my seventeenth birthday, two weeks perhaps, Miss Bell came to call. It was very late, around midnight, but I had a peculiar feeling she was coming for me and I was awake, waiting for her.' Her gaze drifted over to the dining room door, towards the foyer of her home, phantoms of her past putting on a play just for her. 'Voices were raised, doors were slammed. The very next day, Edwina told me to pack my things and prepare to leave for Europe at once. She was taking me on a tour for my birthday.

'I was, as you can imagine, impossibly excited, until we boarded the airplane and I saw the new moon through the window. Something changed in me that evening and I spent the next two weeks in a daze, no idea what was happening. Edwina called it travel sickness and assured me it would pass. On the night of the full moon, I lay on the bathroom floor of our hotel in Florence, screaming and crying as my magic was expelled from my body. The only time my great-grandmother left her bed was to close the door to the bathroom. The next morning, she greeted me as though nothing had happened.'

The tears I'd been holding in slipped over my lower lashes and when I looked over at Lydia, I saw we were all crying. All of us except for Virginia. Strong and proud, she just looked numb.

'Did Catherine know?' I asked. She had claimed the Powells had no knowledge of their magical lineage but it would hardly be the worst lie she ever told me. 'Surely she would've tried to help you?'

'She did not.'

'But surely the two of you talked about it?' I pressed. 'Surely she would've helped you?'

'I couldn't talk about it because I didn't know,' Virginia said. 'Edwina only confessed her actions to me shortly before her death when I fell pregnant with Alexandra, afraid of history repeating. I didn't know whether to believe her or not.'

'That doesn't explain why Catherine didn't say anything,' Lydia protested, shifting away from me by a degree, as though I shared the guilt she had already assigned to my grandmother. 'She could've explained all of it to you.'

Virginia took an unbroken coffee cup from the set in the middle of the table and poured herself a fresh cup.

'The Bells had good reason not to approach me directly,' she said.

'Which was?'

She stirred the hot coffee with a small silver spoon, tapped it twice on the edge of the china cup then set it on the saucer.

'Edwina threatened to kill Catherine, her mother and her grandmother if they did.'

A heavy quiet overwhelmed us once again.

'I suspect it would be quite impossible for me to impress upon you how very strongly Edwina felt about the corrosive effect of magic on her family,' Virginia added, 'but you must believe me when I tell you she was prepared to kill to be rid of it.'

'They could've killed her,' Lydia said with quiet fury. 'They could've protected our magic.'

'Catherine Bell is a formidable woman.' Her grandmother tasted her coffee before adding half a teaspoon of sugar. 'Her antecedents were not quite so ruthless. Your grandmother was not born, nor was she raised, to be the way she is today. Her mother and grandmother were gentler souls. They would never strike against a sister witch.'

'What I don't understand is how you and Catherine have been best friends your whole life,' Lydia said, drumming impatient, dissatisfied fingertips on the table. 'The topic never came up?'

Virginia laughed, the sound light and unexpected. 'Baby, I do realize you find it almost impossible to live with an unexpressed thought, but you'd be amazed at how many conversations a couple of old friends can have about nothing at all. After a while, I did not think of it and I chose not to share the burden with Alexandra.'

'I knew.'

It was barely above a whisper but the silence that followed her statement was deafening. Virginia, Lydia and I sat around the table in varying states of shock, all of us statues. Through the picture window, I noticed clouds gathering overhead.

'Paul told me when we were teenagers,' Alex went on. 'I didn't believe him. He told me his mother made him promise never to discuss magic with me, so naturally he did. You know what Paul was like.'

'No, I don't,' I replied shakily, thinking of my loyal, steadfast father. 'That doesn't sound like him at all.'

'He was different when we were younger,' she said, looking upwards as she wiped her eyes with her napkin. 'Telling Paul Bell not to do something was the surest way you could guarantee it would be accomplished by sundown. He would talk about it from time to time, make wild claims about his crazy witch of a mother, but as we got older he stopped mentioning the magic, only how much he hated his mother. I didn't even take that seriously until you were born. That's when things began to change. That's when I realized he was genuinely afraid of Catherine.'

A crash of lightning sounded outside the house, so close that it rattled the windows in their frames. I looked nervously over to Lydia. Her irises had turned a pale gold, her stare utterly vacant. Alex and Virginia both stood abruptly, Alex's chair falling backwards and clattering loudly against a serving trolley.

'Lydia,' I said, taking her hand in mine. Her skin was cold and clammy to the touch but I knew to her it must feel red hot. 'Lyds, you have to control it.'

'What's happening?' Alex said, standing in front of her mother. 'Make it stop.'

'I'm trying,' I told her, my attention still fully on my best friend. 'She's not doing it on purpose.'

'Make it stop!' Alex said again before racing around the table to grab Lydia's shoulders, shaking her daughter violently. 'Stop it, I said!'

'Alex, no!'

Virginia flew at her daughter, pulling her away just as a white-hot bolt of lightning sliced through the window and ripped the antique dining table into pieces. As the centuries-old mahogany smoked in matchsticks on the floor, Lydia's eyes shifted back to their regular colour and her body slumped in her chair like a fallen ragdoll.

'I can't do this,' Alex muttered, turning away from her only daughter as though she couldn't bear to look at her. 'I just can't.'

'You can and you will,' Virginia said. 'This is who she is.'

But Alex wasn't ready to accept it. She shook her head and pointed at me, an ugly, frightened twist to her lips.

'That is not who she is, it's what she made her!' she yelled, stalking towards the door, her whole body shaking. 'That is not my daughter. Paul was right to take her away from here but it wasn't enough. If only she'd died instead of him, we would all be better off.'

Chapter Twenty-Nine

Alex Powell's words were still echoing in my mind when I left her mother's house. She wasn't wrong. If I'd died instead of my dad, this wouldn't be happening to Lydia now. If he had kept me away until I lost my magic like Virginia, everything would be different. Guilt rattled my bones.

Virginia had insisted on caring for Lydia in her own home. After helping her up to bed, I left them to talk through their past, present and future together. Alex was long gone and when I stretched out a wide net to find her, I found nothing but a blur, a shadow protected by her opal ring and the miles she had already put between herself and Savannah. I hoped, for Lydia's sake, she'd be back.

One of the most beautiful things about my city was how easily you could get lost on purpose. The walk from Madison Square to Lafayette Square, from Lydia's home to mine, could take as little as five minutes or as long as an hour. The sudden storm she'd brought about left the sidewalks shining and the rain made mirrors of the streets. Every green thing seemed brighter and more vibrant as I breathed in the city, warm soil, humid air, plants and flowers and trees. Alex wasn't wrong but she wasn't entirely right either. Magic wasn't something you had, it was something you were. She may not have known but Lydia was born a witch. Now it was my job to see she came into her magic safely and with love.

Jackson's Audi was still outside when I let myself in the front gate but it wasn't the only vehicle parked up by Bell House. Wyn's cherry-red pickup truck was around the corner, crusts of mud splashed up both sides. Wherever he'd been, he'd come back in a hurry.

I found everyone in the kitchen, Ashley overseeing the glowering Jackson and anxious-looking Wyn, a huge jug of iced lavender lemonade on the table between them, though they both nursed empty coffee cups.

'No one needed more caffeine,' Ashley commented, flashing me a warning look. 'But boys will be boys. And by that, I mean boys will be dumber than a box of hair.'

Neither of them spoke as I poured myself a glass of lemonade, sensing the calming herbs Ashley had thoughtfully added alongside the lavender; chamomile, valerian and just a touch of vanilla to encourage patience and harmony. Even if no one else here wanted them, I did.

'What happened?' I asked, empty and angry and relieved and heartbroken all at the same time. 'I asked you not to go alone.'

'And I told you I had to,' he replied, trying and failing not to let his gaze flick over my shoulder to the spot where Jackson lounged against the kitchen counter. 'It was too dangerous for us to be there together. Didn't help anyways, she's gone.'

'We came looking for you, me and Ashley. I couldn't find you, I couldn't even feel you. The only other time that happened was during the phase.'

An entire field of lavender couldn't have calmed my nerves when his mouth contracted and eyes flared.

'Can we have this conversation somewhere else?' he suggested. 'Alone?'

Behind me, I heard Jackson scoff.

'Don't leave on my account.'

'Wasn't about to,' Wyn replied. 'I think you're confused about which one of us should be walking out the door.'

'How do you know she's gone?' I demanded, directing his attention back to the most important subject. 'Did you find something?'

He looked back to me, a little sheepish. 'Not much. I had her scent on the beach and at the store, but aside from that I mostly picked up a whole lot of nothing. Either I'm not experienced enough to catch the trail or she's covering it up somehow, I don't know.'

'Covering it up with magic?'

'I told you already,' he said, lowering his voice. 'A Were would never.'

'Just like a Were could never phase outside a full moon.' I slammed down my glass, sticky lemonade spilling all over the table. 'She isn't playing by your rules, Wyn.'

'You mean Astrid Hansen?'

Three heads all snapped around to face Jackson as he pushed himself up to sit on the kitchen counter. His white T-shirt was still marked with my washed-out blood from the night before, now a watercolour stain, and his long legs dangled down in front of the creamy white cabinets.

'You don't always need magic to be useful,' he said, rapping his knuckles against the cupboard behind his head. 'I got online after you and Lyds headed home and found out more about this woman in fifteen minutes than he did in – what's it been, twelve hours?'

'What else do you know?' I asked, ignoring Wyn's glare.

'That store has been around for years but when I tried to

call the owners listed with the management company, the Harbors, I couldn't get a hold of them. I finally got through to this kid, Kyle, who was running their Instagram and he filled me in. Said he usually helps out on the weekends during school breaks so he messaged the Harbors about coming in over the summer and didn't hear back but they're always kind of flaky so he went by anyway, found Astrid running the joint and got the hell out of there. Said she gave him bad vibes.'

'And he still hasn't heard from the couple who own the place?'

'Says not. No one has. So I went back to the management company and they confirmed the lease had been amended to include an Astrid Hansen at the beginning of May. Also the Harbors paid their rent up front for the next six months which, according to the guy I talked to, they've never done before.'

'And the management company just told you all this?' Wyn said, a disbelieving slant to his eyes.

'It's amazing what someone will tell you if you pretend you're interested in opening an Apple Store,' Jackson replied laughing. 'Someone at the Robertson Group is going to be super pissed when I don't come back with an offer Saffron and River Harbor can't refuse. That guy would've sold out his own mother for a pair of AirPod Max.'

'We have a name,' I said, excited. 'That's a start.'

Wyn didn't seem to agree. When I turned back to him, his stance was stiff and unyielding, his hands curling into fists.

'This is all amazing,' I said to Jackson. 'Why don't you get off home and rest? You must be exhausted. And I think there's some stuff you need to discuss with your grandmother.'

'I'd rather be here with you,' he replied, and Wyn's fists clenched tighter. 'You need me, Em.'

'What I need is all of y'all out of here,' Ashley said, leaving her safe spot by the sink to waft a dishcloth in Jackson's direction. 'I don't know who it is but someone smells worse than the northbound end of a southbound mule.'

Jackson took a surreptitious sniff of his T-shirt and grimaced. 'Maybe I could run home and shower.'

'Fast as you can, if not faster,' Ashley agreed. 'World'll still be turning when you're done. At least in theory.'

'If I hear anything else, I'll come right back,' he promised. 'We'll get to the bottom of this before the next full moon. I won't let another wolf lay a finger on you.'

When he passed through the back door, leaving it open behind him, Wyn was practically growling.

'That boy is getting spicy,' Ashley said, tossing her dishcloth in the air for Wyn to snatch up in his left hand. 'Nothing like a little healthy competition, huh, Fido? Now get out of my kitchen before I kick both your asses.'

Anyone caught out in the rain might not have been thrilled about Lydia's natural disaster temper tantrum but my garden was thrilled. We hadn't had a shower since the night of the full moon and it was parched. Everything was thriving now. The leaves unfurled to meet the sun with new enthusiasm, every blossom tilted up to the sky, the trees stretching out their limbs like they'd just woken from a deep sleep. And right in the middle of all their beauty was one very angry-looking Wyn.

'It's not like I don't know he has feelings for you,' he began, striding up and down the garden, stomping his feet so heavily that the fish in the koi pond all darted off to the furthest corner. 'But he's not even trying to hide it now, is he? And don't tell me I'm being crazy, because we both know I'm not.'

'What I was going to say' – I gave him a look as I placed our glasses of lemonade on the glass top of the table – 'is that it doesn't matter how Jackson feels about anything. What matters is that I love you.'

He glared at me, those impossible eyes, green and grey with flecks of bronze and gold. 'You have no feelings for him whatsoever?'

'He's my friend,' I replied, a strand of hair falling from a hastily secured claw clip. 'That's all.'

'I get it. He's here all the time, I'm not.' Wyn carried on talking as though I hadn't uttered a single word. 'Your families have known each other for ever. On paper, he's the right pick. He's smart and funny, and I know he's a good guy, he would take good care of you.'

'Can you hear yourself?' I whirled around so quickly, my hair clip came undone and flew across the garden, landing in a small patch of primroses. 'Because right now it sounds like you want to date him. What exactly are you trying to do?'

'I'm trying to make it easier,' he yelled. 'Because when you choose him in the end, it's going to kill me.'

'What are you talking about?' I couldn't believe what I was hearing. 'There's no choosing, there's no choice. At the beginning, at the end, it's you, Wyn, it's always and only ever you.'

'Today it's only me,' he said, screwing his eyes shut. 'You don't know what's coming tomorrow.'

Fighting the urge to scream, I wrapped my arms around his neck, my soft cheek against his granite chest, and listened for the sound of his heartbeat, confirmation that this was still my Wyn and not some jealous lookalike.

'If you race to the end,' I said, still holding on to him. 'You miss all the story.'

A sigh raised his chest then he yielded into me, his arms slipping around my back and cradling my head closer to him.

'If it isn't a happy ending, I don't know if I want to read the rest of the book.'

I pulled back to see his forehead creased with anguish. 'What happened to "this is meant to be"?'

'I don't doubt it for a second,' Wyn said. 'But what if "meant to be" isn't "meant to be forever"?'

It sounded a lot like giving up and I wasn't ready to do that, not yet.

'It's whatever we make it,' I said. 'We're agreed, I love you and you love me. Aren't we supposed to be heading out to a drive-in movie right now?'

'Right now we're supposed to be protecting you from a lone wolf,' he amended, and while he wasn't ready to lighten up completely, I felt the shift in him as he blocked out the future and came back to the present. 'If it is Astrid and she's injured, it's going to take longer for her to heal while the moon is waning. Still another nine days until the new moon.'

'Maybe that's why the Wilcuma takes place on the new moon,' I wondered aloud. 'If that's the safest time, while the wolves are most vulnerable?'

The safe cage of his arms loosened around me.

'Should you be telling me that?'

'You're the one who can't share secrets,' I replied, tightening my grip on him. 'I can't think of one single reason why I need to keep anything from you.'

Gently, Wyn broke free of my grip, grasped my forearms and held me out at arm's length. The loss of his body pressed against mine felt like someone had cut off a limb.

'We should tempt fate,' he said, his thumb rubbing against the inside of my wrist. 'All I'm asking is for you to protect yourself.'

'Protect myself from who?'

He didn't answer.

'Are you lying to me?' I asked and when he looked down at the floor, my stomach clenched. 'I know there are things you can't tell me, but I need to know you aren't lying to me. About anything.'

'There's a difference between lying to someone and only telling them what they need to know.'

'And I thought I'd made it very clear that I don't think that difference is worth much. Where were you last night? What happened exactly?'

'I drove back to the house, I looked for the wolf but I didn't find her,' he replied mechanically. 'Like I already told you.'

'Then why couldn't I find you?' I asked, stabbing at my chest with my finger. 'You're always here, I can always feel you, but last night it was like you'd turned off your signal or something.'

'You're asking me why you couldn't use your magic to hunt me down like a dog?'

I took a step back, stung.

'That came out wrong, that's not what I meant,' he said, mouth puckered up as though he were about to curse himself out. 'I'm sorry. I don't know why you couldn't find me, Em, I couldn't feel you either, but there's no reason I can think of that would explain any of this. How she's phasing, how she's hiding, what that might mean. I don't have any more answers than you do.'

'What about your grandpa?' I asked. 'What about the rest of your pack?'

'I don't know.'

'Don't know or can't tell me?'

'Emily, please!' he exclaimed, raking his hands through his hair. 'I'm doing the best I can.'

I clasped my hands, one on top of the other, over my heart, as if I could somehow protect it from the outside in, but it was much too late for that. The mid-morning heat swept over me and all at once, I was so tired I could barely stand. My sleepless nights, the attack at the beach, Virginia's truth, Alex's reaction, it all hit me at the same time. When I looked up at the house, the sun shone directly on the large picture window on the second floor. Catherine's room. It seemed to shimmer with an iridescence, like the glass had been replaced by moonstone.

'You need to rest,' Wyn said, catching me as I swooned against the table, my legs wobbling under my own weight. 'It's been a rough twenty-four hours.'

'It's been a rough year,' I corrected, confused and exhausted and, above all else, unreasonably sad. 'Maybe you should go too. We can talk later.'

'Later today? If the world doesn't end?'

Pinching my shoulders together in a shrug, I nodded and made my way carefully through the garden, calling on the strength of the hollyhocks and hawthorn bush.

'Now who's tempting fate?' I replied, climbing up the kitchen stairs and leaving him in the garden.

The door to Catherine's room opened with a long, loud creaking sound, as if to ask whether or not I really wanted to be in there. I did. I couldn't say why but ever since I stepped back in the house, there was nothing I wanted more than a long soak in the copper clawfoot tub that sat in front of her bedroom window. The weather was too warm, I couldn't remember the last time I'd taken a bath, but the compulsion was irresistible.

It took a little effort to turn the taps, stuck closed from weeks of disuse, but once they were open, the water ran clean and clear. I let it run until it was scalding hot, holding my hand under the stream until my skin turned pink, then red. I needed to wash the last twenty-four hours away. The hotter the water, the better. Without thinking, I tossed in a handful of bath salts from a collection of jars by the brass towel rack, some dried lavender, mugwort, lemon balm and yarrow, then took some of the crystals from the windowsill where they had been bathing in moonlight for a month – tiger's eye, hematite, obsidian, jade and lapis lazuli – and placed them on the wooden tray that lay across the tub.

When the water was almost to the top, I peeled off my sticky clothes and stepped in, barely even flinching at the scorching temperature. My hair floated on the surface as I looked around Catherine's untouched room. The bed was made, her clothes put away. On the antique dresser, I saw a handful of silver framed photographs, one of Catherine and her husband on their wedding day, a baby dressed in blue and then another, dressed in pink. My dad wearing a mortar board and a scowling picture of Ashley that could've been taken at any point between her sixteenth birthday and two months prior. Then, at the very front, there was a photo of me and Catherine, kneeling in the back garden, examining plants. Ashley must've shot it, unless there was a friendly ghost lurking in the house with a Polaroid, but she had never shown it to me. Most likely because we were far from the best of friends when she shot it and yet, she took it anyway. The other photos were all posed and formal, wedding clothes and smiling babies, graduations, birthdays, but this one was more natural. Catherine smiled at me with what looked like genuine affection and I was delighted by whatever praise she was lavishing upon me. It really had been like that, if only for a moment, but those days had truly existed.

I sank down into the water, letting my hair float until it soaked through and sank around my shoulders, only my face breaking the surface. Around the outside of the tub, a circle of white candles flamed into life and even though it was still early in the day and the sun rode high in the sky, the light in Catherine's room dimmed until they were the only source of illumination. The panes of glass in the window turned black and a wave of exhaustion came over me. I closed my eyes and inch by steady inch, slipped under the surface of the water.

When I opened them, I was in Bonaventure Cemetery. Wyn

lay on the floor before me, cut open, his blood blooming in the dirt. Seven figures surrounded us in a circle, the same as before, Catherine, Ashley, Lydia, Jackson, Alex Powell, Wyn's mother and brother, the still unknown man all took one step closer, passing something between themselves. It was the branch-like sword, its silver blade and gold hilt hungry and rusty with blood. Each beheld it with reverence as it passed from person to person, Lydia to Ashley, Ashley to Catherine, Catherine to Jackson, Jackson to Wyn's mother, Wyn's mother to Alex Powell and Alex to the man I had never met. Somewhere in the distance, I heard wolves howling, in victory or anguish, I wasn't quite sure.

'It should've been you,' the man said when the sword fell into his hands, his voice full of gravel and hate. 'In time, it will be.'

He took a step forward into the centre of the circle, holding out the blade and I moved backwards, keeping one hand on Wyn's prone form, but instead of attacking me, he lunged at everyone else, stabbing each of them directly in the heart. One by one, he moved from person to person and no matter how loudly I screamed and begged them to run, they stood their ground, waiting for their untimely deaths, never once taking their eyes off me.

'You are death,' the man declared, slowly sheathing his blade in Jackson's heart as my friend stared back at me, his face contorted in a silent scream. 'All who follow will fail, all who love will lose.'

Finally, when they were all bleeding out into the cemetery ground, he lunged at me, but when I tried to run, black roots twisted up from the earth, tying themselves in knots around my feet and ankles. Even the plants had been turned to darkness in this place, and when I called for my ancestors, I felt nothing. They were gone. The consecrated ground of the Bonaventure corrupted.

'No!' I screamed, delving into the deepest reaches of my magic to free myself. 'This isn't real! You aren't real!'

But it felt real. The black flames running along the Spanish moss kissed my skin with blisters and when the tides roared up from the river, twenty feet tall, I could smell the saltwater. With black fire immolating every tree, running along the Spanish moss, I turned to Catherine where she lay on the ground, dying but not dead.

'You must make the choice,' she whispered, blood dripping from her mouth as she spoke. 'Save this world or end it. Find your peace.'

Find my peace? When everyone I knew and loved was dead on the floor around me?

A rough, leather gloved hand gripped me by the throat and hoisted me into the air, and as the sword pierced my heart, I awoke with a start, gasping for air as I sat up, water splashing onto the floor around the tub.

'You changed your future once, you can change it again.'

Right at the edge of the bed, dressed in her favourite blue silk gown, Catherine beheld me with emerald eyes. Her hair was pinned up away from her exquisite face. She twisted her aquamarine ring around and around on her finger as she spoke.

'He is coming,' she said. 'Lives will be lost. Which lives and in what order, is very much up to you.'

'No one is going to lose their life.' I clung to the side of the tub, my heart pounding. 'Who is he? What does he want?'

Still on the bed, she smoothed imperceptible wrinkles out of her skirt with both hands.

'An end,' she replied. 'To magic.'

'All magic? Not just witches?'

'Like most men who wish to remove something from this world, he doesn't truly understand what he desires.'

'Magic is part of the world,' I murmured, shivering at the

memory of his sword piercing my skin. 'It's part of nature, you can't erase nature. He can't possibly understand what we are, why would anyone try to wipe out something they don't understand?'

'Oh, Emily, that's the only reason they need,' Catherine replied with a disappointed shake of her head. 'Did your father teach you nothing?'

The candlelight pulsed as she stood, walked over to the bathtub and picked a fluffy towel from the brass rack.

'We miss you,' I told her, a confession, as she laid the towel on the side of the tub. 'Me and Ashley. When are you coming back?'

She pushed the wet hair off my face.

'If and when I'm needed.'

'You're needed now.'

'No,' she said. 'My part is done. I brought you here.'

The flames of the candles flared and I looked over at the pictures on the dresser, flames licking at the photograph of Catherine's wedding and the picture of my dad, the images burning away under the glass.

'Protect the blessing and the blessing will protect you,' Catherine instructed. '*When the dead fight back. When the earth consumes. A lie becomes the truth. She will return.*'

Every single candle in the room guttered at once and when my eyes adjusted to the semi-darkness, I was alone. Outside the bedroom window, the sun had set and the sky was dark, pinpricks of stars the only thing illuminating the room now. The carriage clock by the bed said it was past 9 p.m. Half a day had passed since I filled the bath but the water was still hot enough to turn my skin lobster pink. Carefully, I climbed out, searching for crucial evidence my grandmother had ever been here, that I hadn't imagined the whole thing. Had she left the towel on the side of the bath or had I put it there myself?

One thing was certain, the silver frames on her dresser weren't full of ashes when I entered her room. At the end of the bed there was a depression in the quilt, as though someone had been sitting there for some time, watching over me.

And right beside it, Catherine's aquamarine ring.

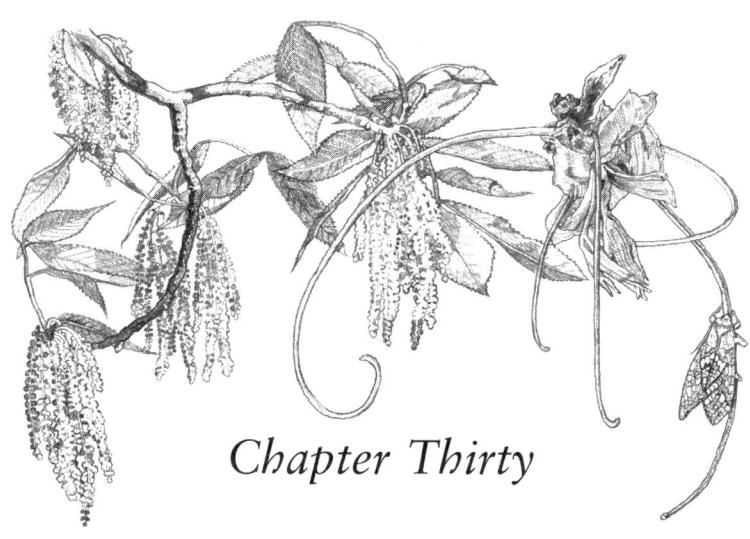

Chapter Thirty

'Em, there's someone at the front door for you.'

'Wyn?' I looked up at Ashley from the kitchen table, heart in my mouth. I'd barely seen him since the difficult conversation we had in the garden three days before. But Ashley glowered at me from the doorway. Whoever it was appeared to be an unwelcome guest.

'The Weres?' I guessed.

'Worse.'

What could be worse?

'The police?' I barely managed to sound out the second word.

'I said *worse*.'

Cocking her head for me to follow, I decided she was right. Waiting on our front doorstep, shielding herself from the sun underneath the portico, was Ileen Stovell.

'Ms Stovell.' I forced myself to sound cheerful, as though she wasn't one of the last people I'd hoped to find waiting for me. 'How nice to see you.'

She waited, anticipating an invitation inside but there was no way I was having this woman in my house. Ashley hovered at my shoulder until she was certain I wouldn't cave then melted away into the parlour, hissing like a cat as she went.

'Can I help you with something?' I asked, all innocence. 'I'm afraid my grandmother is still out of town.'

'Still?'

'Still.'

'Then perhaps I might speak to your aunt if she is the person responsible for you,' she said, as tightly wound as ever.

She was only a small woman but she more than made up for her short stature with an enormous attitude. Combined with the persistent itch that scratched at my magic whenever she was around, I couldn't get her away from the house fast enough.

'No one is responsible for me, I'm seventeen.'

'And still a minor.'

'And more than capable of looking after myself,' I said. 'What can I do for you?'

Any smart woman knew which battles to fight and which to yield, whether it was negotiating my TV time when I was eleven or trying to get Ashley to do literally anything she didn't want to, you had to know when to expend your energy and when it wasn't worth it. Ms Stovell decided to move on.

'I understand you recently visited my home on Hilton Head, according to Virginia Powell, that is.'

'That's right,' I replied, only slightly wounded by her precise blow. My dad would've had me sitting at the desk, writing out a thank you card before we'd left the house but in all the drama, it hadn't crossed my mind. 'It was so kind of Lydia to invite me along as her guest and so kind of you to host us. It's a beautiful home.'

'It is,' she agreed. 'And I wish you and the Powells had left it as you found it. I believe this belongs to you.'

She slid her hand into a large leather purse that hung from

her shoulder, the handle decorated with a twisted silk scarf, and pulled out my Braves jersey. Immediately I held out a hand to grab it back, stunned that I hadn't noticed it was missing. Truly I'd been more than preoccupied but I was never, ever without it, one of the few things I owned that used to belong to my dad. Before I could reach it, Ms Stovell withdrew the jersey.

'Or is it possible this belongs to the young man who accompanied you and the twins to the island?'

'It's mine,' I said tactfully. No need to confirm or deny her gossip, no comment, plead the fifth, nothing to see here.

'It's no business of mine what happens under Catherine's roof,' she replied, still holding on to the shirt. 'But in my house, as a guest of my friends, I'm afraid it's unacceptable behaviour and I'm afraid I have no choice but to inform your grandmother. I'm mightily disappointed in Alexandra and Virginia. What they were doing letting you children run riot is beyond me.'

With that, my tact ran out.

'I'm sorry if you're offended,' I told her, all the strength of Bell House shooting iron through my spine. 'The twins didn't tell me or our friend, also an invited guest of the Powells, that the house came with a set of rules. And like I said, Catherine isn't here. Feel free to let her know when she gets back.'

Her narrow, hawk-like eyes widened and her face turned pale, clashing horribly against her butter yellow blazer and baby blue sundress. It was rude, so rude of me, but I didn't have the time or energy for etiquette.

'If that's it, can I have my jersey back? It belonged to my dad.'

I held out my hand expectantly and almost in shock, she passed it over.

'Wait,' she said, dropping the jersey to the floor and snatching up my hand instead. 'Is that Catherine's ring?'

The instant her skin touched mine, I left the present, a rush of black and then another sunny day, another Ileen Stovell stood on the porch of Bell House, younger and less severe. By my side, two teenagers, one redhead and one brunette. Virginia and Catherine.

'What do you want?' Catherine groaned at the tiny blonde on the doorstep.

'My mama said I could come visit,' Ileen replied, unbearably hopeful and shifting her weight from foot to foot as the two older girls silently debated her response.

'Did we invite you to come visit?' Catherine asked, petulant.

'No, but—'

'Then tell your mama we're too busy today. Come back tomorrow.'

'Tomorrow?' Ileen went from crushed to visibly thrilled in less time than it took for me to cringe. 'Same time or—?'

'Sure,' Catherine said as she closed the door in the other girl's face, Virginia giggling at her elbow. 'Any old time.'

'OK! I'll see y'all tomorrow!' she called, waving at no one, Catherine and Virginia already cackling to each other in the kitchen, making plans to leave for Tybee Island without her at the crack of dawn.

I watched through the window as Ileen skipped away, no idea she was being double-ditched, and felt a pang of sympathy.

'S-sorry,' I stammered as the past disappeared and I found myself shoved violently back into the present. 'I'm sorry.'

'I have not seen your grandmother without that ring since her own mother died,' Ms Stovell said, completely unaware of what I'd seen. The blessing didn't think she needed to relive the memory with me and I wondered if that was an important moment, not a huge defining occurrence, but one of those unpleasant little things that made you who you were, almost against your will. How many times had she been rejected by Catherine and Virginia over the years? Women she still called her friends today, who she invited to her home, looked out for when they were supposedly on vacation. I wondered if their indifference still hurt the same.

'How do you have her ring?' she asked, and I realized she was genuinely worried about Catherine. My heart sank to think she might never know the truth, about what happened to my grandmother or how she felt about her so-called friend.

'It's not Catherine's, it's a replica,' I lied, hiding the jewellery underneath the jersey I retrieved from the floor to avoid further inspection. 'She had it made for my birthday.'

It was obvious she didn't believe me but as my face heated up, the sun became unbearably hot, causing the birds and the trees and Ileen Stovell all to swoon.

'Well, Miss Emily, I can't stand outside in this heat, but I want you to know I have my eye on you as I know your grandmother would prefer it.'

'I'm sure she'll appreciate it. I would invite you in, only I'm literally on my way out the door,' I said, too late for her to believe me. 'If you wanted to come over some other time, I'd love it.'

Something ugly flickered in her memory and I flinched, knowing exactly what it was.

'I have guests right now, I simply cannot commit to anything,' she muttered, backing away from the house. 'Just know I'm watching you, Emily Bell.'

'Appreciate it,' I called as she left, leaving the door open and watching until she was all the way out of sight.

Catherine had her whole life to prepare for my Becoming. I had less than three weeks before Lydia's and only seven days until her Wilcuma.

Not that anyone was doing anything to make my life any easier. Wyn was trying to act as though nothing was wrong, Jackson falling over himself to be of use and Lydia determined to master her magic as soon as possible, resulting in thunderstorms, record high temperatures and a tiny cyclone in Susie King Taylor Square that made the local news. Astrid didn't attack, Wyn was certain she would wait until she was at full strength, but the threat of violence, from her and the man in my visions, lingered around Bell House like a bad smell and my anxiety over Lydia's initiation into the blessing didn't help in the slightest. It was only a month and change since I'd gone through the rituals but it felt like years ago, the memories marring what came before and after. There were no other experienced witches to walk me through the requirements, my favourite ghostly mentor was once again absent, so there was only one place to go.

'Just the basics,' I said, one hand on the door to my craft room, waiting to be granted entry. 'That's all I need. Doesn't need to be a whole production, I just need to get it right.'

But the house knew me better. I'd always been an overachiever when it came to my homework, I was my father's daughter, after all. So when I crossed the threshold into the peaceful space, the desk was already laden with objects, some I recognized, some I did not. A soft white leather journal was positioned in front of the chair and, as I sat, it uncurled itself like a cat waking up from a nap. The pages were blank – or at least they were until I touched them.

'A new moon represents new beginnings,' I uttered under my breath as the words etched themselves into the page in beautiful cursive handwriting I recognized from somewhere. 'A new moon allows us to set our intentions.'

These were the words Catherine had spoken to me at Wormsloe, I was sure of it. As the sentences flowed across the page, my memory sharpened, the wall of trees, the silver dagger, water, earth, fire, air. Flipping through the book, I watched as the pages filled themselves with the correct pronunciation of the incantations, phases of the moon, necessary herbs and crystals, everything I could possibly need to make sure things went smoothly.

'This is exactly it,' I whispered excitedly, smiling at the rippling rainbow-tinted walls. 'Thank you.'

With the journal held tightly to my chest, I shot up to leave but when I tried to open the door, it wouldn't budge.

'Very funny,' I said with a grunt, twisting the handle and pulling as hard as I could. 'Can't very well conduct a Wilcuma if I can't get out of the room, can I?'

The room did not respond. I stepped back from the door and it opened on its own, with a quiet click.

'Appreciate it,' I muttered, and stepped out into the hallway, making it as far as the bottom of the stairs before something told me to check the journal.

I opened the cover to see the first page was blank. And the next. And the next. I thumbed through every page, finding nothing but fresh, untouched, blinding white paper. The soft peach wallpaper warmed up to a peppery pink and I sighed.

'This is the worse practical joke ever.'

Another glance at the book revealed the same blank pages.

With a laborious groan, I turned back to the craft room, the door wide open, waiting for me, and as soon as I stepped inside, the pages of the book were full again.

'Libraries let you take books home,' I said. 'I promise I won't take it out of the house?'

The room replied by slamming the door shut as the chair pulled itself out from under the desk. The book was too precious, the knowledge contained inside too dangerous to risk falling into the wrong hands.

'Message received,' I said, taking my seat and settling in to study. 'Message received.'

Hours later, the doorbell rang, chiming through the cloistered silence of the craft room. Ashley was out again, I'd felt her leave hours earlier, off to another club or class or activity, but the house didn't usually disturb me when I was at work so I closed my books and left the room to investigate, words fading away from the pages as soon as I stood up from the desk.

Waiting patiently in the fading twilight, his face obscured by an enormous bouquet of wildflowers, was Wyn.

'Good evening, Miss Emily,' he said, dipping into a bow. 'I was wondering if you had plans this evening?'

'If by plans you mean staring at the same six words over and over until they lose all meaning then yes,' I replied, my heart soaring into the sky as he brought the flowers inside and placed them on a side table, the whole foyer sighing a soft romantic pink at the sight of them.

'In that case, I have an alternative suggestion.'

He took me by the hand, leading me back out the front door and around to the back of the house. There in the garden, someone had stretched a white sheet against the back wall and set up a projector, connected to a laptop. Two sun loungers sat side by side in front of the screen and the little wrought-iron table I hadn't so much as laid eyes on for the last few busy days was covered in sweets and snacks and sodas. There was even a miniature version of a popcorn machine, the glassed-in kind from the movie theatre.

'I know everything is crazy right now but I want you to know I'm never not thinking about us,' Wyn said, standing behind me, hands on my shoulders. 'You shouldn't have to sacrifice the things you want because of circumstances beyond your control.'

The Witch and the Wolf

'Like a drive-in movie?'

'Since we won't be able to make it over to the drive-in at Beaufort right away, I brought the drive-in to you. And the best part is, you get to pick the movie yourself.'

'This is incredible.' I whirled around to find him smiling, that same old easy smile I'd missed these past few days. 'How did you do all this? When did you do all this?'

'Today and with lots of help,' he replied before giving me the softest, gentlest kiss, any trace of the antagonism between us blowing away. 'Lydia loaned me the popcorn maker and Ashley helped me put up the screen. The projector and the snacks I managed all by myself.'

'And the snacks are the most important part,' I said, eyeing the boxes of concession stand candy, Sour Patch Kids, Milk Duds, peanut and regular M&Ms.

Wyn reached for a box of Junior Mints, tore it open and offered them to me. Truly he knew the way to my heart.

'You're the most important part. No point in any of this if we're not together, if we can't have moments like this.'

It felt so selfish, taking time away from my research to do something just for me, but when I looked at him and he looked at me, I knew he was right. What were we fighting for if not us? All the what ifs in the world wouldn't change that.

'Things might look different for us,' he said, 'than they do for other people. Different doesn't make it wrong, doesn't make it not worth having.'

'Things look exactly as they should,' I told him, putting aside the candy and taking my rightful place in his arms. 'As long as you're here.'

'I'm sorry for acting jealous,' Wyn whispered when his nose brushed against mine.

'I'm sorry you thought there was anything to be jealous of,'

I replied. 'This is the most thoughtful thing anyone has ever done for me. Thank you, I love it.'

Across the square, I heard the cathedral bells chime the hour.

'Sit down,' he said with a light kiss to my lips. 'The movie is about to start.'

I did as I was told for once, settling into my chair as some movie studio's logo appeared on the screen, completely interested in what movie was about to play. My happy ending was sitting beside me, holding my hand and feeding me candy. And I would fight for it until the end.

Chapter Thirty-One

By the time the night of the new moon arrived, I was a mess.

In the mornings, I woke up exhausted and at night, I was so anxious, I couldn't sleep. At least that was one thing working in my favour as I watched the clock in my room tick closer and closer to midnight.

Sitting cross-legged on my bedroom floor instead of in the roll-out bed Ashley made up for her, Lydia was playing with a smoky quartz point as if she were conducting a single-person game of spin the bottle. I put down the book I was pretending to read and watched as she paused to take a drink, pulling snowflakes from a glass of water.

'So cool,' she grinned, heartily smacking her lips.

'Have you heard from your mom today?'

Her grin disappeared.

'Alexandra is playing the yes-no game.'

'Alexandra?' I repeated. 'Ouch.'

While Virginia had been promoted back to grandmother, Alex Powell was no longer afforded the privilege of being called 'mom'. Jackson hadn't mentioned her absence at all and Lydia only suffered talking about her if forced. When she ran out the morning after Lydia's magic manifested, I was sure she'd come right back but she hadn't crossed the state line back into Georgia one time.

'Tell me again about the different kinds of magic?' Lydia was a master at changing the subject. She rolled onto her belly, still toying with the smoky quartz point. 'How many are there?'

'This is as new to me as it is to you,' I said. 'Catherine could harness the elements. She told me about ancestors who could talk to the dead, others who were healers. Most witches specialize in one kind of magic. Yours is manipulating the weather.'

As evidenced again when she accidentally made it hail in the back garden an hour earlier.

'Lydia Powell, weather witch.' Snowflakes settled around her on the floor as she tested the sharp end of the grounding crystal against her fingertip. 'I'm into it. I'm stronger than I was before, faster too.'

'Do you need anything?' I asked, checking the clock again. Almost eleven thirty. Almost time. 'Are you hungry? Do you want something to eat? Do you need the bathroom?'

'No thanks, mom,' she replied, laughing. 'What other abilities will I have?'

'I don't know.'

'Will I be able to see ghosts?'

'No idea.'

'Will I be able to hex people?'

'Even if you could, you probably shouldn't.'

'Will I be able to fly?'

'Lydia.'

I looked at her over the top of my book.

'What?!' She picked up the quartz and tapped it against the end of her nose. 'I need to know these things!'

'Have you ever seen me read someone's mind?'

The Witch and the Wolf

'I haven't seen you do a lot of things,' she replied, waggling her eyebrows up and down. 'Doesn't mean you're not doing them.'

'Believe me, I'm not doing anything you don't know about.'

Dropping the book on my nightstand, I checked my phone, finally working again but there were no messages.

'Wyn won't give it up, huh?' Lydia hopped to her feet gracefully and launched herself onto my bed. 'What a prude.'

'Very funny.' I tapped her arm with my foot and rolled onto my side. 'Things are complicated enough right now, don't you think?'

She pulled herself up the bed until we were face to face and rested her head on her hand, her elbow digging into the pillow.

'Maybe but I hate seeing the both of you all tore up like this and don't you dare tell me you're fine because that dog won't hunt. You want to talk about it? Unless the problem is Jackson because—'

'It is not your brother,' I promised, stopping her before she could start. 'Not that he isn't doing his best to wind Wyn up, but Jackson isn't the issue.'

'Good. I've always been a why choose girlie, but not if it involves my brother.' Lydia pulled a sour face and for a second I was genuinely concerned she was about to bring up her dinner. 'All this macho nonsense would be annoying at the best of times but the way he's acting right now . . . he ain't got the sense God gave a goose. I've told him a thousand times, he's never going to get between the two of you.'

'Could you tell Wyn?'

'Please,' she said, rolling her eyes. 'If he didn't love you so damn much he wouldn't be so mad at my idiot brother.'

It made sense. If Wyn didn't care, he'd be happy to have Jackson's help. When I wasn't shut up in the craft room, trying to memorize as much information as the house and my ancestors were prepared to share, I was working with Lydia to manage her connection to the blessing. The few stolen minutes I had to myself all went to Wyn but somehow, Jackson always seemed to know exactly when to appear and I never sensed him coming, too caught up in everything else that was going on.

'It's all going to work out for the best,' Lydia promised. 'And if it doesn't, I'll whip him up in a tornado and send him to Oz.'

'Don't make me hold you to that,' I said, rolling over and reaching under the bed. I pulled out two small bundles, handing one to Lydia and keeping one for myself. 'This is for you, put it on.'

My sewing skills were not the strongest, but I'd done the best I could without the help of a seamstress. When I'd gone to see the dressmaker who made my Becoming gown, she had altogether too many questions about my grandmother for me to stick around.

'Oh, hell no!' Lydia held up the very simple shift, examining it with extremely judgemental eyes. 'What is this supposed to be? A pillowcase?'

'It's a dress,' I said as I yanked off my pyjamas and pulled my matching dress over my head. 'Be quick, we're on a schedule.'

'On a schedule for what?'

'Can't tell you yet.'

On my nightstand, my phone lit up with one single word. *Here.*

'Oh jeez, is this a witchy thing?' Lydia's excitement whipped up a gust of wind to make her hair dance around. 'Am I getting my broom? Are we going to adopt a cat? I know black is traditional but I'm thinking more of a calico vibe.'

'Lydia Powell, quit talking, put on the dress, and if you need to use the bathroom go now because we've got a long night.'

I gave her my best senior witch stern stare.

The Witch and the Wolf

It had no effect whatsoever.

'OK but I need to grab a soda on my way out, I'm kind of parched,' she replied as she sailed into my bathroom, peeling off her clothes as she went. 'Ooh, and a snack. Maybe some chips and if Ashley has any cookies left over, I would love something sweet as a chaser.'

All those hours I'd spent locked in the craft room, memorizing the language, practising the movements, so afraid I'd do something to mess up this moment. And Lydia wanted to take cookies.

'Note to self,' I muttered as I gathered my things and set off downstairs. 'Be more Lydia.'

Chapter Thirty-Two

'This is it.'

At my direction, Wyn pulled his truck off the road and came to a stop in front of a small cabin I thought I'd forgotten but remembered at once.

'We're getting out here?' Lydia asked.

'We're getting out here,' I confirmed as she tossed back her head to drain her soda. 'Take nothing with you.'

'What about my phone?'

'No.'

'My chips?'

'No chips.'

'But what if Wyn eats them?'

'I solemnly swear I will not eat your chips,' Wyn said, immediately reaching into the bag to steal one. 'At least not all of them.'

'Thank you for this,' I said as she hopped out, leaving the two of us alone in the front of the cab. 'I'm not sure how long we'll be, could be hours.'

'I'll be here.'

He ran his hand down my arm, snapping back when he

reached the blade I had hidden in my woefully sewn sleeve. 'Em?' he said, his sleepy eyes suddenly alert. 'Should I be worried?'

'It's just part of the ritual, no one is going to get hurt.'

The journal I'd spent so long studying assured me of that, but I couldn't quite see how plunging a dagger through my hand would be pain-free. Just like the time I let Lydia do my makeup, I was trying very hard to trust the process.

'No matter what you hear, I want you to stay in your truck,' I told him. 'It may get weird but we'll both be OK.'

'You'd be amazed at how many times I've heard that over the last few months. Starting to think it might be nice to drive into the woods sometime without a "this could get weird" warning up top. We should plan a camping trip.'

'A camping trip with hot running water and a private indoor bathroom?' I asked hopefully.

'We should sleep out in your backyard sometime,' he amended, tenderly brushing his hand against my face. 'Me, you and the stars. Nothing and no one else around.'

'It's a date.' I smiled back, that golden pull sparkling as our lips met.

The spark of wanting him burned through me, fuelled by the magic I already felt rising with the moon. Out of breath, I broke away and rested my fingers against his lips, his ever-changing eyes deep, dark pools of desire.

'Whatever you hear, stay away,' I said again. 'Promise?'

I didn't want to scare him but I was afraid what might happen if a Were tried to follow us under the oaks.

'A wolf has no place in a witch's business,' he replied easily, a statement not judgement, then kissed my fingers and pressed them to my own lips. 'I'll be here, waiting. With the snacks.'

'You are a snack,' Lydia said, appearing at the open window.

'Em, can we get this show on the road already? I want my super powers.'

'Abilities,' I reminded her for the thousandth time as I climbed out the cab. 'Let's hope our ancestors are in a good mood.'

'Woah, the floor is squishy!' Lydia exclaimed, leaping around as we entered the avenue of oaks, her feet bare and her eyes alight. 'This is wild. I must've been to this place damn near a hundred times and I never noticed before.'

The trees arced towards one another, bowing to us as we passed. The Spanish moss hung still, unmoving in the chill night air. I looked up at the interwoven branches and felt an unexpected longing for Catherine's strong comforting presence. She would know what to say right now, she would know what to do.

'I really need you to take tonight seriously,' I told her, shaking my head when she reset her face into a most solemn pout. 'This is the Wilcuma, it's part of your initiation.'

She walked onwards without fear, her head tilted back to take in the static trees.

'Why doesn't the Becoming have a spooky sounding name?'

'It does have another name,' I replied, the knowledge appearing in my mind. 'The original name for the rite is Weorden but our ancestors chose the Becoming.'

'Why?'

'You'll have to ask them.'

'Will I meet them?'

I didn't answer because I couldn't. I didn't know the answer.

'What's going to happen?' Lydia asked. 'Or are we just taking a sweet barefoot stroll?'

She'll see soon enough.

The words whispered through the static leaves but if Lydia heard them, she didn't show it.

The Witch and the Wolf

'We need to keep moving,' I said as we reached the end of the avenue, holding my breath until Lydia passed underneath the final tree without incident. 'We don't have much time.'

'Much time for what?'

'You'll see soon enough,' I said, a strange echo to my voice. 'Follow me.'

By the time we reached the woods, Lydia wasn't speaking to me. The trees trembled with anticipation, branches, boughs and trunks twisting this way and that, opening up a path that had been walked by a hundred witches before me. I thanked them all, my skin electrified, every brush of every leaf sparking a chain reaction in my body I could not and did not wish to control. Doubt had pulled me out of shape but now I was exactly where I was supposed to be. I felt infinite. Our magic sang on the air, loud and clear, and drew us onwards.

'Do you know where we're going?' Lydia asked, breaking the longest silence she'd ever kept in her life. She sounded hushed and uncertain, all of her exuberance smothered by the pitch-black night around us.

'It's this way,' I said with a nod, the path as clear to me as if it were lit up with neon lights. 'Can't you hear it?'

'Hear what?'

I looked back to see her holding onto herself, one arm pulled across her chest and gripping the other tightly.

'You don't need to be afraid,' I said, the ebb and flow of energy directing me. 'Look up.'

She did and she gasped. A velvet sky stretched out across forever, studded with every star that had ever existed. Whatever was about to happen, had already begun and all that time I'd spent studying dissolved into my blood, leaving my conscious mind and seeping into a place where it already seemed to live.

'This is the place.'

My voice was firm and strong. No point lowering it out here, we were completely alone. The woods, the earth, the air and sky, and directly above us the new moon shone down, a pure slice of light and a promise of what was to come.

'Em?' Lydia said as I squatted down to dig my hands into the dirt, silk against my skin. 'Em, what's happening to the trees?'

'They're acknowledging you,' I said without looking up.

Freezing rushes of fear shot out all around her but I couldn't understand why. Everything was perfect. The trees sighed with happiness as they wove themselves into a ring, protecting us from harm. Not even a wolf could touch us here, we were completely safe.

'A new moon represents new beginnings,' I intoned, the words flowing out of me as easily as air. I circled Lydia, so full of love for my friend, for all my sister witches, alive and dead, I could barely breathe. 'A new moon allows us to set our intentions. A new moon welcomes you, Lydia Virginia Sarah Powell. Wilcuma.'

'Wilcuma yourself,' she muttered back, spinning around to keep her eyes on me. 'Can you stop? You're making me dizzy.'

'All of those who came before and all of those to come. We ask you to acknowledge us.'

'Acknowledge me,' Lydia said in a booming voice. 'OK, ow?'

She winced when I took hold of her wrist and pulled her down to the ground until the pair of us knelt in the dirt. The sacred circle drew magic from the moon, funnelling it from the sky to infuse the air around us with an energy so intoxicating, I had to tighten my grip on Lydia's wrist to stop myself from floating away.

'You're hurting me,' she said with tears in her eyes, twisting against my grip, but I couldn't let her go, not when our sisters were so near. 'Em, please, I'm scared, tell me what's happening.'

'Just listen,' I replied, pulling the long, pointed dagger out from my sleeve and placing it on the ground between us. 'Just be.'

The fear in her eyes evolved into terror but it made no sense. Why couldn't she feel the love that surrounded us? The stars burned brighter and I felt Lydia's magic coursing through her as her lips opened and she sucked in the deepest breath.

'What's happening?' I heard her say as the world darkened around me. 'I feel like I'm going to explode and – Emily, your eyes?'

My spirit soared up above the circle and Lydia screamed as though someone was separating her flesh from her bones. Watching from above, I saw myself holding her down. She thrashed around, arms and legs spasming in the dirt, moss and grass and muck staining her white shift. She clawed at my arm and wrist, nails raking my flesh but I couldn't feel it, even as the sleeve of my dress turned scarlet. Reluctantly, I floated back down to my body like a feather, filling myself up to the brim, more than I was before.

'Earth,' I said, sliding her hand into the ground, no longer a solid mass but soft and yielding, like a warm bath.

'Water.'

Rain came pouring down, bathing our bodies, our souls. I turned my face upwards and let the warm water wash me clean.

'Fire.'

I welcomed the flames as they flickered into life, caressing the tops of the trees as they grew, Lydia's screams a world away as they warmed my skin.

'Air.'

The rain stopped and the fire burned out. There was no sound, no heat, no anything. It felt like bliss.

'I can't breathe,' Lydia choked, clawing at her own throat with her one free hand.

Her panic was so strange to me. The whole clearing sparkled, the trees bejewelled, rubies, emeralds and sapphires glinting in the night. We were so close.

'Blood,' I whispered, picking up the dagger.

With the last of the oxygen in her lungs, Lydia screamed as I thrust the blade through my own palm, my blood gushing over her skin. The strength of two hundred years of Bell witches engulfed my body, hurling me forward, face-first. I'd been at this door before, at my Becoming, but I'd only peeked inside. Now it flew wide open and I lay in the dirt, watching golden stars shoot across the sky, smiling up at the universe. Everything was as it should be, everyone where they needed to be. Lydia and I were in perfect harmony with the city that loved us. Savannah wanted us here, both of us. All of us.

'You were born for this,' the first Emma Catherine Bell whispered in my ear. 'We're all so proud.'

I was wrapped in love, pure and unconditional, unable to speak or move but filled with light and energy as the circle filled with witches, my ancestors and Lydia's.

'The blessing welcomes you.'

I sat up, spluttering out a mouthful of dirt I didn't remember taking in. On the ground, the dagger sat between me and Lydia, my blood on its blade, on my dress, on Lydia's skin, as her gold eyes turned white, then black, then brown again, crystal clear and full of new strength.

'Are you OK?' I asked, pulling her into me and holding her so tightly, just for a second I was afraid her bones would break. 'Do you feel different?'

'Yes and no.'

She pulled away from me, staring at the woods around us as if she'd never seen them before. 'I feel complete.'

The Witch and the Wolf

The trees pulled back, releasing us back to the world and as their branches unfurled, the first fall of snow landed on the ground at our feet. Lydia laughed, holding out her hand to catch a pair of identical snowflakes. Smiling, I blew on them gently and watched as they sparkled, shifting into something more permanent. Diamonds.

'They're beautiful,' Lydia said as I unfastened the clasp of her necklace and slid one of the diamond snowflakes onto the chain alongside her locket then added the second to my own. 'Thank you.'

'Don't thank me,' I replied. 'We did it together.'

I stared at her, my friend, my sister, full of something too strong to simply be called love. She beamed, directing the snowflakes as they fell from the sky, making one flurry dance while another hovered in midair.

'We should head back, find Wyn,' I told her, carelessly picking up the dagger blade first. It cut into my palm as Lydia reached to knock it from my grip and I fell backwards into the vision, watching her disappear down a dark tunnel of nothingness.

I saw Virginia Powell, a teenager again, only she wasn't laughing beside my grandmother this time. She was exploding with pain on the tiled floor of an Italian palazzo, her great-grandmother calmly listening to the radio in the next room. Then Alex Powell, underneath the Candler Oak in Forsyth Park with my father. He looked so serious but she was laughing, at least she was until he handed her a dainty opal ring, sliding it onto the middle finger of her right hand and begging her to never, ever take it off. Jackson replaced his mother, walking along the riverfront with a man I didn't recognize. I chased him, calling out his name and when he saw me, he smiled, pulled out a silver sword with a gold hilt and drew it across his own throat before collapsing sideways into the river, his body pulled under the water before I could scream.

'You're back,' Lydia said, when the blessing released me, tossing me back into my body. She took my hand and pulled me up to my feet. 'You're safe.'

I allowed her to take the lead, guiding us out of the woods and back towards the avenue of the oaks, so much closer than they were before.

We were safe. For now.

Chapter Thirty-Three

With everything happening around us, it didn't feel like the right time for a party but Lydia would not be told.

'All I'm saying is, having a party the day before your Becoming really feels like we're asking for trouble,' I pointed out from the easy chair in her bedroom, nestled in among her piles of clothes. 'Can't you have it Friday or Saturday, or wait until the weekend after?'

'The weekend after is ten days after our birthday, no one wants to celebrate ten days late, it isn't the same,' she said, staring at the screen of her laptop and swirling the cursor over a helium tank before clicking add to cart. 'Friday night is Patsy Lunsford's annual back to school party, practically the social event of the season, and Saturday is the first day of the college football season.'

'So?'

She stared back at me, mouth open, eyes blinking.

'In case there was ever any doubt you were not raised in Savannah,' she declared. 'Jackson and I could give away winning lottery tickets at our party and people would still choose the Georgia Bulldogs over us. It has to be Sunday.'

A week had passed since her Wilcuma and now all I could think of was her Becoming ceremony. Wyn and Jackson were in charge of worrying about Astrid Hansen, albeit not together, and my job was to get Lydia safely through the final ritual in one piece. I had more confidence in myself, after the Wilcuma, but every evening, when the moon bloomed slightly bigger in the sky than it had the night before, my confidence in keeping the Weres away diminished.

We'd been agreed the ceremony would take place at Bell House, the safest possible location, and Virginia would attend though she couldn't take Lydia through it herself. While I concerned myself with making sure the whole thing went off without a hitch, Lydia was busy clicking through a party supply website adding more and more items to her cart.

'You can sit there with that frown on your face all day,' Lydia said. 'We're not cancelling. I get that you're worried, really I do, but what's the point in all of this if we're hiding away at home for the next eighty years? Why try to save lives we're not living?'

'It's not only our lives we have to think about.'

'Maybe, but sometimes I think you've forgotten you aren't just a witch. You're a whole person, Em, you have to remember that. I totally respect your commitment but dedication can turn into obsession. Isn't that how Catherine found herself on the wrong path?'

'I know,' I replied, sucking the air in through my teeth. 'But I won't get lost the way she did. I have too much to live for. Catherine didn't have you or Jackson, she didn't have Wyn.'

'She had Virginia, she had her husband, she had Ashley.' Lydia paused and softened her voice to deliver the final blow. 'She had your dad.'

I flinched as though I'd been hit. The truth sometimes hurt more than a physical blow.

The Witch and the Wolf

'Besides' – my best friend glanced at me with shifty eyes, slipping back into a lighter, happier tone – 'it's not only a birthday party. We're celebrating me coming into my full magic.'

'Maybe we don't announce your new status to the entire city,' I suggested, my new diamond pendant tapping against my mother's gold locket. 'Unless you want me to order a cake that says "congrats on being a witch"?'

'I already ordered the banner and the party hats, so, sure, if you don't mind.'

'There's no point arguing with you, I know that.' I sighed when she pumped her fist with success. 'But I have conditions. One, you don't invite the entire town, two, it's over before midnight and three, it has to happen at Bell House.'

'I'm down for everything except for point number two. Midnight is when all the best things happen at parties, everyone knows that. We're turning seventeen not twelve.'

One thing about Lydia Powell, she always got her way. But I wasn't going to let this one go. I didn't have a ton of experience to share with my sister witch but I did know about this.

'After midnight it'll officially be the day of your Becoming,' I told her. 'It's intense, you need to prepare.'

'A girl can't prepare and party at the same time?'

'You tell me,' I replied with an arched eyebrow. 'Weren't you the one who caused a typhoon in her own bathroom yesterday?'

'Excuse me for thinking it might be fun to turn the tub into a jacuzzi,' she muttered. 'Fine, we'll keep a lid on the late-night shenanigans. Everyone out by two a.m.'

'Midnight.'

'One a.m.'

'Midnight.'

'Fine!' she said, throwing up her hands. 'With a small after party for close acquaintances.'

'Tell me y'all aren't planning my own birthday party without me?'

I looked up to see Jackson leaning against the doorjamb, a sly grin on his face. He winked and I returned a tight smile. Ever since her initiation, Lydia had been inclined to stay closer to home than usual. Not that I didn't understand, she was still going through unpredictable growth spurts that got stronger every day. Little flurries of snow appearing whenever she felt too warm, winds whipping up out of nowhere when she wanted her laundry to dry faster, and the skies over the whole city darkening when her favourite author announced a delay to the upcoming final book in her favourite series. But things still felt off between Jackson and me. Or to be more accurate, things were off between Jackson and Wyn, and I was caught in the middle.

'You can't be trusted with party plans and you know it,' Lydia said. 'If it were up to him, we'd have a keg and a Costco pack of Solo cups and that would be it.'

'Not true,' Jackson replied. 'I would also order pizza. Em, you got a sec?'

'She was just leaving.'

'No, I wasn't.'

'If you don't leave, I'll go,' Lydia replied. 'You're killing my vibe.'

When I followed him out of his sister's room, something seemed off. Lydia swore he'd be out all day buying back-to-school supplies and I hadn't heard or sensed him arriving home. As Lydia's magic moulded itself around her, mine felt clearer, more finely tuned. There were so many ghosts in the streets, I could hardly leave the house without walking into someone and everywhere I went, my favourite flowers bloomed months out of season. So how come Jackson Powell had become a walking, talking blank space?

He strolled casually into his room, expecting me to follow. Instead, I lingered in the doorway, one foot in and one foot out. The space was so definitively him, classic with a cool twist, all crisp colours and clean lines, one wall covered in memorabilia, an assortment of ticket stubs, postcards, posters, photographs and sketches. If I tried to do something like that, it would look like a toddler threw the contents of a trashcan at the wall, but Jackson managed to make it look stylish, like something out of a gallery.

'Didn't want to distract Lyds when I know she's studying,' he said as he flicked through a stack of papers on his antique rolltop desk. 'Or at least when she's supposed to be studying. It's Astrid.'

'You've found her?'

'I reckon so.'

Reservations forgotten, I was at his side in half a second as he pulled out a bunch of printouts and handed them to me one at a time.

'Wasn't easy to find much, your girl doesn't like to leave a paper trail. Had to get her name on the magic shop lease, something to do with the alarm company.'

I studied each piece of paper in turn. The first was a copy of the lease, complete with address, phone number and social security number, the second a photograph of an old Victorian house and the third, what looked like a blurry doorbell camera image of the woman from the magic shop.

'All the info on the lease is bogus except the phone number, and that's out of order now. But I did get one hit off of it: a short-term rental down on Jefferson Street. According to the guy who lived downstairs, she damn near set the whole building on fire four or five times, but the landlord never once spoke to her about it.'

The whole thing reeked of magic, whether Wyn believed it or not.

'How did you get all this?' I asked, staring at the photo, my magic prickling at the sight of her. The violet eyes were hard and the rest of her features fell naturally into an antagonistic scowl.

'Friend of a friend. Someone I know from the historical society, used to be a police officer, now he kind of digs into people's lives as a kind of hobby.'

'A kind of hobby where he gets paid a ton of money and has a special licence?'

'Something like that,' he shrugged, as though hiring a private investigator to hunt down a werewolf were a perfectly normal thing to do. 'Also, the neighbour said she had a strong accent. Couldn't say what exactly but definitely not one he could identify, and this dude works in a hotel downtown so nothing obvious. My guy said it sounded like he was doing an impression of Count von Count. Should I be worried about vampires?'

'I'd love to tell you no,' I replied, still studying another photograph of Astrid, standing on a stoop, lit cigarette in one hand, a cell phone pressed up to her ear.

'Great, garlic knots for dinner then,' Jackson deadpanned. 'Strange how she couldn't find a way around the alarm company stuff. She rented a place, a car, seems as though she's got her hands on a phone but there's no trace of her on anyone's records. The landlord for the rental remembered her but couldn't find any paperwork.'

'Where is the alarm company based?'

Jackson held out his hand for the lease and scanned the piece of paper quickly.

'Company address is listed as Tennessee, but the phone number has a +91 area code.'

'And that's not Tennessee.' I frowned. 'Just a theory, but magic has boundaries. If she tripped the alarm and the call centre is outside the US, there's a chance her magic wouldn't be strong enough to stop them from sending someone out to investigate. Catherine had to do some dark stuff to send magic all the way over to Wales.'

'Catching a Were in an administrative error kind of feels like Al Capone being put away on his taxes,' Jackson said. 'Wyn heard anything on his end?'

I shook my head and he made a soft but distinct scoffing sound.

'It's not a competition,' I said with a warning look. 'He's in a tough spot, trying to find out as much as he can without giving us away to Astrid or making the pack suspicious.'

'If he needs to go back to Asheville, I can take care of things here.'

I looked up from the stack of pages to find him leaning casually against the desk, legs crossed at the ankle, hands in his pockets, eyes fixed on me.

'You're doing more than enough,' I assured him, handing the paperwork back.

'Keep them, I have copies.' Lifting his chin, he nodded towards the room across the hallway behind me. 'How's she doing?'

'Better than I did. Feels like I'm racing to keep up with her.'

'You know, I could've driven the two of you out to Wormsloe for that thing last week.'

'Again, it's not a competition,' I insisted, softly this time. 'Lydia couldn't know about it in advance, I didn't want you to have to lie to your own sister, plus I had no idea what to expect.'

'I get it. I don't have magic. You don't need something else to worry about.'

'No,' I corrected. 'I don't want to put people I care about in unnecessary danger.'

Too quickly for me to stop it, the atmosphere between us changed and I was painfully aware of how close we were to his bed, how he couldn't seem to shift his gaze from my lips.

'I'd better go,' I said, slicing through the tension between us with the bundle of paper. 'Thanks for this, I think it's really going to help.'

'Stay for dinner? It's fixing to rain out there.'

'It is?'

Sure enough, the sky outside was darkening rapidly. A regular summer storm or was Lydia fighting with someone on Reddit again?

'Good job I have an in with someone who can take care of the weather. Catch you later.'

'Hey, Em,' Jackson said as I bolted for the door. 'Everything's going to work out, you know, it just is.'

'Oh yeah?' I gave a nervous laugh as I stepped backwards into the hallway. 'Have you been having visions too?'

Framed by the doorway, he smiled at me, easy and sincere.

'Don't need magic to believe in you.'

I flushed with unexpected pride, colour rising in my cheeks as my magic surged through my veins.

'Thanks again for this,' I said, waving the papers at him. 'I'll call if I figure anything out.'

'I'll be waiting.'

It was a promise and a reminder.

'You'd better go,' he said. 'Before the rain comes.'

Still leaning against the desk, Jackson raised one hand in a wave. I mirrored the gesture, taking one last look at my brave, loyal friend. In another life, I would walk in there and kiss him goodbye.

But not in this one, I reminded myself, turning away to run straight down the stairs and out the front door.

Lafayette Square was scarred by the loss of the trees Astrid Hansen chopped down to make her toxic bonfire in Hilton Head. Everyone was talking about the mindless act of vandalism that somehow took place without leaving a trace of evidence. No one saw it happen, no one saw the trees leave the square, no one remembered a thing. Local outrage was still loud enough but it wasn't very committed. There wasn't much the authorities could do without evidence and soon enough, only days later, there was something new to be mad about and the naked north-west corner faded to the back of people's minds unless they were looking right at it. After all, trees would grow back, wouldn't they? I heard people say when I passed by, and thankfully no one was hurt.

No one they knew about.

Still clutching Jackson's evidence, I crouched in the grass and whispered healing words to the stumps she left behind. Recovery had already begun, harsh chunks hacked out by her axe softened and gentle trails of moss soothed the deepest cuts. It wouldn't have been too difficult to strike a bargain with the park and speed up the process. Every other tree for miles around would willingly offer its own energy to return their fallen comrades to their former glory. But inexplicably disappearing trees were one thing, magically reappearing trees were another. Drawing that kind of attention to a place so close to home wasn't a good idea. Kneeling beside the tree stump, I stroked the broad tops of the pale stumps, whispers of Spanish moss and lichen trailing after my fingertips. The trees could wait. Nature was patient. More patient than me.

'Am I interrupting?'

Wyn appeared in front of me, sleepy-eyed and smiling, more relaxed than I'd seen him in what felt like weeks.

'Hi,' I said as he crouched down beside me. 'And yes. We were enjoying a little alone time.'

'Been a long time since I saw you look that peaceful.' He pressed a palm to the trunk, a jolt of heat shooting through the tree and into me. 'Do I have to watch out for every tree now too? I already have enough folks to be jealous of.'

'You don't have to be jealous of anyone or anything. We were just catching up.'

'You and the tree?'

'Maybe chatting was the wrong word,' I said with a blush in my cheeks. 'More like, I was listening to what it had to tell me.'

To his credit, Wyn didn't laugh. Instead, he cocked his head towards the stump and concentrated.

'How does it work?' he asked. 'Do you hear actual words in your head or is it more of a feeling?'

I'd never loved him more.

'You kind of have to tune in to their frequency,' I explained. 'Everything is talking all the time but it doesn't always make sense. Kind of reminds me of when Dad and I would arrive in a new city and I heard everyone talking in a language I couldn't understand. After a while, you start to pick up bits and pieces, and if you stay long enough, eventually, you'd be able to speak it yourself. Just listen. Are any of these trees talking to you?'

He stood up and considered his options with soft eyes before walking all the way over to the tall, proud oak tree that stood across the street from Bell House. The tree he'd been leaning against the first time I'd ever laid eyes on him. I followed, watching as he ran a strong hand over the rough bark, his eyes closed. Pushing up onto my tiptoes, I kissed him softly, his plush firm lips opening against mine in surprise.

'Did the tree tell you to do that?' he asked as his eyelids fluttered open.

'You don't want to know what they said,' I replied, lacing my fingers through his. 'This one has a dirty mind.'

'Then I definitely do want to know what they had to say,' Wyn murmured against my mouth.

Gently pushing me against the tree, he kissed me back, the connection between us growing more urgent and impatient. His body pressed against mine as though he had a very important message to deliver and this was the only way to make sure I properly understood. Surrendering to the sensation, I received it loud and clear.

'Want to come inside?' I asked, my voice breaking as his lips moved to the side of my mouth, my jaw, my throat. 'Ashley should be out for a while.'

'A while isn't going to be long enough,' he replied, teeth nipping against my ear. 'Why don't we go to my place?'

The whole square sighed with delight as his thigh moved between mine and I instinctively clenched against his thick muscular leg. It felt so right, the warmth of him, the beat of his heart in perfect sync with my own. His hands grasped my hips and every leaf on every tree and every frond of Spanish moss chattered excitedly. When he pulled all my hair over my left shoulder and nuzzled into my neck, I struggled to remain upright, and a whole patch of azaleas burst into full bloom beside us.

'Jackson found out some information about Astrid,' I made myself say, sliding out from between him and the tree, chiding the out-of-season flowers as they sheepishly returned to the soil before anyone could see.

'Anything that's going to change what happens to us in the next ten seconds?'

'No,' I admitted. 'But—'

'Then I don't want to hear about Jackson,' he replied. 'It can wait.'

I didn't know if that was true but I badly wanted to believe him.

'Let me run inside for a moment,' I said, tugging on his arm and drawing him quickly across the street to Bell House before a tourist trolley could run us both down. 'I just want to put these papers somewhere safe.'

He made a noise somewhere between a grunt and a groan but came with me anyway, hands never once leaving my body. Stumbling up the front steps, falling over each other, I looked up, expecting the door to swing open for me but it didn't. The house was angry and afraid and in an instant so was I, chilled to the bone by what I saw. Nailed to the front of the door, still warm and bleeding, was the dead body of a recently slaughtered squirrel. Underneath it, five deep claw marks gouged the glossy wood. I instinctively moved away, holding a hand to my abdomen as though the marks were scratched into my flesh rather than my home.

'What the . . .'

'Fuck,' I heard Wyn exhale behind me.

I'd asked a question. He seemed to know the answer.

'What does it mean?' I asked before pressing a hand against my mouth, nauseated by the loss of life pouring down my door and pooling at our feet.

He spun around to search the square but whoever was responsible was long gone now or I'd have sensed them myself. Turning back towards the house, Wyn encircled me in his arms, wrapping me up in a tight, protective embrace, and when he spoke, his words were infused with genuine fear I'd never heard from him before.

'It means they know,' he stated, his whole body trembling. 'It means the wolves are coming for you.'

Chapter Thirty-Four

'This is bad, Em, this is really, really, really bad.'

Wyn hadn't stopped pacing up and down the parlour floor since he pushed me inside, refusing to let me go out and clean up the front door. He shook his head over and over, his whole body a blur of constant movement.

'Let's start at the beginning,' I said, a picture of stillness compared to his perpetual motion. 'Do you know for a fact this is a message from the pack? Maybe it's a threat from Astrid, maybe she knows we've been asking questions about her.'

'No. It's the pack.'

All the energy pulling us together moments ago now pushed us apart. He was full of conflict and I felt the thread between us fraying in real time.

'It means you've been declared prey. The pack has officially accused you of Cole's murder and this is to let you know there will be a trial.'

There would be a trial. The time-slip at Hilton Head. Only that wasn't a trial, it was a witch hunt.

'I always walk in at the best moments,' Ashley said, strolling into the room with a southern woman's eternal answer to bad news, sweet tea and cookies. 'There I was, thinking I had a blissful afternoon all to myself. City council meeting delayed, Armageddon brought forward. Not an equitable exchange. What is going on here?'

'It's good that you're home,' Wyn stalked over to the window, closed the shutters then yanked the curtains closed for good measure. 'Everyone needs to stay inside.'

'Wyn thinks the pack knows I killed Cole,' I told her as he pulled out his phone and turned it off before picking up a pen from the coffee table, poking at a tiny hole in the side, until the sim card popped out. He tucked both items into his back pocket.

'They can track me the regular way anywhere else,' he explained, 'but not here. Gramps mentioned it last time I was home: magic creates blank spots and they exist all over Savannah, that's one of the reasons they were having trouble keeping tabs on Cole. I don't know how far Bell House's wards reach, but we don't need to make things any easier for them.'

'If they know about Em, surely they know about you?' Ashley reasoned. 'The two of you are never apart for more than ten damn minutes.'

'I don't know,' he moaned, head in his hands as he sank down to the sofa. 'I don't fucking know.'

'Tell me about the trial,' I demanded, crawling up beside him on my knees, I had to keep him on track. 'They've accused me. Is anyone else in danger?'

'Anyone considered to have aided or abetted in the death or the cover-up. Even if they don't know about her magic, they'll snatch Lydia just for being in your inner circle. They'll take Ashley and Jackson too. Catherine, if she were still here.'

'Take or . . .?'

He looked at me, grim and afraid. The birds painted on the

walls began to circle, slowly at first then in more erratic orbit as my panic spiralled.

'Just tell us what you can,' I said, taking pains to sound calm when I was flailing inside. 'We need to be prepared.'

'It isn't much. I had one month with the pack. We're not much for sitting around and giving lectures, and if there are books to study, I haven't seen them,' he said, pressing his fingertips into his temples, trying to squeeze out more knowledge than he had. 'There's a council, my mom is the leader, they meet once a month to discuss problems and issue punishments. Mom wanted me to sit in and someone mentioned a trial when they were discussing what happened to Cole . . .'

'When he tried to kill Emily and Catherine, thus getting himself stabbed in the throat and dumped in the river?' Ashley offered before leaning forward to grab a cookie and snap it in two. 'What? Am I wrong? Continue.'

'They didn't know who killed him then, the debate was whether or not an accidental death would still warrant a trial. Most folks figured he got himself shot by a hunter and was too badly injured to heal himself,' Wyn continued, paler than I'd ever seen him. 'From what I recollect, it happens on the night of a full moon, early, before the moon reaches its peak.'

'So before the phase?'

He nodded. 'There will be another message, from an emissary, telling you where to be and when. The pack leader will be the judge.'

'Your mom.' My lips shaped themselves around the words but no sound emerged from my mouth. Wyn didn't respond in any way.

'You know for sure it's your pack?' Ashley asked. 'It could be this lone-wolf asshole trying to scare us into making a mistake.'

'It's them.' Wyn looked sick to his stomach. 'I wasn't sure

at first, the magic around the house threw me for a loop, but I can smell it now. It's my pack for sure.'

'What if I leave?' I suggested. 'Savannah, the US, what if I vanished?'

'Not possible. They have your scent, all the other packs will be informed. You aren't a Were, you can't go to another pack and ask for clemency like an exiled wolf.'

'What if she happened to have a still-beating heart party favour?' Ashley asked.

'I don't think many Weres would look for much of a reason to execute a witch,' Wyn said, stammering out the last couple of words. 'They've given you seven days' notice, they want you to run – it's considered an admission of guilt. Chasing you down is just another part of the hunt. A part they'll enjoy.'

'You can't leave town anyhow,' Ashley said. 'Hate to be the one to point this out, but Lydia's Becoming has to take place on the full moon next Sunday or she loses her magic.'

'So I go through with the trial,' I said, working through my non-existent alternatives in real time. 'And I have to win. Or I'll persuade them to move it or at least to let me complete the ritual before they come to a verdict.'

'Emily, they've already come to a verdict.' Wyn pushed his hands through his hair, frustrated. 'They have declared you responsible for the death of a wolf and the only acceptable retribution is a life for a life. That's why the trial takes place on the full moon. Even if they give you a chance to explain how it happened, the outcome will be the same. They confirm it's you and you die.'

The words echoed around the room, the birds and the trees and the vines and the clouds all whipped up into a frenzy, despairing at the thought. If I died, the Bell family magic died along with me. Wyn reached a hand towards me then hesitated, afraid to make contact.

'From the outside, the Weres might look cruel. From the inside, they're vicious. That's the reason they've managed to stay hidden for so long. Zero tolerance, no mercy. Asking permission to bring another witch into the world before they take you out will only get you killed faster.'

They. Them. As if we were talking about some strange enemy and not his actual family, his blood relations.

'And what about you?' They're in Savannah, you're in Savannah. You can't hide from them forever.'

'If I leave here,' he whispered, words thick with tears we were both willing not to fall, 'I don't know when I'll be able to come back.'

It was like watching someone tear him in two. I nestled into him, pushing his arms up until he had no choice but to let me in, and rested my head on his chest. Tremors of pain ricocheted from his heart and into mine. He was so lost, so churned up inside, and I knew he was searching for a way out, one that would keep us all alive and the two of us together.

'You have to leave,' I said.

'What?'

I extricated myself from his arms and it felt like pulling my own soul from my body. Wyn looked up, blinking, the threat of tears still clinging to his golden lashes.

'Members of your pack are here in Savannah, right now. You don't think they're looking for you? To warn you about the big bad wolf killer?'

'And that's best-case scenario,' Ashley added as Wyn clung to his denial. 'Seems to me if they know so much about Em and her part in Cole's death, they might have a notion about the two of you being such good buddies and all.'

'No, I would know, I would know, I would know,' he said over and over again, convincing us or convincing himself, I wasn't sure. 'They wouldn't allow it, they wouldn't have let me come back. They would've acted before now.'

She looked at him with her head half-cocked to the side.

'You're one hundred per cent sure about that? Completely certain you know what these vicious wolves would do? Your words, Wyn, not mine.'

His shoulders slumped, head hung low.

'You have to leave,' I said again, more forceful, less certain.

What if he went and never came back?

'You told them you met someone down here, right?' I reminded him, pulling what scraps of energy I could find in myself and pushing them into him. 'Go home, tell them we broke up and you don't want to talk about it. If they know about us, if they know what I am, tell them I lied to you and you had no idea. If they don't know, you don't say anything at all.'

'I won't. I won't leave you to save myself.'

Shaking his head again and again, he screwed his eyes shut, as though the gesture was causing him as much pain as the idea. I placed my hands on his thighs and squeezed.

'You have to,' I insisted. 'You staying here makes things more dangerous for both of us. Right now we don't know anything, not really, only that the pack believes I killed Cole. Why do they think that? What do they know? If you go home, you could ask questions, find a way to let me know what to expect. You staying here puts me in more danger.'

'If you care about her as much as you say you do, you'll get into that little red truck of yours and get the hell out of Georgia,' Ashley ordered, much less interested in coddling his feelings. 'You run your ass right back to mama wolf and start listening in, otherwise Em here is as good as cooked.'

He gripped my wrists as though he were hanging over the edge of a cliff and I were the only thing keeping him from falling.

'Please don't ask me to go,' he said. 'I don't want to leave you.'

I noticed the change right away. Before he said he wouldn't leave. Now, he said he didn't want to.

'This is the best chance we have. Me, you, Lydia, all of us,' I told him, nodding. One more push, that's all it would take, and then the worst part would be over. 'Please, Wyn, do it for me.'

'Maybe they'd listen to me,' he mumbled but I shook my head, pressing my fingers to his mouth to stop that thought in its tracks.

'And maybe they'd put you on trial alongside me and kill us both.'

He cupped my face in his hands and wiped away our mingled tears with his thumbs.

'I won't let anyone hurt you, not the pack, not Astrid, not anyone. I don't know how, not yet, but I swear it on my soul. They lied to me my whole life, they held me captive when I wouldn't listen. But if they won't listen to me, I don't have to listen to them. The pack may be my family but you are my life, Emily, without you, everything else is meaningless.'

'This kind of feels like a conversation you could be having in private,' Ashley said, turning away awkwardly in her seat. 'But I do like the energy.'

'We will figure it out,' I agreed, forcing a smile that hurt more than slicing myself open with a knife. Scars I'd thought healed tore open, raw and red and real, on display for all to see. 'I love you, Wyn Evans.'

'I love you, Emily James.'

Words were never supposed to hurt so much.

We were always on a clock but it ran down early this month and I wasn't ready. Would I ever really be ready? Would I ever get used to the pain of watching him leave and hoping he'd come back only so we could do this to each other all over again?

He kissed me one more time, deep and strong, and for a beautiful, fleeting moment, I believed everything was going to work out. Then, without another word, he stood up, walked out of the parlour and through the bloody front door.

'Seems as though the two of you are always saying goodbye,' Ashley said, joining me on the couch and stroking my hair. 'Call me crazy but I'm starting to think love ain't all it's cracked up to be.'

'You're crazy,' I whispered, tears enough to drown an ocean finally falling free when I heard his truck door slam and the engine roar into life.

Chapter Thirty-Five

The Wyn-shaped hole in my life was a chasm, too wide to bridge, impossible to fill. If I looked directly at it, the despair that consumed me was overwhelming, but there wasn't any time to indulge in my own pain. We messaged constantly but didn't dare speak on the phone, not with so many sharp ears around him. The pack had accepted his story and welcomed him home, too anxious and eager to get their newest member completely up to speed before the trial to poke holes in his narrative, not that they were forthcoming with the details. All he could tell me was he'd never seen his mother more focused or his grandfather quite so sad. Not many of the pack had lived through the last trial, he said, but his grandfather had and did not appear to relish the thought of doing so again.

Since he left, I'd barely slept but as long as I didn't look directly at the scar Wyn's absence left on my soul, I could keep moving. The Powells moved into our guest quarters the same day Wyn left town, taking over the three downstairs bedrooms that opened directly out into the garden, their own apartment within Bell House. It made sense. I needed everyone where I could see them and keep them safe, and Lydia needed all the help she could get to hone her magic as best she could before the Becoming. She was already faster and stronger, her senses sharpening every day, but her control over the weather was erratic at best and every time I walked into a room without correcting my permanent scowl, I heard a distant rumble of thunder.

My craft room had become my sanctuary and, once inside, I lost all track of time. It felt like Thursday. Day or night, today, tomorrow or yesterday, I wasn't sure, hours spent poring over the journal that filled itself with all the accumulated knowledge my ancestors had gathered on the Weres. There wasn't much. When I yawned for the third time in a row, I closed the book, admitting defeat for the day and looked up to the impossible skylight in the ceiling. The room was bright with daylight but the sky was dark. Barely any stars, too close to the full moon for the furthest away to break through.

The door to the craft room opened quietly and the lights along the hallway turned themselves half on, guiding me to the kitchen and muffling my footsteps so as not to wake our guests. It was late, although I had no idea how late. The energy of the house was peaceful and at rest, except for one spot in the kitchen. Virginia Powell sat at the kitchen table surrounded by dozens of open glass jars and wielding a stone pestle, the bowl in front of her full of a vivid chartreuse paste.

'Emily,' she said kindly. 'Whatever are you doing out of bed at this hour?'

'I don't actually know what this hour is but I'm extremely hungry,' I replied, heading for the fridge only to be beaten by Virginia. 'I didn't eat dinner. Or lunch. I think I had breakfast?'

'Sit,' she ordered. 'I'll fix you a plate.'

It was nice, to do as I was told for once. Taking a chair at the table, I silently reviewed her poultice. Slippery elm, honey, turmeric and ginger, to treat inflammation and sore muscles. Much of the morning had been spent strengthening the wards around Bell House, burying chunks of black tourmaline and labradorite around the perimeter of our garden. My body ached with the effort. A quick slather of the funky-looking paste would help no end.

'How does it look to you?' Virginia asked, busy assembling a turkey sandwich behind me. 'Your aunt refuses to let me write anything down and I'm having a devil of a time trying to get the measurements right.'

'It looks amazing,' I said. 'Perfect, in fact.'

Brandishing a butter knife, she gave me a look. 'You must be honest with me. It's the only way I'll learn.'

'There's a tad bit too much honey.' I reached across the table to adjust the measurements by adding another pinch of each herb. 'This consistency will stick to the skin better.'

'Marvellous. Just marvellous.'

In companionable quiet, she finished constructing my late-night lunch while I poked a finger in her various concoctions. She would never have access to her magic, but that didn't mean she couldn't be of service to her family's magic.

'Eat,' she said, placing the sandwich in front of me, complete with a radish rosette. 'Can't have you wasting away now, not when there's so much work to do – and your aunt Ashley tells me there is much work on the horizon.'

From the lift of her eyebrows and the prim tightening of her lips that wasn't all Ashley had told her.

'Such a weight to place on young shoulders,' Virginia lamented as she began closing up the open glass jars dotted around the table. 'It really isn't fair.'

'Fair doesn't seem to have much to do with anything these days. If things were fair, a lot of people would still be alive.' I took a bite of the sandwich, sinking my teeth into her fresh-baked, pillowy bread. 'If things were fair, you would have your magic.'

'I don't know about that.'

It was still strange to hear Virginia Powell laugh. I was so used to her stern but delicate persona, discovering this new version of her, a curious, caring woman, was a constant surprise. In her own way, she had tried to protect her family, just like Catherine and her great-grandmother . . . only without the homicidal tendencies.

'Even if there were a way to go back and change the events of the past, I believe I would leave things be. Let the cards fall where they may,' she said. 'It might not look like much to you, but I have had a good life. I loved my husband, my daughter is healthy and I believe happy in her own way. All I can wish for now is the same for Lydia and Jackson. Their path was already set to be a difficult one, and now . . . well.' She pressed her hands into a prayer, fingers intertwined. 'I shall be quite ready to meet my maker knowing I did all I could to protect my grandchildren. That to me is a life well lived.'

I chewed my sandwich thoughtfully. No one made all the right decisions every time but it had never really occurred to me how much she loved her grandchildren. Lydia was forever complaining about her strict rules and adherence to outdated etiquette, and Jackson mostly brushed Virginia off as an out-of-touch guardian but she'd sacrificed so much, for them and before them. Losing her magic, her mother and grandmother, living a lie for so many years, it can't have been easy, but here she was, head held high, loving them the best way she knew how, whether they liked it or not.

'One thing I have learned in this life is that the lion's share of the burden always falls to those who don't deserve it – so often the young,' Virginia added. 'But the worthy always rise to the challenge even when times look bleak. We cannot possibly hope to know what fate has in store for us, Emily, prophecy or no. The darkest days chase the happiest like the dog after the hare. We find love only to lose it, but joy shines brighter against the shadow of pain. One without the other is impossible and knowing that helps us choose to soldier on.'

'Believe me, I'm soldiering,' I said, a hand over my mouth as I swallowed. 'I'm soldiering.'

'I do believe you,' she replied. 'I only wish you didn't have to.'

Under her watchful gaze, I finished every last bite of the sandwich. With a satisfied nod, she picked up my empty plate and took it to the sink, eschewing the dishwasher for a sponge and soap.

'Can't help but notice Jackson hasn't been himself lately.'

'Uh, really?'

'I'd say not.'

Viriginia slipped her elegant hands into a pair of ever present but never used rubber gloves. 'That boy was born with a smile on his face but it's been a sight scarcer than hen's teeth the last few days.'

I didn't know what to tell her. I was as confused about Jackson's behaviour as she was. Ever since they'd moved in, he'd been quiet in a way that made me uneasy, almost as though he'd left the easy-going, charismatic Jackson Powell behind and sent this sullen, suspicious version along in his place.

'I trust my grandchildren implicitly and they trust you,' Virginia said, resting my plate in the drying rack and pulling off the first rubber glove. 'Lydia with her life, Jackson with his heart. It is painfully obvious to the rest of us you do not return his affections.'

The second glove came off with a resounding snap. I opened my mouth to defend myself but she wasn't done.

'Alexandra and your father were fierce friends until the end.

Part of her always loved him, still does to this day. It would be nice to think part of him loved her too, perhaps not in the same way, but it was there. It is my fondest wish that their love lives on in you all.'

Draping the rubber gloves neatly over the drying rack alongside the plate, Virginia returned to the table, one hand on my forearm, understanding written on her face.

'I'm not a tyrant or a fool, I know we can't choose who we love, even if Jackson has yet to learn that lesson. I only ask that you treat him with kindness and respect. Please don't let my grandson take risks for a love he will never see returned.'

'I won't. I would never,' I promised, mortified to have the situation laid out so bare.

'Would that he were having his heart broken for the first time under more ordinary circumstances, but all's fair in love and war, as they say. Or unfair, as the case may be.'

She ran a hand along the kitchen counter as she headed for the door. 'Goodnight, Emily, take the poultice with you and try to get some rest. Burning the candle at both ends makes the room twice as bright but you'll find yourself in the dark twice as fast.'

Chapter Thirty-Six

'Well, y'all might be fiddling while Rome burns but at least you'll be fiddling in style.'

It was Sunday, the day before the full moon. Twenty-four hours until Lydia's Becoming, until the wolves came, and we were about to throw a party. Ashley leaned against the doorframe and whistled at the sight in front of her.

'Is this really our house?'

'It really is,' Lydia said, satisfaction on her face as she surveyed her work. 'And doesn't it look incredible?'

For once, not even Ashley could argue with her. Lydia had oiled and opened up antique room partitions I hadn't known existed, uniting the parlour and our completely unused study, to create an honest to goodness ballroom. Every stick of furniture in the parlour had been moved to the edge of the room, the rugs rolled up and stashed away, and anything breakable safely secured elsewhere. The floors had been polished and there wasn't so much as a single speck of dust to be seen. Even the wallpaper shone a little brighter than it usually did. The house was as pleased and proud of itself as I was. It was easy to imagine the Savannah of old, back when Bell House was first built, ladies in their best gowns, gentlemen in their finery, talking, drinking and dancing. Tonight's affair, I suspected, would look quite different.

'Not to be rude' – Lydia grimaced as she gave my grubby clothes a once-over – 'but you are planning to change, right?'

Ashley grinned. 'Into what?'

'I'm planning to keep watch,' I replied, wiping my dirty hands on my already dirtier T-shirt. 'Do I really need to do full glam for that?'

'Please,' my best friend scoffed with disgust. 'There's nowhere safer in this whole town.'

'Safer without a house full of people. The crowd at the DeSoto was three times your guest list and that didn't stop Astrid from attacking.'

'And the DeSoto is not Bell House. She won't be able to push a single paw through the front door.'

If I'd really wanted to, I could've cancelled the party, but I couldn't bring myself to do it. I wasn't the only one whose life was on the line once the Weres arrived. Lydia, Jackson, Ashley, Virginia, they were all at risk. And if the birth of my best friends wasn't worth celebrating, nothing was.

'As long as we all remember we're working on Cinderella rules,' Ashley instructed when Lydia darted out to straighten up a lightbox directing everyone to exactly where they should leave her gifts. 'Everyone out by midnight, just in case your magic goes bananas and you turn all your little friends into a whole patch of pumpkins.'

'I can think of at least a dozen people who might have that coming,' Lydia muttered under her breath before returning with a dazzling smile. 'But of course, Ashley. Whatever you say, Ashley. You're the boss, Ashley.'

'If that ain't the smartest thing you ever did say.'

Leaving the two of them to stare each other down like a

couple of hyenas, I crossed the room to peek through the shutters. A group of guests were already hovering in the square across from the house, gathering the courage to knock on the door despite the fact they'd all been invited. Bell House had not thrown a party in over twenty years, most of their parents had never so much as set foot over the threshold and in this town, curiosity was hereditary.

'Did I get the wrong day or something? Is this a party or a mother's meeting?'

I turned around to see Jackson emerge from the downstairs bedroom wearing a new outfit and the kind of happy expression I hadn't seen on his face in too long. His inviting cologne surrounded me as he walked up, high-fiving Ashley and ignoring his sister before walking into our new ballroom. I realized I hadn't smelled it since the party at the DeSoto.

'Are y'all planning to leave everyone outside?' he asked. 'No offence, but this isn't much of a party.'

'Offence taken,' Ashley said with a sniff. 'We're not good enough for you, Powell?'

His eyes skirted over me to find her, his smile wavering just for a second.

'Better than I deserve.'

'I'll go open the door,' I offered, flipping down the shutters. The lighting reset itself to create the perfect cosy ambiance and Lydia's party playlist began to hum through hidden speakers. 'Is everyone ready?'

Jackson was the one to answer.

'As we'll ever be.'

He rested his elbow on his twin sister's shoulder, their similarities and differences so apparent when they stood side by side. Lydia's curls were fluffier, coaxed into a perfect halo and tinted honey blonde on the ends while Jackson's held a little tighter, shaved close on the sides still lighter on the ends, lifted by the sun instead of a TikTok hair tutorial. Their wide eyes and full lips had been completely copy-pasted onto each other's features, but the broader planes of Jackson's face gave them more room to settle into his conventional handsomeness. However, Lydia's beauty, especially tonight, was startling. She was already an unbelievable person and she was going to be an incredible witch. I was so proud to call her my friend.

The first trickle of guests brave enough to mount the steps of Bell House were received by an unnerving combination of Ashley's threatening scowl and the twins' effusive hugs. Virginia, like all good parental figures, had sentenced herself to her room downstairs, closed every possible door and informed me, Ashley, Lydia and Jackson she did not want to hear, see or even imagine what might be happening upstairs. As strategies for surviving a teenage party at her age went, it seemed like a good one to me.

The music was so loud and the bass thudded so hard, I could feel it trying to push my heart out of its usual rhythm. The moment Lydia's back was turned, holding court, I slipped out of the ballroom, into the kitchen and out the back door. No one followed. They couldn't, even if they wanted to. The kitchen was spelled to discourage any guests from poking around. The same went for the staircase, the library and pretty much any room that wasn't the ballroom or the powder room, just in case anyone's curiosity got the better of them and they decided to take themselves on a tour of Bell House.

I'd changed my clothes, or at least my shirt, exchanging the party-prep-stained T-shirt for a Lydia-approved tank. The warm night air felt good on my bare arms. The back garden was completely silent and still, and so, restless as I was, I took my patrol around to the front. It was the first time I'd found myself without anything to do in days, weeks maybe, and it was an uncomfortable sensation. The craft room was very much off limits while the house was so full and this definitely wasn't the time to practise my magic. Carpeting the party with wildflowers might not be so bad, but whisking one hundred teenagers away to the eighteenth century seemed like a bad idea.

The magnolia tree stood proud, the tallest branches tickling my bedroom windows, the fist-sized flowers spilling over with the pretty scent of the south.

'How you be, little witch?'

A voice as sweet as honey sailed through the night. Right outside the gate stood a beautiful woman with long braids wrapped up in a patterned headscarf, the sunset sky warming up her already deep brown skin. When she saw me jump, a soft chuckle escaped her plum-painted lips.

'Calm, be calm, you'll find no danger in me,' she said, leaning over the gate to look me over. 'I heard about you. Had to come and see for myself.'

'You've heard about me?' I replied, walking over to meet her. 'I mean, I'm sorry, I think you've got the wrong house.'

'I don't think so. Pleased to meet you, Emma Catherine Bell.'

There was no danger in this woman, not a speck. Close enough to see the spark of her eyes, bright and shiny copper like new pennies, I felt a sense of calm all around her. There was something safe in her that I hadn't known in the longest time.

'I'm Sistah Mariama,' she said, extending a hand my way, warm and kind and strong. 'We've been knowing about you, child. For a long time now.'

'Are you a witch?' I asked.

She cawed at that. 'Don't make me come in there and wash your mouth out with soap and water. I'm no witch. My people are Gullah Geechee. You know what that means?'

Embarrassed, I shook my head.

'Then you better look it up, I'm not Wikipedia. We've been here almost as long as your people, although we made our way to these parts under very different circumstances.'

The shame of what she was saying burned in me. I started to formulate some kind of insufficient apology but she carried on talking over me, not even slightly interested in hearing it.

'Words is only words. No need to waste 'em where they ain't needed. My great-grandmother was a root worker, you know what *that* means?'

'No,' I admitted. 'But I do know it's not a witch.'

'Good girl, you learn quick,' she replied with a chuckle. 'But you ain't know much. My great-grandmother, she knew your people real well, told us to wait on you and here you are. Smaller than I thought you'd be, can't see you plugging up much of a hole in anything, least of all the end of the world. Surely a pretty thing though.'

'You know about the prophecy.'

I hadn't realized how tightly I was clinging to the iron gate until I felt it bend, hot in my hands. 'Are you here to help?'

Behind her, in the square, I saw my oldest ancestor smothering a smile behind her hand and Sistah Mariama clucked with displeasure.

'Y'all be always expecting Black women to save the world. We do our part, honey, more than our fair share, and you tell that spirit lurking in the shadows to leave me be. You do your part, I'll do mine.'

Emma Catherine Bell lowered her head respectfully and took herself away across the park, lingering by the fountain.

'I'm still not entirely clear on exactly what my part is,' I confessed as Mariama started off down the street, her indigo blue dress holding tight to her curves as she went. 'If there's anything you can tell me, I sure would appreciate it.'

The Witch and the Wolf

She ran a hand over the azalea bush on my side of the fence. 'This town is famous for its azaleas. While they sleeping in the ground, you think they know if they going to be pink or orange or red?'

'I think azaleas are less likely to find themselves in the same predicament I'm in,' I replied as politely as I could, and she snickered to herself, nodding as she walked on.

'Most folks forget how powerful a flower can be. That azalea sure is pretty to look at but you eat it and you're going to be sick to your stomach. No one thinking 'bout that while they strolling around, admiring.'

I followed her as far as I could, stopping short when I got to the end of the garden, held back by my own iron railings.

'That's your advice? Don't eat azaleas?'

'It's more than I owe you, little witch.'

Without turning to look back, Sistah Mariama of the Gullah Geechee raised her voice as she crossed the street.

'People underestimate pretty things. Just because they fragile don't mean they ain't got strength all of they own.'

Across the street, the ghost of Emma Catherine Bell watched with reverence as my new friend disappeared around the corner, leaving me in my garden, surrounded by beautiful, fragile flowers.

Chapter Thirty-Seven

'So this is where you've been hiding.'

Jackson closed the door that led from the downstairs bedrooms to the back garden with his elbow, hands full of cans of soda and a paper plate. I'd been sitting outside for a while, watching the sunset in the back garden. The vibrant colours of a summer's day had faded out, the slider shifted all the way to the left on the saturation bar.

'You missed the cake-cutting.' He placed one of the unopened sodas on the table in front of me and sat in the open chair by my side. 'Let me guess, the dance at the DeSoto was so awful, it put you off parties for life?'

'The dance at the DeSoto was great,' I replied as I flipped the tab on the soda. 'At least it was until the end.'

'Yeah, I always hate it when they play that Black Eyed Peas song too.'

The bluish-grey tones of the early evening cooled his skin but nothing could dim his smile. Not when it was at full wattage like it was right now.

'I owe you an apology,' Jackson said, popping his own can while I poked at the cake with a little silver fork.

The Witch and the Wolf

'No, you don't.'

'I really do.' He dropped his head to hide a rueful grin. 'Turns out I made a liar out of myself.'

The cake, one of Ashley's concoctions, was delicious. Double chocolate with hazelnut chocolate frosting and a mass of malt balls on top. For someone who still claimed to despise Lydia Powell, she certainly had gone out of her way to create a cake made of all her favourite things.

'I said I'd be here for you, whatever you need. The last few days have been difficult but that's no excuse, I haven't been a good guest.' Jackson toyed with the tab on his soda can. 'I guess, with everything that's been going on, I'm feeling like a screen door on a submarine and I don't like it one bit.'

'That's crazy,' I said quickly. 'Without you, we wouldn't know anything about Astrid. You've been beyond helpful.'

He scratched the scruff on his chin, half shaking his head. Since the twins moved in I'd noticed he always had a shadow on his jaw by the evening, even if he'd shaved that same day.

'It's funny,' he replied. 'If you'd asked me three months ago, I'd have said my only back-to-school worries would be making the varsity starting lineup and which girl to take to Homecoming. Now I'm living in a magic house, full of witches, and hoping to live past tomorrow.'

I pushed the plate back towards him. 'The witches I can't do much about but you don't need to worry about the rest of it. You're safe here.'

'Can't stay here forever though.'

'You can, actually. As long as you like.'

He looked around the garden, his chest expanding as he breathed in the scent of night blooming jasmine.

'Can't live with you forever,' he corrected. 'Not like this.'

'Jackson, I—' I began but he cut me off with a tight, bittersweet look.

'Please don't. I know how it is. You love him.'

There didn't seem much point in agreeing out loud, making things worse.

'I always thought I was pretty smart,' Jackson said, ducking his head to hide a regretful grin. 'But it turns out I don't know much about anything after all.'

'It's one thing to do good in school, it's another to wake up one day and find out witches and werewolves are running around town and your whole family is caught up in the middle of it,' I replied, reaching across the table. 'I get it, I do. I always thought getting good grades and graduating early meant something. Now I don't know where that kind of thing gets me.'

'It gets you out of first period math on a Monday morning. That's not nothing.'

'See, you're still pretty smart,' I squeezed his hand. 'You don't have to beat yourself up for not having all the answers or for asking questions.'

'Even if those questions are about Wyn?'

'You mean the guy who dropped into your life out of nowhere and is currently hanging out with a whole pack of werewolves on their way to kill us?'

'That would be the one.'

I pulled up my shoulders and inclined my head as I took a sip of my soda. I couldn't quite bring myself to say yes but if I put myself in his shoes, I could see where doubts might creep in. Especially if he had a vested interest in Wyn turning out not to be the good guy after all.

'He's a good guy and I know it,' he admitted with a grimace. 'But there were days when I didn't know what to think. Damn, I can still half convince myself he was the one who attacked us at the dance, and on the beach. Or maybe that's what I want to believe, I don't know.'

'You have to remember he didn't want this,' I insisted. 'If

Catherine and I hadn't met Cole in the cemetery that night, Wyn would never have known his family were Weres. It's not something he can control, it's not something he went looking for. He wasn't given a choice.'

'But that's just it,' Jackson said, attacking the air with his dessert fork. 'He can't control what he is. What if there are other things he can't control?'

'Such as?'

'What if initiating him into the pack wasn't the end of it? What if the other Weres are controlling him somehow?'

I looked up to see the first stars shining down on us. Powerful suns, burning brighter than anything else in the sky, but against the pale rising moon they looked weak.

'No one's controlling him,' I argued. 'No one could make Wyn do anything he doesn't want to do.'

'Are you sure? Are you entirely certain beyond a shadow of a doubt there's no way Weres can influence the behaviour of their pack members?'

It only took a split second of hesitation on my part for him to jump.

'I'm not blaming him, all I'm asking is for you to look at it objectively. At Hilton Head, he ran towards the fire but all you saw was a wolf. You asked him not to go back alone but he went anyway but he couldn't find anything? Not a single trace? And where was he when you found this warning from the pack? Right outside Bell House. At the DeSoto you said yourself it was raining too hard to get a proper look at the wolf. And who showed up two days later?'

Or maybe the night before that, I thought to myself, fighting against the memory of a tall, dark-haired man crossing Lafayette Square.

'There's something else,' Jackson said, slowing himself down, almost as though he didn't really want to say it. 'You killed his brother. Not on purpose, but you did it. You know how I feel about you, Em, but if you hurt Lydia, even accidentally, I would never be able to forgive you.'

All the blood drained from my face.

It's not the same, I wanted to say. But didn't. He couldn't possibly understand. Cole and Wyn had a different relationship to Jackson and Lydia. Cole was literally trying to kill me, there was no other way; Wyn knew it was self-defence and, above all else, Wyn loved me. He loved me, he loved me, he loved me.

A tear slipped over my cheek and I wiped it away quickly, but not before Jackson saw.

'Shit, I came out here to apologize, not make you cry,' he said, shamefaced. 'Forget I said anything. I'm a jealous idiot, a cowardly jealous idiot, looking for the worst in someone because I can't stand losing.'

But it was more complicated than that and we both knew it.

Jackson leaned back, his face contorted with confusion, when the lights of the house caught on something silver against his dark skin. I recognized it at once. Without waiting for permission, I slid my hand inside his shirt and pulled out a silver chain. Dangling from the end was his mother's opal ring.

'This is your mom's.'

Even looking at it for too long was uncomfortable and I let it go, the delicate circlet bouncing off his crisp white shirt.

'She left it in my room before she bailed.' He almost looked embarrassed. 'There was a note, said I should wear it for protection. But like, how is a ring going to protect me against a Were?'

'It isn't,' I replied calmly. 'It's protection against me.'

Now I knew why I'd had trouble sensing his energy. Alex had literally hidden him from me.

The Witch and the Wolf

'Em, I'm only going to ask you once and I swear I won't ask you again,' Jackson said as he slid the opal ring back inside his shirt until it lay flush against his chest. 'Is it at all possible that somehow, maybe against his will, the pack could be controlling Wyn?'

Meeting his eyes in the dark, I felt a shadow of doubt rise up, my scarred heart raked raw one more time.

'It's possible,' I replied, hating myself as night fell all around us. 'Anything is possible.'

Chapter Thirty-Eight

'We could hang out in my room?' Jackson suggested as he followed me, staggering zombie-like back into the house, into the kitchen. 'Watch a movie or something?'

'I wouldn't be very good company.' I was still standing, still in one piece. Just barely. 'Why don't you go back to the party?'

'Same reason you don't want to go back to the party,' he replied. 'Can't say I'm much in the mood.'

It was an understatement to say the least.

The party was a hit, that much was obvious, music rolled through the house until every pane of glass shook. No one else seemed to notice but even the rabbits who lived on the wallpaper in the hallway seemed to be having a good time, hopping around the baseboards, their first social occasion in years.

'Maybe later,' I said, trying on a smile and ignoring the uncomfortable fit. 'I'll come find you.'

'Em, you shouldn't be on your own right now.'

Jackson looked too serious for his seventeen years.

'And you should be enjoying your birthday party,' I replied. 'You could at least try to have fun. You don't want to ruin Lydia's night, do you?'

It was a low blow but he knew when he was beat.

'Fine. I'll go back in, but if you're not down here in an hour, I'm coming to get you,' he told me, pressing himself up against the wall as two girls I vaguely recognized from the party at the DeSoto raced by us. 'Or worse, I'll send Lyds.'

'One hour,' I confirmed, acknowledging the threat. 'You have my word.'

The second I opened my bedroom door, I knew I would break my promise. Sitting on the window seat, staring out at the night sky, was Wyn.

'Emily.'

He leapt to his feet and crossed the room before I'd even let go of the door handle.

'Wyn? What are you doing here?'

He barrelled into me, knocking the back of my head against the door and embracing me so tightly, the breath I'd been holding since I saw him escaped as a gasp, along with the rest of the oxygen in my lungs.

'I couldn't explain it all in a message, I had to see you, had to make sure you were OK, that you were ready.'

The rambled words barely cut through my shock.

'The trial is set for tomorrow, on the full moon, like I said it would be.' Wyn released me just long enough to brand my forehead with his kiss then pulled me back in. 'The pack is coming, Em, the whole pack.'

A trial. My trial. For the murder of Cole Evans.

'You couldn't call?' I replied, trying to find steady ground with a simple question.

'They took my phone.'

A wave of fear threatened to drown me.

'They know?' I whispered. 'About us?'

'No. It's standard before a phase. We have a network that

moves our phones around so we aren't tracked all together in one place.'

'But the wolves change. How can anyone move them around?'

'Only the male wolves have to change,' he said, face buried in my neck, inhaling deeply. 'Female-identifying Weres have more control. Resisting the phase is brutal but two females deny the moon each month to run the network – family members mostly, like my dad, and sometimes a kid who wasn't chosen for initiation. It doesn't matter, what matters is that I got here before them.'

'And they let you go,' I stated slowly.

'Told them I was coming to see my girl.'

'I thought you told them we broke up?'

He released his hold on me, looking down, his forehead creased with confusion.

'Gramps didn't question it. Said something about teenagers breaking up and getting back together all the time and warned me to be at the apartment by dawn.'

I wanted to believe him. I had to believe him. But Jackson's questions rattled back and forth in my mind.

'There was a pack leader meeting this morning, I wasn't allowed inside but I heard enough. Told Gramps I was leaving, got right in my truck and didn't stop.'

'Wyn,' I said, pushing my doubts as far away as I could. 'What's going to happen tomorrow?'

When he growled, the pink painted roses on my walls turned blood red.

'Someone will come to you at midday and issue terms, tell you where to be and when.'

'Here?'

'Anywhere. They'll have eyes on you from dawn.'

It wasn't a reassuring thought.

'They know who you are,' he said. 'They don't need a

twenty-four-seven watch. Even in Savannah with your magic blocking them, the most experienced wolves will be able to hunt you on the day of the phase. Our senses are still heightened in the daytime.'

'So someone will come.' I broke away from him completely, moving to perch on the edge of my bed, creating distance but not clarity. 'Then what? I'm supposed to sit around and wait for them to roll up and rip my heart out? Doesn't sound like a very tempting offer.'

Wyn stood in front of me, his grey shirt crumpled from hours in the car, the laces of his boots untied. His eyes were rimmed red and I realized, with a gut punch of pain, he had been crying in his truck on the way here.

'They'll make it sound like you have a chance, offer to let you bring a second, but whatever sentence is passed down to you will apply to the second also.'

'Meaning they'll kill us both?'

'Weres are forbidden to take human lives. It's a high crime. If you bring a human second and you're found guilty, the pack won't kill them but whoever it is will wish they were dead. They'll take the second's hands, eyes and tongue to prevent them from telling anyone what happened. I'm sure they're hoping you'll bring Ashley, save them the task of hunting her down.'

'Wyn, that's sick.'

'It's beyond cruel,' he agreed. 'And it keeps our secrets.'

'If it's such a crime for Weres to take a human life, how come my killing Cole doesn't count as self-defence?'

'Because a witch isn't a human as far as they're concerned. It won't matter that you didn't know, all they care about is one dead Were versus one living witch.'

I pressed both hands into the mattress but there was no way to steady myself.

'Do they know about Lydia?' I asked, and he shook his head.

'But if they find out, and they will, they'll kill her too. And they'll mutilate Jackson and his mom and anyone else in their family who could potentially continue the line. I know you're strong but it's only you and Lydia, and the whole south-eastern pack is coming to Savannah to kill you and I don't know what to do!'

The last part was a roar. It was only the music blasting downstairs that kept his voice from summoning everyone in the house.

'Do you know how they found out?' I asked. 'Was it Astrid?'

He shook his head again.

'No one mentioned her name.' He sank down at the side of me, my mattress softening under his weight and pushing the two of us together. 'I asked, but they won't tell me. Pack leaders and their council only.'

None of this should've been so alarming. We knew it was coming, knew the wolves would be at my door on the night of the full moon. All I could do was wait.

'We're panicking over nothing,' I said, forcing myself to be calm, one hand clinging to my wooden bedpost. 'We're safe. No one can get into Bell House; they can't touch us here.'

'Are you sure?' he asked, unintentionally echoing Jackson's question as he turned to face me with challenging eyes. 'Are you certain the house can defend you against a whole pack of wolves?'

I looked to my home, the vines that ran up and down my bedroom walls growing at an alarming rate, weaving themselves into a defensive thicket of thorns and building up protection from the inside out.

'She won't go down without a fight,' I told him. 'I wouldn't want to be in the shoes of anyone who showed up here meaning harm to a witch.'

'I don't know what to do.' Wyn stared blankly at the floorboards. 'Do I go back and try to talk my mom down? Do I stay here and try to protect you? We can't run, they'd find us. A wolf hasn't been taken out by a witch in over a century. They're pulling everyone in for this, everyone, dozens of Weres, maybe hundreds. They want to make an example of you, Emily, eradicate the witches for good.'

I instinctively ran my hand through his hair, letting reality sink in. I could stay in Bell House for the full moon but not forever.

'You should go,' I said, even as I curled my fingers in his hair so tightly I felt the tension against his scalp. 'If they arrive while you're here, they'll kill you.'

'Worse. They'll exile me, I'll be a lone wolf. I'd rather be dead.'

'Don't say that,' I ordered. 'Never say that. You wouldn't be alone, you'd have me. You'll always have me, no matter what.'

Wyn twisted against my grip on his hair, his lips finding the inside of my forearm, connecting wherever they could.

'It's not that simple,' he murmured against my skin. 'Living through the phase every month without your pack would tear your soul into pieces. The only wolf exiled from our pack took his own life after the first phase, the pain was too much.'

'What about Astrid?'

'She must be strong,' he admitted. 'But she also attacked you in a public place in the middle of a huge party. You don't think she's gone insane already?'

'There are still things we don't know,' I said, tugging on his arm like a little kid trying to make a grown-up listen when their mind was already made up. 'We still don't know how she's phasing outside the moon cycle. There has to be a part of this picture we haven't seen yet.'

'The part we haven't seen is where they cut your heart out

of your body and I am forced to stand beside my mother and watch!' Wyn yelled.

He leapt up from the bed and stalked off into the middle of the room. With his arms framing his head, each hand clasping the opposite elbow, he stood with his back to me, like he couldn't bear to look at me. Frozen in place, my mind scuttled back an hour or so, Sistah Mariama and her knowing smile.

'Do they know about the prophecy?' I asked.

'Weres don't believe in that kind of magic,' Wyn replied without moving. 'They think to interfere with the natural order is to corrupt nature itself, but they don't know you, Em, they haven't seen the beautiful things I've seen.'

'Or the ugly,' I replied. 'They're right, magic can be used to corrupt. Look at Catherine.'

'That's why I never told them.'

He turned to face me, the weight of all our secrets pressing down on his shoulders as he came to stand before me. He kicked off his boots and laid down on the bed, resting on his side, and the golden cord that tied us together wrapped tighter and tighter as I lay down beside him. Eye to eye, I studied his beautiful face and thought of every promise we'd ever made to each other. The first time I saw him from my window, the first day we spoke, our first kiss, our first fight, waking up in his arms at the beach. Then I thought of the future I'd dreamed for us and tried not to cry when I wondered why the blessing had never granted me a vision that showed me that story. Wyn's eyes had turned soft and hazy, more green than grey as his pupils expanded, drinking me in.

'Do you remember when I said I thought I saw you,' I said, shaking as I found the words. 'The night after the full moon?'

'I was on the mountain. It wasn't me.'

He stroked my face tenderly and my skin prickled under his touch, the exact same feeling as my magic.

'Are you sure?' I asked, aching as I made myself say it. 'This is going to sound crazy, because I know you believe that, but is it possible the pack is using you to get to me without you knowing it?'

Wyn's hand stopped moving, the back of his fingers stilled against my skin.

'Just say no,' I said, calm as I could be. 'Say no, Emily, it isn't possible, there's no way.'

But he didn't. Every muscle in his face contracted at once, tightening until he turned into a statue.

'Wyn?'

No response. The panic that had been bubbling under the surface rose up, calling my name and the room shook gently. Not an earthquake, only a tremor, so slight no one else would notice but to me it was the most tempting invitation. How good would it feel to lose control? How much of a relief to let go?

'Wyn, please,' I said, begging now, fighting my darkest urges and trying to pull him into the light at the same time. 'It was a stupid suggestion. You know where you were, you even remember the phase, you said so yourself.'

'I said I remember most of it, not all of it,' he replied, staring at his own hands as though they belonged to someone else. 'What if they have done something to me? I could be a danger to you and not know it.'

'We're not talking about random Weres.' I seized his face in my hands, forcing him to look at me. 'It's your mother, your own mother. She wouldn't do that to you.'

'Wouldn't she?'

The room shuddered again.

'The way I see it, there are two choices,' he said. 'I go back and we find out the truth, or I stay here and face exile.'

'If you stay here, we'll find a way out of this,' I told him.

'I'll protect you the way you protected me at Hilton Head, the way we will always protect each other.'

There was nothing I could say that would soothe the situation, no more promises to make when I didn't know if they could be kept. Stick or twist, the choice had to be his but he didn't say anything. Instead, he grabbed my shirt and pulled me into a kiss so deep, so powerful, my mind went blank and the world ceased to be. We spoke with our hands instead of words, with no room for misunderstanding, and a sweet heat exploded in my chest when he pushed me back against the pile of pillows at the head of the bed and weighed my body down with his.

He let me lead, dragging his shirt up over his head so my hands could roam over the muscles in his back, learning the topography of his body, memorizing the moments that made him catch his breath, and I liquefied beneath him. I wasn't Emily anymore, or Emma, Paul's daughter or Catherine's witch. I existed only in this moment and only with Wyn. Forehead to forehead, our eyelashes flickered together and my breathing turned shallow. I could've stared into his eyes forever, the pale green and soft grey, the bronze flecks that danced around his pupils, and a new darker ring of desire that created a halo around his iris. We couldn't give up, I wouldn't give up. All I wanted was an escape.

When Wyn reached for the top button of my jeans, I kissed him again and felt myself slip inside his mind to see the exact same love I had for him mirrored right back. We belonged to each other, I was his and he was mine, and I needed to show him how much I loved him just as much as he wanted to show me.

My room filled with a soft pink smoke, hazy and fragrant, as roses grew up the frame of my four poster bed, a blanket of flowers covering my floor and covering the door, wrapping themselves around the wood until it vanished, no way in and no way out. My lips were already tender and bruised but I couldn't get enough, every touch was new, every sensation shocking in the best way. It shouldn't have been a surprise. Of course it felt this good, of course we felt the same way, it was me and Wyn. Each step we took together broke new ground, each breath, each sigh, until I was consumed by him.

Then Wyn paused for a moment, bringing his hands back up to my face, staring at me with wonder, like I was brand new and so precious.

'I love you,' he said, even though he didn't have to.

'I love you,' I said, wishing there were better words, words no one else had ever used before. Those weren't good enough, second-hand and shopworn, whatever this was between us deserved something brand new and never seen, with no one in the world allowed to utter them except for us.

Every moment we had together was sacred and I wouldn't waste a second. All the sounds of the party were far away, all the fear and all the threats left in another world, and the quiet of my room was filled with sharp sighs and sweet gasps and the sound of superfluous clothing hurriedly removed.

The silence didn't break so much as splinter, shattering with the glass in my windowpane. Downstairs, I heard screaming but in my room there was only panic and the low growl of the wolf that stood beside my bed. Huge and grey with gnashing jaws, its eyes were yellow, surrounded by more red than white.

A wolf, a Were, inside Bell House, inside my room.

'What the hell . . .'

Wyn threw his arms out wide, his shirtless body covering mine, too much bare flesh exposed for the present danger. 'You can't be here. This isn't possible.'

The intruder didn't feel like explaining itself. Gashes from the very real thorns protecting the pair of us ran up and down the wolf's sides but still it crouched, mean eyes flickering back and forth from Wyn to me, as if playing a game to make its choice.

'If you touch her, I'll kill you.'

Wyn's words were pure violence but the threat was redundant.

The Were wasn't there for me.

Everything happened so quickly. It lunged, seizing Wyn's shoulder in its jaws, shaking its head to tear through muscle and bone, then tossed him across the room like a chew toy. I didn't scream, I couldn't move, and Wyn didn't make a sound. We stared at each other in shock, his body limp against the frame of my window until the wolf grabbed him again, leapt out into the magnolia tree, leaving nothing behind but a trail of blood.

I stared at the jagged pieces of glass, jutting out of the frame like broken teeth. Wyn was gone. The roses around my bed turned to stone, the field of flowers on the floor burst into flames before dissolving into piles of ash, and finally, when I opened my mouth and screamed, every pane of glass in every window of the house shattered into sparkling sand.

Chapter Thirty-Nine

'Emily?'

When Ashley and Lydia came hurtling through my door, my body was on the floor, imprinted in the stone and ash, but I was not. I hovered somewhere above, close to the ceiling, watching.

'No!' Lydia screamed as she hurled herself at me, grabbing my shoulder as Ashley checked my pulse. I heard thunder and lightning and raised voices.

'She's alive,' Ashley confirmed, pulling up my eyelids and releasing them when she saw the milky irises underneath. 'I think.'

'What do we do?' Lydia turned to my aunt, desperate and afraid. 'Ashley, what do we do?'

'We calm down for a start.'

She sat back on her heels and surveyed the state of my room. The stone roses, the inch-deep carpet of ash, the broken windows. Then she looked up, staring right at me, through me.

'Go downstairs,' Ashley said. 'Tell everyone our boiler exploded, then get them gone and send your brother up here. I need to move Em.'

'Already here,' Jackson replied, careening through the door so fast, he almost tripped over his own feet. He stalled in front of my bed and jerked back at the sight of my motionless body. 'Is she . . .?'

'She needs to be moved,' Ashley repeated. 'I need downstairs emptied *now*.'

Lydia accepted her assignment without further question and raced out of my room, hollering at the top of her voice. The house wanted to help too, encouraging the stragglers out of the parlour and into the streets, all the way off Bell property. It was still reeling from the attack, violated and unsure, and I ran a hand over the chandelier above my bed to soothe it as best I could. My best was all I had now. I hoped it would be enough.

'This better work,' Ashley said through gritted teeth.

Jackson stood close by, carrying my limp body in his arms, as she cautiously raised a hand to the craft room door.

'I don't like you, you don't like me,' she told the blue painted wood. 'But she needs you and I know damn well you need her.'

The door opened slowly, little lights like fireflies guiding the way.

'You can't go in there.'

Ashley thrust out her arm to stop Jackson in his tracks and helped him lower me to my feet, wrapping my arms around her shoulders and bearing my weight herself.

'I don't know if I can go in there,' she said. Then, taking a deep breath, she added, 'Guess we're gonna find out.'

The door slammed shut as soon as we crossed the threshold and Ashley gasped at the beauty of the room, the iridescent walls, the heavenly skylight. As my feet touched the floor, I flew back into my body, eyes snapping open, limbs filled with life.

'Thank you,' Ashley muttered, although I didn't know to whom. 'You're alive.'

The Witch and the Wolf

'It was a Were,' I told her, feeling my way over to the bed on the far side of the room. 'It had to be Astrid.'

'Inside the house?'

I nodded and she looked more afraid than ever.

'She's . . . gone, right? No way she came into Bell House, attacked you and survived.'

'She didn't touch me,' I said lightly as I laid myself down. 'She came for Wyn. I have no idea how she got inside.'

Ashley had more questions but I didn't have time to answer, not when the blessing was calling to me so very loudly. She was still talking when I rolled over and reached for the silver ceremonial dagger. She stopped when I pressed the blade to my skin.

'Emily, don't.'

'Ashley, it's done.'

I drew the point lightly across my palm, a thin line of scarlet springing up against my pale flesh. Holding my palm against my shirt, stained with Wyn's blood, I laid back down and exhaled slowly through pursed lips. The white shell-like walls shimmered, the rainbow shifting through the colour spectrum, from pastel pink to rose red to a deep and menacing maroon-like bruise, throbbing as the cut on my hand pulsed in time with the house's protest. When I fell backwards into the velvet nothingness, it was almost a relief.

At least it was until I saw her.

Astrid Hansen, dark hair, vicious eyes, standing in a kitchen and peering through a round window. She wore black pants and a white shirt, like a dozen other people around her, some of them carrying silver trays. I followed when she pushed through the swinging door and into a huge ballroom, a party. The DeSoto. In a corner, I saw myself talking to Ileen Stovell and Astrid's snarl turned into a smirk. The scene changed. Astrid approached Ms Stovell, offering her a glass of champagne. She took it without paying much attention and didn't notice the small green ball fizzing in the bottom of the glass. Chamomile, lemon balm, something to make her more suggestible. Ms Stovell smiled at Astrid and the darkness rushed back in, stealing me away.

I found myself in a grand house I didn't recognize, the parlour teeming with photographs of people I did. The Stovell family. This was their Savannah home and Astrid Hansen was inside. In a daze, Ileen showed her around, her husband was away in Florida for at least a month, maybe more, no real friends to come calling, no one to intervene on her behalf. Astrid chose a room, Ileen's room, and forced her host to sleep on the floor. From here she watched and waited. From here she made her plans. More moments flashed past, me and Ms Stovell in the square. Eating lunch with Lydia and Alex. Sitting on my balcony with Wyn. Lydia and me in the magic shop.

What came next took me far from Savannah and my body screamed as my spirit soared away across the seas. I was still with Astrid, her protests loud and defiant in her native language. I couldn't understand most of what she said but she was clearly unhappy. Not nearly as unhappy as the woman standing before her. She was a witch and afraid of this version of Astrid, but it hadn't always been that way. There had been a time when she attempted to guide the conflicted young Were along a happier path, a time of empathy, but now she knew she would live to regret it. She knew she would die to regret it. Astrid dropped a palm full of stones on the forest floor and lunged at her mentor, no knife, only the claws at the end of her own fingertips, and slashed at her throat, coating the stones in blood.

I turned away when the light vanished from the witch's eyes and the forest was gone, the blessing leading me back to the void.

'It's not as simple as you thought, is it?' Catherine said, sauntering out of the darkness. 'Protecting those you love.'

The Witch and the Wolf

'What does she want?' I asked, arms reaching out for something solid to hold on to, but there was nothing. We were nowhere.

'What do you think?'

'Where is she now?'

Catherine shrugged.

'Not here.'

She placed her hands on my shoulders and met me, emerald eye to emerald eye. I clutched at her wrists but my hands passed right through.

'I didn't bring you this far only to come this far,' she said. 'If you die, the prophecy fails.'

'You're saying if I die, I can't end the world?'

'I'm saying if you die, you cannot save it.'

My grandmother faded into the distance, and another voice intoned a familiar echo.

'*When the dead fight back. When the earth consumes. A lie becomes the truth. She will return.*'

'Who is she?' I yelled to no one 'Is it you?'

There was no answer.

When I opened my eyes, it was already morning.

Chapter Forty

One way or another, I would've got myself into the Stovells' Savannah home but it was all the easier when Ashley produced a key, bequeathed to Catherine 'in case of emergencies' years ago.

'What exactly are we looking for?' my aunt asked as the key turned in the lock without protest and we let ourselves inside.

'I don't know exactly,' I said, speaking in hushed tones. 'I should probably warn you, there's a chance it won't be anything fun.'

'You mean she's going to want to give me another lecture on the evils of showing your belly button in public?'

I couldn't even raise a laugh. The house was dark, literally and figuratively, all the curtains closed in the middle of the day and a strange gloom hovering that made the hair on my arms stand up. It was also eerily quiet, only the hum of an air conditioning system that wasn't quite up to the task of a Georgia summer breaking the silence.

'Nice place,' Ashley commented, peering around the front hallway. 'Tasteful.'

It was. Nice and tasteful. It was also boiling over with magic.

'How long have the Stovell family been in Savannah?' I

asked, pausing by a low upholstered bench and a rack full of shoes, momentarily wondering if I should take off my sandals. A stupid thought, given how badly I wanted to turn around and run away already.

'A long time, I think. Not as long as us or the Powells. They weren't witches, if that's what you're wondering; Catherine would've mentioned it.'

That much was obvious from the way my grandmother treated Ileen when they were younger. I couldn't believe she'd ever treat another witch or former witch so cruelly. Well, not without what she considered good reason. We were at the door to the parlour when I stopped so suddenly, Ashley almost fell over me.

'What the hell?' she hissed as I turned around and went back to the shoe rack. There, right on top, was the exact same pair of sneakers I'd seen at the Stovells' beach house in Hilton Head. Sweat began to bead on my forehead and my hand closed around the silver and moonstone pin I'd brought in my pocket.

'You shouldn't be here,' I said to Ashley. 'You need to go back to Bell House.'

She picked up a shoe horn, long and elaborately carved out of solid oak with a duck's head cast in brass for a handle.

'I don't think so,' she said, wielding the thing like a baseball bat. 'We're doing this together.'

The parlour door was open, every bit as elegant as you'd expect from a historic southern home, but it was in complete disarray. Glasses, plates, bowls all used and dirty, covered the coffee table and credenza, with half-empty coffee cups lining up and down the mantel over the fireplace. There were clothes too, jackets and sweaters mostly, discarded on the armchairs or the floor, and the sofa was covered in blankets with a pillow at one end.

'This place has to have at least five bedrooms.' Ashley poked at an abandoned black rainslicker with the end of her shoehorn. 'Why would someone bother to camp out in the living room?'

'Best view of the hotel,' I replied, looking out the window and right at the back entrance of the DeSoto.

Ashley continued sorting through the items scattered around the room, the occasional displeased sound squeaking out of her throat.

'Most of these clothes don't look like they'd fit the woman you described,' she said. 'Unless she's going for a super oversized fit.'

'You mean our lone wolf might not be so lone after all?'

It was a harrowing thought and one that posed more questions than it answered.

Ashley picked up a large black hoodie, a long white tank top, a pair of tube socks.

'If she went to the pack, told them about you . . .'

'Then they have Wyn,' I murmured. 'Which means he's safe.'

'But you aren't,' she said sharply. 'Em, get it together, this is not good. A lone wolf is bad, a lone wolf working with a vengeful pack hellbent on ripping out your heart is even worse. I need you to focus—'

Ashley cut herself off by clapping a hand over her mouth.

'What is it?' I asked, rushing over to where she stood, but she quickly moved around the sofa and pushed me away as a bleak call sounded out all around the house.

'You don't need to see it,' she assured me, hurrying me out of the parlour. 'But unless the junior league took up animal sacrifice this season, I think we can officially confirm this is where your wolf has been hiding.'

Back in the hallway, even though I didn't want to let them in, I closed my eyes and listened to the voices clawing at the edges of my mind. There were so many and they were all in pain. Awful, ugly things had happened here and we were nowhere near the worst of them. Every room was hurting from what had happened here and the whorls of magic were so intense, I could almost see them. I hadn't experienced anything so chaotic since I saw the craft room blackened by Catherine's influence. It was as though Astrid had taken that same energy and turned the whole house against nature.

'We need to check the kitchen,' I said, almost sure I saw something move at the end of the hall, turning a corner into the back of the house. 'Or at least I do.'

'You're not leaving me alone out here,' Ashley argued as she trailed after me. 'Whatever is waiting in the kitchen can't be any worse than what I just saw in the parlour.'

She had no idea how wrong she was.

Neither of us screamed. The scene was too sickening for that; any kind of noise would've felt performative, for our benefit only, and poor Ileen Stovell deserved better. In the centre of the kitchen, right by the butcher block table, Ileen's body lay on the floor, all of her limbs protruding at the wrong angles. Ashley physically turned me away, pulling my head to her chest until she heaved and ran out the room, leaving me alone to look again. Not all her limbs. Ileen's hands were missing. Her empty eye sockets stared into eternity and her mouth was open, the tongue cut out, frozen in an endless scream only I could hear.

No hands, no eyes, no tongue, no way she could identify a Were. A task rendered all the more difficult by the wound that ran across her throat, a gaping scarlet slit cut from ear to ear.

'I'm sorry,' I whispered to the unnatural scene, words I was getting too used to hearing and saying. 'I am so sorry.'

Backing out of the room, never once looking away, I found Ashley, crouched in a ball on the bottom step of the stairs, tears pouring down her face.

'I don't know,' she whispered. 'I don't know what to say.'

'There's nothing we can say,' I replied, my turn to soothe her for a change. 'All we can do is try to make sure it doesn't happen to anyone else.'

I was angry, beyond angry. To take Wyn was bad but he was another Were, he was a player in this game and he knew the risks. What Astrid had done to Ileen Stovell was one of the most brutal things I had ever seen, not only the act itself but the meaningless death. Ms Stovell had done nothing to deserve this ugly end other than have the misfortune to be born close in age and location to my grandmother. A whole life spent trying to be someone's friend until she found herself face to face with me at the DeSoto when Astrid happened to be watching. It was senseless and disgusting and I would never allow anything like it to happen again. For weeks, people had been asking me who I wanted to be, what I wanted to do with my life, and I didn't have an answer.

Now I did.

I wanted an end to all this death and violence, whatever the cost. I wanted Wyn, Ashley and my friends to be happy. I wanted to know that on the day I took my last breath, it wasn't the end of a life I had wasted.

Ashley and I stood shakily, leaning on each other as we prepared to leave, before the authorities inevitably arrived. They would never solve what happened here and I knew years from now it would be another ghost story for the tourists of Savannah. Ileen Stovell would always be remembered.

'Do the Stovells have children?' I asked Ashley, pausing by the door as she replaced the shoe horn in the umbrella rack where she'd found it.

'Two daughters. Both moved away, one is in New York, the other somewhere in the Midwest, I think. Poor things.'

'No sons?'

The Witch and the Wolf

'She had a son,' Ashley said with a questioning look. 'He died when he was just a toddler, some kind of terrible allergic reaction, Catherine said, no one could do anything to save him. Said the family was never the same after that.'

At the end of the hallway, Ileen Stovell crouched down beside a little boy, the same blonde hair as her, the same sparkling blue eyes. She whispered something in his ear and he giggled, waving at me, before he pulled away into one of the other downstairs rooms. I raised a hand in return then followed Ashley outside, closing the door on Ms Stovell until the next time we met.

Chapter Forty-One

The Were emissary arrived at exactly midday, just as Wyn said she would.

'Emily Bell,' she said, looking surprised when I opened the front door myself. 'My name is Cerian Price. Do you know why I'm here?'

'I know why you think you're here,' I replied. 'Won't you come in?'

She was alone and while she was on her guard, she wasn't afraid. She truly believed she was on the right side of a fight that needn't exist.

'You'll forgive me for not offering you a drink, I'm a little pressed for time,' I said, arms folded as she scanned the house, mapping it, just in case. 'I imagine you also have places to be.'

'Six feet under our patio,' Ashley commented as she, Lydia and Jackson all emerged from the parlour and flanked me on both sides. Our small but perfectly formed army.

'This place is something else,' Cerian said, craning her neck to get a better look at the third-floor ceiling. 'Can't imagine Wyn in a place like this.'

I flinched at the sound of his name and she smirked.

'I can't imagine you walking out with all your bones intact, so whatever you came here to say, say it.'

Lydia moved forward to stand right beside me and for the first time, Cerian looked concerned. She took a step back towards the door as the house closed it, locked and bolted, with all five of us inside.

'Another witch,' she murmured. 'How?'

'God forbid women have hobbies,' Lydia replied with a theatrical sigh. 'Did you really come here for story time or do you have a message?'

'You know why I'm here.'

She was thrown but not so much she couldn't recover, even though she wasn't pleased to take this message back to the pack. Her stance, solid, feet hip-width apart, hands behind her back. Show no fear. She almost nailed it.

'The Witch known as Emily James Bell hereby stands accused of the murder of Cole Evans, initiated Were, son of pack leader, Pamela Evans, and member of the south-eastern pack,' she declared. 'Your trial will take place tonight, one hour after moonrise in Morrell Park, Savannah, Georgia.'

'That's it?' I looked over at my friends, feigning disappointment. I hoped she couldn't tell how much I was sweating under my black shirt. 'Honestly, I was expecting more fanfare.'

'Right, shouldn't she have a trumpet or something?' Ashley agreed. 'At least a fancy scroll.'

'You are permitted to choose a second,' Cerian continued, frustration turning into anger. 'Should you be unable to stand trial for whatever reason, they will take your place.'

'Guess that's my cue,' Lydia said as she took another step forward. 'It's your lucky day, a try-one-get-one-free deal on witches.'

'One more thing,' the young Were said casually. 'I need an offrian.'

'A what?'

I scowled at my surprise when her face opened up into a beautiful, brilliant smile. She'd caught me off guard and she knew it.

'An offrian. An offering. Witches can't be trusted. We need to take something that will guarantee your presence. More specifically, we need to take someone.'

'You already have Wyn,' I snapped. 'Isn't that enough?'

'Do we? I wouldn't know about that.'

Her poker face was flawless and I couldn't tell whether or not she was lying. She brushed her hair over her shoulder, allowing it to cascade over the front of her plaid shirt. 'Guess he forgot fill you in about the offrian . . . or maybe we forgot to tell him.'

'You knew,' I said softly and she laughed. 'The pack knew about us.'

'Are you really so arrogant you thought we might not?' she replied, a sickened expression written all over her pretty face. 'The pack keeps tabs on new members, especially new members who run away not once but twice to visit some girl down in Savannah where your sick magic still thrives. Fair to say we're a tad more diligent when it's the pack leader's son. Only son, thanks to you. Wyn knew what we wanted him to know. It was a test and he failed, so you won't be the only one on trial tonight.'

'A mother wouldn't punish her son for falling in love. He hasn't done anything wrong,' I said, rage burning inside of me. 'You can't punish him for walking into a trap you set.'

'Oh, honey, you don't know Pamela Evans. You couldn't possibly understand, there is nothing she won't do to protect her pack.'

She was wrong. I did understand. I might not know Pamela Evans but I did know Catherine Bell.

The Witch and the Wolf

'Boy, was his grandpa wrong about you. Not nearly so smart as he thought you were.' The sneer on Cerian's face was full of disdain, not only for me but the wolf she felt had betrayed her too. 'Things might go easier for him if he came willingly. Not that exile is ever easy.'

'What do you mean, if he came willingly?' Jackson cut in, one hand on my shoulder. 'You already have him.'

'What?'

'You took him last night,' I said, and the colours of the wall shifted from peach to pink to red. I was barely able to restrain myself. 'Or Astrid did.'

'Astrid? Your so-called lone wolf? You can quit with that story now; we're not buying it. If there was a lone wolf in our region, the pack would be well aware.'

'Tell that to Ileen Stovell,' Lydia said, but I held my arm out in front of her, cutting her off before she could launch at the Were. She was telling the truth.

'I don't have time for these games,' Cerian declared. 'We'll catch up with Wyn one way or another. Now nominate the collateral before I take someone whether you like it or not.'

'I'll go.'

The speed with which Jackson put himself between me and Cerian knocked the air out of my lungs.

'No, you can't.'

I thought of the promise I'd made to Virginia, Lydia whimpering at my side as he nodded at the two of us.

'Has to be me. Can't be my grandmother, and I'm not going to stand idly by and let Ashley volunteer as tribute.'

'And to think you call yourself a feminist,' Ashley clucked, but her voice broke as Jackson crossed to stand next to Cerian, as though we were setting up a game of Red Rover.

The Were snatched up the collar of his shirt despite the fact he went voluntarily and I knew he would never try to run, even if it meant his life. She had no idea what honour meant, not like Jackson.

'It's all good,' he said, staring hard at me and his sister. 'I was only going to be in the way. Tell Grandmother not to worry, I'll be back tonight.'

'We'll see about that,' Cerian said, yanking him towards the door like a dog on a leash. 'Be seeing ya.'

'Wait!' I rushed at Jackson and threw my arms around his neck, pressing my face close to his. His captor looked away in disgust but Jackson only nodded when I pulled away.

We let them go, Lydia, Ashley and I, standing firm in the foyer as she marched Jackson down the steps, the darkening skies turning all the oaks of Lafayette Square into sinister silhouettes.

'That wasn't part of the plan,' Lydia said shakily, a tease of thunder cracking in the sky. 'We can't let them take him, Em, we can't.'

'The plan has changed.'

I opened my fist to reveal Jackson's silver chain and their mother's opal ring.

'What is it?' Ashley asked, plucking it from my palm to inspect the stones.

'Our advantage,' I replied. 'We just got it back.'

Chapter Forty-Two

The moon was set to rise at 8.21 p.m. and Morrell Park was a twenty-minute walk from Bell House. We had less than an hour between moonrise and the trial to accomplish too many things but we had little choice in the matter.

'This isn't exactly how I imagined conducting my first Becoming ceremony,' I told Lydia as we changed hurriedly in the kitchen. My room was still haunted by the violence of the night before, just stepping inside to retrieve what I needed was difficult enough.

'This should be a celebration, we shouldn't be hurrying through it like this. There are supposed to be gowns.'

'Em, do I look like a gown girlie?' Lydia shucked off her jeans and tank top, trading them for a pair of cargo pants and white long-sleeved shirt. 'Anyway, I've already been to more than my fair share of ceremonies and everyone knows the party afterwards is the best part. This is good. We burn through the yapping and skip straight to the good part.'

Cinching a belt around the carpenter jeans I'd borrowed from Jackson, I frowned.

'I think you might be the first person in history to describe standing trial for murder as "the good bit".'

'Love to be a trendsetter.' She held out her arms and struck a pose. 'Same with the ensemble. Here we have Lydia Powell modelling the finest in Becoming ritual-slash-Were-combat chic. Long sleeves, long pants for practicality, metallic accents for flair and most importantly, pockets for snacks.'

'Snacks and spells,' I corrected. 'Don't get them mixed up.'

Over on the kitchen table, Ashley was lining up the concoctions she and Viriginia had been working on all afternoon, all of them wrapped in muslin bags except for one. The pouch in my back pocket, the smallest of them all but it was already dragging me down.

'Ready?'

Virginia opened the door to the kitchen from the outside, glowing with pride in her long white dress, the traditional Powell family Becoming gown. The only evidence of their connection to the blessing, something so precious even Edwina couldn't bring herself to destroy it. Since Lydia had politely declined the chance to dress up as her great-great-grandmother, Virginia elected to wear it herself, and despite her distress over Jackson's disappearance and Lydia's part in the trial, she still found time to whisper to Ashley how pleased she was to know that the thing still fit.

'I can see the moon,' she said, hurrying us down the steps and into the garden. 'We're ready.'

'You know your lines?' Lydia asked me as I picked up the ceremonial dagger I'd already warned her would be making another appearance.

'Let's hope so,' I replied. 'We don't have time for a dress rehearsal.'

My own Becoming ceremony was not one of my fondest memories. I was determined to ensure that wouldn't be the case for Lydia. Ashley and Virginia waited on either side of the copper arch at the end of the garden, woven with sweet-scented jasmine and morning glory. Time and time again, Catherine told me this ritual was supposed to be a beautiful thing. Time to see if that was true.

Lydia waited, shifting from one bare foot to the other as I passed under the arch. The blessing already alive in both of us. Magic wasn't a limited thing to be sliced up and shared. It was infinite, expanding and deepening as it grew, new possibilities blossoming in both me and Lydia as we took our places.

I searched inside myself for the door, the one that held all the knowledge of my ancestors. I didn't try to force it this time, only bowed my head and waited for it to open. Stop trying and know it is done. See it. Feel it. Our ancestors didn't hesitate. They passed through the open door, filling the garden with their presence and my heart with the knowledge. Lydia couldn't see them yet but I hoped she felt their presence, wishing even more love, even more hope, onto the latest in a long line of beloved sisters.

'Lydia Virginia Sarah Powell,' I said, the words flowing through me. 'Do you accept the blessing as the blessing accepts you?'

The earth was warm beneath my feet, soothing and grounding.

'I do,' Lydia replied, solemn but smiling.

'As the full moon represents wholeness and completion, we ask those who came before us to complete the Becoming and make our daughter whole,' I said, dagger in hand. 'We ask those who came before us to bring her into the blessing. We ask those who came before us to offer her their strength and wisdom and show her the path she must follow.'

I took a step backwards, Lydia's cue to make her choice. Without doubt or hesitation she walked through the archway and, above us, I saw a shower of meteorites shoot across the sky in celebration.

'One last thing.' I held out my hand with an 'I'm sorry' smile.

'Why is there always something gross at the end?' Lydia said, giving me the stink-eye. 'We can't pinky-swear instead?'

'The sooner we get it over with, the better,' I assured her. 'How do you feel?'

She rolled her shoulders like her skin was the wrong size for her body.

'Like I'm about to combust.' Lydia immediately held out her palm. 'Oh wow, I do not care for this part. Hurry up, slice and dice me, baby.'

'This part does burn a little,' I agreed. 'Let's not make it last longer than we need to.'

Without giving her time to think about what came next, I slashed her palm open with the dagger and did the same thing to myself, reopening the same wound I'd given myself the night before.

'We ask those who came before us to bring her into the blessing,' I called, raising my voice as the wind whipped up around us. 'As whole as the moon, she will Become.'

Clasping Lydia's hand in mine, I pulled her into me, embracing her not only as my best friend but as my sister. My blood was her blood, her life was my life. We both belonged to something bigger than ourselves now and I understood, in a very singular way, I would never be alone again.

'I saw them,' Lydia gasped as her knees buckled, leaning against me as Virginia rushed to our side, her eyes full of happy tears. 'My ancestors, the other Powell witches, they were all here.'

'Did you see my mama?' Virginia asked, her stately dignified voice now that of a little girl. 'Did you see Juliet?'

'And Sarah. They're safe and happy and they all love you so much.'

'Then that's all that matters.' She wiped away Lydia's tears while she allowed her own to fall. 'That's all that matters to me.'

'And you?' Ashley asked, pulling me away. 'Anything?'

'Everything,' I breathed, so full of the blessing I thought I might float away. I ached with magic, my skin buzzed like it was on fire. The voices of a hundred sleeping witches called out to me, fading away with the wind but promising to return.

'Then it's time.' Ashley drew in a deep breath and pulled me into a hug. 'I know you always wanted a sister,' she whispered in my ear. 'I wish I'd known how much I needed one. Be safe.'

'I will be,' I promised. 'You have everything you need?'

She nodded. 'I won't let you down.'

Somewhere on the other side of the city, wolves howled.

We were expected.

Shoulder to shoulder and stronger than ever, Lydia and I departed Bell House.

'They might be expecting us but I don't think they're ready,' Lydia said, tossing her head and whipping up a miniature tornado in the palm of her hand. Only minutes since her Becoming and her magic was already sharp and precise.

'Doesn't matter if they're ready, all that matters is that we are. You know the plan, you have everything you need?'

'Get in, get Jackson, get out,' she repeated for at least the hundredth time that day. 'Leave the rest of them to you.'

Without the opal ring, I was able to track Jackson exactly. Whatever magic Astrid was using to hide Wyn, the Weres didn't share it. The pack had convened down by River Street, moving along Factors Walk, where they'd held Jackson in the Cluskey Vaults for most of the day before moving to the park at sundown. I felt sick at the thought of it. Those vaults had dark histories of their own, not only used to hold the goods that came in from the merchant ships, but enslaved people. The wolves most likely couldn't know that, they couldn't hear the screams and cries that called out to me. It was a dark and cursed spot in our beautiful, complicated city, and only served to set the scene for the ugly night ahead.

Lydia and I stalked through the fading twilight as the moon moved higher in the sky. Between us, it was easy to convince people to stay indoors. There was an ever-present threat of thunder, the suggestion of a nightmarish storm. Leaving the house did not make sense, I whispered as we passed by home after home; probably best to stay away from the windows too, close the curtains. Maybe turn in extra early.

'We still don't know where Astrid is,' Lydia said as I opened the door to the empty Pirates' House, all staff and patrons having abandoned ship after the manager became convinced of an unexpected threat of flooding. 'Or what she's done with Wyn.'

'If she's planning to attack tonight, she knows where I am,' I replied. 'No reason why the plan won't work on her the same as it'll work on the others.'

'And you're sure it's going to work?'

I gave her a look as we opened the door to the pirates' tunnels, a maze built for crimping, tricking men into drinking too much and taking their gold then dragging their unconscious bodies down to their ships, long gone from land by the time the men awoke. These tunnels had literally destroyed lives. Tonight, I only hoped they could save some.

'Sure as I can be about anything,' I said, leading the way.

When the hard-packed ground under our feet shifted to an incline, I patted myself down one last time to check everything was where it needed to be. A healing poultice blended just for Wyn, another for Jackson, and in one zipped pocket, the silver and moonstone pin I'd used to kill Cole. Perhaps not the wisest move, bringing the murder weapon to my own trial, but the verdict was in and I'd decided it was better to be armed than not. There were other crystals, other herbs in my pockets and woven into my braid. Protective spells mostly: agrimony for shielding, white willow bark for amplifying lunar magic, and angelica, the herb that bore my mother's name, for protection and courage and more importantly to remind me of the love that brought me into the world when someone else was trying their best to take me out of it. I wore her locket around my neck, the diamond snowflake pendant from Lydia, even Catherine's aquamarine ring. All I'd left behind was the arfvedsonite, the black crystal given to me by my ancestor months ago. Whatever happened, tonight would be something to remember, not forget.

'They're close, I can sense them,' Lydia whispered, slowing her pace and pressing her hand against the roof of the tunnel. 'This is wild.'

'We still don't know exactly how your magic is going to manifest,' I replied, just as quiet. 'Ideally we'd be testing this out at home.'

'Don't worry about me, I always do better in exams than essays. What is it they say? Pressure makes diamonds?'

'We already made diamonds.' I pointed to my necklace and she reached for its twin around her neck. The same locket, the same snowflake and, beside them, her mother's opal ring, humming now with a different kind of magic. For twenty years, it hid Alex from my family. Now, infused with hyssop and wormwood and loaded with aconite, it hid my family from the Weres.

'Can you feel how many of them are up there?' I asked.

'No,' Lydia admitted, scrunching up her face. 'Jackson is

there. Other than him it's not entirely clear. Three, maybe four others? I must be wrong, there must be more.'

'There are more.' I pressed my own palms against the roof, the wooden supports soft and decaying with age but holding together just for us. 'Something is off.'

'You think Jackson kicked their asses?'

Her optimism might've made me laugh if I wasn't so afraid. There were at least a dozen more wolves above us but their energy read so weak, I could barely feel it.

'No way to know exactly what's going on until we get up there,' I said, facing the door with determination. 'Remember, do not let them bite you.'

Her ring wasn't the only thing dosed with aconite; our clothes were still damp to the touch from the hours they'd spent soaking, and Virginia had stitched so much silver thread into the fabric I could see Lydia sparkling even in the dark, but I didn't relish the thought of having to heal a mortal injury we didn't have the time or energy for.

'That's a general rule I like to live by,' she said, testing the two-hundred-year-old door to the riverside. 'On the count of three?'

'On the count of three,' I agreed. 'One, two—'

'Three.'

So much for the element of surprise.

The doors flew open and a rough hand grabbed me by the hair. I gripped the wrist, yelping in pain, yanked out of the tunnel and tossed across the park with too much strength to be human. I landed beside the Waving Girl statue, striking my head on her metal plinth. Stars sparked in front of my eyes as Lydia rolled to a stop by my side, coughing in pain, and crying out when a stained desert boot kicked her in the ribs. Squinting, I tried to focus. All I saw were worn jeans, a soft grey T-shirt, golden tanned skin and wavy, dark ash-coloured hair.

The Witch and the Wolf

I'd been prepared for everything but this.

'Wyn?' I groaned as he dragged me up to my feet.

'Not quite, witch.'

Cole Evans spat in my face then punched me so hard everything went black.

'Next time you kill a wolf, you'd better make sure he stays dead.'

Chapter Forty-Three

As he pulled back his hand to hit me again, someone caught his wrist to stop him.

'Do you want to make it so easy?' Astrid hissed. 'She doesn't deserve a quick death.'

'You're dead,' I managed to say through a throbbing jaw. 'I killed you.'

'You wish,' Cole said with a snarl.

'If I hadn't been there to pull him out the water, you might've come close,' Astrid added. 'Sloppy work. Very sloppy work, Emily.'

She ran her hand down his forearm, stopping at his bicep to squeeze it lovingly. It was too intimate a gesture, almost tender, and clashed with the violence in their posture. They were together, that much was obvious, but when he glanced over at her, I didn't know if I could call the connection between them love. Whatever she returned in her unnatural violet eyes wasn't quite the same.

'It was good of the pack to organize this for us,' she said, lightly flicking her wrist to gesture around the park. 'I like the silver cages, they're a nice touch.'

'And this way we get you and the pack in one fell swoop,' Cole added. 'Two birds, one stone.'

Astrid chuckled and crooked her finger under his chin. 'He loves efficiency, this one. Such a practical man.'

Her English was heavily accented but flawless. Her hair hung stick straight down her back and I wondered if the blood staining her hands belonged to Ileen Stovell, Wyn, or someone else altogether.

'Emily?'

A few feet away, Lydia roused, pressing at a spot on her left temple where a trickle of blood ran down her cheek.

'We don't have much time to chat,' Astrid said regretfully. 'My spells aren't strong enough, not yet, and I don't know how long I can keep these whelps asleep. If they wake up, I'll have to kill them all and that would be messy.'

'But we are going to kill them, right?' Cole sounded concerned. 'You said I could.'

'You want all your vengeance at once?' his girlfriend admonished. 'Efficient but greedy. Yes, Cole, we are going to kill them, but not tonight. Five, six bodies, I can deal with. A hundred wolves at once? Be sensible. Pack leader now, the rest of them later.'

The pack leader. His own mother. Who were their other intended victims?

When Cole dropped me back down to the ground, I reached into the pocket stuffed with spearmint and rue. Clarity and self-belief. I needed both, desperately. Scattered around the park were the bodies of six unconscious Weres, two of them already phased into wolves, four still in human form, one of them Pamela Evans. Behind Astrid, who was crouched over an open suitcase, were two large cages. The bars sparkled brighter than any iron or steel. Solid silver. In the cage closest to me, Jackson crouched in a corner, duct tape over his mouth, yelling wordlessly when our eyes met. Behind him was an enormous, unconscious wolf, its laboured breathing confirming it was alive. In the next, was Wyn, slumped and barely alive, his entire body painted with his own blood. Behind him was another gagged and bound body.

Alex Powell.

'What is she doing here?' I asked, half-crawling and half-dragging myself over to the terrified woman, huddled in a tight ball in the back of the cage. She didn't look up when she heard my voice, and when I got close enough, I saw her skin had been smeared with a mix of herbs and plants, cayenne pepper blended with stinging nettles and fresh aloe. A spell to ward off magic and stop me or Lydia sensing her presence. The mixture had to sting like hell but she seemed too out of it to feel much of anything.

'Don't ask me.' Cole booted the cage until a groan rattled out of his brother. 'She was in there when we found them. Had to make room for little brother though. Makes me sick. Didn't even put up a fight.'

I was so focused on Jackson, Alex and Wyn, I didn't see the dead body behind the cage until Cole kicked the corpse. A young man, maybe twenty, sprawled out on the grass, his neck crooked and open eyes unseeing. Another death on my conscience. Another face I would never forget.

'How did you get into Bell House?' I demanded, filling the question with indignation, refusing to show I was afraid. Grief and blame would have to wait.

'Your precious house is not very pet friendly,' Astrid replied, still busy with the suitcase. 'We only came for him, not you. It took a little finessing, but once the house was certain we meant no harm to any witch and blood or legal relative of the Bell family, we were able to force our way inside. Too trusting. Like you.'

The Witch and the Wolf

She limped over to me, favouring the side where she'd been burned at Hilton Head, her hands slick with a foul-smelling green paste. 'If you hadn't complicated everything by attacking Cole in the cemetery that night, everything would be as it should be by now. Your boy wouldn't be a part of this, none of your friends would have to die.'

'I was defending myself.' Every word I spoke scratched at my throat like a rusty nail. 'I didn't know Cole was a Were.'

The scent of the concoction on her hands made me gag, and I knew, whatever it was, that it would not be pleasant for me.

'Wyn said the wolves don't use magic.' I tried to push myself backwards but there was nowhere to go. My head was still fuzzy and both Astrid and Cole seemed to tower over me, both giants as I sat up with my back to the cage.

'Were by birth, witch by choice.' She almost sang her answer, a disturbingly happy smile on her face. 'Like all of my kind, I was raised to hate witches, but how could I not be curious? So I learned in my own way, practised in my own way. Not born to it in the way you were, no, but if you truly dedicate yourself to any craft until you are cast out by your family and your pack, exiled from your homeland, and you come to hate packs so much it consumes you, then there are a few tricks you can learn.'

She daubed the green paste onto my forehead and I screamed, the whole city shaking with my pain. It was worse than a burn, more like being branded. The triangular mark she made seared itself into my skin until my eyes watered and I retched onto the grass.

'See?' Astrid clapped her hands together in delight then pressed them into her injured left side. 'Unless you are prepared to give everything, you deserve nothing – and I have given *everything* over and over and over. Now it is my turn to get what *I* deserve.'

'Mom?'

Somewhere outside my own agony, I heard Lydia's voice, so tiny and afraid as she shuffled towards her mother. Alex tried to answer but all that came out were more choked sobs.

'Get away from there!' Cole grabbed Lydia by the throat, tossing her away like she weighed nothing, far stronger than a regular Were.

His resemblance to Wyn was so pronounced, each time he looked my way, my heart lurched. Older, but not by much, his hair was longer and darker, and his piercing eyes gleamed gold instead of mossy grey-green, but his face had the same sculptural quality, painstakingly crafted to perfection, full lips, high cheekbones. They even shared the same easy gait. As Cole strolled back to me after inflicting more casual violence on my best friend, my blood churned.

'There's wolf's bane woven into their clothes,' he told Astrid with a laugh. 'Cute.'

'It doesn't hurt?' I asked, my breath still coming in gasps.

He turned his hands palms out to show me the red welts.

'It hurts,' he replied, gold eyes sparkling. 'I just don't care.'

'Amazing what does and doesn't concern you after you've died,' Astrid said in an offhand manner. 'He was dead when I pulled him out the water, but not entirely gone. A spark remained and a spark is enough to burn the world to the ground if you know how to nurture the first flame. The hardest part was staying with him and not ripping your throat out there and then.'

I swiped at the foul tar-like substance on my forehead, the pain never once lessening into something I could live with. Instead of wiping it away, it spread, covering my hands, my forearms. Face down, I tried to whisper to the live oaks that lined the park, to the Spanish moss that swayed in their branches, but received no response.

'You're wasting your energy,' Astrid said when she saw what I was doing. 'They won't help you tonight. Not when you're marked. Ash of a live oak, crushed up selenite, hematite, poppy seed for disorientation, the blood of someone who loves you and the blood of someone who would see you dead. So curious to find both in the same family. I think that's what makes it burn so very badly.'

'If you don't let me help him, your brother is going to die,' I said, turning to Cole. There was no point trying to talk to Astrid, Wyn was right, she was out of her mind. 'Do what you want with me but are you really going to let her kill your brother?'

'A brother who betrayed his pack for the witch who killed me? A brother who kills me again and again, every time he chooses you. As far as I'm concerned, he's already dead.' Cole's foot hovered over my fingers, threatening to crush them if only Astrid would loosen his leash and allow it.

'As far as I'm concerned, they're all dead in the ground. My mother, my family, the whole pack.' His words were flat and dull. 'It's fucked up, all their fake rules, their self-imposed laws. Wolves should be free to do as they wish. We're stronger than ordinary humans, stronger than witches, but we're punished for exercising our natural advantage. I never fit in with them, never felt this supposed kinship they all talked about. Astrid's pack exiled her for asking questions, for being curious about magic. She wanted to make them stronger and they cast her out. What kind of family is that? She helped me see it's all a lie. Weres are nature itself, no one can control us. No egos, no leaders, and the sooner we end the packs, the better.'

'They're worse than witches,' Astrid muttered to herself. 'Always breeding like roaches. You have to cut off the head then make sure you clean up every last one or there will always be another hiding in the shadows, ready to start again.'

'How'd you two crazy kids meet anyhow?'

Cole's head whipped around to see Lydia pushing herself into an upright position, swiping at her bloody mouth with the back of her hand and smearing it all over her face. She looked terrifying.

'Had to be the apps,' she guessed. 'Tinder? Hinge? Psychopaths R Us?'

'That one is weak, ignore her,' Astrid commanded without looking up when Cole sent a menacing howl in her direction. 'Stick to the plan.'

Lydia caught my eye and I nodded as she rolled her mother's ring between her fingers. They couldn't sense the full strength of her magic.

'Astrid found me the first night I arrived in Savannah,' Cole said, gazing at his love with devotion. 'She saw me for who I really was and she didn't turn away. I'd always been unhappy. Difficult, they called me in school, disruptive. Truth is, I was meant for bigger things, we both were. We were meant to be.'

His story was a dark distortion of mine and Wyn's. How could the same universe that brought the two of us together put these monsters in the same place, at the same time?

Astrid approached me, a disappointed look on her face and a glass vial in her hand.

'It would have been nice to have more time with you,' she said, crouching down and brushing her long dark hair behind her ears. 'Natural-born witches are fascinating. I wish I could learn more about your connection to, what do you call it, the blessing? So pretty. It *is* a blessing, to be one with magic the way you are. One you do not deserve. Your magic is too much for you, I think. My way is better.'

'And what exactly is your way?' I jerked away when she raised a hand to my face, touched a finger to my bloody lip then put it in her mouth. Her eyes closed and she sighed with bliss.

'It's a shame, it really is,' she whispered, eyes still closed. 'When you first arrived and I saw you step out of that car, all sweaty and sad, all your belongings in one tiny suitcase, I thought we were the same. Lost. Lonely. I thought maybe we could be friends. So I sent Cole to kill your grandmother and bring you to me, but instead, you killed him. How could I love you after that?'

'Wha - what are you talking about?' I stammered. 'What do you mean?'

Her laugh this time was too close to a cackle.

'Strong but not observant,' she said on a sigh. 'If only you had opened your eyes to the world beyond your grief, beyond yourself. If only you had seen me first.'

Astrid had been watching me all this time. She'd been watching me since my first night in Savannah and I hadn't even noticed. With one delicate finger, she began to paint swirls on my face with the green paste, each swipe bringing fresh tears to my eyes.

'Your grandmother was no better. Self-centred. Impressive,' she admitted with reluctance. 'But ultimately arrogant, like you. Imagine if the three of us could've worked together. What might that have been like?'

'If you were watching, where were you when Catherine tried to drain my magic?' I asked, as defiant as I could be when the thought of this monster lurking in the shadows of Savannah soaked through my skin and into my bones, chilling me to the marrow.

'I was in the Stovell woman's beach house making sure Cole did not die!' Astrid screamed, slapping me so hard my ears rang. 'Because you, always you, have to make things complicated. I had to take the shop to get the supplies I needed to heal him. I could've let the owners live, but once you decided to pay the island a visit, we needed a new place to hide. More death on your hands, Emily, that can't feel good.'

Nothing felt good. The pain that raged around my body came with an unwelcome dose of existential agony and as my vision began to darken and narrow, I felt sure there would never be anything good in the world, ever again.

'Thank you for this.' Astrid recovered herself as she uncorked the glass vial and held it up to my temple, squeezing the broken skin to encourage the trickle of blood. 'My former mentor's blood helped me so much and she did not have half the power you hold. I had not planned to kill her so quickly but perhaps she always knew I would. You could have taught me many things, I think, we could've learned together.'

I laid on my back, staring up at the sky. My magic felt so far away and the pain that sliced through my skin wherever her spell touched was so intense I could hardly think straight. On one side of me, the river rushed onwards, on the other, the city of Savannah lay still. I should've been able to draw power from both, but until I could wash away her spell, I was as good as dead.

'Put the witches together,' Astrid instructed, carefully placing the vial filled with my blood in her suitcase and taking out another. 'We're running out of time before you phase.'

'You said we would do them one at a time,' Cole protested. 'I want the Bell bitch to go last.'

His complaint stood for less than a second. Astrid glared in his direction and immediately Cole grabbed me under my arms, dragging me to where Lydia lay, right between both cages. The post that dug into me didn't fully register until he pulled us up, back to back, and I felt it pressing between both our shoulder blades. He bound us together with thin, plastic-coated wire that cut into the skin at my wrists, my ankles, around my waist and finally, around my throat. Once we were upright, resting against each other, he began to pile up branches of live oak at our feet, concentrating wholly on his task, as if we weren't there. Because we weren't tied to a post, we were tied to a stake. Astrid and Cole were going to burn us at the stake.

I reached into my closest pocket and fumbled with the hidden zipper that held my silver pin. Tucking it away in the palm of my hand, I squeezed until it cut my skin, clenching my jaw as the new, sharp pain sliced through Astrid's spell. Only for a split second, but long enough for me to see a chance.

'Lyds?' I pushed backwards into her and felt her head turn towards me. 'Can you still feel your magic?'

'Only just,' she replied weakly. 'It's not clear but it's there.'

'Good enough,' I said. 'Stay with me.'

The cord around me pulled tight as she brought up her arms in a shrug.

'Where am I going to go?'

'Good point,' I whispered. 'On my cue, you know what to do.'

'Get the bloodstone,' Astrid barked at Cole. 'I need it to spark the flame. Quickly, before the phase begins.'

'You can't control his phase,' I said, Lydia writhing against her ropes behind me.

'Astrid can force my phase but she can't stop it on the full moon, no one could, not even you. I'm too strong,' Cole crowed. 'Which means any minute now, I'm going to tear your head clean off your shoulders.'

'Was it you?' I asked him, my chin jutting out with defiance. I just needed a few more seconds. 'Who attacked me at the DeSoto?'

'And last night,' he confirmed. 'Astrid at the beach, though. I wasn't fully healed or I'd have eviscerated you.'

'Stop telling her things she doesn't need to know!' Astrid yelled. 'Just watch them.'

'Good boy,' Lydia cooed when Cole backed away, his top lip twitching into a snarl. 'Do you know any other tricks? Sit? Fetch? Fuck off?'

The look he gave her made my blood run cold.

'I can't wait to see what your insides look like.'

When he growled this time, it was more animalistic than before. His phase was coming, even without my magic I could see it. But Cole wasn't my only concern. If Wyn and the other wolf phased while locked in their silver cages, Jackson and Alex were as good as dead.

'Cool that you managed to find each other though,' Lydia went on, somehow forcing out a bored yawn. 'The dating pool has to be pretty small when it comes to cry-baby wolf boys and psychotic Eurotrash witch wannabes.'

She'd finally crossed the line. Cole whirled around, arm outstretched and slapped Lydia across the face with the back of his hand.

'I told you to ignore her,' Astrid snapped when he followed up with a boot to the guts. 'This is what she wants. She's new and weak, she doesn't have the same magic as the other one. They're trying to distract you.'

Still half delirious under the fog of her spell, I felt Lydia's hand encircle my wrist and squeeze. Astrid would regret underestimating my friend.

'Bloodstone,' she shouted at him again before approaching me with a pair of gold scissors and a glass vial. 'If you don't mind, Emily, I would like to take a memento.'

'By all means,' I replied, my eyes still on Wyn and Alex as Astrid snipped off a chunk of my red hair before unbuttoning one of my sleeves, sucking in her breath as the aconite in the fabric burned her skin. I waited, holding my own breath until she was close enough, until I could feel the blade of her scissors cold against my throat. Looking deep into her violent, violet eyes, I jabbed the silver pin into her thigh as deep as it would go.

'Lydia!' I yelled over her howl of pain. 'Now!'

A clap of deafening thunder shook the park and a bolt of lightning split the sky in two. As the heavens opened and rain poured down, I saw the precision of her strike. The lightning hit the lock on Jackson's cage and the door swung open. He rolled out onto the wet grass, tearing the tape from his mouth and stumbling straight over to the other cage where Wyn and his mother were beginning to stir.

'Cole!' Astrid's wail was almost as loud as the thunder. 'Help me!'

But he couldn't see her. Lydia's storm thrashed down and the two of them covered their faces with their arms, ducking from raindrops as hard as bullets, rain that saturated Astrid's suitcase, soaking the notebooks full of stolen magic, sweeping the piles of wood at our feet off into the river, and washing away every trace of her spell from my skin. The confusion cleared, searing agony replaced with white-hot anger as I peeled the wires away from my limbs like pieces of wet tissue paper and stepped down from the pyre. I raised my arms to the sky as my magic returned thanks to the rush of the river and thrash of the rain, and stood in front of Astrid Hansen, a witch reborn.

Chapter Forty-Four

'Get your mom out of that cage but if you can, keep Wyn locked in, then get Jackson the hell out of here before that wolf wakes up,' I told Lydia, never taking my eyes off Astrid as she lowered into a crouch, her strange face more lupine than before.

'Only on the condition you kick their ass,' she replied, pushing her sodden hair away from her face.

It was a bargain I was happy to make.

Out the corner of my eye, I saw Cole charge but before he could reach us, I flicked my wrist and a snare of Spanish moss caught him by the ankle, dragging him away, scratching and clawing.

'I know you better than you know yourself,' Astrid said, a threatening bark in the back of her throat. 'You won't kill me.'

'You put people I love in cages and tried to burn me and my best friend alive,' I replied. 'I'm not about to give you a hug and send you on your way.'

'We had nothing to do with the cages. Take that up with the wolves.'

'Oh, I mean to,' I assured her. 'After I deal with you.'

The Witch and the Wolf

Ready for her attack, I silently brokered a deal with the river and the trees. The rain continued to hammer down but I had never seen anything more clearly, the solid sheet of water that blinded Astrid, magnifying the situation for me. My silver pin lay on the floor beside her. It hurt, I was sure of that, but hadn't had the same effect it had on Cole. When he attacked me in Bonaventure, he was a wolf, she was still human. Around her neck, I saw a moonstone necklace, the stones glinting a sickly pink as they caught the light. The moonstones she soaked in the witch's blood. That was how she controlled her phase. I had to remove the necklace.

As I was about to make my move, a huge black blur knocked me off my feet, lunging straight for Astrid. It was the wolf from Jackson's cage.

As strong and as brave as they may be, Astrid was smarter, prepared for a fight in a way the Were wasn't. Flat on her back, sacrificing her forearm to hold its jaws at bay, she drew back her other hand, another piece of jewellery glinting in the moonlight. Five delicate silver rings connected to a bangle around her wrist by fine, sparkling chains. When the wolf raised its head to prepare for the death blow, she thrust her hand upwards, punching through its fur and flesh, through muscle and bone, deep into its chest. The wolf stilled at once, eyes growing large as they realized what had happened far too late to do anything about it.

Not that there was much anyone or anything could do about having their heart torn from their chest.

The wolf fell, body first, head hitting the wet ground with a thud, and Astrid rose. In her hand she clutched their heart, steaming in the pouring rain.

'The wolves would have eaten your heart, Emily Bell,' she said, approaching me with renewed confidence. 'Would you like to taste theirs instead?'

'Thanks but I'll pass,' I said, scrambling to my feet.

'You're my guest. It's only polite to offer you the first bite before I dig in.'

When she opened her mouth and tore into the still-beating organ, blood spurted everywhere, coating her face, her hair, her clothes. I looked away, revolted, and full of pity for the fallen wolf. Astrid tossed the rest of the heart aside like a toddler with a toy she had already tired of, and advanced. I held my ground, one eye on Lydia and Jackson as they pulled their mother out of the cage and dragged her away, the other on Wyn. The sky was black, the moon almost fully risen and his phase would be on him very soon. I took the deepest inhale and pleaded with the elements. My lungs filled with air as I begged the earth, doused in rain, and with fire running through my veins I lifted my arms to the line of trees at the edge of the park. They understood. They agreed. As soon as the Powell family stepped off the grass, their branches wove together to form a boundary, keeping Lydia, Jackson and Alex out, and me, Astrid and the wolves, in.

'For all your magic,' she said, with blood dripping from her mouth. 'It is still so easy to kill a witch. You bleed, you break, you need help to heal. In nature, you are inferior to a Were. You are so fragile.'

'Just because something is fragile doesn't mean it can't be strong,' I told her, forcing myself to stand still, holding my position as she came closer, even as every living thing from the earth to the sky screamed at me to run, run, run.

'Look at you!'

She was laughing now, so close I could see the muscle fibres caught between her teeth. Face-to-face. Eye-to-eye.

'If I had your magic, I would have everything. I would *be* everything.' Astrid growled, her foul breath making me retch. 'This is what makes me so angry, you ungrateful wretch. All the gifts you have been given, and you do nothing with them.

The Witch and the Wolf

The magic is endless, Emily, your fear is the only limit. Do you not understand who you are? A witch powerful enough to end the world and even now you just stand there, doing nothing. You're pathetic. That's why you won't win against me. It's the one thing your grandmother was right about, you aren't prepared to do what is necessary.'

'That's the difference between us,' I replied, forcing myself to stand still as she advanced. 'I don't need to win. I only need you to lose.'

When she lunged forward, I ducked to the side and snatched the moonstone necklace from around her throat. It resisted my grip but only for a second. Astrid's magic was stolen, mine was a gift, and I only wished to return the precious metals and corrupted stones back to the earth where they belonged. Once they understood my intention, the gold melted away, dripping through my fingers, and the moonstones tumbled into the wet grass.

The phase was instantaneous. Before the last stone rolled to a stop, Astrid was something else, half-human, half-wolf, stuck midway, either by accident or design.

'Not smart, Emily,' she snarled before snapping at my outstretched arm and sinking her teeth deep into my wrist. The pain was mind-altering, a thousand times worse than her potion, arteries and tendons severed, an agony like no other. Right away, the world tilted on its axis, everything wrong, everything fading.

'Stupid girl.'

Astrid's voice was full of rage and blood as she released me, tearing through my flesh. I let my arm fall to my side as I staggered backwards, blood gushing out of me.

'This is the part where you're supposed to run away,' she growled.

But I didn't run. I didn't move an inch.

The ground trembled as the first drops of my blood spilled onto the dirt, soaking through the soil, my intentional offering accepted. Then the whole world quaked. The chasm that tore the park in two opened so quickly, Astrid couldn't see what was happening until the earth beneath her feet broke apart, giving her no chance to escape. The Savannah River raged at its banks, the trees that surrounded us bound themselves closer together, and the humid night air roiled. I watched as Astrid fell backwards, her half-wolf hands clawing at nothing, her eyes wide open with panic-stricken surprise, and I remained motionless when the city of Savannah swallowed her whole. The chasm closed, the river calmed itself and her muffled screams were silenced by the night.

'I'm not the one who should've run,' I whispered.

Clutching my wounded wrist, I closed my eyes and bathed in the quiet stillness before crumpling sideways, broken and bloodless.

When the dead fight back. When the earth consumes.

Cole was dead but fought back. The tunnels beneath Savannah had consumed Astrid. Weakened but ready, I steeled myself for what might come next. There had been so many lies, which would become the truth?

The wet grass was a feather bed as I stared blankly at a darkening sky. My arm. The bleeding wouldn't stop, and I was too weak to heal myself. The last time I suffered a Were attack, Catherine had given up her life for mine but there was no one to offer up a sacrifice this time. As my existence ebbed away, a flurry of shooting stars appeared in the sky. So pretty. I couldn't help but sigh at the beauty as I began to bleed out, the wonder of the universe, putting on a show and sparkling just for me.

Not just for me.

A quiet whimper sounded at my side and I turned my head

to see a wolf, one I recognized, looking down on me with the saddest green-grey eyes.

'It's OK,' I told Wyn when he threw his head back and howled. 'Just, stay with me, please?'

He turned around in a circle, tail between his legs, before laying down at the side of me, his body warm, his fur so soft. I didn't know I was crying until I felt his tongue lap the tears from my cheek, and when it all went dark, I realized I had everything I ever wanted.

He was alive. We were together.

I closed my eyes and smiled.

'Oh, honey, please tell me that is not what you wore to conduct a Becoming ceremony?' Catherine shook her head as she tutted, frowning with disappointment. 'Really, there are days when I have to ask myself if I ever taught you anything worth knowing. In one ear and out the other, all of it.'

The stars had disappeared and the soft grass had given way to something cold and hard. Marble. It took me a long moment to realize where I was. The Bell family chapel, underneath our monument in Bonaventure Cemetery. The caskets of our ancestors lined the walls and all the wooden pews glowed in the lamplight. Behind me, the steep stone staircase that led up to the outside world was sealed shut.

'Am I dead?' I asked.

'You look it. Blessed with a gorgeous head of hair and all she does is pull it back in a ponytail. I despair, I really do. Would it kill you to apply a touch of blush before you run off to sacrifice your life?'

I slid down from the altar where I'd awoken and stretched. Nothing hurt. There were no teeth marks on my arm, no rope burns on my wrists.

'You're not dead,' Catherine called from her seat in the front pew. 'Not yet anyway. The way I understand it, this is a spot we Bell witches like to use when we have some thinking between this life and the next.'

'But Astrid bit me.'

I held out my unblemished arm, but it made for poor evidence.

'She did,' my grandmother agreed. 'I saw. As you can imagine, I was not thrilled.'

'I should be dead,' I reasoned, running a finger up and down my intact skin. 'You're sure I'm not?'

With a razor-sharp sigh, she stood and strode towards me, her silk skirt swishing around her long legs. 'Honey, when good things happen to us, it is considered rude to ask why. Do not, as they say, look a gift horse in the mouth.'

'Is this part of my magic?' I asked. 'Am I immune to wolf bites? Because if I am—'

'If you are, that would make me quite the fool, wouldn't it?' Catherine finished for me. 'But it wouldn't change anything, Emily. I would sacrifice my life for yours one hundred times over, whether I knew it was necessary or not.'

My eyebrows flashed up my forehead and my grandmother replied with a sly smile.

'As I believe I mentioned, this is a good spot to do some thinking and I've had nothing but time on my hands.'

'If I'm not dead and you're not dead, then we can leave,' I said, cautiously walking down the aisle and pressing against the solid rock that sealed us in. 'We can go back?'

'You may leave whenever you're ready.' Catherine waved a hand, no big deal. 'I'm going to wait around a while longer. A lady doesn't step out without an invitation.'

'I'm inviting you,' I said uncertainly. 'I'm asking you to come back with me.'

'You're doing wonderful things out there.' She was suddenly beside me, leading me up the stairs that had appeared out of nowhere. A cool night breeze blew in from the open doors of the chapel, and above us I could see the full moon glowing.

'Growing into your magic exactly how I knew you would. My little witch is going to save the world.'

'But what about her?' I asked.

Behind us, in the darkest corner of the chapel, I saw the figure from my nightmares. Tall and emaciated, long stringy hair covering her face. My face.

'*Onginnan,*' she gasped as I cowered behind Catherine, her voice as dry as ashes. '*Onginnan.*'

'Don't you worry about her,' Catherine whispered in her most soothing tone, turning my face away as the wraith-like version of myself melted back into the shadows. 'She's not your concern today.'

But she would be. One day.

'And the man? The man with the dagger that looks like a tree?'

Her lips rolled together, the perfect red lipsticked line disappearing in on itself.

'Another problem for another time. Now go make nice with those mutts before they kill your boy. Make me proud, Emily.'

And with one short, sharp shove, she pushed me through the door and back into the night.

Chapter Forty-Five

The rain had stopped and the night had taken hold of the city, the full moon, a blue moon, hanging low over the river. It was a shame everyone in town was so committed to staying in all evening, I'd never seen such a beautiful sight.

'You're alive.'

Standing over me, Pamela Evans looked as though she might faint.

'But you were bitten,' she said as I rose slowly to my feet. 'You lost so much blood.'

'One thing I've noticed lately, there's always more blood than you think there's going to be,' I replied, testing my arms and legs. Nothing broken, nothing too bruised, the teeth marks on my arm completely healed with just a torn sleeve and bloody mess left behind to show a wound had ever existed. I looked up and offered her a terse smile. 'Shall we get on with the trial?'

'How are you alive?' she asked again, her thick accent dancing up and down the words. 'How can this be?'

'We did have to let your hostages go to avoid them being savagely murdered by Weres who couldn't be held responsible for their own actions,' I told her as the oaks unwound their branches and returned to their regular sentry positions.

As soon as she was able to push through a gap barely big enough for her body, Lydia raced over to my side, weather-beaten but stronger than ever. Jackson hung back, holding his mother upright as he brushed away the last of Astrid's cloaking spell from her skin.

'But in fairness, the wolf I'm supposed to have killed isn't actually dead, so I was thinking maybe declare a mistrial?'

Pamela turned to see her eldest son, a furious wolf still bound to the oaks, raging against the Spanish moss restraints. If I released him, he would try to murder us both. It had to be as obvious to her as it was to me.

'Cole,' she said, her voice a whisper of regret. 'What happened to you?'

'Nothing good,' I answered on his behalf. 'But it was all his choice.'

When Pamela turned back to me, she had resumed her pack leader authority, chin raised, shoulders back. Both her sons took after their mother. They shared her athletic build and unusual dark ash hair. If she spent more time outdoors, her slightly sallow skin would have the same golden tone as theirs. Her eyes though, were different. Or rather, the same. One grey-green, one yellow gold. One for Wyn and one for Cole.

'The lone wolf,' she said. 'Another Were dead at your hands.'

'She's not dead,' I replied, tapping the ground with my foot. 'She's right down here, sealed up in a tunnel. I can take you to her whenever you're ready, she's yours to do with as you please. But before you decide what that is, you should know that she *did* kill a wolf.'

I pointed over to the body that lay between the cages and when she seized up, one hand pressed against her abdomen to keep her from doubling over, I felt her grief.

'Cerian,' she whispered. 'No.'

Her emissary. The Were who came to Bell House to deliver terms and took Jackson with her. She had no reason to help me, only to see what was happening and do what was right.

'Cerian saved my life,' I said quietly, lowering my voice out of respect. 'In case that means anything to you.'

The air hung heavy with Pamela's silence. The empty cages, the dead wolf. One by one, the other Weres awoke, still groggy from whatever spell Astrid had used on them.

'It's an abomination,' Pamela muttered, unhappy and somewhat unwilling to explain herself to me, 'for a Were to use magic. We stick to the natural order of things. We don't interfere like you do.'

'If you can't get the truth of it all from Astrid, maybe you can get it from Cole,' I suggested. 'I don't want to interfere with anything. I'm just trying to live my life, that's all I want.'

As soon as the words were out of my mouth, I understood they were true. What more could anyone ask for? But Pamela was unmoved.

'Until you bring about the end of the world. And what then?'

Beside me, Lydia let out a growl any wolf would be proud of. The pack leader met it with a snarl of her own but Lydia Powell had never been intimidated by anyone, and she wasn't about to start now.

'Wyn said you didn't believe in prophecies,' I said, sending soothing energy Lydia's way. 'If that's not true, you should know killing me won't save anything. Take my life and the world ends. Let me live and we all have a chance.'

Pamela let out a harsh laugh. 'You want me to trust a witch?'

'I want you to trust me. Your emissary died to save my life. I could've killed Cole, I could've killed Astrid. I didn't. Enough people have died.'

The Witch and the Wolf

I thought of Ileen Stovell, the couple at Hilton Head, the witch in Norway and who knew how many others.

A dozen or so women, unphased Weres, appeared at the perimeter of the park and behind them, a whole battalion of wolves. The leader raised her hand in a clenched fist and they all held the line, the unphased Weres struggling almost as much as the wolves.

'Since Cole Evans was not killed, the pack rescinds its accusation,' Pamela declared, loud enough for all the wolves in the park to hear. 'You are free to go.'

'Before I do' – I nodded at the cages when she stood back, her mouth a hard line – 'Astrid said that was your doing.'

'Whatever Wyn told you, he didn't have his facts quite straight,' she answered coolly. 'When a Were is murdered, the punishment is a life for a life, but not your own. Had there not been . . . interference, your sentence would have been to choose which of the cages to open before the moon reached its peak.'

The reality of what she was saying hit so hard I staggered backwards two steps. They were going to make me decide whether to let Wyn phase and maul Alex to death, or save Alex and let her watch Cerian slaughter Jackson.

'That's horrific,' I breathed. 'It's beyond cruel.'

'This is not an age of mercy and I am not a merciful woman.' Pamela stood tall, unwavering in the face of my disgust. 'I make no apologies for doing what must be done. One day you will face difficult decisions and I hope for all our sakes you're strong enough to make them. You may leave. We will do the same when our business is through.'

Lydia put an arm around my shoulders, guiding me away until I threw up my hands to stop her, suddenly aware that something was very wrong. I spun around, glaring at Pamela. There were at least a hundred Weres surrounding the park, but the one quiet wolf that had laid down beside me while I was dying was nowhere to be seen.

'Where is Wyn?'

'A wolf in love with a witch is a danger to his pack.' At last, there was a crack in his mother's voice. 'The traitor, Wyn Evans, will be exiled and his name will not be spoken again.'

'No, you can't,' I protested, pushing my friend away. 'It'll kill him.'

Silently I searched until I found something that felt like him, smothered by another of Astrid's spells, and already in more pain than I could bear.

'One more thing you will have to learn to live with,' Pamela said softly. 'For someone who doesn't want to interfere, you have managed to take both my sons from me. Impressive, witch.'

'You can't exile someone for falling in love,' Lydia yelled when I couldn't find the words. 'That's sick, it's messed up. It's not his fault.'

'Not his fault?' Pamela cackled but I could see the tears in her eyes. 'Then please, I beg you, tell me whose fault is it?'

I had prepared for this eventuality but I wasn't ready.

'It's my fault,' I said, in so much pain I was almost able to believe my whole body had been smeared with Astrid's dark magic again. 'He isn't in love with me, it's magic.'

I thrust out an arm to hold Lydia back when she stepped forward, silently begging her to keep quiet with a quick glance.

'He doesn't love me and I don't love him,' I carried on, spitting out the words faster than I could breathe. If I paused, even for a second, I wouldn't be able to go through with it. 'My grandmother and I, we cursed him. We knew he was from a Were family long before you initiated him and we thought he might be useful, that's all. He could never love me, a wolf could never love a witch.'

'And a witch could never love a wolf,' she replied, eyes boring into me. 'I told them all there had to be more to this.'

'I may be a lot of things but I'm not a complete monster,' I said, choking on my words when she checked over her shoulder and signalled to one of the women at the park's perimeter. 'I don't delight in splitting up families. My mom died when I was a baby, I lost my dad and my grandmother recently. You've already mourned Cole and now you have his mess to deal with. There's no reason for you to lose Wyn. He's a harmless kid. Sweet, really. He's suffered enough.'

Pamela moved towards me, a shred of furious hope in her eyes. She wanted to be convinced but she wasn't, not yet. I had to make her believe me.

'Consider it a peace offering,' I added. 'I'll release him from my magic and in return you and your wolves will stay out of Savannah for good.'

'I want your curse lifted and I want it done now.' She spoke loudly over the murmurings of her pack, her authority not to be questioned. 'We'll see if you're telling the truth.'

She raised her hand and two of the women appeared, dragging Wyn between them. The gaping wound that had almost severed his shoulder from his body when his own brother dragged him from my bed was mostly healed, magically mended by his phase, but somehow he stood before me in human form. All the other males had phased, including Cole, who still howled, high-pitched and hateful, from his prison across the park.

'An exiled wolf does not have the right to phase with his former pack,' Pamela explained, her voice flat and emotionless, as Wyn looked up at me with empty eyes. 'He was unphased. Disorientation is to be expected and better than what's in store for him if you are lying to me.'

'Emily?' Wyn choked out my name, a flicker of light returning to his eyes.

I snatched back a sob. In the depths of his darkest moment, he knew me. When he was a wolf, he knew me. Always and forever, he would know me. But after tonight, he would never, ever forgive me.

'Do it,' his mother commanded. 'Whatever it is, right now.'

'What's happening?' Wyn asked as I reached into my pocket for the healing poultice I'd blended for him. There was no reason to make this hurt any more than it had to. Sprinkling the herbs into the palm of my hand, I smeared them against the still sticky blood on his chest, took his hands in mine and pulled him close.

'Tell him,' Pamela shouted. 'Tell him to his face!'

'I'm sorry,' I whispered, resting my forehead against his then raising my voice for everyone to hear. 'My grandmother cursed you and I used you. This, all of this, it's a lie. I never loved you.'

In his depleted state, he only looked bewildered.

'What are you talking about?'

'It's a spell,' I said, holding back traitorous tears. 'You don't love me, you only think you do because you were useful – and now you're not. In fact, you're a burden. I release you.'

'She's lying,' he said, summoning a scrap of strength to turn around, challenging any wolf that dared look at him. There weren't very many. 'Can't you see? It's so obvious. She's lying so you'll leave us alone.'

When no one responded, he turned back to me, clutching at my face, holding me to him so closely, his perfect features were just a blur.

'Stop it,' he begged as I turned my head away. 'Don't say it. We'll be OK, you and me, one way or another, we'll be OK. Even if they take me away, if they exile me, you know I'll always come back to you. I will always come back to you.'

I let him pull me into his arms one last time, completely still as his hands raked through my hair, grasped my shoulders, trying to find purchase on something that had already slipped out of reach.

'I love you, Emily James,' he said, holding me so tightly I was sure I would break. 'Nothing you can say is ever going to change that.'

'I love you, Wyn Evans,' I breathed, the only words from tonight he would not remember. 'And I wish that were true.'

Without letting go, I looked up to the sky through glassy eyes and summoned the clouds to cover the blue moon, turning it blood red. Around the park, the phased wolves whimpered. Staring at a spot beyond his shoulder, avoiding his chameleon eyes, the constellation of freckles on his nose, the curl of hair by his ear, I spoke one word I'd hoped to never utter.

'*Relēssen.*'

The whole park shook.

'Wyn Evans, I release you.'

The sound that echoed out of his body would haunt me for the rest of my life. A symphony of pain, excruciating to witness, and as Wyn fell to his knees, clutching at his chest, only breathing in long enough to scream out again, I watched. My face impassive, I refused to let myself cry. If so much as a single tear fell from my face, the pack would question my version of events, he would be exiled and this pain, this *agony*, would be for nothing.

After a hundred lifetimes had passed, the clouds moved away from the moon and it lit the park with violent clarity. Wyn lay at my feet, blessedly unconscious. His mother fell to her knees, pressing his hand to her chest.

'Go,' she ordered, without looking up at me. 'We're done.'

'What about Astrid?' I asked, shaking with the effort of ignoring Wyn.

'She's a lone wolf, she's no concern of ours.'

'But she'll die if you leave her down there. There's no way in or out unless I take you.'

'Then she'll die.'

The pack leader stood, drawing herself up to her fullest height, as the two women picked Wyn up from the ground, the pair of them ashen-faced. This was not the evening anyone had been anticipating.

They moved as one, Pamela leading the way out of the park while a group of six or seven subdued Cole, still bound, dragging him behind them while the wolves already phased melted away into the deserted city.

'Em?' Lydia said, her voice breaking through the hush, an unwelcome reminder that the world continued to turn. 'Are you OK?'

'Yes,' I nodded, finding her hand in mine. 'I am.'

It was the second-worst lie I'd ever told.

The Lie

Chapter Forty-Six

'Did it work?'

Ashley met us at the door of Bell House, covered in soot and sweat and worry. I nodded as the four of us traipsed inside, a sorry band of victors.

'Alexandra?' Virginia rushed past us all to her daughter's side. 'What on Earth?'

The twins' mother looked to have taken the worst of it, bruised and bloodied and still shellshocked. Jackson was dazed, burn marks on his wrists from the rope they used to drag him away, sore-looking spots on his face where he'd torn the tape from his skin. Lydia, on the other hand, looked like a goddess, a harnessed storm, leashed lightning. A new witch in thrall to the blessing.

'How come you were there?' she asked her mother as Ashley bundled us all into the parlour, directing everyone to soft spots on which to sit or lay, administering water, tea and whiskey. 'Did they come to Charleston to find you?'

'They didn't have to. I came back to apologize to you.'

Words were still difficult for her, hands shaking as she sipped the warm tea laced with honey and valerian Ashley held to her lips. 'I have behaved monstrously over the last few weeks.'

'We've recently recalibrated the scale of monstrous behaviour,' Jackson stated, sliding down onto the couch beside her. 'You're getting a pass. If only because you punched that Were right in the face.'

'Mom!' Lydia's face lit up. 'You punched a wolf?'

'Well, she didn't listen when I asked nicely,' Alex replied. 'I was parking the car around the corner and there she was, trying to shove my son into the back of some truck with his hands tied. I got a good swing in too, if there hadn't been two more of them, she might not have been so lucky.'

'Remind me never to cross you,' Ashley commented as the Powells crowded around each other, three generations reconnected.

She turned to me, full of the deepest empathy, something I never expected to find in the woman who brought me to Savannah like a lamb to the slaughter four months ago.

'Did it work?' she asked me again. 'Did they believe it?'

'They did,' I confirmed, sucking in my breath when she pulled me into the comfort of her arms. 'So did he.'

Even though she wasn't with us at the park, Ashley had the most important job of all. I knew the only way Wyn would wake up tomorrow still part of his pack was to leave me behind. I also knew he would never do that by choice. Back at Bell House, hidden from the wolves, Ashley had been welcomed back into my craft room, Wyn's blood-soaked shirt in hand, where she performed the ritual I had spent all afternoon perfecting.

At my signal, the dawning of the red moon, she poured out the herbal concoction I had wept over, regretted and prayed we wouldn't need to use for every second of its existence. Aconite to cause as much pain as possible, sage to cleanse his energy, chamomile, vervain and valerian to put him to sleep as quickly as I could and flecks from the black arfvedsonite crystal to make him forget my last words. When he woke, confused and suggestible, he would believe anything his mother told him and he would never want to see me again. But he would be alive and a member of the pack, not living a shadowy half-life as a lone wolf. I'd made my decision before I walked out under the full moon, but after meeting Cole and Astrid, I was certain it was the right one.

'What are you going to do about Astrid?'

Lydia's question pulled me out of a spiral I was keen to avoid for as long as possible. I unzipped one of my pockets and pulled out the handful of bloody moonstones. They rattled in my hand, unnatural and desperate to be undone. The witch whose life she'd ended to cast the spell couldn't rest until I'd reversed the magic but she knew she wouldn't have to wait much longer.

'Leave her where she is.'

Jackson's tone was pitch black. Something in him had changed and it cut a new wound into my heart to hear it. 'You can't let her out, Em. She's a killer.'

'But I'm not,' I said. 'Leaving her down there is a death sentence.'

'You don't need to worry about it.' Lydia straightened as she spoke, looking off to the back of the house as though listening to something we couldn't hear. 'She's gone.'

'Gone as in dead?' Ashley said altogether too hopefully.

'Gone as in taken,' I replied, tuning into the same frequency as Lydia.

Astrid was no longer in the tunnels. She was no longer in Savannah or the state of Georgia.

'Can you tell where?' I asked Lydia, but she shook her head. 'I can't see.'

'Shrouded somehow,' she replied. 'She might be behind the cloaking spell, but she didn't get herself out of the tunnels.'

'It's OK, she won't come back, she knows she can't win against us,' I said with bravado, all four Powells accepting my statement with varying degrees of confidence. They didn't need to worry about this tonight, they'd been through enough. We'd all been through enough. Alex draped her arms around her children, Virginia's watchful eye overseeing as they all closed their eyes, ready to surrender to sleep.

'Emily Bell, you need to rest,' Ashley decreed. 'Do I have to carry you upstairs?'

I shook my head, rising unsteadily to my feet and following her out the room. There was no fight left in me. The walls of the foyer had shifted while we were out, returning to the soft sage green of my arrival in Savannah. Not my colours.

'I saw Catherine tonight,' I said as Ashley and I slowly mounted the grand curved staircase. She stiffened as she walked but did not stop.

'She's back?'

'No. Not yet.'

'It's possible?'

'I think so.'

No one was more difficult to read than Ashley Bell. She sounded hopeful and afraid at the same time, an inscrutable contradiction, to me and I suspected, to herself. Who could know how to feel about this?

'I miss her,' she admitted after a long, thoughtful pause. 'She did terrible things, to me and you and so many people, but still . . .'

I nodded, chewing on my response. 'I miss her too. And I think I understand her a little better now I've done terrible things too.'

Her forehead creased with consternation, green eyes rimmed

with red and the hollows below them darker than I'd ever seen before.

'This feels like a conversation we should have after a good night's sleep,' she said, pushing me gently towards my bedroom door. 'Will you be all right on your own, or do you want a roommate?'

I wouldn't. I wouldn't ever be all right on my own ever again.

'It will get better,' Ashley promised when I didn't answer. 'In time. A long time, maybe, but it will hurt less in the end.'

In the end.

I forced one corner of my mouth into my best impression of a smile. I'd already told the most terrible lie of my life tonight, what was one more?

'You're right,' I agreed, sending her across the hallway. 'Go get some rest, we'll talk in the morning.'

She closed the door but I stayed where I was, fingertips on my door handle, unable to go inside. It was still a mess, still the scene of Wyn's abduction, a brutal blend of love and hate, ruined for me now, maybe forever. As soon as Ashey's door was closed, I turned around and walked back past her room, past Catherine's suite, and stopped at the bottom of the stairs to the third floor.

All of Bell House was beautiful but the ceiling above me might have been the most spectacular part of it all, and the feature I looked at the least. It was painted a deep dense midnight blue and the paint absorbed all the light like velvet. Every constellation of the night sky had been painted in perfect detail, picked out in sparkling silver paint that shone like diamonds. This was where my parents had lived, after they were married. This was where I had spent the first nights of my life. Slowly, as if trudging through molasses, I made my way up the stairs, pulled onwards and pushed back at the same time. The light played differently up here, no lamps I could see, no chandeliers or sconces, just the sparkle of the stars, and when I reached the top step, a perfect circle of stained glass that let in all the glory of the full moon, warm and milky as it spilled onto the floor, illuminated my path. It was easy now, to walk, to breathe, my footsteps following a route I'd taken a thousand times, although never on my own. I'd been carried here, cradled. This was a place where I had been loved with such a passion, it hurt to think about.

The only door opened softly, no creaking or complaining. Unusual for one that had been closed for so long, but I hadn't felt so welcome, it was as though the room didn't want to offend me. All the furniture in the small sitting room was clean and dust-free, the windows shining brightly. Passing through into the bedroom, I recognized everything. A simple wooden bedframe, a cosy rocking chair, an antique crib. My crib. Sinking into the chair, I reached out my hand, my fingertips finding the crib and giving it the lightest push. It swung silently on its own momentum, back and forth, and I watched mesmerized.

Then I let go.

Giving up, giving in, it felt so good and so terrible, just as I'd hoped it would. Shoes kicked to the floor, knees curled up on the chair, I hugged them into my chest to make myself as small as possible, a tiny, tight little ball that no one could hear or harm.

The dead had fought, the earth consumed and tomorrow, my life would become Wyn's truth. Hundreds of miles away, I could still feel his pain. Even unconscious, he was in agony. The tears that fell into the spell as I blended the herbs together were irretrievable and so we would have to share our sorrow, though he would never understand why. I would never be able to sever the connection between us even if it remained a mystery to him. Would he feel it, if I tugged on the thread? Would it

The Witch and the Wolf

confuse him now or make him angry? I couldn't say. When he woke, he would believe my lies, but I knew the truth. I would know it always. And slowly, oh so slowly, it would eat away at me, killing me bit by bit, day by day, knowing the only person I could ever truly love thought me a liar.

Those days would still come, whether I liked it or not. However long I hid up here, the sun would rise and fall, more moons would roll by and I would be needed. A broken-down doll of a girl, carrying the weight of the world on her shoulders.

'Who will be there when I need them?' I whispered to no one, breathing in the sweet floral scent of the room. Jasmine. My dad's favourite because it reminded him of my mom.

I heard the doorbell ring downstairs and ignored it. My work was done for the night. If the clock on the wall kept the correct time, it was two minutes until midnight. No one came with good news at this time of night. Whoever it was could at least wait two minutes, save one problem until tomorrow.

It rang again and I heard doors opening, bedroom and parlour, Ashley and Virginia convening in the foyer, Virginia straightening her hair, Ashley rolling her eyes. Then the front door. Then a pause. The whole house held its breath.

'Emily?' I heard Ashley yell, more like a whisper all the way up here. 'Emily, get down here! You have a visitor.'

As I rolled out of the chair, the clock struck midnight. I didn't bother to straighten up, slouching out the room, barefoot and tear-stained, no longer caring how the world saw me. What did it matter?

Unless, whispered a little voice that somehow survived in the back of my mind, *unless, unless, unless . . .*

She will return.

I picked up my pace, skittering out of my parents' sitting room and turning the corner to the stairs so quickly, I almost slipped. They seemed to go on forever, third floor, second floor, the endless staircase eventually delivering me to the foyer where Virginia held herself awkwardly, backed up against the console table. Ashley clung to the door, white and wild, not sure whether to keep it open or slam it shut.

On the doorstep was a woman. Tall, blonde, blue-eyed. Older than I'd seen her in photographs or visions, but standing right in front of me, very real and very alive.

'Mom?'

Angelica Bell walked through the door and into Bell House. Our faces were a mirror of surprise, mine tainted with shock, hers tinged with delight.

She smelled like jasmine.

'Oh, Emma,' my mother sobbed as she pulled me close, holding me tight. 'Look at you, you're all grown up. My baby, just look at you.'

Upstairs, I heard the clock strike midnight.

It was a new day in Savannah.

Acknowledgements

Thank you to Rowan Lawton and Eleanor Lawlor at The Soho Agency for everything. Proof you don't need to be a witch to work magic. Unless you are witches? None of my business, please carry on.

Thank you to Natasha Bardon, Chloe Gough and Catherine Perks for pulling this book out of my brain and putting it onto the page, and to Anne O'Brien for making the words on the page make sense. Massive thanks to everyone at HarperCollins who had a finger in *The Bell Witches* pie (sorry, gross) especially Fleur Clarke, Vicky Joss and Philippa Cotton, Waterstones for those stunning spredges and The Locked Library for your impossibly beautiful edition that I have happily signed all over the world. Thank you to Fionnuala and the rest of the audio team for the audiobook of my dreams, and to Ashley Haddad for bringing our story to life so beautifully. Jean Marie Kelly, Emily Gerbner, Ariana Juarez and Kamrun Nesa at Harper360, thank you for bringing the Bells to the US and getting me around the country in one piece. @selunchen for the gorgeous art print that captured Emily and Wyn so beautifully.

It's almost impossible to list how many people it takes to

make a book successful in today's world and I am eternally grateful to everyone in every department, editorial, sales, production, warehousing, marketing & PR, design, legal and anyone who ever made a cup of tea or coffee that helped keep this book alive. I used to make those cups of tea and coffee, I know how essential they are.

Thank you to Kevin Dickson and Julie Soto, for the research trips and humouring my Bell Witches tour of Savannah, to Sydney J Shields, Chip Pons, Ali Hazelwood, Kate Goldbeck and Alexandra Vasti for making the US tour so much fun, and to E. Shaver Books, The New Romantics, The Garden District Bookshop, and Lark & Owl for so generously hosting me in spite of flash floods, thunderstorms and my general inability to take anything seriously. Also thank you to every author I have wailed at about this book, in person or online. You helped save my sanity. It helps to know that much like the East High Wildcats, we're all in this together.

Once again, more than half the thanks for this book belongs to the city of Savannah itself, especially the Hamilton-Turner Inn for inspiring Bell House and The Grey for inspiring me to come back for dinner. To Sistah Patt Gunn and Sistah Roz Rouse, Gullah Geechee truth-tellers and incredible human beings, thank you for sharing the realities of Savannah's past with me and everyone else who needs to hear it. To the tour guides from the Davenport House, the Owens-Thomas House, Mercer-Williams House, and Bonaventure Cemetery, as well as every trolley driver, coffeeshop owner, server and street cat, who took the time to talk with me or let me pet them*, I am so grateful.

*Delete as appropriate.

And as ever, thank you to Jeff for supporting me through the deadlines and the research trips, I couldn't do this without you. Well, I probably could but it wouldn't be nearly as much fun. Let's not test the theory.